WHEN WILDERNESS WAS KING

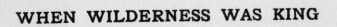

"Toinette!" I whispered passionately, "I would call you by a dearer name—by the dearest of all dear names if I might." Page 386
—*When Wilderness Was King.*

When Wilderness Was King

A Tale of the Illinois Country

By RANDALL PARRISH
Author of "My Lady of the North"

A. L. BURT COMPANY, Publishers
⚜ ⚜ ⚜ NEW YORK ⚜ ⚜ ⚜

CONTENTS

CONTENTS

" **I** SAW a dot upon the map, and a housefly's filmy wing—
They said 't was Dearborn's picket-flag, when Wilderness
was King.

. . . .

I heard the block-house gates unbar, the column's solemn tread,
I saw the Tree of a single leaf its splendid foliage shed
To wave awhile that August morn above the column's head;
I heard the moan of muffled drum, the woman's wail of fife,
The Dead March played for Dearborn's men just marching out of
life;
The swooping of the savage cloud that burst upon the rank
And struck it with its thunderbolt in forehead and in flank,
The spatter of the musket-shot, the rifles' whistling rain,—
The sandhills drift round hope forlorn that never marched again."

—Benjamin F. Taylor.

When Wilderness Was King

CHAPTER I

A MESSAGE FROM THE WEST

SURELY it was no longer ago than yesterday. I had left the scythe lying at the edge of the long grass, and gone up through the rows of nodding Indian corn to the house, seeking a draught of cool water from the spring. It was hot in the July sunshine; the thick forest on every side intercepted the breeze, and I had been at work for some hours. How pleasant and inviting the little river looked in the shade of the great trees, while, as I paused a moment bending over the high bank, I could see a lazy pike nosing about among the twisted roots below.

WHEN WILDERNESS WAS KING

My mother, her sleeves rolled high over her round white arms, was in the dark interior of the milk-house as I passed, and spoke to me laughingly; and I could perceive my father sitting in his great splint-bottomed chair just within the front doorway, and I marked how the slight current of air toyed with his long gray beard. The old Bible lay wide open upon his knee; yet his eyes were resting upon the dark green of the woods that skirted our clearing. I wondered, as I quaffed the cool sweet water at the spring, if he was dreaming again of those old days when he had been a man among men. How distinct in each detail the memory of it remains! The blue sky held but one fleecy white cloud in all its wide arch; it seemed as if the curling film of smoke rising from our chimney had but gathered there and hung suspended to render the azure more pronounced. A robin peeked impudently at me from an oak limb, and a roguish gray squirrel chattered along the low ridge-pole, with seeming willingness to make friends, until Rover, suddenly spying me, sprang hastily around the corner of the house to lick my hand, with glad barkings and a frantic effort to wave the stub of his poor old tail. It was such a homely, quiet scene, there in the heart of the backwoods, one I had known unchanged so long, that I little dreamed it was soon to witness the turning over of a page of destiny in my life, that almost from that hour I was to sever every relation of the past,

2

and be sent forth to buffet with the rough world alone.

There were no roads, in those days, along that valley of the upper Maumee, — merely faint bridle-paths, following ancient Indian trails through dense woods or across narrow strips of prairie land; yet as I hung the gourd back on its wooden peg, and lifted my eyes carelessly to the northward, I saw a horseman riding slowly toward the house along the river bank. There were flying rumors of coming Indian outbreaks along the fringe of border settlements; but my young eyes were keen, and after the first quick thrill of sus-picion I knew the approaching stranger to be of white blood, although his apparel was scarcely less unciv-ilized than that of the savage. Yet so unusual were visitors, that I grasped a gun from its pegs in the kitchen, and called warningly to my mother as I passed on to meet the new-comer.

He was a very large and powerful man, with a matted black beard and an extremely prominent nose. A long rifle was slung at his back, and the heavy bay horse he bestrode bore unmistakable signs of hard travelling. As he approached, Rover, spying him, sprang out savagely; but I caught and held him with firm grip, for to strangers he was ever a surly brute.

"Is this yere Major Wayland's place?" the man questioned, in a deep, gruff voice, reining in his tired

3

horse, and carelessly flinging one booted foot across the animal's neck as he faced me.

"Yes," I responded with caution, for we were somewhat suspicious of stray travellers in those days, and the man's features were not pleasing. "The Major lives here, and I am his son."

He looked at me intently, some curiosity apparent in his eyes, as he deliberately drew a folded paper from his belt.

"No? Be ye the lad what downed Bud Eberly at the meetin' over on the Cow-skin las' spring?" he questioned, with faintly aroused interest.

I blushed like a school-girl, for this unexpected reference was not wholly to my liking, though the man's intentions were evidently most kind.

"He bullied me until I could take no more," I answered, doubtfully; "yet I hurt him more seriously than I meant."

He laughed at the trace of apology in my words.

"Lord!" he ejaculated, "don't ever let that worry ye, boy. The hull settlement is mighty glad 't was done. Old Hawkins bin on the p'int o' doin' it himself a dozen o' times. Told me so. Ye 're quite a lad, ain't ye? Weigh all o' hundred an' seventy, I 'll bet; an' strong as an ox. How old be ye, anyhow?"

"Twenty," I answered, not a little mollified by his manner. "You must live near here, then?"

"Wal, no, but been sorter neighbor o' yourn fer

a month er so back; stoppin' up at Hawkins's she-bang, at the ford, on the Military Road, visitin'; but guess I never met up with none o' your folks afore. My name 's Burns, Ol' Tom Burns, late o' Connecti-cut. A sojer from out West left this yere letter fer yer father at Hawkins's place more nor a week ago. Said as how it was mighty important; but blamed if this was n't the fust chance he 's hed to git it over yere sence. I told him I 'd fetch it, as it was n't more nor a dozen miles er so outer my way."

He held out a square paper packet; and while I turned it over curiously in my hand, — the first letter I had ever seen, — he took some loose tobacco from an outside pocket and proceeded leisurely to fill his pipe.

My mother rolled my father's chair forward into the open doorway, and stood close behind him, as was her custom, one arm resting lightly upon the quaintly carved chair-back.

" What is it, John? " she questioned gently. In-stantly aroused by her voice, I crossed quickly over and placed the packet in my father's thin hands. He turned it over twice before he opened it, looking at the odd seal, and reading the superscription carefully aloud, as if fearful there might be some mistake:

" Major David Wayland,
　　　　Along the Upper Maumee.
　　　　　　Leave at Hawkins Ford
" Important.　　　　on Military Road."

I can see him yet as he read it, slowly feeling his way through the rude, uneven writing, with my mother leaning over his shoulder and helping him, her rosy cheeks and dark tresses making strange contrast beside his pain-racked features and iron-gray hair.

" Read it aloud, Mary," he said at last. " I shall understand it better. 'T is from Roger Matherson, of whom you have heard me speak."

My mother was a good scholar, and she read clearly, only hesitating now and then over some ill-written or misspelled word.

> At FORT DEARBORN, near the head of the
> Great Lake. Twelfth June, 1812.
>
> MY DEAR OLD FRIEND:
>
> I have come to the end of life; they tell me it will be all over by the morrow, and there remains but one thing that greatly troubles me — my little girl, my Elsa. You know I have never much feared death, nor do I in this hour when I face it once more; for I have ever tried to honor God and do my duty as both man and soldier. David, I can scarcely write, for my mind wanders strangely, and my fingers will but barely grasp the pen. 'T is not the grip of the old sword-hand you knew so well, for I am already very weak, and dying. But do you yet remember the day I drew you out of the rout at Saratoga, and bore you away safely, though the Hessians shot me twice? God knows, old friend, I never thought to remind you of the act, — 't was no more than any comrade would have done, — yet I am here among strangers, and there is no one else living to whom I may turn in my need. David, in memory of it, will you not give my little orphan child a home? Your old comrade, upon his death-bed, begs this of you with his final breath. She is all alone here, save for me, and there is no blood kin in all the world

to whom I may appeal. I shall leave some property, but not much. As you love your own, I pray you be merciful in this hour to my little girl.

Your old comrade,

ROGER MATHERSON.

This had been endorsed by another and bolder hand:

Captain Roger Matherson, late of the Massachusetts Continental Line, died at this fort, of fever, fourteenth June, 1812. His daughter is being cared for by the ladies of the garrison.

NATHAN HEALD,

Capt. First Regt. Inf., Commanding.

The tears were clinging to my mother's long lashes as she finished the reading; she was ever tender of heart and sympathetic with sorrow. My father sat in silence, looking far off at the green woods. Presently he took the paper again into his hands, folded it carefully in the old creases, and placed it safely away between the Bible leaves. I saw my mother's fingers steal along the arm of the chair until they closed softly over his.

" The poor little lamb! " she said gently.

My father's old sword hung over the fireplace, and I saw his glance wander toward it, as something seemed to rise choking in his throat. He was always a man who felt deeply, yet said but little; and we both knew he was thinking about the old days and the strong ties of comradeship.

The stranger struck flint and steel to light his

pipe; the act instantly recalled my father to the demands of hospitality.

"Friend," he said, speaking firmly, "hitch to the stump yonder, and come in. You have brought me sad news enough, yet are no less welcome, and must break bread at our board. John," and he turned toward me, "see to friend Burns's horse, and help your mother to prepare the dinner."

Out in the rude shed, which answered as a kitchen during summer weather, I ventured to ask:

"Mother, do you suppose he will take the little girl?"

"I hope so, John," she answered, soberly; "but your father must decide himself. He will not tell us until he has thought it all out alone."

CHAPTER II

THE CALL OF DUTY

IT was upon my mind all through that long afternoon, as I swung the scythe in the meadow grass. I saw Burns ride away up the river trail soon after I returned to work, and wondered if he bore with him any message from my father. It was like a romance to me, to whom so few important things had ever happened. In some way, the coming of this letter out of the great unknown had lifted me above the narrow life of the clearing. My world had always been so small, such a petty and restricted circle, that this new interest coming within its horizon had widened it wonderfully.

I had grown up on the border, isolated from what men term civilization; and I could justly claim to know chiefly those secrets which the frontier teaches its children. My only remembrance of a different mode of life centred about the ragged streets of a

9

small New England village, where I had lived in
earlier childhood. Ever since, we had been in the
depths of the backwoods; and after my father's accident I became the one upon whom the heavier part
of the work fell. I had truly thrived upon it. In
my hunting-trips, during the dull seasons, I learned
many a trick of the forest, and had already borne rifle
twice when the widely scattered settlements were
called to arms by Indian forays. There were no
schools in that country; indeed, our nearest neighbor
was ten miles distant as the crow flies. But my
mother had taught me, with much love and patience,
from her old treasured school-books; and this, with
other lore from the few choice volumes my father
clung to through his wanderings, gave me much to
ponder over. I still remember the evenings when he
read to us gravely out of his old Shakespeare, dwelling
tenderly upon passages he loved. And he instructed
me in other things, — in honor and manliness, in
woodcraft, and many a pretty thing at arms, until no
lad in the settlements around could outdo me in rough
border sport. I loved to hear him, of a boisterous
winter night, — he spoke of such matters but seldom,
— tell about his army life, the men he had fought
beside and loved, the daring deeds born of his younger
blood. In that way he had sometimes mentioned this
Roger Matherson; and it was like a blow to me now
to hear of his death. I wondered what the little girl

would be like; and my heart went out to her in her loneliness. Scarcely realizing it, I was lonely also.

"Has he spoken yet?" I questioned anxiously of my mother, as I came up to the open kitchen door when the evening chores were done.

"No, John," she answered, "he has been sitting there silently looking out at the woods ever since the man left. He is thinking, dear, and we must not worry him."

The supper-table had been cleared away, and Seth, the hired man, had crept up the creaking ladder to his bed under the eaves, before my father spoke. We were all three together in the room, and I had drawn his chair forward, as was my custom, where the candle-light flickered upon his face. I knew by the look of calm resolve in his gray eyes that a decision had been reached.

"Mary," he began gravely, "and you, John, we must talk together of this new duty which has just come to us. I hardly know what to decide, for we are so poor and I am now so helpless; yet I have prayed earnestly for guidance, and can but think it must be God's will that we care for this poor orphan child of my old friend."

My mother crossed the room to him, and bent down until her soft cheek touched his lips.

"I knew you would, David," she whispered, in the tender way she had, her hand pressing back his short gray hair. "She shall ever be unto us as our own little girl, — the one we lost come back to us again."

My father bent his head wearily upon one hand, his eyes upon the candle flame, his other hand patting her fingers.

"It must be all of ten years," he said slowly, "since last I had word of Roger Matherson. He was in Canada then, yet has never since been long out of my mind. He saved my life, not once alone, as he would seem to remember, but three separate times in battle. We were children together in the blue Berkshire hills, and during all our younger manhood were more than brothers. His little one shall henceforth be as my own child. God hath given her unto us, Mary, as truly as if she had been born of our love. I knew that Roger had married, yet heard nothing of the birth of the child or the loss of his wife. However, from this hour the orphan is to be our own; and we must now decide upon some safe means of bringing her here without delay."

He paused. No one of us spoke. His glance slowly wandered from the candle flame, until it settled gravely upon my face as I sat resting on a rude bench fitted into the chimney corner. He looked so intently at me that my mother seemed instantly to interpret his thought.

"Oh, surely not that, David?" she exclaimed, pleadingly. "Not John?"

"I know of no other fit messenger, little woman,"

he answered soberly. "It has indeed troubled me far more than all the rest, to decide on this; yet there is no one else whom I think equal to the task. John is a good boy, mother, and has sufficient experience in woodcraft to make the journey."

"But the savages!" she insisted. "'T is said we are upon the verge of a fresh outbreak, stirred up by this new war with England, that may involve the settlements at any time. You know Burns told you just now, — and he is an old scout, familiar with the West, — that British agents were active along the whole border, and there was great uneasiness among the Indian tribes."

"There is serious promise of danger, 't is true," he admitted, a flash of the old fire in his eyes. "Yet that is scarce likely to halt David Wayland's son. Indeed, it is the greater reason why this helpless orphan child should be early brought to our protection. Think of the defenceless little girl exposed alone to such danger! Nor have we means of judging, Mary, of the real seriousness of the situation to the north and west. War between the nations may very likely arouse the spirit of the savages, yet rumors of Indian outbreak are always on the lips of the settlers. Burns himself was upon his return westward, and did not seem greatly troubled lest he fail to get through. He claimed to live at Chicagou Portage, wherever that may be. I only know it is the extreme frontier."

My mother did not answer; and now I spoke, my cheeks aflame with eagerness.

"Do you truly mean, sir, that I am to go in search of the little girl?" I asked, barely trusting my own ears.

"Yes, John," my father replied gravely, motioning me to draw closer to his chair. "This is a duty which has fallen to you as well as to your mother and me. We can, indeed, but poorly spare you from the work at this season; yet Seth will be able to look after the more urgent needs of the farm while you are absent, while he would prove quite useless on such a mission as this. Do not worry, Mary. Friend Burns is well acquainted with all that western country, and he tells me there is scarcely a week that parties of soldiers, or friendly Indians, do not pass along the trail, and that by waiting at Hawkins's place for a few days John will be sure to find some one with whom he may companion on the long journey westward. He would himself have accompanied him, but must first bear a message to friends at Vincennes. It is now some weeks since Roger Matherson died, and we shall prove unworthy of our trust if we delay longer in sending for his daughter."

Though my mother was a western woman, patient and long habituated to sacrifice and peril, still her eyes, fixed upon my face, were filled with tears, and the color had deserted her cheeks.

"I know not why it should be so, David," she

urged softly; "but in my heart I greatly fear this trip for John. Yet you have ever found me ready to yield wherever it seemed best, and I doubt not you are right in your decision."

At any other time I should have gone to her with words of comfort and good cheer; but now my ambition was so aroused by this impending adventure as to permit me to think of nothing else.

"Is it so very far, father, to where I must go?" I questioned, eagerly. "Where is this Fort Dearborn, and how am I to journey in reaching there? 'T is no garrison of which I have ever heard."

"Bring me the map your mother made of this country, and the regions to the westward," he said. "I am not over clear in regard to the matter myself, although friend Burns, who claims to know all that country, gave me some brief description; but I found him most chary of speech."

I got the map out of the great square cupboard in the corner, and spread the paper flat upon the table, placing knives at each corner to hold it open. I rolled his chair up before it, and the three of us bent our heads over the map together, our faces glowing in the candle flame. It was a copy made by a quill from a great government map my mother had seen somewhere in her journeying westward; and, though only a rude design, it was not badly done, and was sufficiently accurate for our purpose. Much of it was still blank; yet the main open trails had been traced with care, the principal fords over the larger streams were marked, and the various government posts and trading settlements distinctly located and named. Searching for the head of the Great Lake, we were not long in discovering the position of the fort called Dearborn, which seemingly was posted upon the western shore, nearly opposite another garrison point at the mouth of the St. Joseph river. We were able to trace with clearness the military road that had been constructed northward from Fort Wayne, our nearest government post; but the map failed to exhibit evidence of any beaten track, or used trail, leading westward and around the head of the lake. There were numerous irregular lines which denoted unnamed streams, but by far the larger portion of the territory extending to the west beyond Fort Wayne had been simply designated as " forest land " and " unexplored."

"Friend Burns tells me there is a trail used by both troops and savages, which he has traversed several times," my father explained, as he lifted his eyes from the map; " but it is not over plain, nor easily followed, as communication with the Fort is mostly maintained by means of the waterways to the northward. The overland journey, however, will prove speedier, besides being less liable to disaster for one unaccustomed to boats. How soon can John be ready, mother?"

Her voice trembled, and I felt the pressure of her hand upon my sleeve.

"It will take all of the morrow, David, to prepare his clothing properly," she replied, with the patient resignation of the frontier. "There is much that will need seeing after."

"Then John will start the next dawn. You had best ride the brown colt, my son; he is of good breed, and speedy. Seth shall accompany you until you find suitable companionship at Hawkins's. He will bring back word of how you started, and that knowledge will greatly comfort your mother."

He paused, and held out his thin hands.

"You go upon this strange journey willingly, my son?"

"Yes, father."

"You will be both kind and thoughtful with Roger Matherson's little girl?"

"She shall be to me as my own sister."

I felt the confiding clasp of his fingers, and realized how much to him would be a successful termination of my journey.

"Kiss your mother, John," he said, a trustful look coming into his kindly eyes. "We must all be astir early on the morrow."

Beneath the rived shingles of my little room, under the sloping roof, how I turned and tossed through those long night hours! What visions, both asleep and awake, came to me, thronging fast upon my heated brain, each more marvellous than its fellow, and all alike pointing toward that strange country which I was now destined by fate to travel! Vague tales of wonder and mystery had come floating to me out of that unknown West, and now I was to behold it all with my own eyes. But marvellous as were my dreams, the reality was to be even more amazing than these pictures of boyish imagination. Had I known the truth that night, I doubt greatly whether I should have had the courage to face it.

At last the gray dawn came, stealing in at the only window, and found me eager for the trial.

CHAPTER III

A NEW ACQUAINTANCE

I DREW rein upon the upper river bank, before we finally plunged into the dark woods beyond, and glanced back. I had to brush the gathering tears from my eyes before I could see clearly; and when I finally rode away, the picture of that dear old home was fixed in my memory forever. Our house stood near the centre of an oak opening, — a little patch of native prairie-land, with a narrow stream skirting it on one side, and a dense fringe of forest all about. The small story-and-a-half cabin of hewn logs, with its lean-to of rough hand-riven planks, fronted to the southward; and the northern expanse of roof was green with moss. My father sat in the open doorway, his uplifted hand shading his eyes as he gazed after us; while my mother stood by his side, one arm resting upon the back of his chair, the other extended, waving a white cloth in

19

farewell. Rover was without, where I had bidden him remain, eagerly watching for some signal of relenting upon my part. Beyond stood the rude outbuildings, silhouetted against the deep green. It was a homely, simple scene, — yet till now it had been all the world to me.

With a final wave of the hand, I moved forward, until the intervening trees, like the falling of a curtain, hid it all from view. Seth was astride the old mare, riding bareback, his white goat-like beard hanging down his breast until it mingled with her mane, while his long thin legs were drawn up in the awkward way he had. He was a strange, silent, gloomy man, as austere as his native hills; and we rode on with no exchange of speech. Indeed, my thoughts were of a nature that I had no wish to share with another; so it was some time before the depth of loneliness which oppressed my spirits enabled me to feel even passing interest in the things at hand.

"I'd hate like thunder ter be a-goin' on your trip, Maester John," volunteered Seth at last, solemnly turning on the mare's broad back to face me.

"And why?" I asked, wonderingly; for the man's rare gift of silence had won him a certain reputation for deep, occult knowledge which I could not wholly ignore. "It will bring me the sight of some wonderful country, no doubt."

His shrewd gimlet eyes seemed fairly to pierce

me, as he deliberately helped himself to tobacco from a pouch at his waist.

"Wal, that may all be, Maester John; but I've heerd tell ther is some most awful things goes on out yonder," and he swung his long arm meaningly toward the west. "Animyles sich as don't prowl raound yere, man-yeatin' snakes as big as thet tree, an' the blood-thirstiest salvages as ever was. An' arter a while ther ain't no more trees grows, ther lan' is thet poor, by gosh! jist a plumb dead levil er' short grass, an' no show ter hide ner nuthin'.."

"Were you ever there, Seth?" I questioned with growing anxiety, for I had heard some such vague rumors as these before.

"Me? Not by a dinged sight!" he replied, emphatically. "This yere is a long way further west thin I keer 'bout bein'. Ol' Vermont is plenty good 'nough fer this chicken, an' many 's ther day I wish I was back ther. But I hed a cousin onct who tuk ter sojerin' 'long with Gineral Clarke, an' went 'cross them ther prairies ter git Vincennes frum the British. Lor'! it must a' bin more ner thirty year ago! He tol' me thet they jist hed ter wade up ter ther neck in water fer days an' days. I ain't so durn fond o' water as all thet. An' he said as how rattlesnakes was everywhere; an' ther Injuns was mos' twice es big es they be yere."

"But Clarke, and nearly all of his men, got back safely," I protested.

"Oh, I guess some on 'em got back, 'cause they was an awful lot in thet army, mighty nigh two thousand on 'em, Ephriam said; but, I tell ye, they hed a most terrible tough time afore they did git hum. I seed my cousin whin he kim back, an' he was jist a mere shadder; though he was bigger ner you whin he went 'way."

"But Fort Dearborn is much farther to the north. Perhaps it will be better up there."

"Wuss," he insisted, with a most mournful shake of the head, "a dinged sight wuss. Ephriam said es how the further north ye wint, the tougher it got. He saw an Injun from up near the big lake — a Pottamottamie, or somethin' like thet — what was nine fut high, an' he told him es how the rivers in his kintry was all full o' man-eatin' critters like snakes, an' some on 'em hed a hundred legs ter crawl with, an' cud travel a dinged sight faster ner a hoss. By gosh! but you bet I don't want none on it. Your father must 'a' been plum crazy fer ter sind ye way out ther all 'lone, — jist a green boy like you. What ye a-goin' fer, enyhow?"

I explained to him the occasion and necessity for my trip, but he shook his head dubiously, his long face so exceedingly mournful that I could not remain unaffected by it.

"Wal," he said at length, carefully weighing his words, "maybe it's all right 'nough, but I've got my doubts jist the same. I 'll bet thet ther gal is jist one o' them will-o'-the-wisps we hear on, an' you never will find her. You 'll jist wander 'round, huntin' an' huntin' her, till ye git old, or them monsters git ye. An' I 'll be blamed if ever I heerd tell o' no sich fort as thet, nohow."

Seth was certainly proving a Job's comforter; and I was already sufficiently troubled about the final outcome of my adventure. Hence my only hope of retaining any measure of courage was to discountenance further conversation, and we continued to jog along in silence, although I caught him looking at me several times in a manner that expressed volumes.

We camped that night in the dense heart of some oak woods, beside a pleasant stream of clear, cool water. Late the following evening, just as the sun was disappearing behind the trees, our wearied horses emerged suddenly upon the bank of a broad river, and we could discern the dim outlines of Hawkins's buildings amid the deepening shadows of the opposite shore.

Upon one thing I was now fully determined. Seth should start back with the first streak of the next dawn. His long face and dismal croakings kept me constantly upon nettles, and I felt that I should face the uncertain future with far stouter heart if he were out of my sight. Firm in this resolve, I urged my horse to splash his reluctant way through the shallows of the ford; and as our animals rose on the steep bank

of the western shore, we found ourselves at once in
the midst of a group of scattered buildings. It seemed
quite a settlement in that dim light, although the
structures were all low and built of logs. The largest
and most centrally located of these was evidently the
homestead, as it had a rudely constructed porch in
front, and a thin cloud of smoke was drifting from its
chimney. As I drew nearer, I could perceive the reflection of a light streaming out through the open
doorway.

No one appeared in answer to our shouting, — not
even a stray dog; and, in despair of thus arousing the
inhabitants, I flung my rein to Seth, and, mounting
the doorstep, peered within. As I did so, a shiny,
round, black face, with whitened eyes and huge red
lips, seemed to float directly toward me through the
inner darkness. It was so startling an apparition that
I sprang back in such haste as nearly to topple over
backward from the steps. Heaven alone knows what
I fancied it might be; indeed, I had little enough time
in which to guess, for I had barely touched the ground,
— my mind still filled with memories of Seth's grotesque horrors, — when the whole figure emerged into
view, and I knew him instantly for a negro, though I
had never before seen one of his race. He was a
dandified-looking fellow, wearing a stiff white waistcoat fastened by gilded buttons, with a pair of short
curly mustaches, waxed straight out at the ends; and

he stood there grinning at me in a manner that showed
all his gleaming teeth. Before I could recover my wits
enough to address him, I heard a voice from within
the house, — a soft, drawling voice, with a marked
foreign accent clinging to it.

"Sam," it called, "have you found either of the
scoundrelly rascals?"

The darkey started as if shot, and glanced nervously back over his shoulder.

"No, sah," he replied with vigor, "dat Mistah
Hawkins am not yere, sah. An' dat Mistah Burns has
gone 'way fer gud, sah. But dar am a gemman yere,
sah, — "

"What!" came a surprised ejaculation that
caused the negro to jump, and I heard a chair overturned within. "A gentleman? Sam, don't deceive
me! For the love of Heaven, let me see him. May I
be bastinadoed if it has n't been three months since
my eyes beheld the last specimen! Sam, where was
it I saw the last one?"

"Montreal, sah."

"By Saint Guise! 't is gospel truth," and the
speaker strode forward, candle in hand. "Here, now,
you ace of spades," he cried impatiently, "hold the
flame until I bid this paragon of the wilderness fit
welcome in the name of Hawkins, who strangely
seems to have vanished from the sylvan scene. Alas,
poor Hawkins! two gentlemen at one time, I greatly

fear, will be the death of him. Would that his good friend Burns might be with him on this festive occasion. Ye gods, what a time it would be!"

As the black hastily reached out for the candlestick, his erratic master as quickly changed his mind.

"No," he muttered thoughtfully, drawing back within the hall; "'t is far more fit that such formal greeting should occur within, where the essentials may be found with which to do full courtesy. I will instead retire. Sam, bid the gentleman meet me in the banquet hall, and then, mark you, thou archfiend of blackness, seek out at once that man Hawkins in his hidden lair, and bid him have ample repast spread instantly, on pain of my displeasure. By all the saints! if it be not at once forthcoming I will toast the scoundrel over his own slow fire."

"Seth," I said to my staring companion, as soon as I could recover from my own surprise, "find a place for the horses somewhere in the stables, and come in."

"Where is your master to be found?" I questioned of the black, whose air of self-importance had been resumed the moment he was left alone.

"Second door to de right, sah," he answered, gazing curiously at my deerskin hunting-shirt as I pressed by.

I had little difficulty in finding it, for all that the way was totally dark, as the fellow within was lustily carolling a French love-song. I hung back for a moment, striving vainly to distinguish the words.

Without pausing to make my presence known, I opened the door quietly, and stepped within. The room was not a large one, though it occupied the full width of the house; and the two lighted candles that illumined it, one sitting upon a table otherwise bare, the other occupying the rude dresser in the far corner, revealed clearly the entire interior.

The sole occupant of the room sat upon a corner of the table, one foot resting on the floor, the other dangling carelessly. Hardly more than a year my elder, he bore in his face the indelible marks of a life vastly different. His features were clear-cut, and undeniably handsome, with a curl of rare good-humor to his lips and an audacious sparkle within his dark eyes. His hat, cocked and ornamented in foreign fashion, lay beside him; and I could not help noting his long hair, carefully powdered and arranged with a nicety almost conspicuous, while his clothing was rich in both texture and coloring, and exhibited many traces of vanity in ribbon and ornament. Within his belt, fastened by a large metal clasp, he wore a pearl-handled pistol with long barrel; and a rapier, with richly jewelled hilt, dangled at his side. Altogether he made a fine figure of a man, and one of a sort I had never met before.

If he interested me, doubtless I was no less a

study to him. I could see the astonishment in his eyes, after my first entrance, change to amusement as he gazed. Then he brought a white hand down, with a smart slap, upon the board beside him.

"By all the saints!" he exclaimed, "but I believe the black was right. 'T is the face of a gentle, or I know naught of the breed, though the attire might fool the very elect. Yet, *parbleu!* if memory serves, 't is scarcely worse than what I wore in Spain."

He swung down upon his feet and faced me, extending one hand with all cordiality, while lips and eyes smiled pleasantly.

"Monsieur," he said, bowing low, and with a grace of movement quite new to me, "I bid you hearty welcome to whatsoever of good cheer this desert may have to offer, and present to you the companionship of Villiers de Croix. It may not seem much, yet I pledge you that kings have valued it ere now."

It was a form of introduction most unfamiliar to me, and seemed bristling with audacity and conceit; but I recognized the heartiness of his purpose, and hastened to make fit response.

"I meet you with much pleasure," I answered, accepting the proffered hand. "I am John Wayland."

The graceful recklessness of the fellow, so conspicuous in each word and action, strongly attracted me. I confess I liked him from his first utterance, although mentally, and perhaps morally as well, no two men of our age could possibly be more unlike.

"Wayland?" he mused, with a shrug, as if the sound of the word was unpleasant. "Wayland?— 't is a harsh name to my ears, yet I have heard it mentioned before in England as that of a great family. You are English, then?"

I shook my head emphatically; for the old wounds of controversy and battle were then being opened afresh, and the feeling of antagonism ran especially high along the border.

"I am of this country," I protested with earnestness, "and we call ourselves Americans."

He laughed easily, evidently no little amused at my retort, twisting his small mustache through his slender fingers as he eyed me.

"Ah! but that is all one to me; it is ever the blood and not the name that counts, my friend. Now I am French by many a generation, Gascon by birth, and bearing commission in the Guard of the Emperor; yet sooth, 't is the single accursed drop of Irish blood within my veins that brings me across the great seas and maroons me in this howling wilderness. But sit down, Monsieur. There will be both food and wine served presently, and I would speak with you more at ease."

As he spoke he flung himself upon a low settee, carelessly motioning me toward another.

"On my word," he said, eying me closely as I crossed over to the bench, "but you are a big fellow for your years, and 't is strength, not flabby flesh, or I know not how to judge. You would make a fine figure of a soldier, John Wayland. Napoleon perchance might offer you a marshal's baton, just to see you in the uniform. *Parbleu!* I have seen stranger things happen."

"You are now connected with the French army?" I questioned, wondering what could have brought him to this remote spot.

"Ay, a Captain of the Guard, yet an exile, banished from the court on account of my sins. *Sacre!* but there are others, Monsieur. I have but one fault, my friend, — grave enough, I admit, yet but one, upon my honor, and even that is largely caused by that drop of Irish blood. I love the ladies over-well, I sometimes fear; and once I dared to look too high for favor."

"And have you stopped here long?"

"Here — at Hawkins's, mean you? Ten days, as I live; would you believe I could ever have survived so grievous a siege?" and he looked appealingly about upon the bare apartment. "Ten days of Hawkins and of Sam, Monsieur; ay! and of Ol' Burns; of sky, and woods, and river, with never so much as a real white man even to drink liquor with. By Saint Louis! but I shall be happy enough to face you across the board to-night. Yet surely it is not your purpose to halt here long? "

" Only until I succeed in joining some party travelling westward to the Illinois country."

" No! is that your aim? 'T is my trip also, if Fate be ever kind enough to bring hither a guide. *Sacre!* there was one here but now, as odd a devil as ever bore rifle, and he hath taken the western trail alone, for he hated me from the start. That was Ol' Burns. Know you him? "

" 'T was he who brought the message that sent me here; yet he said little of his own journey. But you mention not where you are bound? "

" I seek Fort Dearborn, on the Great Lake."

" That likewise is to be the end of my journey. You go to explore? "

" Explore? Faith, no," and he patted his hand upon the bench most merrily. " There are but two reasons to my mind important enough to lure a French gentleman into such a hole as this, and send him wandering through your backwoods, — either war or love, Monsieur; and I know of no war that calleth me."

Love, as he thus spoke of it, was almost an unknown term to me then; and, in truth, I scarcely grasped the full significance of his meaning.

" You seek some lady, then, at Fort Dearborn? " I asked, for his tone seemed to invite the inquiry.

"Ay!" with quickened enthusiasm; "'t is there Toinette has hidden herself for this year or more, — Toinette, on my word as a French soldier, the fairest maid of Montreal. I have just discovered her whereabouts, yet I shall win her ere I traverse these trails again, or I am not Villiers de Croix."

"I travel thither to bring back a little orphan child with me," I explained simply, in response to his look, "and will most gladly aid you where I can."

Before he could answer, Hawkins, a gaunt, silent frontiersman, together with Sam, entered the room, bearing between them our evening meal.

CHAPTER IV

CAPTAIN WELLS OF FORT WAYNE

E tarried at the table a considerable time, — not because of any tempting variety in the repast, as the food furnished was of the coarsest, but for the sake of companionship, and because we discovered much of passing interest to converse about. De Croix had travelled widely, and had seen a great variety of life both in camp and court. He proved a vivacious fellow, full of amusing anecdote, — a bottle of rich wine drawn from his own private stock so stimulating his imagination that I had little to do but sit and listen. Yet he contrived to learn from me, — how, I hardly know, — the simple story of my life, and, indeed, assumed a certain air of patronizing superiority, boasting unduly of his wider experience and achievements in a way that somewhat nettled me at last, as I began to comprehend that he was merely showing off his genteel graces the better to exhibit his contempt for my provincial narrowness. I did not permit this really to anger me, for our views upon such matters were totally different, and I could not help feel admiration for the brilliant and audacious fellow.

The black waited upon us while we ate and drank, moving noiselessly across the rough floor, so keenly observant of his master's slightest wish as to convince me the latter possessed a temper which upon occasion burst its bounds. Yet now he was surely in the best of humors; and with the coming of our second bottle, after the remains of the repast had been removed, he sang several love-songs in his native tongue, the meaning of which I could only guess at.

"Saint Guise!" he exclaimed at last, flinging one booted foot over the table corner. "You are a very sphinx of a fellow. You deny being English, yet you have all the silence of that nation. I am hungry, Monsieur, for the sweet sound of the French tongue."

"'T is a language of which I know little," I answered, striving to speak pleasantly, although his manner was becoming less and less to my liking. "I have met with your *coureurs de bois* in plenty, and picked up sufficient of their common phrases to enable me to converse on ordinary themes with them; yet I confess I find it difficult to follow your speech."

"*Canaille,*" he returned, in tone of undisguised

contempt, " Canadian half-breeds, the very offscour-
ings of our people. *Sacre!* but you should know us
at home, Monsieur, — we are the conquerors of the
world!"

I wish I could picture to you how he said this.
Simple as it now reads, he made it vital with meaning.
The insolent boast was uttered with such a swagger
that my face instantly flushed, and he noted it.

" Is it not true, Monsieur?" he asked quickly, his
own blood heated by the wine. " I tell you, the whole
of Europe has trembled, and will again, at the nod of
our Napoleon. Why, even over here we had to come
with our legions to help you repel the redcoats. Saint
Guise! but it was the Frenchmen who made you a
nation."

" Ay! but only that they might revenge themselves upon England," I retorted blindly, " and the
force sent merely hurried a result already inevitable;
yet we gave you a slight touch of our own quality in
'98 that stung a bit, I warrant."

" Bah! a ship or two. 'T was well for you that
our army was so closely engaged elsewhere, or the
story would have a different ending."

We were both of us upon our feet by this time,
glaring at each other across the board, our faces hot
with the ill-restrained passion of youth. A word more
from either would surely have precipitated matters;
but before it could be spoken the door leading into the

hallway was hurriedly flung aside, and, without apology for the intrusion, two men strode forward into the glare of light.

"Serve supper here, Hawkins," commanded the first, his back still turned toward us. "Anything you may chance to have in the house, — only let there be little delay."

He was a tall, dark-featured man, smoothly shaven, as swarthy as an Indian, with stern dark eyes, thick coarse hair, and an abrupt manner born of long command. His companion, of lighter build and younger face, was attired in a travel-stained uniform of blue and buff; but he who was evidently the leader was so completely wrapped within the folds of a riding-cloak as to reveal nothing of rank other than his unmistakable military presence and bearing. Turning from the door, he swept a penetrating glance over us, loosening the clasp of his cloak as he did so.

"I regret having thoughtlessly interrupted your quarrel, gentlemen," he said brusquely, "but this appears to be the sole excuse for a public-room in the place. However, my services are at your command if they be desired in any way."

De Croix laughed, perfectly at his ease in a moment.

"'T is scarce so serious," he explained lightly. "A mere interchange of compliments over the respective merits of our nations in war."

The stranger looked at him intently, and with some manifest disapproval.

"And yours, no doubt, was France," he said shortly.

De Croix bowed, his hand upon his heart.

"I have worn her uniform, Monsieur."

"I thought as much, and fear my sympathies may be altogether with your antagonist in the controversy. Yet what's the use of wasting life like that? Surely there is fighting enough in this world of ours for such young blades, without inventing cause for quarrel. Come, sit down once more, and join with us in whatsoever cheer our landlord may provide."

As he spoke, he flung aside his cloak, revealing beneath merely the well-worn dress of a frontiersman, with an army sword-belt buckled about the waist.

"Come, Walter," he called to his companion, who remained standing, "there is to be no touch of ceremony here to-night. Gentlemen, I am Captain Wells, formerly of the army, now Indian agent at Fort Wayne; and this is Sergeant Jordan."

The Frenchman bowed gracefully, and extended a card across the table. The other glanced at it carelessly.

"Ah! De Croix; pleased to meet you. Think I heard some of our officers speak of seeing you a month ago at Detroit, — McBain or Ramsey, I have forgotten which."

"I recall a game of cards with a Lieutenant Ramsey, a rather choleric Scotchman, with a magnificent capacity for strong whiskey."

The Captain turned inquiringly toward me, and I hastened to name myself.

"Wayland, did you say?" he asked, with deepened interest. "'T is not a common appellation, yet I once knew a Major by that name in Wayne's command."

"My father, sir," I asserted proudly.

With quick impulsiveness he extended his hand.

"As noble a soldier as I have ever known," he exclaimed heartily. "I served with him in two campaigns. But what are you two young fellows doing here? for it would be hard to conceive of a more disheartening place of residence. Surely, De Croix, you are not permanently located in this delightful spot?"

"The saints forbid!" ejaculated the other, with an expression of horror that caused the younger officer to smile. "Yet I have already survived ten days of it. We seek to join some party bound westward, either to Fort Dearborn or beyond."

The elder officer smiled gravely, as his stern eyes wandered thoughtfully over our faces in the candlelight.

"You will scarcely find those who go beyond," he said, at last, slowly. "That is our extreme frontier;

and even this post, I hear it rumored, is to be abandoned shortly. Indeed, I am now proceeding thither, hoping to escort a niece safely eastward because of that very probability. I can offer you naught save companionship and guidance upon the journey; yet if you needs must go, you may ride with us and welcome. But 't is my first duty to advise you strongly against it."

"You look for trouble?" I asked, for his words and manner were grave.

"I am not one easily alarmed," he answered, scanning our faces as we fronted him; "but I have lived long among the Indians, and know them well. This new war with England will not pass without atrocities along the border, and in my judgment we are now on the eve of a general uprising of the savages. It will surely come with the first news of British success, and 't is the fear of reverses at Dearborn that has hurried me westward. You, sir," and he turned toward me, "are young, but it is evident you have been bred to the frontier, so you will realize what it may mean to us if we be caught in the Illinois country by such an uprising."

I bowed, deeply impressed by his earnestness.

"I have, indeed, seen something of savage warfare, and know much of its horror," I replied stoutly. "Yet what you say of the possible future only makes more urgent my duty to press on."

" And you? " he asked De Croix.

" Faith, Captain," was the instant reply, " it is the gentle hand of love which leads me westward, and never yet did a true Frenchman hesitate in such a quest because danger lurked between."

Wells smiled grimly.

" Then my conscience is left clear," he exclaimed heartily; " and if you ride with me to death, 't is of your own choosing. However, glad enough we have cause to be thus to gain two more fighting men. I have a party of Miamis travelling with me, and I doubt not there will be ample work for all before we return. Here comes supper; let us eat, drink, and be merry, even though to-morrow it be our fate to die. 'T is the best border philosophy."

CHAPTER V

THROUGH THE HEART OF THE FOREST

E lingered long over the wine, — for that which De Croix had furnished proved excellent, and greatly stimulated our discourse. Yet, I must confess, it was drunk chiefly by the Frenchman and Jordan; for Wells barely touched his glass, while I had never acquired a taste for such liquor. De Croix waxed somewhat boastful, toward the last; but we paid small heed to him, for I was deeply interested in Captain Wells's earlier experiences among the savages, which he related gravely and with much detail. Jordan proved himself a reckless, roistering young fellow, full of high spirits when in liquor; yet I formed an impression that he stood well in his commander's favor, for the latter warned him kindly to be more abstemious.

However late it may have been when we finally sought rest, we were early astir the next morning.

I despatched Seth upon his return journey to the farm, bearing under his girdle as cheerful a note of farewell as I could frame; and then, though it was scarce later than sun-up, the rest of us were fairly upon the westward trail. There were in the party thirty Miami Indians, strong, lusty-looking warriors, most of them. The larger portion of them travelled in our advance, under command of one of their chiefs; a smaller detachment acting in similar manner as a rear-guard. The white men, as well as the negro, who controlled a pack animal heavily laden with his master's baggage, were on horseback; and it pleased me greatly, — for I was young and easily flattered, — to have Captain Wells rein in his horse at my side as soon as we were safely across the ford, leaving the Frenchman either to companion with Jordan or ride alone.

I looked at De Croix curiously, as he moved forward with slow carelessness in our front, for he had kept the entire company waiting outside the house for half an hour in the gray dawn while he curled and powdered his hair. Doubtless this was what so disgusted Wells, whose long black locks were worn in a simple queue, tied somewhat negligently with a dark cord. I almost smiled at the scowl upon his swarthy face, as he contemplated the fashionably attired dandy, whose bright-colored raiment was conspicuous against the dark forest-leaves that walled us round.

" I have heard it claimed these gay French beaux

fight well when need arises," he commented at last, thoughtfully; "but 't is surely a poor place here for flaunting ribbons and curling locks. Possibly my fine gentleman yonder may have occasion to test his mettle before we ride back again. Sure it is that if that time ever comes he will not look so sweet."

"You make me feel that we go forward into real peril," I said, wondering that he should seem so fearful of the outcome. "Have you special reason?"

"The Miamis have already been approached by Indian runners, and their young men are restless. It was only because I am the adopted son of Big Turtle, and a recognized warrior of their tribe, that these have consented to accompany me; and I fear they may desert at the first sign of a hostile meeting," he answered gravely. "There is an Indian conspiracy forming, and a most dangerous one, involving, so far as I can learn, every tribe north of the Ohio. Now that war with England has actually been declared, there can no longer be doubt that the chiefs will take sides with the British. They have everything to gain and little to lose by such action. The rumor was at Fort Wayne, even before we left, that Mackinac had already fallen; and if that prove true, every post west of the Alleghanies is in danger. I fear that death and flame will sweep the whole frontier; and I frankly acknowledge, Wayland, my only hope in this expedition is that, by hard travel, we may be able to reach Chicagou

43

and return again before the outbreak comes. Tom Burns, an old scout of Wayne's, and a settler in that country, was at Fort Wayne a month since with an urgent message from the commandant at Dearborn. I tell you frankly, it will be touch and go with us."

"Chicagou?" I questioned, for the word was one I had heard but once before and was of an odd sound.

"Ay! old Au Sable called it the Chicagou portage long before the fort named Dearborn was ever established there. 'T is the name the French applied to a small river entering the Great Lake from the west at that point."

"Have you journeyed there before?"

"Once, in 1803. I held Indian council on the spot, and helped lay out the government reservation. 'T is a strange flat country, with much broken land extending to the northward."

Little by little our conversation lapsed into silence; for the narrow trail we followed was a most difficult one, and at times taxed our ingenuity to the utmost. It led through dense dark woods, fortunately free from underbrush, skirted the uncertain edges of numerous marshes in the soft ooze of which the hoofs of our horses sank dangerously, and for several miles followed the sinuous course of a small but rapid stream, the name of which I have forgotten. There were few openings in the thick forest-growth, and the matted branches overhead, interlaced with luxuriant wild vines, so completely shut out all vestige of the sun that we toiled onward, hour after hour, in continuous twilight.

What mysterious signs our guides followed, I was not sufficiently expert in woodcraft to determine. To my eyes, — and I sought to observe with care, — there was nowhere visible the slightest sign that others had ever preceded us; it was all unbroken, virgin wilderness, marked only by slow centuries of growth. The accumulation of moss on the tree-trunks, as well as the shading of the leaves, told me that we continued to journey almost directly westward; and there was no perceptible hesitancy in our steady progress, save as we deviated from it here and there because of natural obstacles too formidable to be directly surmounted.

We skirted immense trees, veritable monarchs of the ages, hoary with time, grim guardians of such forest solitudes; climbed long hills roughened by innumerable boulders with sharp edges hidden beneath the fallen leaves, that lamed our horses; or descended into dark and gloomy ravines, dank with decaying vegetation, finally halting for a brief meal upon the southern edge of a small lake, the water of which was as clear and blue as the cloudless August sky that arched it. The sand of the shore where we rested was white as snow, yet De Croix had his man spread a cloak upon it before he ventured to sit down, and

with care tucked a lace handkerchief about his throat
to prevent stray crumbs from soiling the delicate yellow of his waistcoat.

"One might fancy this was to be your wedding
day, Monsieur," observed Wells, sarcastically, as
he marked these dainty preparations, and noted with
disgust the attentive negro hovering near. "We
are not perfumed courtiers dancing at the court of
Versailles."

De Croix glanced about him carelessly.

"*Mon Dieu*, no," he said, tapping the lid of a
richly chased silver snuff-box with his slender fingers.
"Yet, my dear friend, a French gentleman cannot
wholly forget all that belongs to the refinements of
society, even in the heart of the wilderness. Sam, by
any foul chance did you overlook the lavender water?"

"No, sah; it am safe in de saddle-bags."

"And the powder-puff, the small hand-mirror,
and the curling-iron?"

"I saw to ebery one ob dem, sah."

De Croix gave a deep sigh of relief, and rested
back upon the cloak, negligently crossing his legs.

"Captain," he remarked slowly and thoughtfully,
"you've no idea the trouble that negro is to me.
Would you believe it? he actually left my nail-brush
behind at Detroit, and not another to be had for love
or money this side of Montreal! And only last night
he mislaid a box of rouge, and, by Saint Denis! I

hardly dare hope there is so much as an ounce of it in the whole party."

" I rather suspect not," was the somewhat crusty reply; " yet if a bit of bear's grease could be made to serve your turn, we might possibly find some among us."

" I know not its virtue," admitted the Frenchman gravely; " yet if it reddens the lips it might be useful. But that which I had came from the shop of Jessold in Paris, and is beyond all price."

We were ten days upon this forest journey, from the time of our crossing the Maumee; and they were hard days, even to those of us long habituated to the hardships of border travel. Indeed, I know few forms of exertion that so thoroughly test the mettle of men as journeying across the wilderness. There are no artificial surroundings, either to inspire or restrain; and insensibly humanity returns to natural conditions, permitting the underlying savage to gain ascendency. I have seen more than one seemingly polished gentleman, resplendent with all the graces of the social code, degenerate into a surly brute with only a few hours of such isolation and the ceaseless irritation of the trail. Yet I must acknowledge that De Croix accepted it all without a murmur, and as became a man. His entire plaint was over the luxuries he must forego, and he made far more ado about a bit of dust soiling his white linen than about any real hardship of the march. 'T is my memory that he rather grew upon us; for his natural spirits were so high that he sang where others swore, and found cause for amusement and laughter in much that tested sorely even the Indian-like patience of Wells. He was like a boy, this gayly perfumed dandy of the French court; but beneath his laces and ribbons, his affectations and conceits, there hid a stout heart that bade him smile where other men would lie down and die. He companioned mostly with Jordan as we journeyed, for Wells never could become reconciled to his mincing ways; yet I confess now that I began to value him greatly, and longed more than once to join with the two who rode in our advance, cheering their wearisome way with quips of fancy and snatches of song. He knew it too, the tantalizing rascal, and would frequently send back a biting squib over his shoulder, hoping thus to draw me away from the silent grimfaced soldier beside whom I held place.

It was truly a rough and wild journey, full enough of hardship, and without adventure to give zest to the ceaseless toil. I know now that we made a wide detour to the southward, trusting thus to avoid any possible contact with prowling bands of either Pottawattomies or Wyandots, whom our friendly Miamis seemed greatly to dread. This took us far from the regular trail, rough and ill-defined as that was, and plunged us into an untrodden wilderness; so that there were times when we fairly had to cut our way through the twisted forest branches and tangled brakes of cane with tomahawks and hunting-knives. We skirted rocky bluffs, toiled painfully over fallen timber, or waded ankle deep in softened clay, in the black gloomy shadows of dense woods which seemed interminable, meeting with nothing human, yet constantly startling wild game from the hidden coverts, and feeling more and more, as we advanced, the loneliness and danger of our situation, — realizing that each league we travelled only added to the length and peril of our retreat if ever disaster came or Fort Dearborn were found deserted.

Captain Wells, naturally grave and silent from his long training among savages, grew more and more reticent and watchful as we progressed, riding often at my side for hours without uttering a word, his keen eyes warily searching the dark openings upon every hand as if suspecting that each spot of gloom might prove the chosen place for an ambuscade. Our Indian allies moved like shadows, gliding over the ground noiselessly; and the occasional outbursts of merriment from De Croix and his equally reckless companion grew gradually less frequent, and appeared more forced. The constant and never-ending toil of our progress, the depressing gloom of the sombre primeval forest on every side of us, the knowledge of possible peril lurking in each league of this haunted silence, weighed upon us all, and at last closed the lips of even the most jovial of our number.

It was the tenth day, as I remember, — though it may have been later, for I have no writing to guide me concerning dates, — when we emerged into a broad valley, treeless save for a thin fringe of dwarfed growth skirting the bank of a shallow stream which ran almost directly westward. I cannot describe how sweet, after our gloomy journey, the sunlight appeared, as we first marked it play in golden waves over the long grass; or the relief we felt at being able to gaze ahead once more and see something of the country that we were traversing. 'T was like a sudden release from prison. Our jaded horses felt with us the exhilaration of the change, and moved with greater sprightliness than they had shown for days. As the sun began its circle downward, vast rolling hills of white and yellow sand arose upon the right of our line of march, — huge mounds, many of them, glistening in the sunshine, some jagged at the summit, others rounded as if by art, so unusual in form and presence that I ventured to address our leader regarding them, as he rode with his head bent low and a far-off look in his eyes.

"The sand?" he questioned, glancing up as if startled at the sound of my voice. "Why, it has been cast there by the stormy waves of the Great Lake, my lad, and beaten into those strange and fantastic shapes by the action of the wind. Doubtless 't is the work of centuries of storms."

"Are we, then, so close to the lake?" I asked eagerly, — for I had never yet seen so large a body of water, and his description fired my imagination.

"'T is but just beyond those dunes yonder, and will be still nearer when we come to camp. Possibly you might reach the shore before dark if you exercise care, — for there is danger of becoming lost in that sand desert. Those hills seem all alike when once you are among them."

"What is it that so greatly disturbs your Miamis?" I ventured to ask, for I had been noticing for some time that they were restless and travelling poorly. "They have been counselling now for two hours."

He glanced aside at me in apparent surprise.

"Why, boy, I thought you were bred to the border; and can you ask me such a question? Do you observe nothing, like that fine gentleman yonder? What have we been following since first we entered this valley?"

"An old Indian trail."

"True," he exclaimed, "and one that has been traversed by a large war-party, bound west, within twelve hours."

"How know you this?"

"By a hundred signs far plainer than print will ever be to my eyes. In faith, I thought those fellows

out yonder would have summoned me to council long
ere this, instead of threshing it out among themselves.
They are bolder warriors than I deemed, though they
will doubtless revolt in earnest when we camp. We
shall have to guard them well to-night."

As he paused, his eyes fixed anxiously upon our
Indian allies, De Croix began to hum a popular tune
of the day, riding meanwhile, hat in hand, with one
foot out of the stirrup to beat the time. Then Jordan
caught up the refrain, and sang a verse. I saw one or
two of the older Indians glance around at him in grave
displeasure.

"The young fools!" muttered Wells, uneasily.
"I shall enjoy seeing if that French popinjay keeps all
of his fine airs when the hour for stern work comes."

He lifted his voice.

"Jordan!"

The young soldier instantly ceased his song, and
turned in his saddle to glance back.

"The time has come when I must insist on less
noise, and more decorum upon the march," Wells said
sternly. "This is not Fort Wayne, nor is our road
devoid of danger. Captain de Croix, I shall have to request you also to cease your singing for the present."

There was that in his voice and manner which
forbade remark, and we rode on silently. I asked:

"But you have not explained to me how you
learned all this of which you spoke?"

"By the use of my eyes, of course. It is all simple; there are marks beside the beaten trail, as well as in its track, which prove clearly the party ahead of us to be moving westward, that it travelled rapidly, and was certainly not less than a hundred strong, with ponies and lodge-poles. Not more than a league back we passed the evidences of a camp that had not been deserted longer than twelve hours; and when we crossed the river, a feather from a war-bonnet was lying in the grass. These are small details, yet they tell the story. That feather, for instance, was dropped from a Pottawattomie head-dress, and no doubt there are warriors among those Indians yonder who could name the chief who wore it. It simply means, my lad, that the savages are gathering in toward Dearborn, and we may reach there all too late."

"Is the way yet long?" and my eyes sought the horizon, where the sun hung like a red ball of fire.

"We should be there by the morrow," he answered, "for we are now rounding the head of the Great Lake. I wish to God I might see what fate awaits us there."

Young and thoughtless as I was in those days, I could not fail to realize the depth of feeling which swayed this stern, experienced man; and I rode on beside him, questioning no more.

CHAPTER VI

FROM THE JAWS OF DEATH

THINK it must be in the blood of all of New England birth to love the sea. They may never have seen it, nor even heard its wild, stern music; yet the fascination of great waters is part of their heritage. The thought of that vast inland ocean, of the magnitude and sublimity of which I had only the vaguest conception, haunted me all that afternoon; and I scarcely removed my eyes from those oddly constructed mounds of drifted sand, striving vainly to gain, through some depression between them, a fleeting glimpse of the restless waters that had helped to shape them into such fantastic forms.

As the sun sank, angry red in our faces, presaging a storm, the course of the little stream we had been following drew in closer toward these grotesque piles, and the trail we followed became narrower, with the sluggish current pressing upon one side and that odd bank of gleaming sand upon the other. In a little open space, where quite a carpet of coarse yellowish grass had found lodgment, beneath the protecting shadow of a knot of cottonwoods, we finally made camp, and proceeded to prepare our evening meal. Determined to strike north through those guarding sand-dunes, and reach the shore of the lake if possible before final darkness fell, I hastily crowded my pockets with food, and looked eagerly around for some congenial companion. Captain Wells, whom I should have preferred to be with me, was deep in conference with one of the Miami chiefs, and not to be disturbed; Jordan had seemingly been detailed to the command of the night-guard; so, as a last resort, I turned aside and sought De Croix. I found him seated cross-legged on a blanket beneath one of the cottonwoods, a silver-backed mirror propped against a tree-butt in his front, while the obsequious darkey was deliberately combing out his long hair and fashioning it anew. The Frenchman glanced up at me with a welcoming smile of rare good-humor.

"Ah, sober-face! and have you at last mustered courage to break away from the commander of this most notable company?" he cried mockingly. "'T is passing strange he does not chain you to his saddle! By Saint Guise! 't would indeed be the only way in which so dull a cavalier would ever hold me loyal to his whims. Friend Wayland, I scarce thought you would ever thus honor me again; and yet, 't is true, I have had an ambition within my heart ever since we first met. 'T is to cause you to fling aside those rough habiliments of the wilderness, and attire yourself in garments more becoming civilized man. Would that I might induce you, even now, to permit Sam to rearrange those heavy blond locks à la Pompadour. Bless me! but it would make a new man of you."

"Such is not at all my desire, Monsieur," I answered, civilly. "I came now merely to learn if you would walk with me through these dunes of sand before the daylight fades."

He looked out, idly enough, across that dreary expanse of desolation, and shrugged his shoulders.

"Use the other powder, Sam, the lighter colored," he murmured languidly, as if the sight had wearied him; "and mind you drop not so much as a pinch upon the waistcoat."

Then he lifted his eyes inquiringly to mine.

"For what?" he asked.

"To look forth upon the Great Lake. Captain Wells tells me 't is but a brief and safe walk from here to the shore-line."

"The lake? — water?" and the expression upon his face made me smile. "Mon Dieu, man! have you become crazed by the hard march? What have I ever said in our brief intercourse that could cause

56

you to conceive I care greatly for that? If it were
only wine, now!"

"You have no desire to go with me, then?"

"Lay out the red tie, Sam; no, the one with the
white spots in it, and the small curling-iron. No,
Monsieur; what you ask is impossible. I travel to
the west for higher purpose than to gaze upon a
heaving waste of water. *Sacre!* did I not have a full
hundred days of such pleasure when first I left France?
My poor stomach has not fairly settled yet from its
fierce churning. Know ye not, Master Wayland, that
we hope to be at this Fort Dearborn upon the morrow,
and 't is there I meet again the fair Toinette? Saints!
but I must look my best at such a time, not worn and
haggard from tramping through the sand. She was
ever a most critical maid in such matters, and has not
likely changed. 'T is curled too high upon the right
brow, you black imp! and, as I live, there is one hair
you have missed entirely."

Realizing the uselessness of waiting longer, I
turned my back upon his vanity, and strode off alone.
It is not my nature to swerve from a purpose merely
because others differ in desires; and I was now determined to carry out my plan. I took one of the narrow
depressions between two mounds of sand and plunged
resolutely forward, endeavoring to shape my course
as directly northward as the peculiarities of the path
would admit. To my mind, there was little to fear

from the hostile Indians, as every sign proved them to be hastening westward in advance of us; while I was too long accustomed to adventure to be easily confused, even in the midst of that lonely desolation.

I soon found the walking difficult; for I sank to the ankles with each step, while the soft sliding sand rolled beneath me so as to yield no solid foothold. The irregularity of the mounds continually blocked my passage, and caused me to deviate in direction, so that I grew somewhat bewildered, the entire surface bearing such uniformity of outline as to afford little guide. Yet I held to my original course fairly well, for I could pilot somewhat by the dim north star; and it was not long before my alert ears caught the pounding of surf along the shore-line. Much encouraged, I pressed forward with greater rapidity, ignoring the lanes between the dunes, and clambering over the mounds themselves in my eagerness to reach the lake before the complete closing down of night.

At last I topped a particularly high ridge that felt solid to the feet; and as I did so the wind came, hard and biting, against my face. There, just below me, not fifty feet away, were rolling the great waves, white-capped and roaring, pounding like vast sledges upon the anvil of the sand. My entire being thrilled at the majestic sight, and for the moment I forgot everything as I gazed away across those restless, heaving waters, seemingly without limit, stretching forth into the dim northward as far as the eye could reach, until water and sky imperceptibly met and blended. Each advancing wave, racing toward the beach, was a white-lipped messenger of mystery; and the vast tumultuous sea, rolling in toward me out of that dark unknown, with its deep voice of thunder and high-bursting spray, breathed the sublimest lessons of the Infinite to my soul. It awed, impressed, silenced with the sense of its solemn power. No dream of ocean grandeur had ever approached the reality now outspread before me, as this vast inland sea tossed and quivered to the lashing of the storm-wind that swept its surface into fury.

To the left and right of where I stood motionless, curved the shore-line, a seemingly endless succession of white shining sand-hills, with the sloping shingle up which the huge breakers tossed and rolled in continuous thunder and foam, rising, breaking, receding, chasing each other in gigantic play. How savagely strong it all looked! what uncontrollable majesty lived in every line of the scene! The very suggestion of tremendous power in it was, to my imagination, immeasurably increased by its unutterable loneliness, its seemingly total absence of life; for not a fin rose above the surface, not a wing brushed the air overhead. The sun, sinking slowly behind the rim of sand, shot one golden-red ray far out into that tumbling waste, forming a slender bridge of ever-changing light that seemed to rest suspended upon the breaking crests of the waves it spanned. Then, gradually, stealthily, silently, the denser curtain of the twilight drew closer and closer, and my vista narrowed, as the shadows swept toward me like black-robed ghosts.

I turned about reluctantly, to retrace my steps while the dim light yet lingered. Some unseen angel of mercy it must have been that bade me pause, and led me gently down the steep bank to the water's edge, where the sharp spray lashed my cheeks. If this be not the cause, then I know not why I went; or why, once being there, I should have turned to the right, and rounded the edge of the little bay. Yet all of this I did; and God knows that many a time since I have thanked Him for it upon my knees.

I saw first the thing bobbing up and down behind a bare wave-washed rock that lifted a hoary crown close beside the water's edge. A branch from off some tree, I thought, until I had taken a half-dozen curious steps nearer, and felt my heart bound as I knew it to be a boat. My first thought, of course, was of hostile Indians; and I swept the sand-hills anxiously for any other sign of human presence. The world about me was soundless except for the ceaseless roaring of the waves, and there was not even a leaf within my sight to flutter. I crept forward cautiously, seeing no footprints on the smooth sand, until my searching eyes rested upon a white hand, dangling, as if lifeless, over the boat's gunwale. Forgetting everything else in the excitement of this discovery, I sprang hastily forward and peered within the boat.

It was an awkward and rudely-formed water-craft, with neither mast nor oars, yet of fair size, broad-beamed and seaworthy. In the forward part lay the body of a woman; curled up and resting upon the boat's bottom, the head buried upon the broad seat so that no face was visible, with one hand hidden beneath, the other outstretched above the rail. So huddled was her posture that I could distinguish few details in the fading light; yet I noted that she wore a white upper garment, and that her thick hair flowed in a dense black mass about her shoulders.

For a moment I stood there helpless, believing I gazed upon death. She either moved slightly, or the waves rocked the boat so as to somewhat disturb her posture. That semblance of life sent my blood leaping once more within my veins, and I leaned over and touched her cautiously.

"Oh, go away! Please go away!" she cried, not loudly, but with a stress of utterance that caused me to start back half in terror. "I am not afraid of you, but either take my soul or go away and leave me."

"For whom do you mistake me?" I asked, my hand closing now over hers.

"For another devil come out of the black night to torture me afresh!" she answered, never once moving even to my touch. "Ah, what legions there must be to send forth so many after the soul of one poor girl! 'T is not that I shrink from the end. Death! why, have I not died a hundred deaths already? Yet do I trust the Christ and Mother Mary. But why does the angel of their mercy hold back from me so long?"

Was she crazed, driven mad by some extremity of suffering at which I could only guess? That oarless boat, beached amid the desolation of sand and the waste of water, alone told a story to make the heart sick. I hesitated, not knowing what I had best say. She lifted her head slowly, and gazed at me. I caught one glimpse of a pale young face framed in masses of black dishevelled hair, and saw large dark eyes that seemed to glow with a strange fire.

"You, — you cannot be a devil also," she said, stammeringly. "You do not look like those others, — are you a man?"

I bowed in silence, astounded by her words and appearance.

"Yet you are not of the garrison, — not of Dearborn. I have never seen your face before. Yet you are surely a man, and white. Holy Mother! can it indeed be that you have come to save me?"

"I am here to serve you by every means in my power," I answered soberly, for the wildness of her speech almost frightened me. "God, I truly think, must have led me to you."

Her wonderful eyes, questioning, anxious, doubtful, never once left my face.

"Who are you? How came you here?"

"I am named John Wayland," I replied, striving to speak as simply as might be, so that she would comprehend, "and form one of a small party travelling overland from the east toward the Fort. We are encamped yonder at the edge of the sand. I left the camp an hour ago, and wandered hither that I might look out upon the waters of the Great Lake; and here, through the strange providence of God, I have found you."

She glanced apprehensively backward over her shoulder across the darkened waters, and her slight form shook.

"Oh, please, take me away from it!" she cried, a note of undisguised terror in her voice, and her hands held out toward me in a pitiful gesture of appeal. "Oh, that horrible, cruel water! I have loved it in the past, but now I hate it; how horribly it has tortured me! Take me away, I beg, — anywhere, so that I can neither see nor hear it any more. It has neither heart nor soul." And she hid her face behind the streaming hair.

"You will trust me, then?" I asked, for I had little knowledge of women. "You will go with me?"

She flung the clinging locks back from her eyes, with an odd, imperious gesture which I thought most becoming, holding them in place with one hand, while extending the other frankly toward me.

"Go with you? Yes," she replied, unhesitatingly. "I have known many men such as you are, men of the border, and have always felt free to trust them; they are far more true to helpless womanhood than many a perfumed cavalier. You have a face that speaks of honor and manliness. Yes, I will go with you gladly."

I was deeply impressed by her sudden calmness, her rapid repression of that strange wildness of demeanor that had at first so marked her words and manner. As I partially lifted her from the boat to the sand, she staggered heavily, and would have fallen had I not instantly caught her to me. For a single moment her dark eyes looked up confidingly into mine, as she rested panting against my shoulder, and I could feel her slender form tremble within my arms.

"You are ill — faint?" I questioned anxiously.

She drew back from me with all gentleness, and did not venture again to attempt standing entirely without support.

"I am ashamed so to exhibit my weakness," she murmured. "I fear I am greatly in need of food. What day is this?"

"The twelfth of August."

"And it was the night of the tenth when I drifted

out of the mouth of the river. Ever since then I have been drifting, the sport of the winds and waves."

"Sit you down here, then," I commanded, now fully awakened to her immediate need. "The sand is yet warm from the sun, and I have food with me in my pockets."

CHAPTER VII

A CIRCLE IN THE SAND

**HAVE** since thought it almost providential that my food supply was so limited; for, after first asking me if I had eaten all I required, she fell upon it like a famished thing, and did not desist until all was gone. A threatening bank of dark cloud was creeping slowly up the northern sky as we were resting, but directly overhead the stars were shining brilliantly, yielding me sufficient light for the study of her face. She was certainly less than my own age by two or three years, a girl barely rounding into the slender beauty of her earliest womanhood, with hints of both in face and form. She was simply dressed, as, indeed, might naturally be expected in a wilderness far removed from marts of trade; but her clothing was of excellent texture, and became her well in spite of its recent exposure, while a bit of rather expensive

lace at the throat and a flutter of gay ribbons about the wrists told plainly that she did not disdain the usual adornments of her sex. And this was quickly shown in another way. She had not yet completed her frugal meal when her mind reverted to her personal appearance, and she paused, with heightened color, to draw back her loosened hair and fasten it in place with a knot of scarlet cord. It was surely a winsome face that smiled up at me then.

"I feel almost guilty of robbery," she said, "in taking all this food, which was no doubt intended for your own supper."

"Merely what chanced to be left of it," I answered heartily. "Had I so much as dreamed this stretch of sand was to yield me such companionship, I should have stinted myself more."

An expression of bewildered surprise crept into her eyes as I spoke.

"Surely you are not a mere *coureur de bois,* as I supposed from your dress," she exclaimed. "Your expression is that of an educated gentleman."

I smiled; for I was young enough to feel the force of her unconscious flattery.

"I believe I can prove descent from an old and honorable race," I said; "but it has been my fortune to be reared in the backwoods, and whatever education has come to me I owe to the love and skill of my mother."

My frankness pleased her, and she made no attempt to disguise her interest.

"I am so glad you told me," she said simply. "My mother died when I was only ten, yet her memory has always been an inspiration. Are you a Protestant?"

This unexpected question took me by surprise; yet I answered unhesitatingly, "Yes."

"I was educated at the Ursuline Convent in Montreal. It was my mother's dearest wish that I should take the vows of that order, but I fear I am far too frivolous for so serious a life. I love happy things too well, and the beautiful outside world of men and women. I ran away from the Sisters, and then my father and I voyaged to this country, where we might lead a freer life together."

"Here?" and I glanced questioningly about me into those darkening shadows which were momentarily hemming us in more closely.

"To Fort Dearborn," she explained. "We came by boat through the straits at the north; and 't was a trip to remember. My father brought out goods from Canada, and traded with the Indians. I have been in their villages. Once I was a week alone with a tribe of Sacs near Green Bay, and they called me the White Queen. I have met many famous warriors of the Wyandots and Pottawattomies, and have seen them dance at their council. Once I journeyed as far west as the Great River, across leagues and leagues of prairie," and her face lighted up at the remembrance. "Father said he thought I must be the first white woman who had ever travelled so far inland. We have been at Dearborn for nearly a year."

She rose to her feet, and swept her eyes, with some anxiety, around upon dim mounds of sand that appeared more fantastic than ever in the darkness.

"Had we not better be going?" she asked. "There is surely a storm gathering yonder."

"Yes," I answered, for I had not been indifferent to the clouds steadily banking up in the north. "Yet you have not told me your name, and I should be most glad to know it."

The girl courtesied mockingly, as though half inclined to laugh at my insistence.

"What is a name?" she exclaimed. "'T is not that for which we greatly care. Now I — I am simply Mademoiselle Antoinette, — at least, so most of those I care for call me; and from now on, the very good friend of Master John Wayland."

I was deeply conscious that I blushed at her words and manner; but with it there arose an instant query in my mind: could this be the fair Toinette whom De Croix sought so ardently? I greatly feared it; yet I resolved I would not mention his name to her.

"It has a decided French sound," I stammered.

She laughed at my tone, with a quick shrug of her shoulders.

"And pray, why not, Monsieur? Have you such a prejudice against that great people that you need speak of them with so glum a voice? Ah, but if I must, then I shall endeavor to teach you a higher regard for us."

"That may not prove so hard a task," I hastened to assure her; "though I was surprised, — you speak English with so pure an accent that I had not dreamed you other than of my own race."

"My father was of English blood," she answered more gravely; "but I fear you will find me quite of my mother's people, if ever we come to know each other well. But hark! that was surely thunder! We have loitered too long; the storm is about to break."

It was indeed upon us almost before she ceased speaking. A sudden rush of wind sent my hat flying into the darkness, and whipped her long black hair loose from its restraining knot. I had barely time to wrap my hunting-jacket closely around her shoulders, when the rain came dashing against our faces.

I drew her unresistingly around the edge of the nearest sand-pile; but this supplied poor protection against the storm, the wind lashing the fine grit into our faces, stinging us like bits of fire. I tried to ex-

cavate some sort of cave that might afford us at least
a partial shelter; but the sand slid down almost as
rapidly as I could dig it out with my hands.

"Oh, let us press on!" she urged, laying her
hand upon my arm in entreaty. "We shall become
no wetter moving, and your camp, you said, was only
a short distance away."

"But are you strong enough to walk?" And as
I leaned forward toward her, a quick flash of vivid
lightning, directly overhead, lit both our faces. I
marked she did not shrink, and no look of fear came
into her eyes.

"I am quite myself once more," she answered
confidently. "It was despair and loneliness that so
disheartened me. I have never been timid physically,
and your presence has brought back the courage I
needed."

There was a natural frankness, a peculiar confidence, about this girl, that robbed me of my usual
diffidence; and as we struggled forward through the
dampening sand, her dress clinging about her and
retarding progress, I dared to slip one arm about her
waist to help in bearing her along. She accepted this
timely aid in the spirit with which it was offered,
without so much as a word of protest; and the wind,
battering at our backs, pushed us forward.

"Oh, that troublesome hair!" she exclaimed, as
the long tresses whipped in front of our faces, blinding

71

us both. " I have never before felt so much like sacrificing it."

" I beg that you will not consider such an act now," I protested, aiding her to reclaim the truants, " for as I saw it before the darkness fell, your hair was surely worthy of preservation."

" You laugh at me; I know I must have been a far from pretty sight."

" Do you wish me to say with frankness what I thought of your appearance under such disadvantages? "

She glanced at me almost archly, in the flash of lightning that rent the sky.

" I am really afraid to answer yes, — yet perhaps I am brave enough to venture it."

" I have never been at court, Mademoiselle, and so you may not consider my judgment in such matters of much moment; but I thought you rarely beautiful."

For a moment she did not attempt to speak, but I could distinctly feel the heaving of her bosom as I held her hard against the assault of the wind, and bent low hoping to catch an answer.

" You are sincere and honest," she said at last, slowly, and I felt that the faint trace of mockery had utterly vanished from her soft voice. " 'T is manifest in your face and words. You speak not lightly, nor with mere empty compliment, as would some gilded courtiers I have known; and for that reason I do value your opinion."

"You are not angry at my presumption?"

"Angry? — I?" and she stopped and faced me, holding back her hair as she did so. "I am a woman, Monsieur; and all women, even those of us hidden here in the wilderness, like best those who admire them. I do not know that I am as beautiful as you say, yet other men have often said the same without being pressed for their opinion. No, I am not angry, — I am even glad to know you think so."

"And you surely do know?" I insisted, with a courage strange to me.

"Yes," she answered, but her eyes fell before my eagerness; "you are not one who has yet learned to lie, even to women. 'T is a relief to know there are such men still in the world."

We had come to a full halt by this time.

"Do you have any idea where we may be?" she asked, peering anxiously about, and perhaps glad to change the tone of our conversation. "I cannot note a landmark of any kind. These sand-hills seem all alike."

"I believe we have kept to the southward, for we have merely drifted with the storm; but I confess my sole guidance has been the direction of the wind, as these sand-lanes are most confusing. If there were the slightest shelter at hand, I should insist upon your waiting until the rain was over."

"No, it is better to go on. I am now wet to the skin, and shall be warmer moving than resting on this damp sand."

We must have been moving for an hour, scarcely speaking a word, for the severe exertion required all our breath. The rain had ceased, and stars began to glimmer amid the cloud-rifts overhead; but I knew now that we were lost. She stopped suddenly, and sank down upon the sand.

"I am exhausted," she admitted, "and believe we are merely moving about in a circle."

"Yes," I said, reluctantly; "we are wasting our strength to no purpose. 'T will be better to wait for daylight here."

It was a gloomy place, and the silence of those vast expanses of desolate sand was overwhelming. It oppressed me strangely.

"Let me feel the touch of your hand," she said once. "It is so desperately lonely. I have been on the wide prairie, at night and alone; yet there is always some sound there upon which the mind may rest. Here the stillness is like a weight."

Possibly I felt this depressing influence the more because of my long forest training, where at least the moaning of limbs, fluttering of leaves, or flitting of birds brings relief to the expectant senses; while here all was absolute solitude, so profound that our breathing itself was startling. The air above appeared empty and void; the earth beneath, lifeless and dead. Although neither of us was cowardly of heart, yet we instinctively drew closer together, and our eyes strained anxiously over the black sand-ridges, now barely discernible through the dense gloom. We tried to talk, but even that soon grew to be a struggle, so heavily did the suspense rest upon our spirits, so oppressed were we by imaginings of evil. I remember telling her my simple story, gaining in return brief glimpses of her experiences in Canada and the farther West. She even informed me that orders had been received, the day before she became lost upon the lake, to abandon Fort Dearborn; that an Indian runner — whom she named Winnemeg — had arrived from General Hull at Detroit, bringing also news that Mackinac had fallen.

"Doubtless your absence has greatly worried them also," I said.

"Oh, no; none of them knew my plight. Possibly some may miss me, but they will naturally suppose I have been at Mr. Kinzie's house all this time. I have been there often for weeks together, and they have frequently urged me to take shelter with them. You see it is far safer there than at the Fort, for even the most hostile Indians remain on friendly terms with Mr. Kinzie and his family. He has been there so many years, and is so just a man in his dealings with them. 'T is really strange to see how he leaves his house unguarded, while the garrison at the Fort is almost in a state of siege. It makes it hard to realize how imminent is the danger. Yet they are terribly alarmed at the Fort, and I fear with cause. Even Mr. Kinzie feels the situation to be critical. There were fully three hundred Pottawattomie warriors encamped without the Fort two days ago; and they were becoming bold and impudent, — one chief even firing his gun in Captain Heald's office, thinking to frighten him into furnishing them with liquor."

"But the Fort is strong?" I asked. "It is capable of resisting an attack?"

"I should suppose so," she answered, hesitatingly; "but that is not a matter upon which a girl may judge. I fear, however, all is not harmony among its defenders. I know that Captain Heald and Ensign Ronan do not agree, and I have heard bitter words spoken by other officers of the garrison."

I thought she did not care to speak more about this matter, and we drifted off upon other topics, until I felt her head sink slowly down upon my shoulder, and knew she slept. I sat there still, pillowing her tenderly upon my arm, when the gray light of the dawn stole slowly toward us across the ridges of sand and revealed the upturned face.

CHAPTER VIII

TWO MEN AND A MAID

HE emotion I felt was new and strange to me; for though I had known little of young women, yet as I looked upon her in that dim light of dawn I found myself wondering if I already loved this strange girl. Fair as her face certainly was, its beauty rendered even more striking by the pallor of her late exposure and the blackness of her dishevelled hair, it was her frankness and confidence which most appealed to me. She had held all my thoughts through the long hours of watchfulness as I sat there quietly, feeling the rise and fall of her regular breathing, and thrilled by the unconscious caress of stray tresses as they were blown against my cheek. How she trusted me, stranger though I was! Yet it was through no lack of knowledge of the great world of men, for this young girl had known court gallants and rough soldiery, soft-spoken courtiers and boastful men-at-arms.

77

So the night through I dreamed of what might be; and when the light finally came slowly reddening the eastern sky, I feasted my eyes unchecked upon that sweet upturned face, and made a rash vow that I would win her heart.

I was still mirroring her image in my memory, forgetful of all else, — the broad white brow, the long dark lashes resting in such delicate tracery against the smooth velvet of the cheek now slightly flushed, the witching pink of the ear, the softly parted lips between which gleamed the small and regular teeth of ivory, the round white throat swelling ever so slightly to her breathing, — when a sudden shout of surprised recognition aroused me from my reverie, and I looked up to see Jordan topping the sand-bank in our front, and waving his hand to some one beneath him and out of sight.

"See here, De Croix!" he cried, excitedly, "the prodigal has had good cause to lag behind. He has found the lost fairy of this wilderness."

Before I could relieve myself of my burden, — for the mockery of his words angered me, — the Frenchman appeared at his side, and glanced down where his companion's finger pointed. For a moment he gazed; then he murmured a sharp French oath, and strode heavily down the sand-bank. There was a look in his face that caused me to lay the girl's head back upon the sand and rise hastily. The sudden movement awoke her, and her dark eyes looked up in startled confusion. By this time I had taken a quick step forward, and faced De Croix.

"This lady is under my protection," I said, a bit hotly, not relishing the manner of his approach, "and any disrespect from either of you will be unwarranted."

He paused, evidently surprised at my bold front, and his lip curled contemptuously.

"Ah, my young game-cock!" he ejaculated, surveying me curiously. "So you have spurs, and think you can use them? Well, I have no quarrel with you, but perchance I may have more reason to be the protector of this young lady than you suppose. Stand aside, Monsieur."

She had risen from the sand, and now stood erect beside me. I saw Jordan grinning in great enjoyment of the scene, and that De Croix's eyes were full of anger; but I would not stir. In my heart I felt a dull pain at his words, a fear that they might prove too true; but I remained where I was, determined to take no step aside until she herself should judge between us.

"Will you stand back, Monsieur?" he said, haughtily, dropping his hand upon the hilt of his rapier, "or shall I show you how a gentleman of France deals with such impertinence?"

If he thought to affright me with his bravado, he reckoned ill of my nature, for I have ever driven badly;

my blood seems slow to heat, though it was warm enough now.

"If the lady wishes it, you may pass," I answered shortly, my eyes never leaving his face. "Otherwise, if you take so much as another step I will crush every bone in your body."

He saw I meant it, but there was no cowardice in him; and the steel had already flashed in the sunlight to make good his threat, when she touched me gently upon the shoulder.

"I beg you do not fight," she urged. "I am not worthy, and 't is all unneeded. Captain de Croix," and she swept him a curtsey which had the grace of a drawing-room in it, "'t is indeed most strange that we should meet again in such a spot as this. No contrast could be greater than the memory of our last parting. Yet is there any cause for quarrel because this young gentleman has preserved my life?"

De Croix hesitated, standing half-poised for attack, even his glib tongue and ready wit failing as she thus calmly questioned him. Indeed, as I later learned, there was that of witchery about this young girl which held him at bay more effectually than if she had been a princess of the royal blood, — a something that laughed his studied art to scorn. She noted now his hesitancy, and smiled slightly at the evidence of her power.

"Well, Monsieur, 't is not often that your lips

fail of words," she continued, archly. "Why is it I am made the subject of your quarrel?"

The slight sarcastic sting in her voice aroused him.

"By all the saints, Toinette!" he exclaimed, striving to appear at his ease, "this seems a poor greeting for one who has followed you through leagues of forest and across oceans of sand, hopeful at the least to gain a smile of welcome from your lips. Know you not I am here, at the very end of the world, for you?"

"I think it not altogether unlikely," she replied with calmness. "You have ever been of a nature to do strange things, yet it has always been of your own sweet will. Surely, Monsieur, I did never bid you come, or promise you a greeting."

"No," he admitted regretfully, "'t is, alas, true"; and his eyes seemed to regain something of their old audacity. "But there was that about our parting,— you recall it, Toinette, in the shadow of the castle wall?—which did afford me hope. No one so fair as you can be without heart."

She laughed softly, as though his words recalled memories of other days, pressing back her hair within its ribbon.

"Such art of compliment seems more in place at Montreal than here. This is a land of deeds, not words, Monsieur. Yet, even though I confess your conclusion partially true, what cause does it yield

6

why you should seek a quarrel with my good friend, John Wayland?"

"You know him, then?" he asked, in quick astonishment.

"Know him! Do you think I should be here otherwise? Fie, Captain de Croix, that you, the very flower of the French court, should express so poor a thought of one you profess to respect so highly!"

He looked from one to the other of us, scarce knowing whether she were laughing at him or not.

"*Sacre!*" he exclaimed at last. "I believe it not, Mademoiselle. The boy would have boasted of such an acquaintance long before this. You know him, you say, — for how long?"

"Since yester even, if you must know. But he has a face, Monsieur, a face frank and honest, not like that of a man long trained at courts to deceive. 'T is for that I trust him, and have called him friend."

"You may rue the day."

"No, Captain de Croix," she exclaimed, proudly. "I know the frontiersmen of my father's blood. They are brave men, and true of heart. This John Wayland is of that race." And she rested one hand lightly upon my arm.

The motion, simple as it was, angered him.

"You ask why I sought quarrel," he said sternly. "'T was because I suspected this uncouth hunter had wronged you. Now I understand 't was of your own choice. I wish you joy, Mademoiselle, of your new conquest."

I felt the girl's slight form straighten, and saw his bold eyes sink beneath the flame of her look.

"Captain de Croix," and every sentence stung like the lash of a whip, "those are cowardly words, unworthy a French gentleman and soldier. Did you leave all your courtesy behind in Montreal, or dream that in this wilderness I should cringe to any words you might speak? You wish the truth; you shall have it. Three days ago, through an accident, I drifted, in an oarless boat, out from the river-mouth at Fort Dearborn to the open lake. None knew of my predicament. A storm blew me helpless to the southward, and after hours of exposure to danger, and great mental anguish, I was driven ashore amid the desolation of this sand. This comrade of yours found me scarce alive, ministered to my sore need, protected me through the hours of the night, stood but now between me and your ribaldry, counting his life but little beside the reputation of a woman. He may not wear the latest Paris fashions, Monsieur, but he has proved himself a man."

"I meant not all I said, Toinette," he hastened to explain. "You will forgive, I know, for I was sorely hurt to find that some one else had done the duty that was plainly mine. Surely no rude backwoodsman is to come between us now?"

She glanced from the one to the other, with true French coquetry.

"Faith, I cannot tell, Monsieur," she said, gayly; "stranger things have happened, and 't is not altogether fine clothes that win the hearts of maidens on this far frontier. We learn soon to love strength, and the manly traits of the border. On my word, Monsieur, this John Wayland seems to have rare powers of body; I imagine he might even have crushed you, as he said."

"Think you so?" he asked, eying me curiously. "Yet 't is not always as it looks, Mademoiselle."

It came so quickly as to startle me. I was wondering at the smile that curled his lips, when he sprang upon me, casting his arms around my waist, and twining one leg about mine. The shock of this sudden and unexpected onset took me completely by surprise, and I gave back sharply, scarce realizing his purpose, till he had the under-hold, and sought to lift me for a throw. 'T was my weight alone that saved me, together with the rare good fortune that I had been leaning upon my gun.

As the breath came back to me, we locked grimly in a fierce struggle for the mastery. I had felt the straining grip of strong arms before, but De Croix surprised me, — he was like steel, quick of motion as a wildcat, with many a cunning French wrestling trick that tried me sorely. I heard a quick exclamation of surprise from the girl, a shout of delighted approval from Jordan, and then there was no sound but the harsh trampling of our feet and the heavy breathing. De Croix's effort was to lift me to his hip for a throw; mine, to press him backward by bodily strength. Both of us were sadly hindered by the sliding sand on which we strove. Twice I thought I had him, when my footing failed; and once he held me fairly uplifted from the ground, yet could not make the toss. 'T was a wild grapple, for when we had exhausted all the tricks we knew, it came to be a sheer test of physical endurance. Then, for the first time, I felt myself the master, — though he was a man, that gay French dandy, and never did my ribs crack under the pressure of a stronger hand. But I slowly pressed him back, inch by inch, struggling like a demon to the last, until I forced his shoulders to the sand.

For a moment he lay there, panting heavily; then the old frank and easy smile came upon his lips.

"Your hand, monsieur," he said; "that is, if it yet retains sufficient strength to lift me."

Upon his feet he brushed the sand from out his long hair, and bowed gallantly.

"I have done my very best, Mademoiselle. 'T is defeat, but not disgrace, for I have made your giant puff to win. May I not hope it has won me restoration to your good graces?"

CHAPTER IX

IN SIGHT OF THE FLAG

T would have been impossible not to respond to his sparkling humor and good-nature, even had the girl been desirous of doing otherwise. From the first I felt that she liked this reckless courtier, whose easy words and actions made me realize more deeply than ever my own heaviness of thought and wit.

As he stood there now, bowing low before her, his clothing awry and his long hair in disorder from our fierce contest, she smiled upon him graciously, and extended a hand that he was prompt enough to accept and hold.

"Surely," she said mockingly, "no maid, even in the glorious days of chivalry, had ever more heroic figures to do battle for her honor. I accept the *amende,* Monsieur, and henceforth enroll you as knight at my court. Upon my word," and she looked about at the desolate sand-heaps surrounding us, "'t is not much to boast of here; nor, in truth, is Dearborn greatly better."

She paused, drawing her hand gently from his grasp, and holding it out toward me.

"Yet, Captain," she continued, glancing at him archly over her shoulder, "I have likewise another knight, this wood ranger, who hath also won my deep regard and gratitude."

De Croix scowled, and twisted his short mustache nervously.

"You put a thorn beside every rose," he muttered. "'T was your way in Montreal."

"A few hundred miles of travel do not greatly change one's nature. Either at Dearborn or Montreal, I am still Toinette. But, Messieurs, I have been told of a camp quite close at hand, — and yet you leave me here in the sand to famish while you quarrel."

The tone of her voice, while still full of coquetry, was urgent, and I think we both noted for the first time how white of face she was, and how wearily her eyes shone. The Frenchman, ever ready in such courtesies, was the first to respond by word and act.

"You are faint, Toinette," he cried, instantly forgetful of everything else, and springing forward to give her the aid of his arm. "I beg you lean upon me. I have been blind not to note your weakness before. 'T is indeed not a long walk to our camp from here, — yet, on my life, I know nothing of where it lies. Jordan," he added, speaking as if he were in command, " lead back along the path we came. *Sacre !* the old bear was gruff enough over the delay of our search; he will be savage now."

I know not how Jordan ever found his way back, for the sliding sand had already obliterated all evidences of former travel; but I walked sullenly beside him, leaving De Croix to minister to the needs of the girl as best he might. I felt so dull beside his ready tongue that, in spite of my real liking for the fellow, his presence angered me. 'T is strange we should ever envy in others what we do not ourselves possess, ignoring those traits of character we have which they no less desire. So to me then it seemed altogether useless to contend for the heart of a woman, — such a woman, at least, as this laughing Toinette, — against the practised wiles of so gay and debonair a cavalier. I steeled my ears to the light badinage they continued to indulge in, and ploughed on through the heavy sand at Jordan's heels, in no mood for converse with any one.

We came upon the camp suddenly, and discovered Captain Wells pacing back and forth, his stern face dark with annoyance. At sight of me, his passion burst all restraint.

"By God, sir!" he ejaculated, "if you were a soldier of mine, I would teach you what it meant to put us to such a wait as this! Know you not, Master Wayland, that the lives of helpless women and children may depend upon our haste? And you hold us here in idleness while you wander along the lake-shore like a moonstruck boy!"

Before I could answer these harsh words, the girl stepped lightly to my side, and standing there, her hand upon my arm, smiled back into his angry eyes. I do not think he had even perceived her presence until that moment; for he stopped perplexed.

"And am I not worth the saving, Monsieur le Capitaine," she questioned, pouting her lips, "that you should blame him so harshly for having stopped to rescue me?"

His harsh glance of angry resentment softened as he gazed upon her.

"Ah! was that it, then?" he asked, in gentler tones. "But who are you? Surely you are not unattended in this wilderness?"

"I am from Fort Dearborn," she answered, "and though only a girl, Monsieur, I have penetrated to the great West even farther than has Captain Wells."

"How know you my name?"

"Mrs. Heald told me she believed you would surely come when you learned of our plight at the Fort, — it was for that she despatched the man Burns with the message, — and she described you so perfectly that I knew at once who you must be. There are not so many white men travelling toward Dearborn now as to make mistake easy."

"And the Fort?" he asked, anxiously. "Is it still garrisoned, or have we come too late?"

"It was safely held two days ago," she answered, "although hundreds of savages in war-paint were then encamped without, and holding powwow before the gate. No attack had then been made, yet the officers talked among themselves of evacuating."

For a moment the stern soldier seemed to have forgotten her, his eyes fastened upon the western horizon.

"The fools!" he muttered to himself, seemingly unconscious that he spoke aloud; "yet if I can but reach there in time, my knowledge of Indian nature may accomplish much."

He turned quickly, with a sharp glance over his military force.

"We delay no longer. Jordan, do you give this lady your horse for to-day's journey, and go you forward on foot with the Miamis. Watch them closely, and mark well everything in your front as you move."

"But, Captain Wells," she insisted, as he turned away, "I am exceedingly hungry, and doubt not this youth would also be much the better for a bit of food."

"It will have to be eaten as you travel, then," he

answered, not unkindly, but with all his thought now fixed on other things, " for our duty is to reach Dearborn at the first moment, and save those prisoned there from death, and worse."

I shall always remember each detail of that day's march, though I saw but little of Toinette save in stolen glances backward, Wells keeping me close at his side, while De Croix, as debonair as ever, was her constant shadow, ministering assiduously to her wants and cheering her journey with agreeable discourse. I heard much of their chatter, earnestly as I sought to remain deaf to it. To this end Wells aided me but little, for he rode forward in stern silence, completely absorbed in his own thoughts.

During the first few hours we passed through a dull desolation of desert sand, the queerly shaped hills on either side scarcely breaking the dead monotony, although they often hid from our sight our advance scouts, and made us feel isolated and alone. Once or twice I imagined I heard the deepening roar of waves bursting upon the shore-line to our right, but could gain no glimpse of blue water through those obscuring dunes. We were following a well-worn Indian trail, beaten hard by many a moccasined foot; and at last it ran from out the coarser sand and skirted along the western beach, almost at the edge of the waves. 'T was a most delightful change from the cramped and narrowed vision that had been ours so long. Our faces were now set almost directly northward; but I could not withdraw my eyes from the noble expanse of water heaving and tumbling in the dazzling sunlight. Indeed, there was little else about our course to attract attention; the shore in front lay clear and unbroken, bearing a sameness of outline that wearied the vision; each breaking wave was but the type of others that had gone before, and each jutting point of land was the picture of the next to follow. To our left, there extended, parallel to our course of march, a narrow ridge of white and firmly beaten sand, as regular in appearance as the ramparts of a fort. Here and there a break occurred where in some spring flood a sudden rush of water had burst through. Glancing curiously down these narrow aisles, as we rode steadily onward, I caught fleeting glimpses of level prairie land, green with waving grasses, apparently stretching to the western horizon bare of tree or shrub. At first, I took this to be water also; until I realized that I looked out upon the great plains of the Illinois.

The Captain was always chary of speech; now he rode onward with so stern a face, that presently I spoke in inquiry.

"You are silent, Captain Wells," I said. "One would expect some rejoicing, as we draw so close to the end of our long journey."

He glanced aside at me.

"Wayland," he said slowly, "I have been upon

the frontier all my life, and have, as you know, lived
in Indian camps and shared in many a savage cam-
paign. I am too old a man, too tried a soldier, ever
to hesitate to acknowledge fear; but I tell you now,
I believe we are riding northward to our deaths."

I had known, since first leaving the Maumee, that
danger haunted the expedition; yet these solemn
words came as a surprise.

"Why think you thus?" I asked, with newly
aroused anxiety, my thoughts more with the girl behind than with myself. "Mademoiselle Toinette tells
me the Fort is strong and capable of defence, and
surely we are already nearly there."

"The young girl yonder with De Croix? It may
be so, if it also be well provisioned for a long siege,
as it is scarce likely any rescue party will be despatched
so far westward. If I mistake not, Hull will have no
men to spare. Yet I like not the action of the savages
about us. 'T is not in Indian nature to hold off, as
these are doing, and permit reinforcements to go by,
when they might be halted so easily. 'T would ease
my mind not a little were we attacked."

"Attacked? by whom?"

He faced me with undisguised surprise, a sarcastic smile curling his grim mouth. His hand swept
along the western sky-line.

"By those red spies hiding behind that ridge of
sand," he answered shortly. "Boy, where are your

eyes not to have seen that every step we have taken this day has been but by sufferance of the Pottawattomies? Not for an hour since leaving camp have we marched out of shot from their guns; it means treachery, yet I can scarce tell where or how. If they have spared us this long, there is some good Indian reason for it."

I glanced along that apparently desolate sandbank, barely a hundred feet away, feeling a thrill of uneasiness sweep over me at the revelation of his words. My eyes saw nothing strange nor suspicious; but I could not doubt his well-trained instinct.

"It makes my flesh creep," I admitted; "yet surely the others do not know. Hear how the Frenchman chatters in our rear!"

"The young fool!" he muttered, as the sound of a light laugh reached us; "it will prove no jest, ere we are out of this again. Yet, Wayland," and his voice grew stronger, "the red devils must indeed mean to pass us free, — for there is Fort Dearborn, and, unless my sight deceive me, the flag is up."

I lifted my eyes eagerly, and gazed northward where his finger pointed.

CHAPTER X

A LANE OF PERIL

E passed a group of young cottonwoods, the only trees I had noted along the shore; and a few hundred feet ahead of us, the ridge of sand, which had obscured our westward view so long, gradually fell away, permitting the eye to sweep across the wide expanse of level plain until halted by a distant row of stunted trees that seemed to line a stream of some importance. As Captain Wells spoke, my glance, which had been fixed upon these natural objects, was instantly attracted by a strange scene of human activity that unfolded to the north and west.

The land before us lay flat and low, with the golden sun of the early afternoon resting hot upon it, revealing each detail in an animated panorama wherein barbarism and civilization each bore a conspicuous part. The Fort was fully a mile and a half distant, and I could distinguish little of its outward appear-

95

ance, save that it seemed low and solidly built, like a stockade of logs set upon end in the ground. It appeared gloomy, grim, inhospitable, with its gates tightly closed, and no sign of life anywhere along its dull walls; yet my heart was thrilled at catching the bright colors of the garrison flag as the western breeze rippled its folds against the blue background of the sky.

But it was outside those log barriers that our eyes encountered scenes of the greatest interest, — a mingling of tawdry decoration and wild savagery, where fierce denizens of forest and plain made their barbaric show.

No finer stage for such a spectacle could well be conceived. Upon one side stretched the great waste of waters; on the other, level plains, composed of yellow sand quickly merging into the green and brown of the prairie, while, scattered over its surface, from the near lake-shore to the distant river, were figures constantly moving, decked in gay feathers and daubed with war-paint. Westward from the Fort, toward the point where a branch of the main river appeared to emerge from the southward, stood a large village of tepees, the sun shining yellow and white on their deer-skin coverings and making an odd glow in the smoke that curled above the lodge-poles. From where we rode it looked to be a big encampment, alive with figures of Indians. My companion and I both noted, and spoke together of the fact, that they all seemed braves; squaws there may have been, but of children there were none visible.

Populous as this camp appeared, the plain stretching between it and us was literally swarming with savages. A few were mounted upon horses, riding here and there with upraised spears, their hair flying wildly behind them, their war-bonnets gorgeous in the sunshine. By far the greater number, however, were idling about on foot, stalwart, swarthy fellows, with long black locks, and half-naked painted forms. One group was listening to the words of a chief; others were playing at la crosse; but most of them were merely moving restlessly here and there, not unlike caged wild animals, eager to be free.

I heard Captain Wells draw in his breath sharply.

"As I live!" he ejaculated, "there can be scarce less than a thousand warriors in that band, — and no trading-party either, if I know aught of Indian signs."

Before I could answer him, even had I any word to say, a chief broke away from the gathering mass in our immediate front, and rode headlong down upon us, bringing his horse to its haunches barely a yard away.

He was a large, sinewy man, his face rendered hideous by streaks of yellow and red, wearing a high crown of eagle feathers, with a scalp of long light-colored hair, still bloody, dangling at his belt. For a moment he and Captain Wells looked sternly into each other's eyes without speaking. Then the savage broke silence.

"Wau-mee-nuk great brave," he said, sullenly, in broken English, using Wells's Indian name, "but him big fool come here now. Why not stay with Big Turtle? He tell him Pottawattomie not want him here."

"Big Turtle did tell me," was the quiet answer, "that the Pottawattomies had made bad medicine and were dancing the war-dance in their villages; but I have met Pottawattomies before, and am not afraid. They have been my friends, and I have done them no wrong."

He looked intently at the disguised face before him, seeking to trace the features. "You are Topenebe," he said at last.

"True," returned the chief, with proud gravity. "You serve me well once; for that I come now, and tell you go back, — there is trouble here."

Wells's face darkened.

"Have I ever been a coward," he asked indignantly, "that I should turn and run for a threat? Think you, Topenebe, that I fear to sing the death-song? I have lived in the woods, and gone forth with your war-parties; am I less a warrior, now that I fight with the people of my own race? Go take your warning to some squaw; we ride straight on to Dearborn, even though we have to fight our way."

The Indian glanced, as Wells pointed, toward the Fort, and sneered.

"All old women in there," he exclaimed derisively. "Say this to-day, and that to-morrow. They shut the gates now to keep Indian on outside. No trade, no rum, no powder, — just lies. But they no keep back our young men much longer." His face grew dark, and his eyes angry.

"Why you bring them?" he asked hotly, designating our escort of Miamis, already shrinking from the taunts of the gathering braves. "They dog Indians, bad medicine; they run fast when Pottawattomie come."

"Don't be so certain about that, Topenebe," retorted Wells, shortly. "But we cannot stop longer here; make way, that we may pass along. Jordan, push on with your advance through that rabble there."

The Indian chief drew his horse back beside the trail, and we moved slowly forward, our Indian guides slightly in advance, and exhibiting in every action the disinclination they felt to proceed, and their constantly increasing fear of the wild horde that now resorted to every means in their power, short of actual violence, to retard their progress. As they closed in more closely around us, taunting the Miamis unmercifully, even shaking tomahawks in their faces, with fierce eyes full of hatred and murder, I drew back my horse until I ranged up beside Mademoiselle Antoinette, and thus we rode steadily onward through that frenzied, howling mass, the girl between De Croix and me, who thus protected her on either side.

It was truly a weary ride, full of insult, and perchance of grave peril had we faced that naked mob less resolutely. Doubtless the chiefs restrained their young men somewhat, but more than once we came within a hair's-breadth of serious conflict. They hemmed us in so tightly that we could only walk our horses; and twice they pressed upon Jordan so hard as to halt him altogether, bunching his cowardly Miamis, and even striking them contemptuously with their blackened sticks. The second time this occurred, Captain Wells rode forward to force a path, driving the spurs into his horse so quickly that the startled animal fairly cut a lane through the crowded savages before they could draw back. Naught restrained them from open violence but their knowledge of that stern-faced swarthy soldier who fronted them with such dauntless courage. Hundreds in that swarm had seen him before, when, as the adopted son of a great war-chief of the Miamis he had been at their side in many a wild foray along the border.

"Wau-mee-nuk, the white chief," passed from lip to lip; and sullenly, slowly, reluctantly, the frenzied red circle fell back, as he pressed his rearing horse full against them.

How hideous their painted faces looked, as we slowly pushed past them, their lips shrieking insult, their sinewy hands gripping at our stirrups, their brandished weapons shaken in our faces. With firm-set lips and watchful eyes I rode, bent well forward, so as best to protect the girl, my rifle held across my saddle pommel. Twice some vengeful arm struck me a savage blow, and once a young devil with long matted hair hanging over his fierce eyes thrust a sharpened stake viciously at the girl's face. I struck with quick-clinched hand, and he reeled back into the mass with a sharp cry of pain. My eyes caught the sudden dazzle, as De Croix whipped out his rapier.

"Not that, Monsieur!" I cried hastily, across her horse's neck. "Use the hilt, not the blade, unless you wish to die."

He heard me above the clamor, and with a quick turn of the weapon struck fiercely at a scowling brave who grasped at his horse's rein. He smiled pleasantly across at me, his fingers twisting his small mustache.

"'T is doubtless good advice, friend Wayland," he said, carelessly, "but these copper-colored devils are indeed most annoying upon this side, and I may lose my temper ere we reach the gate."

"For the sake of her who rides between us, I beg that you hold in hard, Monsieur," I answered.

" 'T would be overmuch to pay, I imagine, for a hot brain."

I glanced at her as I spoke, scarcely conscious even then that I had removed my eyes from the threatening mob that pressed me, though I know I must have done so, for I retain the picture of her yet. She rode facing me, although her saddle was of the old army type with merely a folded blanket to soften its sharp contours, and her foot could barely find firm support within the narrow strap above the wooden stirrup. She sat erect and easily, swaying gently to the slow step of the horse. Her face was pale, but there was no evidence of timidity in her dark eyes, and she smiled at me as our glances met.

" You are surely a brave girl, Mademoiselle! " I exclaimed, unable to restrain my admiration. " 'T is a scene to try any nerves."

" Yet almost worth the danger," she returned softly, " to realize what men can be in such stress of need. You are the real — Beware of that half-breed, Monsieur! "

Her last words were a quick warning, yet my eyes were already upon the fellow, and as he dodged down, knife in hand, to aim a vicious lunge at the forward leg of her horse, I brought the stock of my rifle crunching against his shoulder. The next instant we had passed over his naked body as he lay gasping in the trail.

"See!" she cried, with eagerness. "The gates are opened!"

We were possibly a hundred yards from the southern front of the stockade, when I glanced forward and saw the level ground between a seething mass of savage forms, so densely wedged together as to block further progress. I could see hundreds of brown sinewy arms uplifted from a sea of faces to brandish weapons of every description, and marked how the Miamis cowered like whipped curs behind the protection of Wells's horse, while close beside him stood Jordan, erect and silent as if on parade, a rifle grasped in his hands, his head bare, a great welt showing redly across his white forehead.

A little party, hardly more than twenty infantrymen, marched steadily out from the open gateway of the Fort. The first file bore bayonets fixed upon their guns, and the naked savages fell slowly back before the polished steel. It was smartly done, and it thrilled my blood to note with what silent determination that small band of disciplined men pressed their way onward, passing through the threatening mass of redskins as indifferently as if they had been forest trees. A young, smooth-faced fellow, wearing a new officer's uniform, led them, sword in hand, a smile of light contempt upon his lips.

"Clear the space wider, Campbell!" he said sternly, to the big corporal at his side. "Swing your files to left and right, and push the rabble out of the way."

They did it with the butts of their guns, laughing at the brandished knives and tomahawks and the fierce painted faces that scowled at them, paying no apparent heed to the taunts and insults showered from every side. There were some stones thrown, a few blows were struck, but no rifle-shot broke the brief struggle. The young officer strode forward down the open space, and fronted our advance.

"I presume this is Captain Wells, from Fort Wayne?" he said, lifting his cap as he spoke.

"It is," was the reply, "and I am very glad to find that you still hold Fort Dearborn."

The other's frank and boyish face darkened slightly, as if at an unpleasant memory.

"'T is no fault of some," he muttered hastily; then he checked himself. "We are glad to greet you, Captain Wells," he added, in a more formal tone, glancing about upon us, "and your party. I am Ensign Ronan, of the garrison; and if you will kindly pass between my guard lines, you will find Captain Heald awaiting you within."

Thus we rode freely forward, with the guarding soldiery on either side of us, their faces to the howling savages; we passed in at the great southern gate, and halted amid the buildings of old Fort Dearborn.

CHAPTER XI

OLD FORT DEARBORN

T makes my old head dizzy to recall the events of that hour across the years that have intervened. Possibly I, as I write these words, am the only person living who has looked upon that old stockade and taken part in its tragic history. What a marvellous change has less than a century witnessed! Once the outermost guard of our western frontier, it is now the site of one of the great cities of two continents. To me, who have seen these events and changes, it possesses more than the wonderment of a dream.

That day, as I rode forward, I saw but little of the Fort's formation, for my eyes and thoughts were so filled with those frenzied savages that hemmed us about, and the cool deployment of the few troops that guarded our passage-way, that everything else made but a dim impression. Yet the glimpse I obtained, even at that exciting moment, together with the subsequent experiences that came to me, have indelibly

impressed each detail of the rude Fort upon my
memory.

It stands before me now, clear-cut and prominent,
its outlines distinct against the background of blue
water or green plains. In that early day the Fort was
a fairly typical outpost of the border, like scores of
others scattered at wide and irregular intervals from
the Carolina mountains upon the south to the joining
of the great lakes at the north, forming one link in the
thin chain of frontier fortifications against Indian
treachery and outbreak. It bore the distinction,
among the others, of being the most advanced and
exposed of all, and its small garrison was utterly
isolated and alone, a forlorn hope in the heart of the
great wilderness.

The Fort had been erected nine years before our
arrival, upon the southern bank of a dull and sluggish
stream, emptying into the Great Lake from the west,
and known to the earlier French explorers as the river
Chicagou. The spot selected was nearly that where
an old-time French trading-post had stood, although
the latter had been deserted for so long that no rem-
nant of it yet lingered when the Americans first took
possession, and its site remained only as a vague tra-
dition of those Indian tribes whose representatives
often visited these waters.

The earliest force despatched by the government
to this frontier post erected here a simple stockade

of logs. These were placed standing on end, firmly planted in the ground and extending upward some fifteen feet, their tops sharpened as an additional protection against savage assailants. This log stockade was built quite solid, save for one main entrance, facing to the south and secured by a heavy, iron-studded gate, with a subterranean or sunken passage leading out beneath the north wall to the river, protected by a door which could be raised only from within. The enclosure thus formed was sufficiently large to contain a somewhat restricted parade-ground, about which were grouped the necessary buildings of the garrison, the quarters for the officers, the soldiers' barracks, the commandant's office, the guard-house, and the magazine. These rude structures were built in frontier style, of cleaved logs, and with one exception were but a single story in height, so that their roofs of rived shingles were well below the protection of the palisade of logs. Besides these interior buildings, two block-houses were built, each constructed so that the second story overhung the first, one of them standing at the southeast and one at the northwest corner of the palisaded walls. A narrow wooden support, or walk, accessible only from one or the other of these block-houses, enabled its defenders to stand within the enclosure and look out over the row of sharpened logs.

At the time of our arrival the protective armament of this primitive Fort, besides the small-arms of the garrison, consisted of three pieces of light artillery, brass six-pounders of antique pattern, relics of the Revolution. Outside the Fort enclosure, only a few yards to the west along the river bank, stood the agency building, or, as it was often termed, "goods factory," built for purposes of trading with the Indians, so that it would not be necessary to open the Fort to them. This agency building was a rather large two-story log house, not erected for any purposes of defence. Along the southern side of the stream, in both directions, the soldiers had excavated numerous root-houses, or cellars, in which to store the products of their summer gardens, — these excavations fairly honeycombing the bank.

Such was Fort Dearborn in August of the fatal year 1812. It stood ugly, rude, isolated, afar from any help in time of need. Its nearest military neighbor lay directly across the waters of the Great Lake, where a small detachment of troops, scarcely less isolated than itself, garrisoned a similar stockade near the mouth of the river. Saint Joseph. To the westward, the vast plains, as yet scarce pressed by the adventurous feet of white explorers, faded away into a mysterious unknown country, roamed over by countless tribes of savages; to the northward lay an unbroken wilderness for hundreds of leagues, save for a few scattered traders at Green Bay, until the military outpost at Mackinac was reached; to the eastward rolled the waters of the Great Lake, storm-swept and unvexed by keel of ship, an almost unsurpassable barrier, along whose shore adventurous voyagers crept in log and bark canoes; while to the southward alternating prairie and timber-land stretched away for unnumbered leagues the Indian hunting-grounds, — broken only by a few scattered settlements of French half-breeds.

From the walls of the Fort the eye ranged over a dull and monotonous landscape, nowhere broken by signs of advancing civilization or even of human presence. A few hundred yards to the east the waves of Lake Michigan broke upon the wide, sandy beach, whence the tossing waters stretched away in tumultuous loneliness to their blending with the distant sky. Southward, along the shore of the lake, the nearly level plain, brown and sun-parched, soon merged into rounded heaps of wind-drifted sand, barely diversified by a few straggling groups of cottonwoods. To the westward extended the boundless prairie, flat and bare as a floor, except where the southern fork of the little river cut its way through the soft loam, and gave rise to a scrubby growth of cottonwood and willow; while northward, across the main body of the river, the land appeared more rugged and broken, and somewhat heavily wooded with oak and other forest trees, but equally devoid of evidences of habitation.

In all this wide survey from the little knoll on

which the Fort stood, five houses only were visible. These were built roughly of logs in the most primitive style of the frontier, and, with a single exception, were now deserted by their occupants, who had retreated for safety to the stockade of the Fort. The single exception was the larger and more ambitious dwelling standing on the north bank of the river, occupied by John Kinzie and his family, himself an old-time Indian trader, whose honesty and long dealing with the savages had made him confident of their friendship and fidelity. At one time, however, so threatening had become the strange bands that flocked in toward Dearborn, as crows to a feast, he also deserted his home, and, with those dependent upon him, sought refuge within the Fort walls; but, influenced by the pledge of the Pottawattomies, and believing that safety lay in trusting to their friendship, they had returned to their own house. The other cabins were scattered to the westward of the stockade, close to the river bank. These dwellings had been occupied by the families of Ouilmette, Burns, and Lee, respectively; while the last named owned a second cabin, built some distance up the south branch of the river, and occupied by a tenant named Liberty White.

The prospect was in truth depressing to one accustomed to other and more civilized surroundings. A spirit of loneliness, of fearful isolation, seemed to hover over the restless waters upon the one hand, and those vast silent plains on the other; sea and sky, sky and sand, met the wearied eye wherever it wandered. The scene was unspeakably solemn in its immensity and loneliness; while irresistibly the thought would wander over those fateful leagues of prairie and forest that stretched unbrokenly between this far frontier and the few scattered and remote settlements that were its nearest neighbors.

It was not until some time later that these sombre reflections pressed upon me with all their force. After the excitement of our first boisterous greeting was over, and I found opportunity to lean across the top of the guarded stockade and gaze alone over the desolate spectacle I have endeavored to describe, I could feel more acutely the hopelessness of our situation and the danger threatening us from every side. But at the moment of our entrance, all my interest and attention had been centred upon the scenes and persons immediately about me. It was my first experience within the stockaded walls of an armed government post. The scene was new to my young senses, and, in spite of the excitement that still heated my blood, I looked upon it with such absorbing interest as to be forgetful for the moment even of the fair girl who rode in at my side.

The dull clang of the heavy iron-bound gate behind us was a welcome sound after the fierce buffetings of our perilous passage; yet it only partially shut off the savage howlings, while above the hideous uproar came the sharp reports of several guns. But the instant bustle and confusion within scarcely allowed opportunity to notice this disorder; moreover, there had come to us a sense of safety and security, — we were at last within the barriers we had struggled so long to gain. However the savage hordes might rage without, we were now beyond their reach, and might take breath again.

Our little party, closely bunched together, with Wells and the timorous Miamis at its head, surged quickly through between the bars, and came to a halt in an open space, evidently the parade-ground of the garrison, the bare earth worn smooth and hard by the trampling of many feet. A tall flag-pole rose near the centre, and the wavering shadow of the banner at its top extended to the eastern edge of the enclosure. Out from the log-houses which bordered this enclosure there came a group of people to welcome us, — officers and soldiers, women neatly dressed and with bright intelligent faces, women of rougher mould attired in calico or deerskin, hardy-looking men in rude hunter's garb, picturesque French voyageurs wiry of limb and dark of skin, an Indian or two, silent, grave, emotionless, a single negro, and trailing behind them a number of dirty, delighted children, and dogs of every breed and degree. It was a motley gathering, and appeared almost like a multitude as it hurried forth into the open parade-ground, and surged joyfully about us, all eager to welcome us to Dearborn, and hopeful that we brought them encouragement and relief. We were of their own race, a link between them and the far-distant East; and our coming told them they were not forgotten.

The odd commingling of tongues, the constant crowding and scraps of conversation, the volley of questioning from every side, was confusing and unintelligible. I could gain only glimpses here and there of what was going on; nor was I able to judge with any accuracy of the number of those present. I looked down upon their appealing, anxious faces, with a sad heart. In some way the sight of them brought back thoughts of the savage, howling mob without, clamoring for blood, through which we had won our passage by sheer good-fortune; of those leagues of untracked forest amid whose glooms we had ploughed our way. I thought of these things as I gazed upon the helpless women and children thronging about me, and my heart sank as I realized how great indeed was the burden resting upon us all, how frail the hope of safety. Death, savage, relentless, inhuman death in its most frightful guise with torture and agony unspeakable, lurked along every mile of our possible retreat; nor could I conceive how its grim coming might long be delayed by that palisade of logs. We were hopeless of rescue. We were alone, deserted, the merest handful amid the unnumbered hordes of the vast West.

Swift and terrible as this conception was when it swept upon me, it grew deeper as I learned more fully the details of our situation.

Just in front of where I lingered in my saddle, the crush slightly parted, and I noticed a tall man step forward, — a fair man, having a light beard slightly tinged with gray, and wearing the undress uniform of a captain of infantry. A lady, several years his junior, stood at his side, her eyes bright with expectancy. At sight of them, Captain Wells instantly sprang from his horse and hastened forward, his dark face lighted by one of his rare smiles.

"Captain," he exclaimed, clasping the officer's hand warmly, and extending his other hand in greeting to the lady, "I am glad indeed to have reached you in time to be of service; and you, my own dear niece, — may we yet be permitted to bring you safely back to God's country."

I was unable to catch the reply of either; but I noted that the lady flung her arms about the speaker's neck and kissed his swarthy cheek.

Then Captain Wells spoke more loudly, so that his words reached my ears.

"But, Heald," he said, "what means all this litter of garrison equipment lying scattered about? Surely you have no present intention to leave the Fort, in face of that savage mob out yonder?"

"'T is the orders of General Hull," was the low

and somewhat hesitating response, "and the Potta-wattomie chiefs have pledged us escort around the head of the lake. But this is no place to discuss the matter. As soon as possible I would speak with you more fully in my office."

The look of undisguised amazement upon Wells's face startled me; and as I glanced about me, wondering whom I might take counsel with, I was astonished to note the horse that Toinette had ridden standing with empty saddle. De Croix, negligently curling his mustache between his slender fingers, gazed at me with a blank stare.

"Where is Mademoiselle?" I questioned anxiously, as he remained silent. "Surely she was with us as we came in!"

"Pish! of course," he returned carelessly; "if she chooses to dismount and rejoin her friends, what has that to do with John Wayland? Cannot the girl so much as move without your permission, Monsieur?"

The words were insolent, not less than the manner that accompanied them. Instantly there flashed upon me the thought that this Frenchman sought a quarrel with me; but I could conceive no reason therefor, and was not greatly disposed to accommodate him.

"'T was no more than curiosity that urged my question," I answered, assuming not to notice his bravado. "I was so deeply interested in other things as to have forgotten her presence."

"Something no lady is ever likely to forgive," he interjected. "But what think you they propose doing with us here?"

As if in direct answer to his question, the young officer who had met us without now elbowed his way through the throng, until he stood at our horses' heads.

"Gentlemen," he said, with a quick glance into our faces, "dismount and come within. There is but little to offer you here at Dearborn, we have been cut off from civilization so long; but such as we possess will be shared with you most gladly."

De Croix chatted with him in his easy, familiar manner, as we slowly crossed the parade; while I followed them in silence, my thoughts upon the disappearance of Toinette and the Frenchman's sudden show of animosity. My glance fell upon the groups of children scattered along our path, and I wondered which among them might prove to be Roger Matherson's little one. At the entrance of one of the log houses fronting the parade, — a rather ambitious building of two stories, if I remember rightly, with a narrow porch along its front, — an officer was standing upon the step, talking with a sweet-faced woman who appeared scarce older than seventeen.

"Lieutenant Helm," said Ronan, politely, "this is Captain de Croix, of the French army."

He presented De Croix to Mrs. Helm, and then turned inquiringly toward me.

" I believe I have failed to learn your name? "

"I am simply John Wayland," I answered, and, with a glance at my face, Lieutenant Helm cordially extended his hand.

"We are greatly pleased to welcome you both," he said earnestly, but with a grave side-glance at his young wife, "though I fear we have little to offer you except privation and danger."

"How many have you in the garrison?" I questioned, my eyes upon the moving figures about us. "It looks a crowd, in that narrow space."

"They are all there who are able to crawl," he said, with a grave smile. "But in this case our numbers are a weakness. In the garrison proper we have four commissioned officers, with fifty-four non-commissioned officers and privates. To these may be added twelve settlers acting as militiamen, making a total defensive force of seventy men. But fully twenty-five of these are upon the sick-list, and totally unfit for active duty; while we are further burdened by having under our protection twelve women and twenty children. It almost crazes one to think of what their fate may be."

"Your defences look strong enough to keep off savages," broke in De Croix, "and I am told there is a sufficiency of provisions. Saint Guise! I have seen places where I had rather reside in my old age; yet with plenty of wine, some good fellows, and as lovely women as have already greeted me here, 't will not prove so bad for a few weeks."

Helm glanced at him curiously; then his gaze, always gravely thoughtful, wandered back to me.

"We are to evacuate the Fort," he said quietly.

"Evacuate?" echoed the Frenchman, as if the word were displeasing. "'T is a strange military act, in my judgment, and one filled with grave peril. Does such decision come from a council?"

"There has been no council," broke in Ronan, hastily. "The commander has not honored his officers by calling one. Such were the orders as published on parade this morning."

He would have added more, but Helm warned him by a sudden look of disapproval.

"I understand," he explained quietly, "that the instructions received from General Hull at Detroit were imperative, and that Captain Heald was left no discretion in the matter."

"I have not yet discovered the man who has seen the orders," exclaimed the Ensign hotly, "and we all know it means death."

Helm faced him sternly.

"A soldier's first duty is obedience," he said shortly, "and we are soldiers. Gentlemen, will you not come in?"

CHAPTER XII

THE HEART OF A WOMAN

S I sat in the officers' quarters, listening to the conversation regarding existing conditions at the Fort and the unrest among the Indians of the border, my thoughts kept veering from the sudden and ungracious disappearance of Mademoiselle to the early seeking after that hapless orphan child for whose sake I had already travelled so far and entered into such danger. Evidently, if I was to aid her my quest must be no longer interrupted.

With characteristic gallantry, De Croix had at once been attracted toward Lieutenant Helm's young and pretty bride, and they two had already forgotten all sense of existing peril in a most animated discussion of the latest fashionable modes in Montreal. I was not a little amused by the interest manifest in her soft blue eyes as she spoke with all the art of a woman versed in such mysteries, and at the languid air of elegance with which he bore himself. Meanwhile, I answered as best I might the flood of questions addressed to me by the two officers, who, having been shut out from the world so long, were naturally eager for military news from Fort Wayne and from the seat of government. As these partially ceased, I asked:

" Has a date been set for the abandonment of the Fort? "

" We march out upon the fifteenth," was Helm's reply, " the day after to-morrow, unless something occurs meanwhile to change Captain Heald's plans. I confess I dread its coming, much as I imagine a condemned man might dread the date of his execution," and his grave eyes wandered toward his young wife, as if fearful his words might be overheard by her. " There are other lives than mine endangered, and their peril makes duty doubly hard."

" Lieutenant," I said, recalled to my own mission by these words, " I myself am seeking to be of service to one here, — the young daughter of one Roger Matherson, an old soldier who died at this post last month. He was long my father's faithful comrade in arms, and with his dying breath begged our care for his orphan child. It has come to us as a sacred trust, and I was despatched upon this errand. Can you tell me where this girl is to be found? "

Before he could frame a reply, for he was somewhat slow of speech, his wife, who had turned from

De Croix, and was listening with interest to my story,
spoke impulsively.

"Why, we have been wondering, Mr. Wayland,
where she could have gone. Not that we have worried,
for she is a girl well able to care for herself, and of a
most independent spirit. She disappeared very suddenly from the Fort several days ago; we supposed
she must have gone with my mother when Mr. Kinzie
took his family back to their home."

"With Mr. Kinzie?" I questioned, for at that
moment I could not recall hearing the name. "May
I ask where that home is?"

"He is the very good step-father of my wife, and
one she loves as truly as if he were her own father,"
answered Helm, warmly; "a man among a thousand.
Mr. Kinzie is an Indian trader, and has been here for
several years, if indeed he be not the first white settler, for old Pointe Au Sable was a West Indian
mulatto. His relations with these savages who dwell
near the Great Lake, and especially those of the Pottawattomie and Wyandot tribes, are so friendly that
he has felt safe to remain with his family unguarded
in his own home. They have always called him Shaw-
nee-aw-kee, the Silver-man, and trust him as much as
he trusts them. He is, besides, a great friend of Sau-
ga-nash, the half-breed Wyandot; and that friendship
is a great protection. His house is across the river, a
little to the east of the Fort; it can easily be seen

from the summit of the stockade. But we have had
no direct communication for several days; the orders
have been very strict since the gates were closed. It
is not safe for our soldiers to venture outside except
in force, and neither Kinzie nor any of his family have
lately visited us. Doubtless they feel that to do so
might arouse the suspicion of their Indian friends."

"But are you sure they are there, and safe? And
do you believe the one I seek will be found with
them?"

"Smoke rises from the chimney, as usual, and
there was a light burning there last evening. We do
not know certainly that your friend is there, but think
such is the case, as she was extremely friendly with
a young French girl in their employ named Josette La
Framboise."

I sat in silence for some time, thinking, and neg-
lectful of the conversation being carried on around
me by the others, until we were called to supper by
the soldier who officiated as steward for the officers'
mess. I remember many details of the situation, as
they were frankly discussed in my presence while we
lingered at the table; yet my own reflections were
elsewhere, as I was endeavoring to determine my duty
regarding the safety of her whom I had come so far to
aid. Surely, my first object now must be to ascertain
where she was, in order to be at her service when the
hour for departure came. Nor had I any time to spare,

if we were to march out on the fifteenth. I cannot describe, at this late day, how strangely my allegiance wavered, in that hour, between the unknown, unseen girl, and the fair, vivacious Toinette. My heart drew me toward the one, my clear duty to the other; and I could see no way out of the dilemma except to find Elsa Matherson without delay, in order that the two should be close together where, as need arose, I could stand between them and whatever of evil impended.

I fear I was an indifferent guest, for I was never nimble of tongue, and that night I was more silent than usual. However, De Croix most effectually hid my retirement by his rare good-humor and the sparkling badinage with which he concentrated all attention upon himself, and was consequently soon in the happiest of moods. I know not how the fellow succeeded in working the miracle, but he sat at the board, upon Mrs. Helm's left hand, powdered and curled as if he were gracing a banquet at the Tuileries. His ruffled shirt, glittering buckles, and bright blue waistcoat, were startling amid such homely surroundings; while his neatly folded handkerchief of lace exhaled a delicate perfume. Deeply as I was immersed in my own thoughts and plans, I could not help admiring his easy grace, and more than once forgot myself in listening to his marvellous tales and witty anecdotes.

He was detailing a recent scandal of the French court, passing delicately over its more objectionable

features, when I grasped the opportunity to slip unobserved from the room into the open of the parade-
ground. It proved a dark night without, but the
numerous lights in the surrounding buildings, whose
doors and windows were open, sufficiently illumined
the place, so that I found my way about with little
difficulty. A group of soldiers lounged at the open
door of the guard-house, and I paused a moment to
speak with one, a curly-headed lad, who sat smoking,
his back resting easily against the logs.

"Are the outer gates ever opened at night?" I
asked.

He glanced up at me in surprise, shading his eyes
to be assured of my identity before speaking.

"Scarcely either day or night now, sir," he replied,
respectfully, "but between sunset and sunrise they are
specially barred, and a double guard is set. No one
can pass except on the order of Captain Heald."

"In which direction is the Kinzie house?"

He pointed toward the northeast corner of the
stockade.

"It is just over there, sir, across the river. You
might see the light from the platform; beyond the
shed yonder is the ladder that leads up into the block-
house."

Thanking him, I moved forward as directed, found
the ladder, and pushed my way up through the narrow
opening in the floor of the second story. The small

square room, feebly lighted by a single sputtering
candle stuck in the shank of a bayonet, contained half
a dozen men, most of them idling, although two were
standing where they could readily peer out through
the narrow slits between the logs. All of them were
heavily armed, and equipped for service. They looked
at me curiously as I first appeared, but the one who
asked my business wore the insignia of a corporal,
and was evidently in command.

"I wish to look out over the stockade, if there is
no objection. I came in with Captain Wells's party
this afternoon," I said, not knowing what their orders
might be, or if I would be recognized.

"I remember you, sir," was the prompt response,
"and you are at liberty to go out there if you desire.
That is the door leading to the platform."

"The Indians appear to be very quiet to-night."

"The more reason to believe them plotting some
fresh deviltry," he answered, rising to his feet, and
facing me. "We never have much to disturb us upon
this side, as it overhangs the river and is not easy of
approach; but the guard on the south wall is kept
pretty busy these last few nights, and has to patrol
the stockade. The Indians have been holding some
sort of a powwow out at their camp ever since dark,
and that's apt to mean trouble sooner or later."

"Then you keep no sentry posted on the platform?" I asked, a thought suddenly occurring to me.

"Not regularly, sir; only when something suspicious happens along the river. There's nobody out there now excepting the French girl, — she seems to be fond of being out there all alone."

The French girl? Could it be possible that he meant Toinette? I was conscious of a strange fluttering of the heart, as I stepped forth upon the narrow footway and peered along it, searching for her. I could distinguish nothing, however; and as I slowly felt my way forward, testing the squared log beneath me with careful foot and keeping hold with one hand upon the sharpened palisades, I began to believe the corporal had been mistaken. The door, closing behind, shut off the last gleam of light, and I was left alone in utter darkness and silence, save for the low rumble of voices within the Fort enclosure, and the soft plashing below where the river current kissed the bank at the foot of the stockade.

I had gone almost the full length of that side, before I came where she was leaning against the logs, her chin resting upon one hand, her gaze turned northward. Indeed, so silent was she, so intent upon her own thought, I might have touched her unnoticed in the gloom, had not the stars broken through a rift in the cloud above us, and sent a sudden gleam of silver across her face.

"Mademoiselle," I said, striving to address her with something of the ease I thought De Croix would exercise at such a moment, "I meant not to intrude upon your privacy, yet I am most glad to meet with you once more."

She started slightly, as though aroused from reverie, and glanced inquiringly toward me.

"I supposed my visitor to be one of the guard," she said pleasantly; "and even now I am unable to distinguish your face, yet the sound of the voice reminds me of John Wayland."

"I am proud to know that it has not already been forgotten. You deserted me so suddenly this afternoon, I almost doubted my being welcome now."

She laughed lightly, tapping the ends of the logs with her finger-tips.

"Have you, then, never learned that a woman is full of whims, Monsieur?" she questioned. "Why, this afternoon your eyes were so big with wonder that they had forgotten to look at me. Truly, I spoke to you twice to aid me from the saddle; but you heard nothing, and in my desperation I was obliged to turn to the courtesy of Captain de Croix. Ah, there is a soldier, my friend, who is never so preoccupied as to neglect his duty to a lady."

"It was indeed most ungallant of me," I stammered, scarce knowing whether she laughed at me or not. "Yet my surroundings were all new, and I have not the training of De Croix in such matters."

"Pah! 't is just as well. I am inclined to like you

as you are, my friend, and we shall not quarrel; yet, with all his love for lesser things, your comrade has always shown himself a truly gallant gentleman."

I made no answer to these flattering words, for I felt them to be true; yet no less this open praise of him, falling from her lips, racked me sorely, and I lacked the art to make light of it.

"The soldiers in the block-house tell me you come here often," I ventured at last, for the dead silence weighed upon me. "You have never seemed to me like one who would seek such loneliness."

"I am one whom very few wholly comprehend, I fear, and surely not upon first acquaintance," she answered thoughtfully, "for I am full of strange moods, and perhaps dream more than other girls. This may have been born of my early convent training, and the mystic tales of the nuns; nor has it been lessened by the loneliness of the frontier. So, if I differ from other young women, you may know 't is my training, as well as my nature, that may account for it. I have led a strange life, Monsieur, and one that has known much of sadness. There are times when I seek my own thoughts, and find liking for no other company. Then I come here, and in some way the loneliness of water and plain soothe me as human speech cannot. I used to love to stand yonder by the eastern wall and gaze out over the Great Lake, watching the green surges chase each other until they burst in spray along the beach. But since I went adrift in the little boat, and felt the cruelty of the water, I have shrunk from looking out upon it. Monsieur, have you never known how restful it sometimes is to be alone? "

" My life has mostly been a solitary one," I answered, responding unconsciously to her mood, and, in doing so, forgetting my embarrassment. " It is the birthright of all children of the frontier. Indeed, I have seen so little of the great world and so much of the woods, that I scarcely realize what companionship means, especially that of my own age. I have made many a solitary camp leagues from the nearest settlement, and have tracked the forest alone for days together, so content with my own thought that possibly I understand your meaning better than if my life had been passed among crowds."

" Ah! but I like the crowds," she exclaimed hastily, " and the glow and excitement of that brighter, fuller life, where people really live. It is so dull here, — the same commonplace faces, the tiresome routine of drill, the same blue sky, gray water, and green plains, to look upon day after day. Oh, but it is all so wearisome, and you cannot conceive how I have longed again for Montreal and the many little gaieties that brighten a woman's world. There are those here who have never known these happier things; their whole horizon of experience has been bounded by garrison palisades; but 't is not so with me, — I tasted of the sweet wine once, when I was a girl, and the memory never leaves me."

"Yet you are often happy?"

"'T is my nature, Monsieur, a legacy of my mother's people; but I am not always gay of heart when my lips smile."

"And the coming of the French gallant has doubtless freshened your remembrance of the past?" I said, a trifle bitterly.

"It has indeed," was her frank admission. "He represents a life we know so little about here on the far frontier. To you, with your code of border manliness, he may appear all affectation, mere shallow insincerity; but to me, Captain de Croix represents his class, stands for the refinements of social order to which women can never be indifferent. Those were the happiest days of my life, Monsieur; and at Montreal he was only one among many."

She was gazing out into the black void as she spoke, and the slowly clearing skies permitted the starlight to gleam in her dark eyes and reveal the soft contour of her cheek.

"You do not understand that?" she questioned finally, as I failed to break the silence.

"I have no such pleasant memory to look back upon," I answered; "yet I can feel, though possibly in a different way, your longing after better things."

"You realize this sense of loneliness? — this absence of all that makes life beautiful and worth the living?"

"Perhaps not that, — for life, even here, is well worth living, and to my eyes the great sea yonder, and the dark forests, are of more interest than city streets. But in one sense I may enter into your meaning; my thought also is away from here, — it is with a home, scarcely less humble than are our present surroundings, yet it contains the one blessing worth striving after — love."

"Love!" she echoed the unexpected word almost scornfully. "'T is a phrase so lightly spoken that I scarce know what it may signify to you. You love some one then, Monsieur?" and she looked up at me curiously.

"My mother, Mademoiselle."

I saw the expression upon her face change instantly. "Your pardon," she exclaimed, hastily. "'T was not the meaning I had thought. I know something of such love as that, and honor you for thus expressing it."

"I have often wondered, since first we met, at your being here, seemingly alone, at this outermost post of the frontier. It seems a strange home for one of your refinement and evident delight in social life."

"'T is not from choice, Monsieur. My mother died when I was but a child, as I have already told you. I scarce have memory of her, yet I bear her

name, and, I am told, inherit many of her peculiarities.
She was the daughter of a great merchant at Montreal, and the blood of a noble family of France flowed
in her veins. She gave up all else to become my
father's wife; nor did she ever live to regret it."

Her voice was so low and plaintive that I hesitated to speak; yet finally, as she ceased, and silence
fell between us, I asked another question:

"And 't was then you voyaged into this wilderness with your father?"

"I have never since left him while he lived," she
answered softly, her head resting upon her hand.
"But he also has gone now, and I merely wait opportunity to journey eastward."

"He was a trader, you told me once?"

"A soldier first, Monsieur; a true and gallant
soldier, but later he traded with the Indians for furs."

I felt that she was weeping softly, although I
could see but little, and I leaned in silence against the
rough logs, gazing out into the black night, hesitating
to break in upon her grief. Then a voice spoke rapidly
at the farther end of the stockade, and a sudden glow
of light shot like an arrow along the platform. I
turned quickly, and there in the open doorway, clearly
outlined against the candle flame, stood De Croix.

CHAPTER XIII

A WAGER OF FOOLS

T looks a narrow walk, my friend," he said rather doubtfully, peering forward with shaded eyes, " and 't is dark as Erebus; yet gladly will I make the venture for hope of the reward."

The door closed behind him, shutting off the last vestige of light; and we, with our eyes accustomed to the gloom, could mark his dim outline as he advanced toward us. His actions belied his words, for he moved with all his accustomed jauntiness along the uncertain foot-way, barely touching the top of the palisades with one hand to guide his progress. He was almost upon the girl before he perceived either of us; and then his earliest words surprised me into silence.

" Ah, Toinette! " he cried eagerly, " I fear I must have kept you waiting overlong; yet I was with Mrs.

Helm, — a most fair and charming bride, — and scarce noted the rapid passage of time."

"I naturally supposed it was a woman," she answered, with what I interpreted as a strained assumption of indifference, "as that has ever been your sufficient reason for breaking faith with me."

"Do not interpret it so, I beg," he hastened to implore. "Surely, my being a few moments in arrears is not a matter sufficiently serious to be called a breakage of faith. I do assure you, Toinette, you were never once absent from my thought."

"Indeed?" she exclaimed incredulously, and with an echo of suppressed laughter in her voice. "Then truly you are far more to be commiserated on this occasion than I, for in truth, Monsieur de Croix, I have not missed you over-much. I have enjoyed most excellent company."

"The mysterious spirits of the starry night?" he questioned, looking out into the darkness, "or the dim figures of your own imagination?"

"Very far from either," she retorted, with a laugh; "a most substantial reality, as you are bound to confess. Master Wayland, is it not time for you fitly to greet Captain de Croix? He may deem you lax in cordiality."

I can perceive now how dearly the laughing witch loved to play us one against the other, hiding whatever depth of feeling she may have had beneath the surface

of careless innocence, and keeping us both in an un-
certainty as aggravating as it was sweet. I could not
read the expression upon De Croix's face in the gloom,
yet I saw him start visibly at her almost mocking
words, and there was a trace of ill-suppressed irritation in his voice.

"Saint Guise! 'T was for that, then, he left us
so mysteriously," he exclaimed, unconsciously uttering
his first thought aloud. "But how knew he you were
to be here?"

Before she could answer, I spoke, anxious to relieve her of embarrassment; for 't was ever my nature
to yield much without complaint.

"As it chances, Captain de Croix, she did not
know," I said, standing back from the palisades where
he could see me more clearly. "I left the table below
with no thought of meeting Mademoiselle, and came
out on this platform for a different purpose. As you
know, I am visiting Dearborn upon a special mission."

"Ah, true," and I could feel the trace of relief
in his voice as he instantly recalled my story. "You
also sought a girl in this wilderness, — may I ask, have
you yet found trace of her?"

I heard Mademoiselle move quickly.

"A girl?" she asked in surprise. "Here, at
Dearborn?"

"She was at Dearborn until very lately, but they
tell me now I must seek for her at the Kinzie house.

It was for the purpose of marking its position from the Fort that I came up here."

For a moment no one of our voices broke the strained silence. I was troubled by this knowledge of a pre-arranged meeting between these two, yet felt it was nothing with which I had a right to interfere. This careless French girl, whom I had known for scarcely two days, was not one to be easily guided, even had I either reason or excuse for attempting it.

" 'T is strange," she said, musingly, " that she has never so much as spoken to me about it; yet she was always shy of speech in such matters."

" Of whom do you speak, Toinette? " questioned De Croix.

" Of Master Wayland's young friend with the Kinzies," she answered, the old sprightliness again in her voice. " I know her very well, Monsieur, — a dear, sweet girl, — and shall be only too glad to speed you on to her. Yet 't is not so easy of accomplishment, hemmed in as we are here now. Yonder is the light, Master Wayland; but much of peril may lurk between. 'T is not far, were the way clear; indeed, in the old days of peace a rope ferry connected Fort and house, but now to reach there safely will require a wide detour and no little woodcraft. There were patrols of savages along the river bank at dusk, and it is doubtful if all have been withdrawn."

I looked as she pointed, and easily distinguished

the one glittering spark that pierced the darkness to the north and east. I wondered at her earlier words; yet they might all be true enough, for I knew nothing of this Elsa Matherson. Before I could question further, De Croix had interfered, — eager, no doubt, to be rid of me.

"Upon my soul!" he exclaimed recklessly, "if I could voyage here from Montreal to win but a smile, it should prove a small venture for our backwoods friend to cover yonder small distance. *Sacre!* I would do the deed myself for one kiss from rosy lips."

I have wondered since what there was about those words to anger me. It must have been their boastful tone, the sarcasm that underlay the velvet utterance, which stung like salt in a fresh wound. I felt that from the summit of his own success he durst laugh at me; and my blood boiled instantly.

"You are wondrous bold, Monsieur," I retorted, "when the matter is wholly one of words. I regret I cannot pledge you such reward, so that I might learn how you would bear yourself in the attempt."

He stared at me haughtily across the shoulder of the girl, as if doubting he heard aright.

"You question my courage to venture it?"

"It has been my experience that the cock that crows the loudest fights the least."

"Oh, hush, Messieurs!" broke in Mademoiselle, her voice showing suppressed amusement. "This

platform is far too narrow to quarrel upon; and, besides, the condition of the wager is most easily met, —
that is, if my lips be deemed of sufficiently rosy hue."

I know I stood with opened mouth, so astounded
by these mocking words as to be stricken dumb; but
not so De Croix. The audacity of his nature made
eager response to the bold challenge.

"Do you mean what you say, Toinette?" he
asked, striving to gain a view of her face in the
darkness.

"Do I? And pray, why not?" she questioned
lightly. "One kiss is not so very much to give, and
I shall never miss it. 'T is duller here than at Montreal, and no doubt 't will greatly interest me to witness the race. Surely it will prove a better way to end
your foolish quarrel than to shoot each other. But
come, Messieurs, why do you hesitate so long? is not
the prize enough?"

He bowed gallantly, and took her hand.

"'T would be the ransom of a king," he answered;
"though first I wish to know the terms of this contest
more clearly."

She looked out into that silent and lonely night,
her eyes upon the distant gleam, and instinctively our
glances followed hers. It was a dull desolation, with
no sound, no movement, in all the black void. The
stars gleamed dull on the water of the river beneath
us, and we could dimly see the denser shadow of the

opposite shore; beyond this, nothing was apparent
save that distant candle flame. What lay between, —
what strange obstruction of land, what ambushed foes,
— neither of us had means of knowing. We could
simply plunge into the mystery of it blindfolded by
the fates. Yet to draw back now would brand either
of us forever with the contempt of her who had challenged us so lightly.

"'T is all simple enough," she said at last, her
eyes glowing with quick excitement. "The goal is
yonder where that light glows so clearly, though I
warn you the longest way round may prove the surest
in the end. To the one of you who reaches there first
and returns here, I am to give one kiss as a measure
of reward. I care not how it may be accomplished,
— such minor matters rest with your own wits."

"But the young girl we seek," he insisted; "must
she also be brought here upon the return?"

"Pish! what care I what may be done with the
girl? Besides, she is far safer from the savages there
than she would be here."

I saw De Croix lean far out over the sharpened
palisades and peer downward. The movement gave
me instantly a thought of his purpose, and, unnoticed,
I loosened the pistol-belt about my waist and silently
dropped it upon the platform. Whatever desperate
chance he might choose to take, I was determined now
to equal.

"Doth the water of the river come to the very foot of these logs?" he asked, unable to determine in the darkness.

"No, Monsieur, the earth slopes downward for some feet, yet the current is at this bank, and gives much depth of water at the shore."

"But of what width is the strip of earth between?"

"Perhaps the length of a tall man."

"Saint Guise! 't is well I thought to ask!" he explained jauntily. "And now, Mademoiselle, if you will but kindly hold this coat and sword, I shall strive to show you how highly I value the prize offered, and what a French gentleman can do for love."

I fully grasped his purpose now, and even as he turned toward her, holding out the valuables he hesitated to lose, I scaled the low barrier in my front, planted my feet firmly between the pointed stakes, and sprang boldly into the darkness.

CHAPTER XIV

DARKNESS AND SURPRISE

I T was a greater distance to the water than I had supposed, but I struck at last fairly enough, and went down until I thought I should never come up again. As I rose to the surface and shook the moisture from my face and ears, a light laugh rang out high above me, and Mademoiselle's clear voice cried mockingly:

"The backwoodsman has taken the first trick, Monsieur."

I saw De Croix's body dart, like a black arrow, far out into the air, and come sweeping down. He struck to my left, and a trifle behind me; but I waited not to learn just how. With lusty strokes I struck out for the north shore. It was a hard swim, for my deerskins held the water like so many bags, and the current, though not rapid, was sufficiently strong to make me fight valiantly for every foot of way. I came out, panting heavily, upon a low bank of soft mud, and crept cautiously up under the black shadow of some low bushes growing there. I took time, as I rested, to glance back, hoping thus to learn more of the direction I should follow; for the Kinzie light was no longer visible, and my struggle with the current had somewhat bewildered me. I neither saw nor heard anything of De Croix; but the flame of the candle gleaming through the narrow slits of the block-house told me clearly where it stood, while a wild yelling farther to the southward convinced me that our Indian besiegers were yet astir and concocting some fresh deviltry at their camp. With a half-uttered prayer that they might all be there, I hastily pressed the water from my soggy clothes and plunged forward into the unknown darkness. A big cottonwood, as from its shape I judged it to be, rose against the stars in my front, — a dim outline swaying slightly in the westerly wind, and I took it as my first guide-mark, moving over the rough unknown ground as rapidly and silently as possible.

The soft moccasins I wore aided me greatly, nor were there many trees along the way to drop twigs in the path to crackle under foot; yet I found the ground uneven and deceptive, rifted with small gullies, and more or less bestrewn with stones, against which I stumbled in the darkness. I was too thoroughly

trained in the stern and careful school of the frontier
not to be cautious at such a time, for I knew that silence and seeming desolation were no proof of savage
desertion; nor did I believe that Indian strategy would
leave the north of the Fort wholly unguarded. Any
rock, any black ravine, any clump of trees or bushes,
might well be the lurking-place of hostiles, who would
only too gladly wreak their vengeance upon any hap-
less straggler falling into their hands. I was unarmed,
save for the long hunting-knife I carried in the bosom
of my shirt; but my thought was not of fighting, —
it was to get through without discovery.

To De Croix I gave small consideration, save that
the memory of the wager was a spur to urge me
forward at greater speed. The place was strangely,
painfully still; even the savage yelling of the distant
Indians seemed to die away as I advanced, and nothing
broke the oppressive silence but an occasional flutter
of leaves, or my own deep breathing. I had gone, I
take it, half or three-quarters of a mile, not directly
north, but circling ever to the eastward, seeking thus
to reach the house from the rear, when I came to a
sharp break in the surface of the land, somewhat
deeper and more abrupt than those before encountered.
It seemed like a cut or ravine made by some rush of
water lakeward; and, as I hesitated upon the edge of
it, peering across and wondering if I had better risk
the plunge, my eyes caught the blaze of the Kinzie

light scarce a hundred yards from the opposite bank of the ravine.

Assured that I was headed right, I stepped off with a new confidence that, for the moment, conquered my usual prudence, — for the steep bank gave way instantly beneath my weight. I grasped vainly at the edge, fell heavily sidewise, and rolled like a great log, bruised and half-stunned, into the black gorge below. I remember gripping at a slender bush that yielded to my touch; but all the rest was no more than a breathless tumble, until I struck something soft at the bottom, — something that squirmed and gripped my long hair savagely, and pushed my head back with a grasp on the throat that nearly throttled me.

It was all so sudden, so unexpected, that for the moment I was helpless as a child, struggling merely from the natural instinct of preservation to break free. I could perceive nothing, the darkness was so intense; yet as I gradually succeeded in getting my hands loose, I wound them in long coarse hair, pressed them against bare flesh, heard deep labored breathing close to my face, and believed I was struggling with a savage.

It was a question of mere brute strength, and neither of us had had the advantage of surprise. I could feel the sharp prick of my own knife as he hugged me to him, but I dare not reach for it, and I held his arms so tightly that he lay panting and struggling as if in a vise. It was an odd fight, as we turned

and tossed, writhed and twisted among those sharp
pointed rocks like two infuriated wild-cats in the dark,
neither venturing to break hold for a blow, nor having
breath enough in our bodies for so much as a curse.
My adversary struck me once with his head under the
chin, so hard a blow that everything turned red before
me; and then I got my knee up into the pit of his
stomach and caused him to quiver from the agony of
it; yet the fellow clung to me like a bull-terrier, and
never so much as whined.

It was never my nature to yield easily, and I felt
now this struggle was to cost his life or mine; so I
clinched my teeth, and sought my best to push back
the other's head until the neck should crack. But if
I was a powerful man, this other was no less so, and he
fought with a fierce and silent desperation that foiled
me. We dug and tore, gouged and struck, digging our
heels into the soft earth in a vain endeavor to gain
some advantage of position. My cheek, I knew, was
bleeding from contact with a jagged stone, and I was
fast growing faint from the awful tension, when I felt
his arms slip.

"My God!" he panted. "The devil has me!"

So startled was I by these English words, that
I loosed my grip, staring breathlessly through the
darkness.

"Are you white?" I gasped, so weakened I could
scarce articulate.

For a moment he did not answer, but I could hear his breath coming in gasps and sobs. Then he spoke slowly, his voice hoarse from exertion.

"By the memory of Moses! I was once, — but that squeeze must have turned me black, I'm thinkin'. An' ye're no Injun?"

"Not so much as a feather of one," I retorted. "But that is what I took you to be."

We were both sitting up by this time, he with his back against the bank, both of us panting as if we could never regain our breath, and eagerly seeking to see each other's features in the gloom. Any attempt at conversation was painful, but I managed at last to stammer:

"You must be a whalebone man, or I'd have broken every rib in your body."

"An' I'm not a bit sure ye did n't," was the response, uttered between puffs. "'T was the worst grip ever Ol' Tom Burns had squeeze him, — an' I've felt o' bars mor' nor oncet. Who may ye be, anyhow, stranger? an' for what cause did ye jump down yere on me?"

There was a trace of growing anger in his tone, as remembrance of the outrage returned to his mind, which caused me to smile, now that I could breathe less painfully. It seemed such a ludicrous affair, — that dark struggle, each mistaking the purpose and color of the other.

DARKNESS AND SURPRISE

"My name is Wayland," I made haste to explain, "and I left the Fort but now, hoping by this roundabout route to reach the Kinzie place and return under cover of darkness. I slipped on the edge of the bank up yonder, and the next thing I knew we were at it. I can assure you, friend, I supposed myself in the arms of a savage. You say your name is Burns?"

"Ol' Tom Burns."

"What? It is not possible you are the same who brought a message to Major Wayland on the Maumee?"

"I reckon I am," he said, deliberately. "An' be you the boy I met?"

"Yes," I said, still doubtful. "But how came you here?"

"Wal, here's whar I belong. I've bin a sorter huntin' an' trappin' yer'bouts fer goin' on nine year or so, an' I built a shanty to live in up yonder by the forks. I hed n't much more nor got home frum down east, when the Injuns burnt thet down; an' sence then I ain't bin much o' nowhar, but I reckon'd I'd go inter ther Fort to-morrow and git some grub."

He spoke with a slow, deliberate drawl, as if not much accustomed to converse; and I pictured him to myself as one of those silent plainsmen, so habituated to solitude as almost to shun companionship, though he had already let drop a word or two that made me deem him one not devoid of humor. Suddenly I thought of De Croix.

"Has any one passed here lately?" I asked, rising to my feet, the old emulation throbbing in my veins. "A white man, I mean, going north."

"Wal," he answered slowly, and as he also stood up I could make out, what I had not noted in our previous meeting, that he was as tall as I, but spare of build; "I ain't seen nuthin', but some sort o' critter went ploughin' down inter the gulch up yonder, maybe ten minutes 'fore ye lit down yere on me. Dern if I know whether it were a human er a bar!"

"Will you show me the nearest way to the Kinzie house?"

"I reckon I'll show ye all right, but ye bet ye don't git me nigher ner a hundred foot o' the door," he returned seriously. "John Kinzie's a mighty good man, stranger, but he an' Ol' Tom Burns ain't never hitched worth a cent."

We climbed silently, and came out together upon the top. A slight beam of light crept along through the open door of the log house just in front of us, and for the first time I caught a fair view of my companion. He was a tall, gaunt, wiry fellow, typical in dress and manner of his class,—the backwoodsmen of the Southwest,—but with a peculiarly solemn face, seamed with wrinkles, and much of it concealed beneath a bushy, iron-gray beard. We eyed each other curiously.

"Dern if ever I expected ter meet up with ye agin in no sich way as this," he said shortly. "But thet 's the house. Be ye goin' ter stay thar long?"

"No," I answered, feeling anxious to have his guidance back to the Fort, "not over five minutes. Will you wait?"

"Reckon I may as well," and he seated himself on a stump.

No one greeted me at the house, not even a dog; though I could see figures moving within. Either the occupants felt that an assumption of confidence was their best security, or experienced no fear of Indian treachery, for I rapped twice before there was any response. A young girl, with a face of rare beauty and a pair of roguish black eyes, peered out curiously. At sight of a stranger she drew back slightly, yet paused to ask:

"Did you wish to see some one here?"

"I am seeking for a young girl," I answered, wondering if this could possibly be she, "and they told me at the Fort I should probably find her here. May I ask if you are Elsa Matherson?"

For a moment she looked out at me, as if I might be an escaped lunatic. Then she turned her face over her shoulder toward those within.

"Mr. Kinzie," said she, "here 's another man looking for Elsa Matherson."

CHAPTER XV

AN ADVENTURE UNDERGROUND

HEAVILY-BUILT man in shirt-sleeves, with a strong, good-humored face, and a shock of gray hair, appeared beside the girl in the doorway.

" 'T is not the same scamp that kissed you, Josette," he exclaimed, after examining me intently in the dim light, "but I doubt not he may prove of similar breed, and it behooves you to be careful where you stand."

"Has De Croix been here?" I questioned, scarcely deeming it possible he could have outstripped me in our race through the night.

"I know not the rascal's name," was the reply, in the man's deep voice, "but certain I am there was one here scarce ten minutes agone asking after this same Matherson girl. Saint James! but she must have made some sweet acquaintances, judging from the looks of

her callers! Josette has been rubbing the fellow's kiss
off her lips ever since he caught her unawares."

"He was a dandified young fellow?" I urged, impatient to be off, yet eager to be sure.

The girl laughed lightly, her roguish eyes ablaze
with merriment.

"He might be sometime, Monsieur," she cried,
evidently glad to talk, "but to-night he reminded me
of those scare-crows the farmers near Quebec keep in
their fields; a little chap, with a bit of turned-up
mustache, and a bright eye, but rags, — gracious,
such rags as he wore!"

'T was De Croix, there could be no doubt of it,
— De Croix, torn and dishevelled by his mad rush
through the darkness, but with no shred of his reckless
audacity gone. There was naught left me now but
to race back upon his trail, hopeful for some chance
that might yet allow me to come in first on the return
journey. In my throat I swore one thing, — the grace-
less villain should never collect his reward at both
ends of his journey. He had already stolen the sweets
from Josette's red lips, but he should never claim those
of Mademoiselle. I lingered for but a single question
more.

"But this Elsa Matherson, — she is not here,
then?"

"No," returned Mr. Kinzie, somewhat gruffly,
"and has not been since the closing of the gates of the

Fort. I think you are a parcel of mad fools, to be chasing around on such an errand; yet humanity leads me to bid you come in. There is not a safe foot of ground to-night for any strange white man within three hundred miles of Dearborn."

I glanced about me into the black shadows, startled at his solemn words of warning. Away to the southward a faint glimmer told of the location of the Fort; farther to the west, a sudden blaze swept up into the sky, reflected in ruddy radiance on the clouds, and the thought came to me that the savages had put torch to the deserted cabin on the south branch of the river.

" No doubt 't is true," I answered hastily; " yet, whatever the danger may be, I must regain the stockade before dawn."

I saw him step forward, as if he would halt me in my purpose; but, wishing to be detained no longer, my thoughts being all with De Croix and Mademoiselle, I turned away quickly and plunged back into the darkness.

" You young fool! " he called after me, " come back, or your life will be the forfeit! "

Without so much as answering, I ran silently in my moccasins to the spot where I had left Ol' Tom Burns. He sat upon his stump, motionless, apparently without the slightest interest in anything going on about him.

" Ol' Kinzie was gol-dern polite ter ye, sonny," he

commented. "Reckon if an Injun was a scalpin' me right on his front doorstep he 'd never hev asked *me* ter walk inside like that! He an' me sorter drew on each other 'bout a year ago, down at Lee's shebang; an' he don't 'pear ter fergit 'bout it."

"Show me the nearest safe passage to the Fort," I said, interrupting him, almost rudely.

He got up slowly, and cast his eyes with deliberation southward.

"Oh, thar ain't no sich special hurry, I reckon," he answered with an exasperating drawl. "We 'll be thar long afore daylight, — perviding allers we don't hit no Injuns meantime, — an' the slower we travel the less chance thar is o' thet."

"But, friend Burns," I urged, "it is a racing matter. I must reach there in advance of another man, who has already been here ahead of me."

"So I sorter reckoned from what I heerd; but ye need n't rip the shirt off ye on thet account. The feller can't git in thar till after daylight, nohow. Them sojers is too blame skeered ter open the gates in the dark, an' all the critter 'll git if he tries it will be a volley o' lead; so ye might just as well take it easylike."

The old man's philosophy seemed sound. De Croix would certainly not 'gain admittance until he could make himself known to the guard, and, carefully as the stockade was now patrolled, it was hardly probable he would be permitted to approach close enough for identification during the night. De Croix was no frontiersman, and was reckless to a degree; yet his long training as a soldier would certainly teach him a measure of caution in approaching a guarded fort at such a time.

" 'T is doubtless true," I admitted, "yet I shall feel safer if we push on at once."

" Ye called the feller De Croix, did n't ye? " he asked. " Is it the French dandy as was at Hawkins's? "

" Yes," I answered, " and I guess you don't care much to help *him*."

Burns wasted no breath in reply, but moved forward with noiseless step. Glancing back, I could clearly perceive Kinzie framed in the light of his open door. The vivacious French lass stood beside him, peering curiously out across his broad shoulders. Then we sank into the blackness of the ravine, and everything was blotted from our sight.

Burns evidently knew the intricacies of the path leading to the Fort gate, for I soon felt my feet upon a beaten track, and stumbled no more over the various obstacles that rendered my former progress so uncertain. My guide moved with excessive caution, as it seemed to me, frequently pausing to peer forward into the almost impenetrable darkness, and sniffing the night air suspiciously as if hoping thus to locate any lurking foes when his keen eyes failed in the attempt. So dark was it that I had almost to tread upon his heels in order to follow him, as not the slightest sound came from his stealthy advance. As he surmounted the steeper inclines of land, I was able to perceive him dimly, usually leaning well forward and moving with the utmost caution, his long rifle held ready for instant use. As we drew nearer the river, — or where I supposed the river must be, for I could distinguish but little of our position, — he swerved from the footpath we were following, and the way instantly grew rougher to our feet.

"Reckon we'd better hit the crick a bit below the Fort," he muttered, over his shoulder; "less likely ter find Injuns waitin' fer us thar."

"You think there are savages on this shore?"

He turned partially, and peered at me through the darkness.

"I never heerd tell as Injuns was fools," he answered briefly. "In course thar's some yere, an' we're almighty likely ter find 'em."

On the bank of the river, which I could see dimly by the faint light of a star or two that had broken through the cloud-rifts, he paused suddenly, sniffing the air like a pointer dog.

"The gol-dern fools!" he muttered, striking his rifle-butt on the ground with an expression of disgust. "They've gone and done it now!"

"Done what?" I questioned, almost guessing his meaning as a pungent odor assailed my nostrils. "That smells like rum!"

"'T is rum. Dern if ever I see whar the A'mighty finds so many blame idjits ter make sojers of! Them ar' fellers in the Fort wer n't in tight 'nough pickle, with a thousand savages howlin' 'bout 'em, so they 've went an' poured all their liquor inter the river! If I know Injun nature, it jist means the craziest lot o' redskins, whin they find it out, ever was on these yere plains. I bet they make thet fool garrison pay mighty big fer this job!"

"You mean the destruction of the liquor will anger them?"

"Anger? It 'll drive 'em plum crazy, — they 'll be ravin' maniacs! It 's the hope o' spoils thet 's held 'em back so long. They 've wanted the Fort to be 'vacuated, so as they could plunder it, — thet 's been the song o' the chiefs to hold their young men from raisin' ha'r. But come, sonny, thar 's nothin' gained a-stayin' here, an' dern me if I want ter meet any Injun with thet thar smell in the air. I don't swim no river smellin' like thet one does. We 'll hev ter go further up, I reckon, an' cross over by the ol' agency buildin'."

We crept up the edge of the stream, keeping well in under the north bank, and moving with the utmost caution, for the chances were strong that this portion

of the river would be closely watched by the redskins.
We met with no obstacle, however, nor were we apparently even observed from the stockade, as we
slowly passed its overhanging shadow. I could distinguish clearly its dark outlines, even making out a
head or two moving above the palisades; but no hail
of any kind rang out across the intervening water, and
we were soon beyond the upper block-house, where
a faint light yet shone. We could see the dim shape
of the two-story factory building, looking gloomy and
deserted on the south shore. Burns lay flat at the
water's edge, studying the building intently; and his
extreme caution made me a bit nervous, although I
could scarcely determine why, for I had thus far
marked not the slightest sign of danger.

"I reckon we'll hev ter risk it," he said at length,
as he bound his powder-horn upon his head with a
dark cloth. "Come right 'long arter me, and don't
make no splashin'."

He slipped off so silently that I scarcely knew he
was gone, until I missed the dark outline of his figure
at my side. With all possible caution, I followed him.
The current was not strong, but I partially faced it,
and struck out with a long, steady stroke, so that my
progress, as nearly as I could judge, was almost directly across the stream. Burns had been completely
lost to my sight, although as I looked along the
slightly glistening water I could see for some distance

ahead. I remember a black log bearing silently down upon me, and how I shrank from contact with it, fearful lest it might conceal some human thing. Soon after it had swirled by, my feet touched the shelving bank, and I crept cautiously up into the overhanging shadow. Burns was there, and had already reconnoitred our position; for my first knowledge of his presence came when he slowly lowered himself down the bank until he lay close beside me.

"They're thar," he said, soberly. "Thought most likely they wud be."

"Indians?" I asked, doubtfully, — for I had an impression the factory might be garrisoned by some of our own people.

"Sure; I heerd as how the sojers hed been drawed in, an' naturally reckoned the Injuns would n't be over-long findin' it out. 'Nother fool thing fer the sojers ter dew."

He paused, listening intently. In the silence, above the slight sound of the running water, I felt sure I could distinguish voices speaking not far distant.

"It's no place yere ter stay," he whispered, his lips close at my ear. "Reckon best thing we kin dew now is to find one o' the sojers' root-caves somewhar along the bank, an' crawl in thar till daylight. The Injuns ain't so likely to bother us when the guards kin see 'em from the Fort. They don't want no out-'n'-out fuss, to my notion, till they kin git inter the stockade

for good. Creep 'long yere with me, sonny, an'
't won't be far till I find a hole somewhar thet 'll hide
us fer awhile anyhow."

We crawled slowly along, snake-fashion, at the
edge of the river, for perhaps thirty feet, our movements hidden by the high and slightly overhanging
bank at our left. The night was so dark that Burns
relied more upon feeling than sight to guide him.
At last he stopped suddenly.

"Here's one o' 'em," he said. "Crawl along in,
sonny; thar's lots o' room after ye go a foot er two."

It was the merest hole dug into the bank, roughly
lined with irregular bits of rock, which opened out
into quite a cellar about a yard from the surface. The
air within felt somewhat chill and damp, as I put my
head cautiously down the narrow opening; but there
seemed no cause for fear, and I crept nimbly forward,
feeling my way as I advanced along the rude mud
walls. I could hear Burns behind me on his hands
and knees, puffing slightly as he squeezed through the
small aperture that led into the larger chamber.

I had advanced perhaps two yards without reaching the end of this odd underground apartment, when
suddenly, and directly in my front, there sounded a
deep, hollow, unearthly groan. The sound was so
terrifying that I stopped with chilled blood and beating heart, gripping my knife-hilt and peering forward
into the dark as frightened as ever I was in my life.

I heard Burns gasp and half turn; then, before I could move, even had I dared venture such a thing, an instantaneous flash lit up the black interior. I caught one confused glimpse of a huge object, topped with a head of tumbled hair, of two flapping wings stretching out upon either side, and then the impenetrable curtain of the dark hid everything once more. Sweat bathed me in cold drops; nor could I have moved a limb to save my life. Behind me Burns was muttering what might have been a prayer; when the thing groaned again, a hollow, awful moan, thrilling with agony, that sent me grovelling upon my face as nearly dead as one could well be and yet breathe and know.

CHAPTER XVI

"FRANCE WINS, MONSIEUR!"

OR the moment, every muscle of my body seemed paralyzed. I distinctly heard the creature moving in my direction, and I backed away violently, actuated only by the thought of instant escape into the open air. But Burns blocked the solitary passage.

"Back out of here, for God's sake!" I managed to exclaim through parched lips. "That devil-thing is coming this way!"

He struggled desperately in the darkness, tugging madly at some obstacle, an oath smothered on his lips. I waited and listened, every nerve on edge.

"Dern it all, but I can't!" he groaned at last. "My blame ol' gun hes got wedged, and won't give an inch."

Then a half-smothered laugh rippled out of the gloom just in front of me.

"Heaven protect me, but it's Wayland!" came a voice, and the laughter broke into a roar of merriment.

"Mon Dieu! Mon Dieu! This will be the death of me!"

The voice, choked and muffled as it was, sounded strangely hollow in that dark cave; yet it had a familiar tone. So surprising was the situation, that I could only stare into the black void, speechless. It was Burns who realized the need of action.

"Whoever the dern fool is," he growled, his voice hoarse with anger, "choke the wind out of him, or his blame howling will bring every Injun on the river yere!"

"De Croix!" I exclaimed quickly, aroused to recollection by the seriousness of the situation, "stop that infernal racket, or the two of us will throttle you!"

He puffed and gurgled, striving his best to smother the sense of ludicrousness that mastered him. To me there was small cause for merriment; the supreme terror of those moments merged into hot anger at the deception, and I crept forward eager to plant my hand upon the rascal's throat.

"What French mockery is this?" I exclaimed, my hand hard upon his arm. "Think you, Captain de Croix, that you can play such tricks in this wilderness, and not be made to pay for them?"

I felt him tremble under my fierce grasp; yet

it was not from fear, for my words only served to loosen his laughter once more. Burns now broke in, shoving the barrel of his long rifle forward over my shoulder till he struck the Frenchman a blow that effectually silenced him.

"You chattering ape!" he said, growling like an angry bear, "another yawp like that, and I'll blow a hole clean through you! Now, you French ninny, tell us what this means, an' be quick about it if ye want ter save yer hide!"

De Croix did not answer, but he ceased to laugh, and panted as if the breath had been knocked out of him. Another impatient movement by Burns led me to speak up hastily in his defence.

"Wait," I said, laying my grasp upon his gun, "he has no breath left with which to make reply. 'T is the French gallant who raced with me, the same whom you met at Hawkins's Ford; and no doubt he felt good reason to play the ghost here in this dark pit."

"Ay," panted De Croix painfully, "I truly thought the savages were upon me, and sought to frighten them by the only means I could devise. *Sacre!* but you hit me a sore blow in the ribs! If I have frightened you, 't was no worse than the terror that took me at your entrance here."

For a time none spoke, and no sound, save De Croix's labored breathing, broke the silence. Burns had turned slightly, and I knew was listening intently

163

for any sound without. Apparently satisfied that the noise made by us had not been overheard, he asked in his old deliberate drawl:

"How in thunder, Mister Parly-voo, did ye git up thet thar combination, anyhow?"

I heard the Frenchman chuckle, and pinched him as a warning to be careful. He answered, in his reckless, easy way:

"'T was all simple enough behind the scenes, Messieurs. I but took some old sacking discovered here, and used it as a robe, standing my hair well on end; and a flash of powder made the scene most realistic. The thing indeed worked well. I would I had a picture of Master Wayland's face to show Toinette!"

This chance mention of her name recalled me to myself. The undecided wager was yet to be won, and the night was now nearly spent. There came to me a sudden determination to risk a rush through the darkness to the Fort gates, rather than chance any further defeat at the hands of this rash gallant. Yet prudence bade me question somewhat further before I ventured upon so mad a deed.

"No doubt 't was most happy from your point of view, Monsieur. From ours, it was less so; and instead of laughing, you might better be thanking your lucky stars that you did not pay more dearly for such folly. But what brought you here? Why have you failed to reach the stockade?"

"Sacre!" he muttered carelessly, " but I had a fierce enough run for it as it was. Why did I not reach the stockade? Because, my friend, I am no real ghost to be invisible in the night, nor am I a bird to fly. 'T was in the shadow of that big building yonder that I ran into a nest of those copper-colored fiends, and 't was nip and tuck which of us won, had I not, by pure good luck, chanced to stumble into this hole, and so escape them. Perchance they also thought me a ghost, who knows? But, be that as it may, they were beating the river bank for me in the flesh, when you came creeping here."

We lay flat on the floor, the three of us, our eyes fastened upon the faint light that began to stream in through the entrance. I could hear Burns muttering to himself, as is often the way with men who lead lives of solitude; and every now and then De Croix would shake silently at the recollection of what had just occurred. I minded neither of them, but chiefly planned how best I might outwit De Croix and win the prize offered by Mademoiselle. The promise of dawning day was in the outer air, too dim as yet to render our faces visible. Suddenly the slight draft of air veered, and swept a tiny breath of smoke into my nostrils. It came so quickly that I scarcely realized its significance until Burns scrambled to his knees with a growl.

" God! the devils have run us to cover!" he cried,

sullenly. "They have started a fire to smoke us out!"

It hardly needed a moment to prove this true; the thin smoke grew more and more dense, filling the narrow entrance until we lay gasping for breath. De Croix, ever the most impulsive, was the first to act.

"Parbleu!" he gasped, pulling himself forward with his hands. "Better Indians than this foul air! If I die, it shall at least be in the open."

To remain longer cooped in that foul hole was indeed madness; and as soon as I could I followed him, rolling out of the entrance to the water's edge, fairly sick with the pressure upon my lungs, and caring so little what the end might be, provided I might first attain one breath of pure air, that before I gained strength to resist I was prisoner to as ill-looking a crew of savages as ever my eyes encountered. The villains triced us firmly with thongs of skin, and sat us up against the bank like so many puppets, dancing about before us, snapping their dirty fingers in our faces, and treating us to all manner of taunts and insults. 'T was done so quickly as to seem a dream, had I not smarted so sorely from the blows dealt me, and my limbs chafed where the tight cords were drawn.

I recall glancing aside at Burns; but his seamed and puckered face remained emotionless, as the red devils rolled him over till he stared straight up at the sky, now gray with coming dawn. The sight of De

Croix almost set me laughing, which won for me a
kick from the brute who had me in special charge.
The Frenchman was surely no court dandy now; his
fancy clothing clung to him in rags, while the powder-
flash within the cellar had blackened his face and made
sad havoc with his gay mustache. He endeavored
to smile at me as our eyes met, but the effort produced
only what seemed like a demoniac grin.

" 'T is a hard life, Monsieur," I could not forbear
remarking, " and will hardly remind you of Versailles."

His form stiffened in its bonds, as if the words
spurred his memory of other days.

" A French soldier smiles at fate, wherever it
overtakes him," he answered, a touch of pride in his
voice. " Besides, the game is not played out, — I may
yet prove the first one in. But see! if I mistake not,
here comes the chief of all these devils."

The new-comer strode down the high bank alone,
and was greeted noisily by our captors. It was the
same Indian that had halted Captain Wells the day
previous; and he looked us over with a contemptuous
sneer that curled his lips and transformed the whole
expression of his hideously painted face. I noted that
he paid but small heed to either De Croix or myself,
contenting his vengeance with sharp kicks at our prostrate bodies; but as he came to Burns, he paused,
bending down till he could peer into the old borderer's
upturned face.

"Bah! I know you," he said, brokenly. "You Ol' Burns. Stake down in village for you."

The old man neither moved his head nor gave the slightest sign that he had heard.

"Squaw eat heart," went on the Indian, prodding him with his stick; "feed bones to dog. All white men go that way now, — Ol' Burns first."

"Topenebe," was the quiet reply, as the victim rolled over until he half-sat against the bank, "I had the pleasure o' kickin' ye once down on the Kankakee, an' should be mighty glad ter do it agin. I reckon as how ye don't feel over friendly ter me, but ye 're simply wastin' yer breath tauntin' me. Any time yer derned old fire is hot, I 'm ready to dance."

These calm words angered the warrior, and he spat at him; then he turned and grunted an order in his own language. With blows of their sticks the Indians got us on our feet; but when they sought to drive us up the steep bank to the prairie, Ol' Burns balked and absolutely refused to move.

"Not one dern step, Topenebe," he swore grimly, "with these yere things on my legs. I 'm no pony ter be hobbled, an' blame if I 'll jump 'long fer any redskin. Ye kin carry me, if ye ain't too lazy; but, by thunder! thar 'll be no walkin' till ye cut them bonds."

Blows, curses, and threats failed alike to budge the old man. He simply sat down and smiled grimly at them; and we followed his example, dimly perceiving there must be a purpose in it. Sheer obstinacy wins many a battle, and when we went up the bank our lower limbs were free, although to my mind we were as hopelessly bound as ever. Not so with Burns. I chanced to press close to him, as we came out upon the prairie, and he muttered a quick word into my ear.

" See how they herd us in the shade of the Agency! They are not yet ready to let the sojers know whut they 're re'lly up to. Not an Injun will go beyond thet line long enough to be seen. Be ready to run fer it as soon as I say ' Go,' an' tell the Frenchman."

I succeeded in making De Croix understand, by means of the mongrel French at my command, which seemed not to be intelligible to the savages; and we moved forward at as slow a gait as our vigilant guards permitted, with every muscle tense for the coming strain. We were bunched together, with no pretence of order on the part of our captors; indeed, they seemed to be of various minds over what was to be done with us, though Topenebe exercised sufficient control over his mongrel followers to compel at least partial obedience to his orders. We tramped along to the west of the factory, the walls of which shut off all view of the Fort, a half-dozen of the savages about us, while the chief stalked on a few feet in advance.

We had almost reached the southwestern corner of the big Agency building, and Topenebe had already taken a step to the right, carefully keeping the log walls as a protection between our movements and the eyes of the garrison, when Burns, shaking off the Indians nearest him, bounded suddenly forward and struck Topenebe with his head, hurling the fellow by his side over backward as he passed.

"Run for the gate!" he yelled.

Like an arrow from the bow, I shot around the Agency corner, and raced for the stockade, De Croix, running like a deer, barely a foot behind me. I never dreamed, in that moment of intense action, that Burns was not also coming, — that he had deliberately sacrificed himself in order to hold back the savages and give us the better chance for life. Behind arose the sound of struggle, but there was no indication of pursuit, and as I rounded the end of the stockade the lower gate swung open just before me and I glanced back, half pausing as I realized the old borderer had not followed us; then some one tripped me, and I fell headlong. With a sudden rush, De Croix swept by.

"France wins, Monsieur!" he cried back in mocking triumph, as I staggered to my knees.

CHAPTER XVII

A CONTEST OF WITS

HOUGH I was never of hasty or violent temper, it was quite as well that I failed to gain a sight of De Croix as I passed the posts and the sentry clanged the gate behind me. The Frenchman's scurvy trick would have heated cooler blood than mine; nor was my spirit soothed by the harsh fall I suffered. But De Croix had not waited; nowhere along the bare sunlit parade was he visible. I saw nothing but a squad of grinning soldiers lounging beside the barracks, until Captain Wells, issuing from the guard-house door, caught sight of me and came forward.

"Back, are you, Master Wayland?" he said gruffly, and 't was easy to see he did not approve of my escapade. "I scarcely thought to see you here again with so full a head of hair, after I learned of your mad wager. Providence must indeed take special care of fools. Have the redskins captured our French friend?"

"He entered a step in my advance."

A gleam of amusement played over his swarthy face.

"Ah, and so you let him win!" he exclaimed; "he, a mere voyager from the courts, unused to forest play! Such remissness deserves the guard-house, at the very least. Come, how happened it that this gay sprig outfooted you?"

"'T was but a trick," I retorted, aroused by these contemptuous words, "and one I shall make him pay well for. But I pray you cut these bands and set me free."

I think he had not noticed them before; but now, as he quickly drew his knife across the deerskin thongs, his whole expression changed.

"'T is Indian tying," he said earnestly; "you have been in the hands of the savages?"

"Ay!" and the memory of it instantly brought back the recollection of the sacrifice that had won us our freedom. "There were three of us taken at daylight on the river bank, beyond the factory building. De Croix and I escaped through the efforts of one who is still a prisoner, and marked for torture."

Many were gathering about us by this time, anxious to learn whatever news I brought from without; but it was Captain Heald himself who now pushed his way through the throng until he fronted me.

"Who was it?" he asked, sharply. "We have lost no men!"

"His name is Burns, sir. I ran across him just back of the Kinzie house."

"Burns? Ol' Tom Burns?"

"Yes, sir."

Heald laughed, a look of evident relief on his haggard features.

"We shall not have to worry much as to his fate," he said, turning toward Wells. "You remember the fellow, William? He was one of Mad Anthony's scouts, and came west with you in 1803 when you first held council here."

The other nodded, a twinkle of pleasant recollection in his eyes. "Remember him?" he repeated. "I am not likely ever to forget him. He it was who brought me your message at Fort Wayne a month ago. My sympathies in this case are entirely with the Indians. There are likely to be things happening when Ol' Tom is around, unless he has lost his versatility and nerve in recent years. Come, my lad, give us the details of the story, for it must be worth the hearing if Ol' Burns played a leading part. He is as full of tricks as a dog of fleas."

I repeated the story briefly, for I was now eager to be away before De Croix could dress and claim his wager. I knew well the conceited coxcomb would never seek the presence of Mademoiselle until he had shed the rags he wore on entering the Fort. I remember yet that throng of faces, anxious yet amused, peering over each other's shoulders to get a better view of me as I talked, and constantly augmented as the word passed quickly about the garrison that we had safely returned from our midnight adventures.

"You will send aid to him?" I questioned, as I concluded, my eyes fixed appealingly upon Captain Heald.

"Not I," was the prompt and decisive rejoinder. "No soldier of this command shall leave the stockade until the hour for our final departure. The fellow had a chance to come in here with the others before the gates were closed, but was obstinate as a mule, and must now take the consequences. But you need not worry about Ol' Tom, my boy; he'll circumvent those red devils in some way, you may rest assured, nor would he even thank us for interference. I have no force with which to control the horde of savages that surround us here. A clash of arms would be their excuse for immediate attack, and might mean death and torture to the whole garrison. Our only hope lies in being permitted to pass out without armed collision; and to do this requires that we ignore such hidden deeds. 'T was a mad prank of yours last night, and might have involved us all in common ruin. Go this

time free, except for these words of censure; for you
are not directly under my orders. Another such attempt, subversive of all discipline, and the gates of
Dearborn will be closed against you."

These harsh expressions stung me, but I felt them
in a measure merited, and made no reply.

" 'T was but the act of a boy, Heald," interposed
Wells kindly, resting his hand upon my shoulder,
" and you will find the lad well worth having when
time of trial comes."

I slipped away through an opening in the curious
throng, and hastened across the open parade toward
the messroom. I felt dust-covered and bruised from
my rough experiences, and hoped to discover oppor-
tunities for a bath. The building called the mess-
room was long, running nearly half the length of the
stockade, built like the others of logs, two stories in
height, and containing a number of rooms. The single
flight of stairs, opening just within the porch, was exceedingly rude, and built without any protecting rail.
I hesitated a moment when fairly within the entrance,
scarce knowing which way to turn in search of what
I sought; but as I waited there, a light step sounded
upon the bare floor above, and glancing up, with
quickened beat of the heart, my eyes caught the soft
drapery of a woman as she stepped on the upper stair.

I could scarcely have retreated had I wished to
do so, though I realized instantly who it was, and drew

back against the wall, so that she came down, singing lightly to herself, without noticing my presence until we were face to face. It was a picture to touch the heart of any man, and abide forever in the memory. I saw the sunlight as it streamed through an upper window along the rough log wall and flecked her white dress with ever-changing spots of quivering gold, and, as she drew nearer to my standing-place, played softly amid the masses of her dark-brown hair, giving it a tinge of glory. How daintily fair she was! how archly sweet looked the clear girlish face under the coquettish sweep of the broad hat! and with what unconscious grace she moved down the rude stairway, one white hand steadying her against the brown logs, the other gathering her draperies so close that I could not be blind to the daintily slippered foot that shyly peeped below the petticoat of ruffled silk. I may not have loved her then as I learned to do in later days, but my heart throbbed riotously at her presence, and I stood forgetful of all else.

As she turned aside at the foot of the stairs, she saw me, and the color deserted her face, only to return instantly in deeper volume, while her tell-tale eyes hid themselves behind long lashes.

"And are you indeed returned, Master Way-land?" she asked quickly, conquering her first emotion with a proud uplifting of her head. "You surprised me greatly. I think I first mistook you for a ghost come back to haunt me for having despatched you on so perilous a quest. You cannot know how I have been scolded for doing such a thing; yet surely you would have gone, even if I had failed to encourage it."

"Perhaps so, Mademoiselle," I answered, hoping I might lead her to speak with greater seriousness; "but it was the hope of the reward that spurred me forward."

"Ah, of course," she said deliberately ignoring her own offer, and with a reckless toss of her head, "you sought a fair girl for whose sake you have travelled far. Pray tell me, Monsieur, — I am so curious to know, — do you truly think Josette fairer than I?"

She spoke so lightly, smiling softly into my eyes, that I hardly detected the faint tinge of regretful sarcasm in her low voice.

"Josette, you ask me? Why, Josette is indeed a most charming girl, Mademoiselle; but to my mind there can be no comparison between her and you, for you are the fairest woman I have ever known."

Her dark eyes were full upon me, and I saw her parted lips move as if she would speak. But no words came, and we stood there silent except for the nervous tapping of her foot against the floor. Her look of seriousness changed into a smile.

"By my faith, but you pay compliments with so grave a countenance, Monsieur, that I hardly know how to receive them. Most men whisper such things with a light laugh, or a twinkle of the eye, and I know their words to be empty as bubbles of air. But you, — why, you almost make me feel you are in earnest."

"And I am," I interrupted, longing to seize her hand as I knew De Croix would have done, and pour forth the words that burnt upon my lips. "I have not been privileged to see much of the great outside world, Mademoiselle, — the world of courts and cities, — nor do I know how lovely its women may be; but no ideal formed in dreams satisfies me as you do. I know naught of idle compliments, nor the graces of a courtier; but my words are from the heart."

"I do truly believe and trust you, John Wayland," and she gave me her hand. "But let us talk of this no longer. My vanity is already more than satisfied by your frank and honest speech. And so you found Josette?"

"Yes," I answered, scarce noting what it was I said, so puzzled was I by her quick retreat.

"And that meeting, perchance, was so pleasant that it has taken your thought from all else? It must indeed be so, or why is it that Master Wayland doth not claim of me the stake of the wager?"

"Because," I stammered, greatly embarrassed by her roguish questioning eyes, "I fear it has not been fairly won."

"Not fairly won?" she echoed, puzzled by my

tone and manner. "Surely you have made the trip, and the terms were plain. Really, Monsieur, you do not think I would withhold so small a reward from the winner?"

"But there was another, — the prize was destined for him who came back first."

"And has Captain de Croix returned also?"

"We arrived together, Mademoiselle, but it was his good fortune to be earliest through the gate."

'T was good to see how her face lit up with the amusement this reply afforded her.

"Pish! but you are in truth the most marvellous man I ever knew. 'T is good to meet with such open honesty; and when did maid ever have before so unselfish a cavalier to do her honor? Monsieur, I greatly doubt if Captain de Croix will prove so thoughtful when his hour comes."

"You are right, Toinette," broke in a voice at my back. "I know not what Master Wayland may be yielding up so easily, but, like the Shylock of your William Shakespeare, I am here to claim my pound of flesh."

I wheeled and faced him, standing firmly between his approach and the girl, my blood instantly boiling at the familiar sound of that drawling voice.

"I have refused to accept from Mademoiselle what I had not fairly earned," I said, with quiet emphasis, "and so, no doubt, will you."

There was that about my words and action that astonished him, and for the moment his old audacity was gone as he swept a puzzled glance over our faces. I have often reflected upon the contrast we must have presented to her sight as we stood there, — for De Croix had donned his best attire, and was once again resplendent in frills and ribbons, with heavily powdered hair.

"Oh, most certainly, what I have not earned," he said at length, "but the kiss promised is surely mine by every right, as I was the first in."

"'T was done by a most scurvy trick."

"Poof! what of that? 'T is the same whether the goal be won by wit and strategy, or mere fleetness of foot. Toinette will make no such fine distinction, I warrant you."

"Mademoiselle," and I turned toward the smiling girl, who seemingly enjoyed our interchange of compliments, "what may have been your understanding of this wager?"

"Why," she answered slowly, endeavoring to recall the details to mind, "Captain de Croix declared he would willingly make the trip for a touch of rosy lips, and in a spirit of venture I promised that whichever of you two first completed the journey and returned here should obtain such reward."

"There, 't is plain enough," he cried, stroking his mustache complacently, "and I have won."

"Most surely you have," I retorted, "and the reward has already been given you."

"Been given?" she questioned, "and by whom?"

"The girl Josette."

She looked from the one to the other of us, puzzled for a brief moment at the odd situation. Then, as her eyes settled upon De Croix's flushed and angry face, she laughed gaily, even as she daintily drew aside her skirts to pass us by.

"Pish, Monsieur!" she cried, shaking her finger at him, "I doubt it not. No, you need not deny it, for 't is but one of your old-time tricks, as I knew them well at Montreal. 'T would be no more than right were I even now to reward Master Wayland, for he hath truly won it, — yet for that I will delay awhile."

And with a flash of her dark eyes that held us speechless, she was gone.

CHAPTER XVIII

GLIMPSES OF DANGER

F any trace of anger held place in my heart, it utterly vanished as I noted the bewildered surprise with which De Croix gazed after Mademoiselle's departing figure.

"*Sacre!*" he exclaimed presently, turning toward me, his face flushed, and forgetful of all his well-practised graces. "'T was an unworthy trick, Master Wayland, and one I am not likely to forget."

"'T was a moment ago," I answered, in great good-humor at his discomfiture, "that you claimed wit was as important a factor as fleetness of foot in the winning of a race. I did no more than illustrate your theory, Monsieur."

The humor of it failed to touch him, and there was a direct menace in his manner which caused me to fall back a step in the narrow passage and front him warily.

"No boor of the woods shall laugh at me!" he exclaimed, his eyes aflame with passion, "be the cause love or war. What mean all these sly tricks of speech and action? — this hurried message to the ear of Mademoiselle? By my faith, you did not even pause to wash the dust from off your face before you sought her company. 'T is strange such intimacy could spring up between you in so short a time! But mark you this, Master Wayland, once and for all; I have not voyaged here from Montreal to be balked in my plans by the interference of an uncouth adventurer. I give you now fair warning that if you ever step again between Toinette and me, naught but the decision of steel shall end our quarrel."

That he was indeed in deadly earnest, and indulged in no vain threat, I well knew; his passion was too strongly painted on his face. My own temper rose in turn.

"I hear your words, Monsieur," I returned coldly, "and care no more for them than for a child's idle boasting. There is naught between Mademoiselle and me that the whole world might not know. We are good friends enough, but if by any chance love should be born from that friendship, no French gallant, though he sport a dozen swords, shall come between us. Win her if you can by reckless audacity and lavishness of perfume, but dream not to frighten me away from her presence by the mutterings of bravado. I am the son of a soldier, Monsieur, and have myself borne arms in battle."

"You will fight, then?"

"With pleasure, whenever the occasion arises," I replied slowly, struggling hard to keep back more bitter words. "But I see none at present, and, if I mistake not, all our skill at arms will soon be needed to save this girl, as well as ourselves, from savage hands."

I know not how we would have parted, for 't was evidently his wish to goad me on to fight; and there are times when passion overwhelms us all. But at that moment I heard the soft rustle of a dress, and wheeled to face the fair young wife of Lieutenant Helm. It was plain she had been weeping; but De Croix, ever quicker than I in such matters, was first to accost her in words of courtesy. A pretty face to him was instant inspiration.

"We bow to you, Madame," he exclaimed with excessive gallantry, doffing his hat till it swept the stairs; "your coming makes the very sunshine a brighter gold."

"I trust it may bring peace as well," she answered, striving to smile back at him, although trouble yet shadowed her sweet face; "surely my ears caught the sound of harsh words."

"A slight misunderstanding, which will hardly grow to any serious end," he protested.

"I trust not, gentlemen, for the time is come when

we women at Dearborn surely need you all to protect us. Our case already appears desperate."

"Has something new occurred," I questioned anxiously, "that makes you more alarmed?"

Her eyes, grown strangely serious once more, swept our faces.

"You may neither of you comprehend this in its full meaning as clearly as I do," she returned gravely, "for I am frontier-bred, and have known the Indian character from childhood. We have long been acquainted, in my father's family, with many of the chiefs and warriors now encamped around us. We have traded in their villages, lived with them in their smoke-stained tepees on the great plains, and trusted them as they showed faith in us. You, I learn," and she looked at me more intently, "were at my father's house no later than last night. In spite of rumors of war and tightly guarded Fort-gates, you found his door wide open to whosoever might approach, with never a dog to bark at an intruder, be he white or red. This is because the Silver-man has always dealt fairly with the Indian, and won his respect and gratitude in return. Now, in time of peril this trader dares to believe in their good faith toward him and his. 'T is because of this I know so well all that is going on without, and have been able to inform Captain Heald of much his scouts were unable to discover. From the first there have been two factions among the savages gathered yonder; and whether we live or die may depend upon which counsel prevails among them — that of peace or that of war. Until within an hour I have hoped it might be peace, — that the older chiefs would hold their young men in control, and the red wampum be not seen at Dearborn. Twenty minutes ago one of the noblest advocates of peace, — a Pottawattomie warrior named Black Partridge, — sought interview with Captain Heald, and his words have shown me how desperate indeed has our situation become."

"He threatened?" broke in De Croix, his hand upon his sword-hilt.

"Nay, Monsieur, 't is not the way of an Indian, nor is Black Partridge one to indulge in vain words. I have known him long; in childhood I sat upon his knee, and believe him so friendly to the whites that naught but a sense of duty could move him otherwise. Yet, as I say, he came just now to the commandant of this garrison, and returned a medal once given him by the government. It was done sadly, and with deep regret, — for I overheard his speech. He said: 'Father, I come to deliver up to you the medal I wear. It was given me by the Americans, and I have long worn it in token of our mutual friendship. Our young men are resolved to imbue their hands in the blood of the whites. I cannot restrain them, and I will not wear a token of peace while I am compelled to act as an enemy.'"

She stopped, her agitated face buried in her hands, and neither of us spoke. The solemnity of her words and manner were most impressive.

"You feel, then, that the die is cast?" asked De Croix, all lightness vanished from his voice.

"I believe we march forth from these walls to our death to-morrow."

"But why," I protested, "should you, at least, take part in such hazard? Your father's family, you tell us, will be safe from attack. Surely, that home might also prove your refuge?"

The little woman, with the face of a girl, looked up at me indignantly through her tears.

"Lieutenant Helm marches with the troops," she answered quietly, "and I am his wife."

I retain no memory, at this late day, of what conversation followed. I know that De Croix in his easy carelessness about the future, sought to laugh at her fears and restore a feeling of hopefulness; but all my thoughts were elsewhere, — upon the grave dilemma in which we found ourselves, and my duty to these helpless ones upon every side.

I must have left the two standing there and conversing, though just how I moved, and why, is dim to me. I recall crossing the bare parade, and noting the company that formed the little garrison drawn up in the shadow of the south stockade. At any other time I should have paused in interest, for military evolutions always attracted my attention; but then I had no sense other than that of mental and physical exhaustion from the hours of toil and lack of rest. Owing to my absence the night before, no quarters had been assigned me; but finding the barracks of the troops unoccupied, and yielding to imperative need, I flung myself, without undressing, upon a vacant bunk, and lay there tossing with the burden of intense fatigue.

And then how the thoughts I sought to banish thronged upon me! No effort of my will could shut them out. I went over again and again the quarrel with De Croix, the incidents of the night, the solemn words of Mrs. Helm. Little by little, each detail clear and absolute, there unrolled before my mind's view the picture of our situation. I saw it as a frontiersman must, in all its grim probabilities. The little isolated Fort was cut off from all communication, held by a weakened garrison. Hope of rescue there was none. Without were already gathered hundreds of warriors attracted by rumors of war and promise of pillage; and these were growing in number and increasing in ferocity each day. I had ridden through them once, when their mood was only to annoy, and realized with a shudder of horror what it would mean to face them in our retreat, with all restraint of their chiefs removed. I thought of those long leagues of tangled forest-land stretching between us and the nearest border settlements, of ambuscades, of constant and harassing attack on the ever-thinning column as we fought for each foot of the way. Once my mind dwelt for an instant upon the quiet home I had left on the banks of the Maumee; as my eyes filled at the memory I drove it from me, for the present necessity was all too stern to permit indulgence in such weakness.

'T was of the women and children I thought most, and their probable fate if we failed to win a passage. The half-framed thought of such a possibility made my heart throb with dread apprehension, as I set my lips together in firm resolve. What had become of Roger Matherson's orphan child? 'T was indeed strange that I could gain no trace of the little girl. At the Fort they said she was with the Kinzies, at Kinzies' they told me she was at the Fort. It was, as Seth had prophesied, like seeking after a will-o'-the-wisp; yet surely she must be in the flesh somewhere. My plain duty was to find her at once; and I resolved to take up the task anew that day, and question every one I met till some trace yielded to my persistency. However, I needed first to sleep; but as I resolutely closed my eyes, there came gliding into my memory another face, — an arch, happy face, with softly rounded cheeks and dark laughing eyes, a face that mirrored a hundred moods, and back of them all a sweet womanly tenderness to make every mood a new and rare delight. Toinette! — never before was woman's name so pleasant to my lips. Ignorant as I was in mysteries of the heart, I knew not clearly whether I loved her, though this I knew beyond cavil, — no savage hand should ever touch her while I lived; and if I had to fight each step of the path from that accursed spot to Wayne, I swore within my heart she should come safe through. Her gentle memory was with me when all the rest yielded to the drowsy god, and in sheer exhaustion I slept — to dream.

CHAPTER XIX

A CONFERENCE AND A RESOLVE

O my mind, the risk would be extreme; and I greatly doubt the wisdom of the step."

"But, William, what other alternative offers us any hope?"

"I confess I know not, for your last mistake has greatly aggravated the situation."

I sat up hastily, for seemingly these words were spoken at the very side of the bunk on which I lay. As I glanced about me I saw the room was vacant; so I knew the conference thus accidentally overheard must be taking place in an adjoining apartment. I was thoroughly awake when Captain Heald's voice spoke again.

"You say a mistake, — what mistake?" he questioned, as though aggrieved. "I have done no more than simply obey the orders of my superior officer."

"That may be true," broke in the gentler tones of Lieutenant Helm, "but of that we are unable to judge, for not one of your officers has been privileged to see those orders."

"You shall see them now. If I have been remiss in taking you into my confidence in these grave matters, it has been because of certain malcontents in the garrison with whom I hesitated to confer."

There was a rustle of paper, and Heald read slowly. I failed to distinguish the opening words, but as he reached the more important portion of the document his utterance grew deeper, and I heard distinctly this sentence:

"Evacuate the post if practicable, and in that event distribute the property belonging to the United States in the Fort, and in the factory or agency, to the Indians in the neighborhood."

There was a pause as he concluded. Captain Wells spoke first.

"To my mind, these orders are not positive, and leave much to your discretion. Who brought the message, and when?"

"A Wyandot named Winnemeg. He reached here on the ninth."

"I have heard the name, and believe him worthy of confidence. Did you advise with him?"

"Ay! Though he had no oral message from General Hull, he counselled immediate evacuation. I also felt such action to be wise; but things were in such

192

condition within the Fort, — so large a number of helpless women and children to be provided for, and so heavy a proportion of the garrison on the sick-list, — that I found it impossible to act promptly. The Indians gathered so rapidly without, and assumed so hostile a manner, that I thought it suicidal to attempt a march through the wilderness, encumbered as we should be, without some positive understanding with their chiefs."

"I can easily comprehend all this, and that you have sought to act for the best," was Wells's comment; "but I fail to realize how you hoped to appease those same Indians by the wanton destruction last night of the liquor thrown into the river. It was done in direct opposition to the orders you have just read, and is bound to increase the hatred of the savages. You may be sure they are not ignorant of the contents of your despatch, and must resent the destruction of property they consider their own."

"'T was done upon the advice of two of their leading chiefs."

"Indeed! Which two?"

"Topenebe and Little Sauk."

"The two biggest devils in that whole Pottawattomie camp, and the head and front of their war-party! Their purpose is clear enough to my mind, and seamed with treachery. Well, Heald, from my knowledge of Indian nature I must say that whoever goes forth now to confer with yonder redskins has a desperate mission; but if you are still determined upon such a conference, I will take my chances with you. 'T is given unto man but once to die."

"No, William," replied Captain Heald, with more firmness. "It is your part to remain here in protection of your niece, my wife; and if my own officers refuse to volunteer in this service, I shall go forth alone to meet the chiefs. It is my duty as commandant."

"Two of your officers are here," said Wells, "and they can probably answer for themselves. Ensign Ronan is not present."

"He is acting as officer of the day," returned Heald, somewhat stiffly, "and is therefore not eligible for such service. Perhaps one of the officers here present possesses courage enough for the venture?"

Apparently neither cared to express himself, after such an insinuation. At last one, whose voice I recognized as that of Surgeon Van Voorhis, gave utterance to his refusal.

"As the only medical officer of the garrison, I feel justified in declining to go upon so desperate an expedition," he said gravely. "It would expose not only my own life to unnecessary peril, but the lives of many others as well."

"And what say you, Lieutenant Helm? Have you also personal scruples?"

A CONFERENCE AND A RESOLVE

I could detect a tremor in the younger officer's voice, as he answered promptly.

"Captain Heald has before this seen me in time of danger," he said quietly, "and can have no reason for ascribing cowardice to me. But I will frankly say this, sir, and with all respect to my commanding officer, I believe such conference as now proposed with the hostile Indians yonder, at this late day, to be perfectly useless, and that every hour's delay since the receipt of orders to evacuate the post has only tended to increase our danger and lessen our hope of escape. I feel now that our only chance of safety lies in defending this stockade against attack until a rescue party from the East can reach us. I have a young wife among the women of this garrison; to her I owe allegiance, as well as to the flag I serve. Feeling as I do, Captain Heald, as a soldier I will obey any command you give, and will go forth upon this mission if ordered to do so, either in your company or alone; but I cannot volunteer for such service. I believe it to be foolhardy, and that whoever undertakes it goes forth to almost certain death."

"Then I shall go alone," said Heald, sternly; "nor do I look forward to any such disastrous ending to so open a mission of peace."

"Wait," broke in Wells, impulsively. "I have a final suggestion to make, if you are resolved to go. There rode in my party hither a rattle-brained gallant,

195

bearing a French commission, who ought to prove sufficiently reckless to lend you his companionship. Faith! but I think it may well suit the fellow. Besides, if he wore his French uniform it might have weight with the reds."

"Who is he?" asked Heald, doubtfully. "I seem not to have memory of him."

"He calls himself Captain Villiers de Croix, and holds commission in the Emperor's Guard."

Scarcely were the words spoken when I was on my feet, all vestige of sleep gone from my eyes. De Croix was hardly a friend of mine, since late developments, but he had been my comrade for many a league of hard forest travel, and I was unwilling to have him carelessly sacrificed in a venture regarding the danger of which he knew nothing. Besides, I counted on his sword to aid in the defence of Mademoiselle. I understood thoroughly the desperate chances of Indian treachery that lay before such a commission as was now proposed. It was rash in the extreme; and only the terrors of our position could sanction such an experiment. The savages that hemmed us in were already in an ugly mood, and fully conscious of their power. To go forth to them, unarmed and uninvited, as Captain Heald coolly proposed doing, was to walk open-eyed into a trap which treachery might snap shut at any time. It was not my purpose to halt De Croix, nor to stand between him and any adventure he might choose to undertake; but I could at least warn him, in a friendly spirit, of the imminent danger such a thing involved.

With this thought in mind, I ran hastily across the open parade into the officers' mess-hall, hoping I might find him loitering there. To my hasty glance, the place appeared deserted; and I drew back, wondering where to turn next in search. As I hesitated on the threshold, the low voice of Mademoiselle fell upon my ear; and at that moment she emerged from behind the curtain which divided the officers' quarters.

"May I hope you are seeking me?" she asked, graciously; "for it has been most lonely here all day, — even Captain de Croix seems to have forgotten my existence."

"It was De Croix I sought," I answered, somewhat nettled by her prompt reference to him; "and doubtless you are well able to give me trace of him."

She studied me keenly, marking an angry note in my voice that I sought vainly to disguise.

"Forever a quarrel?" she said, regretfully. "Do you know, Master Wayland, I had thought better of you. Surely it is not your nature to be a brawler, and always seeking opportunity to show the strong hand! What has Captain de Croix done now to make you seek him so vengefully?"

"'T is not in quarrel," I explained, — I fear with ill grace, for her words in his defence were little inclined to mollify me. "You may indeed have so poor conception of me as to misinterpret my coming; yet in truth I seek De Croix in friendship, hoping that I may by a chance word serve him."

"Indeed! what danger threatens, that he needs to be warned against?"

I hesitated; for, now that my blood had somewhat cooled, my mission seemed a bit foolish.

"I insist upon knowing," she continued haughtily, her eyes full upon mine, "or I shall believe you sought him for hostile purpose, and would deceive me by fair words."

"Mademoiselle," I answered gravely, "you do me wrong. Only a few moments ago I chanced to overhear a discussion, by the officers of this Fort, regarding a commission to go forth and hold council with the Indians. Captain Heald is determined upon such a course; but none will volunteer to accompany him, because of the grave danger of savage treachery. The Frenchman's name was mentioned as one reckless enough to join with such a party; and I sought to warn him ere he accepted blindly. He is hardly a friend of mine, — yet it seems no more than fair that he should know the full measure of his peril before saying ' yes.'"

She came impulsively forward, with quickly extended hand, her face aglow.

"You are indeed a true heart, John Wayland, and

have shamed me rightly. I know well the deceit and treachery of Indian nature, and can understand the peril such a party would run. Promise me that you will prevent Captain de Croix from becoming one of them."

" I ? " I exclaimed in perplexed surprise; " I can do no more than warn him."

" But you must do more! " she cried imperatively. " He will surely go if asked. A warning such as you propose would only stir his blood. I beg you to use your wits a little, so that he may know nothing of it."

I looked at her, deeply hurt by the interest so openly displayed.

" You are wondrously aroused for the Frenchman's safety, Mademoiselle! "

" Yes, though not as you may fancy. Captain de Croix came here for my sake, even though no word of mine gave him reason for doing so. For this reason I could never forgive myself if harm befell him on such a journey. 'T would be as if I had lured him to his death. So 't is for my sake, not his, that I ask the favor."

I leaned against the log wall and thought quickly, her anxious eyes never leaving my face. There came into my mind a conviction that the girl really loved him; and this made the struggle harder for me to serve him. Nor did I see clearly how it could well be done, save through a sacrifice of myself, such as I had never intended.

"Surely," she urged, "your wits will conceive some way in which it may be done?"

"Yes," I answered, eager now to hide my own feeling from her; "'t is not hopeless. You desire that he be kept within the Fort, ignorant of this commission?"

"I do; 't is the only way."

"Very well, it shall be done, Mademoiselle. No, I need no thanks from you. Only do this simple thing, which, I am sure, you will find no hardship, — keep Captain de Croix from any possible contact with others for an hour. Your eyes will prove sufficient, no doubt, to enchain him that long; if not, use other measures."

"But what will you do?"

"That does not count. 'T is the result, not the means, that must content you. I have my plan, and it will work; but I cannot stay here longer to discuss it. Only do your part well, and I pledge you the safety of De Croix."

I left her standing there, the light of questioning still in her eyes; but I wished mainly to be safely away, where I might hide my own sudden heart-ache in the energy of action.

CHAPTER XX

IN THE INDIAN CAMP

IT cut me deeply to think that this girl would willingly sacrifice me to save the French gallant from injury, and an anxiety to escape her presence before I should speak words I might always regret caused me to leave with scant ceremony. Yet I was none too soon; for scarce had I stepped without the door when I met Lieutenant Helm ascending the steps.

"Ah, Wayland!" he said, catching sight of me, "do you happen to know where I am most likely to find Captain de Croix?"

"He is scarcely to be disturbed at present, unless the matter be truly urgent," I replied, my plan hastily sketched in mind. "Have you arranged a banquet in honor of the Frenchman?"

"No such good fortune," was the grave response. "Captain Heald desires his company upon an immediate mission to the Pottawattomie camp."

"Oh, is that all? Well, Captain de Croix will hardly be found sufficiently recovered from his late adventure to enter upon another one so early. 'T is in my thought he either sleeps or is prinking himself for more pleasant conquests. But why worry him? In my judgment, no poorer choice could be made for so serious a task as you propose. He is a mere French courtier, — brave enough, and rash, I grant, yet without knowledge of Indian ways and treachery. Might not I answer better as his substitute?"

"You?"

"Ay! and why not? I am frontier-bred, long trained in woodcraft and savage ways, and surely far better fitted for such a task than is this petted darling of the courts. Were it a flirtation, now, the post might be truly his."

"'T is true, you would be my choice; but do you realize the peril involved?"

"Fully, my friend, yet scarce think it so desperate as you imagine. It is my judgment the savages yonder are seeking bigger game than so small a party would afford, and will therefore allow us to go free. However, if it should prove otherwise," and I spoke the words with a sore heart as I recalled what had just occurred, "I am a lone man in the world, and to such an one death is not so terrible, even at Indian hands. Come, I will go with you to confer with Captain Heald, and offer him my services. He can do no more than refuse."

Helm offered no further objection, doubtless feeling it useless in my venturesome mood; and we crossed the parade together without speaking.

Captain Wells was the first to see me as we entered, and some instinct told him instantly of my purpose.

"Ah, Wayland, my boy! I have been troubled lest you might chance to hear of our plight, and jump in. Come now, lad! 't was not you we sent after, nor can we use you in so grave a matter."

"And pray, why not?" I questioned, a little touched by this evidence of kindness, yet firmly determined to keep my pledge to Mademoiselle. "I am a better man for such deeds than the Frenchman, and am eager to go."

"So this is not your Captain de Croix?" said Captain Heald, eying me curiously. "Saint George! but he is a big fellow, — the same who made the race last night, or I mistake greatly. And what is this man's name?"

"It is John Wayland," I answered, anxious to impress him favorably; "a frontiersman of the Maumee country, and fairly skilled in Indian ways. I have come to volunteer my services to go with you."

"You are anxious to die? have the spirit of a Jesuit, perchance, and are ambitious of martyrdom?"

"Not unusually so, sir, but I think the danger

overrated by these gentlemen. At least, I am ready
and willing to go."

"And so you shall, lad!" cried the old soldier,
striking a hand upon his knee. "You are of the race
of the long rifles; I know your kind well. Not another
word, William! here is a man worth any twenty of your
French beaux strutting with a sword. Now we start
at once, and shall have this matter settled speedily."

The earliest haze of the fast-descending twilight
was hovering over the level plain as we two went forth.
In the west, the red tinge of the sun, which had just
disappeared below the horizon, lingered well up in
the sky. Against it we could see, clearly outlined in
inky blackness, the distant Indian wigwams; while
to the eastward the crimson light was reflected in
fantastic glow upon the heaving surface of the lake.
For a moment we paused, standing upon the slope of
the mound on which the Fort was built, and gazed
about us. There was little movement to arrest the eye.
The dull, dreary level of shore and prairie was deserted; what the more distant mounds of sand or
the overhanging river banks might hide of savage
watchers, we could only conjecture. Seemingly the
mass of Indian life, which only the day before had
overflowed that vacant space, had vanished as if by
some sorcerer's magic. To me, this unexpected silence
and dreary barrenness were astounding; I gazed
about me fairly bewildered, almost dreaming for the

moment that our foes had lifted the long siege and departed while I slept. Heald no doubt read the thought in my eyes, for he laid a kindly hand upon my sleeve and pointed westward.

"They are all yonder, lad, at the camp, — in council, like enough. Mark you, Wayland, how much farther to the south the limit of their camp extends than when the sun sank last night? Saint George! they must have added all of fifty wigwams to their village! They gather like crows about a dead body. It has an ugly look."

"Yet 't is strange they leave the Fort unguarded, so that the garrison may come and go unhindered. 'T is not the usual practice of Indian warfare."

"Unguarded? Faith! the hundreds of miles of wilderness between us and our nearest neighbor are sufficient guard. But dream not, my lad, that we are unobserved; doubtless fifty pair of skulking eyes are even now upon us, marking every move. I venture we travel no more than a hundred yards from the gate before our way is barred. Note how peaceful the stockade appears! But for the closed gates, one would never dream it the centre of hostile attack. Upon my word, even love-making has not deserted its log-walls!"

I lifted my eyes where he pointed, and even at that distance, and through the gathering gloom, I knew it was De Croix and Mademoiselle who overhung those eastern palisades in proximity so close.

The sight was as fire to my blood, and with teeth clinched to keep back the mad utterance of a curse, I strode beside Captain Heald silently down the declivity to the deserted plain below.

It is my nature to be somewhat chary of speech, and to feel deeply and long; but if I doubted it before, I knew now, in this moment of keen and bitter disappointment, that my heart was with that careless girl up yonder, who had sent me forth into grave peril apparently without thought, and who cared so little even now that she never lifted her eyes from the sparkling water to trace our onward progress. Anger, disappointment, disgust at her duplicity, her cruel abuse of power, swept over and mastered me at the moment when I realized more deeply than ever my own love for her, and my utter helplessness to oppose her slightest whim. No Indian thongs could bind me half so tightly as the false smiles of Toinette.

Plunged into this whirlpool of thought, I moved steadily forward at Captain Heald's shoulder, unconscious of what might be taking place about us, and for the moment indifferent to the result of our venture. But this feeling was not for long. Scarcely had our progress taken us across the front of the deserted agency building, and beyond the ken of the sentinels in the Fort, when a single warrior rose before us as from the ground, and blocked the path. He was a short, sturdy savage, bare to the waist save for a chain of teeth which dangled with sinister gleam about his brawny throat, and, from the wide sweep of his shoulders, evidently possessed of prodigious strength. He held a gun extended in front of him, and made a gesture of warning impossible to misapprehend.

"What seeks the White Chief?" he questioned bluntly. "Does he come for peace or war?"

The query came with such grave abruptness that Heald hesitated in reply.

"Never since I have been at Dearborn have I sought war," he replied at last. "Little Sauk knows this well. We travel now that we may have council of peace with the chiefs of the Pottawattomies. See!" and he held up both empty hands before the Indian's eyes, "we are both unarmed, because of our trust in the good faith of your people."

Little Sauk uttered a low grunt of disapproval, and made no motion to lower his threatening rifle.

"Ugh! You talk strong! Did any Pottawattomie send to White Chief to come to council?"

"No," admitted Heald. "We come because it is the wish of the Great Father of the white men down by the sea that we talk together of the wrongs of the red men, and make proposals of peace between us. There is no cause for these rumors of war, and the Great Father has heard that the Pottawattomies are dissatisfied, and it has made him sad."

The Indian looked from one to the other of us

in the growing darkness, and made a gesture of contempt.

"The real Great White Father wears a red coat, and is friend to the Pottawattomie," he said with dignity. "He no lie, no shut Indian out of Fort, no steal furs, no throw rum in river. Who this man, White Chief? He no soldier, — he long-knife."

"Yes, he is a frontiersman, and came to the Fort yesterday with Wau-me-nuk, bringing word of greeting from the Great Father to the Pottawattomies. He goes now with me to council. May we pass on to your camp?"

For a moment Little Sauk did not answer, stepping closer in order that he might better scan my features. Apparently satisfied by the keen scrutiny, he turned his broad back upon us and strode off with contemptuous dignity.

"Come," he said shortly; and without further word we followed across that dim plain and through the thickening darkness.

The Indian's step was noiseless, and his figure cast the merest shadow; but as we moved onward others constantly joined us, stalking out of the black night like so many phantoms, gliding silently in their noiseless moccasins across the soft grass, until fully a dozen spectral forms hedged our pathway and kept step to every movement. It was a weird procession, through the shifting night-shadows; and although I could catch but fleeting glimpses of those savage faces and half-naked forms, the knowledge of their presence, and our own helplessness if they proved treacherous, caused my heart to throb till I could hear it in the painful silence like the beat of a drum. Now and then a guttural voice challenged from the darkness, to be instantly answered by those in advance, and another savage glided within our narrowed vision, scanned us with cruel and curious eyes, and fell in with the same silent, tiger-like tread of his fellows.

It was not long that we were compelled to march thus, the gathering warriors pressing us closer at each step; and it was well it proved so soon ended, for the grim mockery set my nerves on edge. Yet the change was hardly for the better. Just before reaching the spot where the river forked sharply to the southward, we came to the upper edge of the wigwams, and into a bit of light from their scattered fires. There rushed out upon us a wild horde of excited savages, warriors and squaws, who pushed us about in sheer delirium, and even struck viciously at us across the shoulders of our indifferent guard, so that it was only by setting my teeth that I held back from grappling with the demons. But Heald, older in years and of cooler blood, laid restraining hands upon my arm.

" 'T is but the riff-raff," he muttered warningly. " The chiefs will hold them back from doing us serious harm."

As he spoke, Little Sauk uttered a gruff order, and the grim warriors on our flank drove back the jeering, scowling crowd, with fierce Indian cursing and blows of their guns, until the way had been cleared for our advance. We moved on for two hundred yards or more, the maddened and vengeful mob menacing us just beyond reach of the strong arms, and howling in their anger until I doubted not their voices reached the distant Fort.

We came to a great wigwam of deer-skin, much larger than any I had ever seen, with many grotesque figures of animals sketched in red and yellow paint upon the outside, and clearly revealed by the blazing fire without. A medicine-man of the tribe, hideous with pigment and high upstanding hair, sat beating a wooden drum before the entrance, and chanting wildly to a ferocious-looking horde of naked savages, many bleeding from self-inflicted wounds, who danced around the blaze, the leaping figures in the red glare making the scene truly demoniacal. Little Sauk strode through the midst of them, unheeding the uproar, and flung aside the flap of the tent.

"White Chief and Long Knife wait here," he said sternly. "Come back pretty soon."

There was nothing to be seen within, excepting some skins flung carelessly upon the short trodden grass. We sat down silently upon these, gazing out through the narrow opening at the blazing fire and the numerous moving figures constantly crowding closer about the entrance, both of us too deeply immersed in thought to care for speech.

The black shadows upon the tepee cover told me that guards had been posted to keep back the rabble from intrusion, and once I saw signs of a brief struggle in front when the swarm had grown too inquisitive and were forced back with scant ceremony. The weird dance and incantation continued; and although I knew but little of the customs of the Pottawattomies, there was a cruel savagery and ferocity about it which I felt held but little promise of peace.

"'T is the war-dance," whispered Heald in my ear, "and bodes ill for our purpose. See! the red wampum is in the fellow's hand."

As I bent forward to catch the gleam of it in the flames, a new figure suddenly flitted past our narrow vista, between us and the wild circle of dancers. It was a woman, attired in fanciful Indian dress; but surely no Pottawattomie **squaw** ever possessed so graceful a carriage, or bore so clear a face.

"Captain!" I ejaculated eagerly. "Did you see that white woman there, with the long skirt and red hair?"

"Ay!" he answered as though he scarce had faith in his own eyes. "I marked not the color of her hair, but I saw the lass, and, by Saint George! she looked to me like old Roger Matherson's daughter."

CHAPTER XXI

A COUNCIL OF CHIEFS

WAS on my feet in an instant, forgetful of everything excepting my duty to this girl whom I had come so far to find, and who now was plainly a prisoner in Indian hands. At the entrance of the tepee, a scowling warrior pushed me roughly back, pretending not to understand my eager words of expostulation, and, by significant gesture, threatening to brain me with his gun-stock if I persisted. A slight return of reason alone kept me from striking the fellow down and striding over his prostrate body. While I stood struggling with this temptation, Captain Heald grasped me firmly.

"Are you mad, Wayland?" he muttered, dragging me back into the dark interior of the tepee. "For God's sake, don't anger these fellows! Think of all the helpless lives depending on the success of our errand here! What is the girl to you?"

" I will wait," I answered, calmed by his earnestness, and ashamed of my boyish impetuosity; "but I am here at Dearborn seeking this young woman, whom I had supposed rather to be a young child. Her father was my father's dearest friend, and wrote us from his death-bed asking our protection for her."

"You are Major Wayland's son, — I remember the circumstances now, and that I endorsed such a letter. 'T is most strange. This girl disappeared from Dearborn some days ago. Mrs. Heald heard the matter discussed among the ladies of the garrison, and then all supposed her to be at John Kinzie's in company with Josette La Framboise; yet I would almost have sworn I saw her again, and not two hours ago, within the Fort. By Saint George! the glimpse I got just now makes me doubt my own eyesight. She was ever an odd creature, — but what can bring her here, walking so freely about in this camp of vengeful savages?"

I could not answer him; the mystery was beyond my clearing. Only, if this was the Elsa Matherson for whom I had sought so long, surely God had in some way led me on to find her; nor should any peril turn my quest aside.

I had hardly time for this resolve, ere the flap of the tepee was held back by a dark hand, and in grimly impressive silence warrior after warrior, plumed, painted, and gaudily bedecked with savage

ornaments, stalked solemnly within, circled about us
without sign of greeting, and seated themselves cross-
legged upon the bare ground. The uplifted door-skin
permitted the red flames from without to play freely
over their stern, impassive faces, and shone back upon
us from their glittering eyes. It was an impressive
scene, their stoical demeanor breathing the deep solemnity of the vast woods and plains amid which their
savage lives were passed; nor could one fail to feel
the deep gravity with which they gathered in this
council of life or death. To them it was evident that
the meeting was of most serious portent.

I saw only two faces that I recognized in that
red ring, — Topenebe and Little Sauk. I knew, however, it was probable there were some great chiefs
among that company; and I marked especially two,
one with long white hair, and a tall, slender, rather
young fellow, having two wide streaks of yellow down
either cheek.

The Indians sat motionless, gazing intently at
us; and I swept the entire dark circle of scowling
faces, vainly endeavoring to find one hopeful glance,
one friendly eye. Open hatred, undisguised distrust,
implacable enmity, were stamped on every feature.
Whatever our plea might be, I felt convinced that
the chiefs were here only to carry out their own purposes and make mock of every offering of peace.

After several moments of this painful silence, the

chief with the long white hair deliberately lighted a large pipe drawn from his belt. It was curiously and grotesquely fashioned, the huge bowl carved to resemble the head of a bear. He drew from the stem a single thick volume of smoke, breathed it out into the air, and solemnly passed the pipe to the warrior seated upon his right. With slow deliberation, the symbol moved around the impassive and emotionless circle, passing from one red hand to another, until it finally came back to him who had first lighted it. Without so much as a word being uttered, he gravely offered it to Captain Heald. I heard, and understood, the quick sigh of relief with which my companion grasped it; he drew a breath of the tobacco, and I followed his example, handing back the smoking pipe to the white-haired chief without rising, amid the same impressive silence.

The Indian leader spoke for the first time, his voice deep and guttural.

" The Pottawattomies have met in council with the White Chief and the Long Knife," he said soberly, " and have smoked together the peace-pipe. For what have the white men come to disturb Gomo and his warriors? "

I gazed at him with new interest. No name of savage chief was wider known along the border in those days, none more justly feared by the settlers. He was a tall, spare, austere man, his long coarse hair whitened by years, but with no stoop in his figure. His eyes, small and keen, blazed with a strange ferocity, as I have seen those of wildcats in the dark; while his flesh was drawn so closely against his prominent cheek-bones as to leave an impression of ghastliness, as of a corpse suddenly returned by some miracle to life. With dabs of paint across the forehead, and thin lips drawn in a narrow line of cruelty, his face formed a picture to be long remembered with a shudder.

It was easy enough to see that Captain Heald felt uncertain how far to venture in his proposals, though he spoke up boldly, and with no tremor in his voice. His long frontier experience had taught him the danger that lay in exhibiting timidity in the face of Indian scorn.

"Gomo," he said firmly, "and you other Chiefs of the Pottawattomies, there has never been war between us. We have traded together for many seasons; you have eaten at my table, and I have rested by your fires. We have been as brothers, and more than once have I judged between you and those who would wrong you. I have remembered all this, and have now come into your camp through the night, without fear and unarmed, that I might talk with you as friends. Am I not right to do this? In all the time I have been the White Chief at Dearborn, have I ever done wrong to a Pottawattomie?"

He paused; but no warrior made reply. A low guttural murmur ran around the line of listeners, but the bead-like eyes never left his face. He went on:

"Why should I fear to meet the Pottawattomies, even though word had come to me that their young men talk war, and seek alliance with our enemy the red-coats? The Chiefs have seen war, and are not crazed for the blood of their friends. They will restrain such wild mutterings. They know that the White Father to the east is strong, and will drive the red-coats back into the sea as he did when they fought before. They will ally themselves with the strong one, and make their foolish young man take up arms for their friends."

Still no one spoke, no impassive bronze face exhibited the faintest interest. It was as if he appealed to stone.

"Is this not so?"

"The White Chief has spoken," was the cold reply. "His words are full of eloquence, but Gomo hears nothing that calls for answer. The White Chief says not why he has come and demanded council of the Pottawattomies."

A low murmur, expressive of approval, swept down the observant line; but no man among them stirred a muscle.

"I came for this, Gomo," said Heald, speaking now rapidly, and with an evident determination to trust all in a sentence and have it over with, for it was clear the savages were in no mood for diplomatic evasion: "to ask your guidance and protection on our march eastward on the morrow. I come to the Pottawattomies as friends; for I fear we may meet with trouble on the way, from roving bands of Wyandots and Miamis, and we are greatly burdened by our women and children. It is to ask this that I and the Long Knife are here."

"You say the White Father is strong, and will drive the red-coats into the sea: did he at Mackinac?"

"There was treachery there."

"Ugh! Why, if White Father so strong, you leave Fort and go way off?"

"Because just now I can serve him better elsewhere; but we shall come again."

"My young men have rumor that Detroit go like Mackinac."

"It is untrue; your young men bring false news."

Gomo turned and looked about him upon the expectant warriors; and, as if the glance was an invitation to free speech, one sitting half-way across the circle asked gruffly:

"Why you pour out rum, if you love Pottawattomie?"

"Because I am only the White Chief at Dearborn," returned Heald, facing the questioner, "and, like Peesotum who asks, have higher chiefs elsewhere whom I must obey. What they tell me I have to do."

"White Chief lies!" was the short, stern answer. "Winnemeg brought no such word."

So furious were the many dark, glowering faces, that I braced myself, thinking the next moment would be one of struggle for life or death; but Gomo held them motionless with a wave of his hand. He rose slowly to his feet, and faced us with grave dignity.

"It is true, as Peesotum says," he said impressively. "The White Chief has used a double tongue to the Red man; yet we will deal fairly with him, for he has come to us in peace. White Chief, there is to be war between us; 't is the will of our young men, and the red wampum has passed among our lodges and the lodges of our brothers the Wyandots. Yet when you unlock the gates we will go forth with you and your people, around the sweep of the water. Such is the will of the Great Spirit, and the decision of the Pottawattomie in council of chiefs."

Heald looked about upon the scowling circle with disbelief so clearly expressed in his eyes, that Gomo, reading it, turned to his warriors and called upon them one by one to say if he spoke the truth. I heard him speak thus to Little Sauk, Black Bird, Topenebe, Mankia, Pipe Bird, Peesotum, and Ignance; and each answered with the low grunt of assent. He fixed his eyes upon the younger Indian who had already attracted my attention by the manliness of his face as well as the yellow stripes that disfigured him.

" And you, Black Partridge? "

" I have already spoken to the White Chief in his own wigwam, and given back the medal of the Americans," was the grave response. " I have no more to say."

I confess these words chilled me, as I recalled their meaning; and Heald half rose to his feet as though he would protest, but not a stolid face among the warriors changed in expression. Gomo drew his robes more closely about his gaunt figure in simple but impressive dignity.

" Doth Shaw-nee-aw-kee go east also with the white men? " he asked.

" I have not of late conferred with the Silver-man. He has been at his own lodge, and doubtless you may know his purpose better than I."

" We wish him to stay. He good man; Potta-wattomie's friend."

The Indian stood motionless, his eyes watching keenly the expression of each face. He added slowly:

" The White Chief hears the promise of the Potta-wattomies. It is enough. He can go forth in peace upon the morrow, with all his warriors, squaws, and pappooses, and the people of my nation will walk with them as guards. It is our pledge; we will counsel no longer."

A COUNCIL OF CHIEFS

At a simple commanding gesture of his long arms, the circle melted away through the narrow opening as silently as it had gathered, the dark figure of each warrior silhouetted for an instant against the red glare of the fire, before it suddenly disappeared in the darkness beyond. At last Little Sauk alone stood between us and the blaze.

"Come," he commanded gruffly, "White Chief go back to his people."

Enclosed by that same phantom guard of savages, we passed out through the limits of the camp; but now the rabble paid not the slightest heed to our presence. Our mission known, and no longer a mystery, they treated us with the stolid indifference of Indian contempt. I walked with eyes alert upon either side of our path for another glimpse of that girlish figure that I had seen before so dimly; but we traversed nearly the full length of the tepee rows before I saw any one that at all resembled her. Even then, I was far from certain, until the sudden leaping up of a dying fire reflected on her crown of auburn hair, and set my heart to throbbing.

"Little Sauk!" I cried, in my excitement clutching his naked arm, "who is that white girl yonder, and how comes she here?"

The startled Indian sprang aside, flinging me from him with a violence that showed his giant strength.

221

"No white girl," he protested, vehemently. "Pottawattomie."

"No Pottawattomie has hair like the sunset," I retorted. "Come, I would speak with the girl."

For an instant I saw the bead-like eyes of the savage glittering in the darkness and wandering where I pointed. He faced me doggedly.

"Long Knife leave Indian maid alone," he said grimly. "Long Knife go Fort; no talk."

I was in a mood to resist the fellow's dictation, and reckless enough of consequences at that moment to take the chance; but Heald interfered.

"You can serve her far better, lad, in that way," he muttered hastily. "We shall not always be two to twelve."

With teeth gritted to keep back the fierce anger that shook me, I strolled sullenly on, not even venturing to glance back lest I should give way. It was thus we reached the Fort gate, and entered, leaving our dusky escort to slink back into the night. An anxious crowd met us. It was Wells who questioned first.

"So those devils have let you go unharmed? What answer made the savages?"

"They pledge us safe convoy around the head of the lake."

"They do? Who spoke the words of the pledge?"

"Old Gomo himself, and it was ratified by each of the chiefs in turn."

"They are lying dogs, — all but one of them. What answered Black Partridge?"

Heald made no response; and Wells wheeled impetuously to me.

"Come, lad, the truth, — what reply did Black Partridge make to this Indian mummery?"

"He said, 'I have already spoken to the White Chief in his own wigwam, and given back the medal of the Americans, and have nothing more to say.'"

For a moment the old Indian soldier stared at me, his stern face fairly black with the cloud in his eyes. He brought his clinched hand down hard against the log wall.

"By God! it is treachery!" he exclaimed fiercely, and turned and walked away.

CHAPTER XXII

THE LAST NIGHT AT DEARBORN

T was evident that preparations were even then well under way for retreat the following morning. Trunks and boxes, together with various military stores and arms, strewed the sides of the parade-ground; farther back, a number of wagons, partially filled, stood waiting the remainder of their loads. Men and women were hastening back and forth, and children were darting through the shadows, their little arms piled high with bundles, and making play, as children ever will, of what was to prove an awful tragedy. A large fire, burning brightly before the deserted guard-house, cast its ruddy glow over the animated scene, checkering the rude walls with every passing shadow.

I noticed, as I slowly pushed my way along, that the soldiers worked seriously, with few jests on their lips, as if they realized the peril that menaced them; while many among the women, especially those of the humbler sort, were rejoicing over the early release from garrison monotony, and careless of what the morrow might bring of danger and suffering.

A few steps from the gate, I paused for a moment that I might watch their flitting figures, the incessant bustle being a positive relief after the dull and ghostly silence without. My mind, — though I strove to cast the thought aside, — was still occupied with the mystery of Elsa Matherson; but the more I dwelt upon it, the less I was able to penetrate the secret of her strange presence in the Indian camp, or devise any scheme for reaching her. The ache in my heart made me dread to meet again with Mademoiselle Toinette, lest I should utter words of reproach which she did not deserve; for, sad as such a confession was, I had to acknowledge that she had a perfect right to protect the man she loved, even at my cost.

Nor did I greatly desire to run upon De Croix. I knew his temper fairly well, and doubtless by this time he had learned the story of my interference, and would be in fit mood for a quarrel. Still, as seems often to be the case at such a time, before I had taken a dozen steps away from the gate, I met him face to face. It was a jaunty picture he made in the glare of the fire, the fine gentleman sauntering lazily about, with hat of bleached straw pushed rakishly upon his powdered hair, and a light cane dangling at his wrist, as fashionably attired as if he were loitering upon the boulevards of an August evening, his negro man a yard behind, bearing a silken fan which flashed golden in the radiance. At sight of him, I stopped instantly, ready enough to resent attack if that had been his purpose, though anxious to avoid violence for the sake of Mademoiselle. But he merely laughed as he surveyed me critically, swinging his bamboo stick as if it were a whip-lash.

"*Parbleu,* Master Wayland!" he said, seeming in rare good-humor, "I this moment learned of your safe return. 'T would have been an excellent joke had the savage found excuse to retain you out yonder, to form a part of one of their delightful entertainments! Fit revenge, indeed, for the foul deceit you played upon me!"

"Think you so, Monsieur?" for his easy words relieved me greatly. "It would have been one less arm for our defence."

"With safe convoy guaranteed by the Indian chiefs, that loss would make small odds," he replied carelessly. "But, truly, that was a most scurvy trick you played to gain the wager which was offered me. But for the happy ending, I should be sorely tempted to break this cane across your shoulders in payment therefor."

"Indeed!" I said; "the act might not be as easily

accomplished as you imagine. But what mean you by happy ending? Had the savages roasted me over a slow fire, I should hardly be here for the pleasure of your chastisement."

He laughed lightly, his eyes wandering carelessly over the throng of figures in front of us.

"Saint Guise! I thought not about your predicament, but rather of the happiness which came to me in the society of Mademoiselle. In faith, she was most gracious with her favor. 'T is thus you did me a great kindness, friend, and have won my gratitude."

The words were as stinging as he meant them to be, for I marked his quick glance into my face. So I held my resentment well in check, and smiled back at him, apparently unconcerned.

"Then we are again even, Monsieur," I returned quietly, "and can start anew upon our score. But why should I remain here to discuss matters of such small import, with all this work unfinished which fronts strong men to-night? I will break my long fast, and turn to beside these others."

He seemed to have further words to say; but I minded him not, and pushed past, leaving him to saunter where he willed, accompanied by his black satellite. If I could not win Mademoiselle, as I now felt assured from his boastful speech I could not, I might at least work for her greater safety and comfort;

and there was much I could do to help in burying my own disappointment.

For all that, it was a night to live long in the memory, — that last night we spent at Dearborn. It remains a rare jumble in my mind, — its varied incidents crowding so fast upon each other as to leave small room for thought regarding any one of them. Without, the dim black plain stretched away in unbroken solemnity and silence; nor did the sentinels posted along the walls catch glimpse of so much as a skulking Indian form amid the grass and sand. A half-moon was in the sky, with patches of cloud now and then shadowing it, and in the intervals casting its faint silver over the lonely expanse and tipping the crest of the waves as they crept in upon the beach. The great Indian village to the westward was fairly ablaze with fires; while the unending procession of black dots that flitted past them, together with the echo of constant uproar, showed that the savages were likewise astir in eager preparation for the morrow. We could hear the pounding of wooden drums, mingled with shrill yells that split the night-air like so many war-missiles. Only those above, upon the platform, could mind these things; for the bustle within the enclosure below continued unabated until long after midnight.

The report of our mission spread rapidly, and the pledge of protection given by the chiefs greatly heart-

ened the men, so that they worked now with many
a peal of laughter and careless jest. The women and
children, ever quick to feel the influence of the soldiers,
responded at once to this new feeling of confidence,
which was encouraged by the officers, however they
may have secretly doubted the good-faith of the savages. So the children tumbled about in the red glare
of the flames, the soldiers swung their traps into the
waiting wagons with good-natured badinage, their
brawny breasts bare and glistening with sweat in the
hot night; while, as the hour grew late and discipline
sensibly relaxed, the women danced in the open and
sang songs of home.

It was hard enough to realize what it all meant, —
what hardship and suffering and death lay just before
these rejoicing people; what depths of cruel treachery
and murder lurked for them so few hours away. We
did not suspect it then; not even those among us who
had long learned the deceit of Indian nature could
unroll the shadowing veil of that morrow and reveal
the forthcoming tragedy of those silent plains. I remember that, doubtful as I felt about the future, I
could look on with interest at the busy scene, and that
more than once a smile lay upon my lips. What an
odd variety of figures that congested place disclosed!
what strange life-histories were having their culmina-
tion there! I saw Ensign Ronan, young, slender,
smooth of face, appearing scarce more than a boy, his

short fatigue-jacket buttoned to the throat in spite of the heat, hurrying here and there in his enthusiasm, ever upon his lips some happy phrase to take the sting from his word of command. Lieutenant Helm, calm but observant of every detail, moved in and out among the busy throng, every now and then stealing aside to speak a word of encouragement to his young wife, who stood watching by the mess-room door. There was quite a bevy gathered there, officers' wives for the most part, gazing in mingled interest and apprehension upon the scene. I marked among them Josette, who had come in that evening with the Kinzies; and as I drew yet nearer the group, a sudden blazing up of the fire yielded me a glimpse of Mademoiselle, and I turned hastily away, unwilling still to greet or be greeted by her.

Gaunt frontiersmen stalked about, having little to save and nothing to do, with the inevitable long rifle held in the hollow of the arm; Captain Wells's Miamis skulked uneasily in dark corners, or hung over the embers to cook some ration yet unused, their dark skins and long coarse hair a reminder to us of the hostiles who watched without. Captain Heald, in company with Captain Wells and John Kinzie, the latter conspicuous by his white beard, stood long in deep converse near the barracks, leaning against the black logs. I felt the two latter were urging some change of plan; but in the end Wells left in vexation, almost in anger, striding across the parade-ground to the northern block-house.

In the shadow of the south stockade, some one was softly playing upon a violin, the sweet notes stealing up through the wild hubbub in strains of silvery sound. Close upon one side of the fire, forgetful of the heat in their deep interest, two young soldiers were engrossed in a game of cards, while a group of comrades commented freely on the fortunes of the play. Scarcely a yard distant, a grizzled old sergeant, — a veteran of the great war, no doubt, — bent above a book held open upon his knee, the shape of which bespoke a Bible; while on the other side a bevy of children were romping with their dogs or playing with sharp knives in the hard ground. A woman over by the gate lifted a sweet contralto voice in an old-time love-song, and had hardly lilted the opening line before others joined her, making the night resound to the tender melody. I saw the soldiers pause in their work to beat time, and marked the dark forms of the sentries above on the palisades as they leaned over to listen, every heart set throbbing with the memory of days gone by.

"Man is indeed a strange animal," said a voice beside me, and I turned to greet Ensign Ronan. "He can sing, laugh, and jest, in death's very teeth."

"'T is better, surely, than to cry," I commented. "But these do not so much as dream of death; the pledge of the Pottawattomies has brought renewed hope."

"Yes, I know; though I confess I have little faith in it. And there will be plenty of danger about us before we see Fort Wayne, even if they pass us in safety around the lake. There will be leagues of travel through hostile territory. That," he added, "is, to my mind, the only sensible way of preparation for the morrow."

He pointed to the old sergeant seated beside the fire with his Bible; and I glanced into his boyish face with no little surprise.

"Some remark Surgeon Van Voorhis made caused me to deem you indifferent in such matters."

"No doubt," he said, dryly. "If one does not subscribe to the creeds, he is written down a heretic. I have laughed at folly, and so have won the reputation of being an unbeliever. Yet, Wayland, if we ride forth to a savage death to-morrow, no one will meet it with more faith in Christ than I. The years indeed have not left me spotless, but I have never wavered from the great truths my mother taught me. I know not the future, lad, but I believe there is ever mercy for the penitent."

In an instant my own thought spanned the leagues of forest to my distant home; and I choked back a sob within my throat.

"It is our mothers' love that makes us all better

232

men," I said gravely. " And whatever may befall us upon the morrow, that God of whom they taught us will be true."

" The words are spoken in the right spirit," he returned, soberly, " and have the soldier ring I like best to hear. If it chance that we both come forth from this venture in life, I should be most glad to know you better."

I was deeply touched by his open, manly spirit, and especially impressed with his frank adherence to the Christian faith, — something too uncommon in that day along the border.

" 'T is rather my wish to begin friendship before that time of trial," I said eagerly, and with extended hand. " We shall fight the better for it when the hour for fighting comes; and if it be God's will to guide us safely through the wilderness, a friendship thus cemented in peril will have the strength of comradeship."

The young man's strong and thoughtful face lighted up; but his eyes were resting upon the form of the sentry above us, and he did not speak.

" Ronan," I questioned, somewhat doubtfully, " I have long wished to ask you the cause of the friction that apparently exists between Captain Heald and the officers of this garrison; but have felt it none of my business. I cannot but realize you are not in his good graces, although he appears to me to be a brave and capable man."

"He is both," was the instant and manly reply; "for all that, he has constantly turned for counsel in military matters to others than his own officers, — why, I know not, unless he considered us unworthy of his confidence. Instead of confiding his orders to us, and asking judgment upon his plans, he has been swayed from the beginning by Indian advice; and it is only natural for us to resent such unjust and discourteous treatment. Moreover, each move thus far made has proved to be a mistake, and we must suffer from them in silence and without remedy."

"He does indeed seem strangely headstrong," I admitted reluctantly, recalling to mind the words uttered in the room beyond my bed; "but surely his conference with the chiefs has resulted well, and is proof of his good judgment."

The young officer turned quickly and faced me, his eyes full of emotion. "That remains to be decided," he exclaimed. "Such old frontiersmen as Captain Wells and John Kinzie say that pledge only hides black treachery. They urged him most earnestly, for an hour to-night, to reconsider his decision, and give up the immediate evacuation of the post. But he fully believes he can put faith in those lying, murderous hounds out yonder. So certain is Kinzie of trouble, that he has sworn to march forth with us, sending his family away by boat, in hope that his influence may hold back the savages from open attack;

while Wells declares that he will ride forth with blackened face, as becomes a Miami who goes to certain death in battle. These men are no fools, no strangers to savage warfare and Indian deceit, — yet in spite of their warning, Captain Heald persists in driving us forth into the very fangs of the wolves. Brave! ay, he is indeed brave to the point of rashness; but this bids fair to be a fatal bravery to all of us who must obey his orders."

The intense bitterness of these words shocked me and held me dumb, — the more so, as I could not be insensible to their truth. As I lifted my eyes, I beheld, crossing the parade through the mass of equipment scattered here and there, De Croix and Mademoiselle. With a half-muttered excuse, I drew hastily back into the protecting shadow of the stockade; and as they slowly passed, I heard him jesting lightly, and saw her laughing, with a side-glance up at his face.

With these words of warning from Ronan's lips yet ringing in my ears, such reckless thoughtlessness of the danger encircling us astounded me; and I drew farther back, less willing than ever to make one of them. Deep in my heart, I knew this was no time for careless laughter or happy jest.

CHAPTER XXIII

THE DEATH-SHADOW OF THE MIAMIS

IT was after midnight when I finally ceased my labors, feeling I had performed my fair share of the hard work of preparation. By this time everything was comparatively quiet within the stockade enclosure; the wagons were piled with all that could be loaded before morning, and many of the wearied soldiers had flung themselves upon the ground to snatch what rest they might before the early call to march. The women and children had disappeared, to seek such comfort as was possible amid the ruins of their former quarters; and only the sentries remained alert, pacing their solemn rounds on the narrow walk overlooking the palisades and the silent plain without.

Physically wearied as I was, my mind remained intensely active, and I felt no desire for sleep. I do not recall that I gave much thought to the perils of our situation. One grows careless and indifferent to danger, — and in truth I looked forward to no serious trouble with the Indians upon the morrow's march through the sand-dunes; not that I greatly trusted to those reluctant pledges wrung from the chiefs, but because I felt that if properly handled in that open country our force was of sufficient fighting strength to repel any ordinary attack from ill-armed savages, my long border experience rendering me a bit disdainful of Indian courage and resourcefulness. So it was that my restless mind dwelt rather upon other matters more directly personal. I could not put away the thought of the half-seen girl flitting about amid the dusk of the Pottawattomie camp, especially as Captain Heald had declared her to be Elsa Matherson. I was surprised to discover that she I sought, instead of being a mere child, was a woman grown; for in this we were all deceived by the words of her father. What did she there, passing with such apparent freedom from restraint among those fierce warriors? and how was I ever to reach her with any hope of rescue, even if she desired it? There was evidently a mystery here which I could never solve through idle musing; and yet I could but ask myself where lay my graver duty, — beside this single woman, who seemingly needed no defender, or with the many helpless ones who must march forth on the morrow on that long and dangerous passage through the wilderness? Indeed, what hope could I cherish of aiding the young girl, if I now deserted these others, and endeavored alone to penetrate that Indian camp in search of her?

Then came another thought. It was of Mademoiselle.

It was this that effectually halted me. To whomsoever else she might have given her heart, she was still the one for whom I was most glad either to live or die; and in spite of De Croix, I would ride at her side on the morrow, within striking distance of any prowling hostile. Let the Matherson girl wait; my arm belonged first of all to the defence of Mademoiselle.

Busied with these thoughts, and endeavoring to adjust this decision with my conscience, I passed out upon the platform, that I might look forth once more upon the moonlit waters of the lake. There were a few dim figures to be seen, leaning over the logs; but I supposed them to be members of the night-guard, and, feeling no desire for companionship, I halted in a lonely spot at the northeastern corner of the stockade. How desolate, how solemnly impressive, was the scene! To the north all was black in the dense night, the shadows of the scattering trees obscuring the faint glow of the moon and yielding little of detail to the searching eye. Even the single ray of light which the evening previous had blazed forth as a friendly beacon from the Kinzie home, was now absent. I could vaguely distinguish the dim outlines of the deserted house in the distance, and noticed a large boat moored close to the bank beneath the Fort stockade, — doubtless the one in which the fugitives expected to venture out upon the lake on the morrow.

It was the wide stretch of water, gleaming like silver, that fascinated me, as it always did in its numberless changing moods. What unutterable loneliness spoke to the soul in those unknown leagues of tossing sea! how far the eye wandered unchecked, searching vainly for aught to rest upon other than glistening surge or darkling hollow! The mystery of the ages lay unexpressed in those tossing billows, sweeping in out of the black east, making low moan to the unsympathetic and unheeding sky. Deeper and deeper the spirit of unrest, of doubt, of brooding discontent, weighed down upon me as I gazed; life seemed as aimless as that constant turmoil yonder, a mere silver-tinted heaving, destined to burst in useless power on a shore of rock, and then roll back again into the mighty deep.

I leaned over the palisades, sunk deep in revery of home, recalling one by one the strange incidents of the last month that had so curiously conspired to cause a total upheaval of my life; and for the moment I grew oblivious of my surroundings. A mere lad, knowing little of himself and less of life, had ridden westward from the Maumee; a man, in thought and character, leaned now over that beleaguered stockade of Dearborn.

I was recalled to actualities by a light touch on the sleeve of my shirt, and a half-laughing, half-petulant voice at my elbow.

"Well, Master Laggard! do I not show you great honor in thus seeking you out, after your avoidance of me all these hours?"

I glanced aside into the fair face and questioning eyes, noting at the same time that De Croix stood only a step beyond her in the shadows.

"I have been very busy, Mademoiselle," I tried to explain; "it has been a time when every strong hand was needed."

"Fudge!" was the indignant rejoinder. "Did I not perceive you loitering more than once to-night, — though each time I drew near, hopeful of a word of greeting, it was to behold you disappear as if by magic? Do I flatter you by thus showing my interest? Yet 't was only that I might have explanation, that I sought you thus. Come, confess that you feared my just resentment for going forth on so perilous a trip without telling me of your plans."

"'T was not altogether that," I answered, for dissembling was never an easy task for me, "as I only did what I believed would most please you. Nor have I anything to regret in my action, now that we have

thus gained the pledge of the Pottawattomies for protection upon the march."

She watched me closely as I spoke, and I wondered if she realized ever so dimly the impulse of lov-
ing service that had inspired my deed. Whether 't was
so or not, her whole mood quickly changed.

"I must admit you are a constant puzzle to me,
John Wayland, — yet rather an interesting one withal.
For instance, here is Josette, who did assure me but
an hour ago that your very name was unknown to
her, although, if memory serves, you asserted only
yesterday that you were seeking her from the
Maumee country. Perhaps, sir, you can explain the
contradiction?"

"It was not altogether as you have stated it,
Mademoiselle," I stammered, confused by the direct-
ness of her attack. "I said nothing of knowing this
Josette, and you have deceived yourself in the matter.
I came here seeking a young girl, 't is true, but found
no trace of her until a few hours ago, most curiously,
in the heart of that Indian camp yonder."

"You found her there? How strange!"

"Most strange indeed, Mademoiselle, especially
as she appeared to enjoy perfect liberty among the
savages."

"You spoke with her?"

"Not a word; it was only a glimpse I caught of
her in the firelight, and when I sought to go to her

the warriors interfered and forced me back. But Captain Heald, who saw her at the same time, assured me 't was the one I sought."

" 'T is small wonder, then, you could stand here at my very side so long, and yet see me not, or remain indifferent to my presence," she said, drawing slightly back. "Come, Captain de Croix, let us walk to the other corner of the stockade, and leave Master Wayland to dream of his mysterious beauty undisturbed."

"You misapprehend me," I cried, awakened by her words, but more by De Croix's smile. "She has no such hold upon my memory as that, for until to-night I had supposed her a mere child. I knew not you were upon the platform, believing the forms I saw in the gloom to be those of the night-guard. What dark figure is that, even now leaning over the logs yonder?"

It was De Croix's deeper voice that made answer.

" 'T is Captain Wells; and we found him in no mood for conversation. Seemingly he hath small faith in the pledges of the chiefs."

"My own hope rests far more upon our skill at arms, Monsieur," I answered directly; "for I have known Indian treachery all my life. They may keep faith with us to-morrow, for John Kinzie has great influence with them for good; nevertheless, I shall oil my gun carefully before riding forth."

It was in his eyes to make reply; but before

it could come the girl between us uttered a cry so piercing that it set us gazing where her finger pointed out across the lake.

"Look there, Messieurs! Did ever mortal behold so grewsome a sight before? What means the portent?"

It is before me now, in each grim, uncanny detail, — though I know well that my pen will fail to give it fit description, or convey even feebly a sense of the overwhelming dread of what we saw. Nature has power to paint what human hand may never hope to copy; and though, as I now know well, it was no more than a strange commingling of cloud and moon in atmospheric illusion, still the effect was awe-inspiring to a degree difficult of realization within the environments of peace and safety. To us, it appeared as a dreadful warning, — a mysterious manifestation of supernatural power, chilling our blood with terror and striking agony into our souls. Up from the far east had rolled an immense black cloud, rifted here and there by bars of vivid yellow as electric bolts tore it asunder. Moonlight tipped its heavy edges with a pale spectral gleam; and as it swiftly rose higher and higher into the sky, blotting out the stars, it seemed to dominate the entire expanse, hovering over us menacingly, and assuming the shape of some gigantic monster, with leering face and cruel mouth, bending forward as if to smite us with huge uplifted hand.

243

Perchance our tensioned nerves may have exaggerated the resemblance, but nothing more horribly real have my eyes ever beheld.

For a moment I cowered, like a nerveless craven, behind the logs, gazing up at that awful apparition, that mocking devil's-face, as a man fronts death in some terrible and unexpected form. It seemed as if the breath of the creature must be pestilence, and that it would smite us gasping to earth, or draw us helplessly struggling within its merciless clutch. A prayer trembled on my lips, but remained unuttered, for I could only stare upward at the mighty, crawling thing now overshadowing us, my arms uplifted in impotent effort to avert the crushing blow.

I could hear the girl sob where she had sunk upon the platform, and caught one glimpse of De Croix, his face yellow in the weird glare as he stared in speechless terror out over the water, his hands clutching the palisades. It was Captain Wells, who had been standing near us, who first found voice.

"'T is the Death-Shadow of the Miamis!" he cried, in choked accents, striding toward us along the narrow plank, and pointing eastward. "I knew it must come, for our doom is sealed."

What centuries of Indian superstition rested behind the fateful utterance, I know not; but facing that horrible spectre as we did, his words held me in speechless awe. In the blood of us all such terrors linger to unman the bravest; and for the moment such fright and panic swept me as I have never known before or since. I, who have laughed at death even in the hour of torture, sank in deadly agony before that mystery of light and shadow, as if it indeed foreshadowed the wrath of the Great Spirit.

The sobs of Mademoiselle recalled me somewhat to myself, and led me to forget my own terror that I might help to relieve hers.

"I beg you, fear not," I urged, though my voice trembled and my lips were dry. "Come, Mademoiselle," and I found her hand and clasped it, feeling the touch a positive relief to my unstrung nerves, "look up and see! the cloud is even now breaking asunder, and has already lost much of its form of terror. Mind not the words of Captain Wells; he has been raised among the Indians, and drunk in their superstitions. De Croix, arouse yourself, and help me to bring courage to this girl."

He drew back from his grip on the palisades, as if, by sheer power of will, he forced his fascinated eyes from the cloud-bank, shivering like a man with an ague fit.

"*Sacre!* did ever human eyes behold so foul a thing!" he cried, his voice shaking, his hand shading his face. "'T will haunt me till the hour I die."

"Bah! 'T will all be forgotten with return of daylight," I was quick to reply; for had found relief

245

in action, and could perceive already that the clouds were becoming shapeless and drifting rapidly southward in a great billowy mass. " Do not stand there moping like a day-blind owl, but aid me to make Mademoiselle see the foolishness of her fears."

The sting of these words moved him more than a blow would have done; but as he knelt beside her, I noted there was little of the old reckless ring in his voice.

" 'T is indeed true, Toinette, — 't was but a cloud, and has already greatly changed in aspect. 'T will be no more than cause for laughter when the sun gilds the plain, and will form a rare tale to tell to the gallants at Montreal. Yet, Saint Guise! 't was grewsome enough, and my knees quake still from the terror of the thing."

Mademoiselle was as brave and cool-headed a girl as ever I knew; but so thoroughly had she been unnerved by this dreadful happening, that it was only after the most persistent urging on our part that she consented to be led below. There, at the foot of the ladder, I stepped aside to permit De Croix to walk with her across the parade; but she would not go without a word of parting.

" Do not think me weak and silly," she implored, her face, still white from the terror, upturned to me in the moonlight. " It was so spectral and ghastly that I gave way to sudden fear."

"You need no excuse," I hastened to assure her. "When the thing frightened De Croix and me, and even set so old a soldier as Captain Wells to raving, it was no wonder it unnerved a girl, however brave she might prove in the presence of real danger. But you can sleep now, convinced it was naught but a floating cloud."

She smiled at me over her shoulder, and I watched the pair with jealous eyes until they disappeared. I noticed Captain Wells standing beside me.

"You thought I raved up yonder," he said gravely; "to-morrow will prove that my interpretation of the vision was correct."

"You believe it a prophecy of evil?"

"It was the warning of the Great Spirit — the Death-Shadow of the Miamis. Never has it appeared to men of our tribe except on the eve of great disaster, the forerunner of grave tragedy. We ride forth from these gates to death."

It was plain that no amount of reasoning could change his Indian superstition; and with a word more of expostulation I left him standing there, and sought a place where I might lie down. Already the numbing sensation of supernatural fear had left me, for in the breaking up of that odd-formed cloud I realized its cause; and now the physical fatigue I felt overmastered all else. I found a quiet corner, and, with a saddle for a pillow, was soon fast asleep.

CHAPTER XXIV

THE DAY OF DOOM

*IFTEENTH August, 1812.* — My hand trembles and my pen halts as I write the words; for the memory of those tragic hours, far distant as they are now, overmasters me, and I see once again the faces of the dead, the mutilated forms, the disfigured features of the hapless victims of savage treachery. Were I writing romance merely, I might hide much of detail behind the veil of silence; but I am penning history, and, black as the record is, I can only give it with strict adherence to truth. I dread the effort to recall once more the sad incidents of that scene of carnage, lest I fail to picture it aright; but I can tell, and that poorly, only of what I saw within the narrowed vista of my personal experience, where the fate of the day found me. Out of the vortex of so fierce and sudden a struggle, the individual, battling

madly for his own life, catches but hasty and confused glimpses of what others may do about him or in other portions of the field; and there has been much recorded in what men call the history of that day's battle, about which I know nothing. Nor shall I attempt to tell much more than the simple story of what befell me and those who faced the danger close at my side.

In spite of the early bustle around me, incident to the preparations for departure, I slept late, stupefied by intense fatigue. The sun was already high, painting with gold the interior of the western wall of the stockade, when some unusual disturbance aroused me, so that I sat up and looked about, scarce realizing for the moment where I was. The parade was alive with moving figures; and I instantly marked the cheery look on the faces of those nearest me, as if the entire garrison rejoiced that the hour for departure had at last arrived. The northern half of the little open space was filled with loaded wagons of every description, to which horses, mules, and even oxen, were being rapidly hitched; while women and children were clambering in over the wheels, perching themselves upon the heaps of camp accoutrements, and rolling up the canvas coverings in order that they might the better see out and feel the soft refreshment of the morning air.

The officers of the post were moving here and there among the throng of workers, grave of face, yet

249

making no effort to curb the unusual gaiety of the enlisted men. For the time, all reins of discipline seemed relaxed. The few settlers and plainsmen who had gathered within the Fort for protection looked on stolidly, either lying in the shade of the log wall or lounging beside their horses already equipped for the trail; while the Miamis were gathered restlessly about their breakfast fires, their faces unexpressive of emotion, as usual, although many among them had blackened their cheeks in expectation of disaster.

Evidently the hour fixed upon for our final desertion of Fort Dearborn was close at hand; and I hastened to seek opportunity for a bath and breakfast. I do not recall now, looking back after all these years upon the events of that day, any dreading of the future, or serious thought of the coming ordeal. The bustle of excitement about me, the high spirits of the men, were like a tonic; and I remembered only that we were east-bound once more, and my chief concern was to be ready to ride out promptly with the column.

It could not have been far from nine o'clock when every preparation was completed, and the echoing bugle called the laggards from their quarters into the open parade. The officers, already mounted, rode about quietly, assigning each driver and wagon to position in the marching column, and carefully mustering the troops. The many sick of the garrison were brought forth from the barracks in their blankets, and

gently lifted to places beside the women and children
in the loaded wagons; while the men fit for active duty
fell in promptly along the southern wall, the right of
their slender column resting opposite the barred entrance. I was assigned to ride with the rear-guard
beside the wagons, in company with the few settlers
and fifteen of the Miamis under command of Sergeant
Jordan. Captains Heald and Wells, the latter with
face blackened so that at first glance I scarcely recognized him, took position at the head of the waiting
column in front of the closed gates, and they sat there
on their horses, facing us, and watching anxiously our
rather slow formation.

John Kinzie joined them, his features grave and
careworn, a long rifle in his hands; while the ladies
of the garrison, plainly dressed for the long and hard
journey, came forth from their several quarters and
were assisted to mount the horses reserved for them.
De Croix accompanied Mademoiselle, attired as for a
gay pleasure-ride in the park, and gave her his gloved
hand to step from into the saddle, with all the gallantry
he might have shown a queen. I knew this was no
boy's play before us now; and, crushing back my
natural diffidence, I spurred my horse boldly forward
until we ranged up beside her, even venturing to un-
cover in polite salute.

Never did I see her look fairer than beneath the
shade of the wide-brimmed hat she had donned to keep

the hot sun from her clear cheeks; nor was there the slightest vestige of last night's terror lurking in the laughing eyes that flashed me greeting.

"I surely know of one sad heart amid this gay company," she exclaimed, "for while we rejoice at being once more bound for civilization, Master Wayland looks most truly mournful; doubtless his thought is with her who has turned Indian for a time."

Her careless bantering tone nettled me; but I was quick enough to answer, having no wish to awaken her fears as to the safety of our journey.

"'T is true, Mademoiselle. I dislike greatly to leave in peril one I have journeyed so far to seek; nor can I banish from my mind the thought that perhaps I am failing in my duty toward her. Yet surely you have small cause for complaint, as I have, instead, deliberately chosen to ride here at your side, in order that I may be near to defend you should occasion arise, — provided always that my presence shall meet your wishes and approval."

She bowed as best she could in her high-peaked saddle, shooting a mischievous glance from me to the unconcerned and self-satisfied face of the Frenchman.

"I am indeed most gratified and happy, Monsieur, thus to feel myself the object of such devotion; but I greatly fear you will prove but a poor companion on the journey if you wear so glum a look. Captain de Croix is full of wit and good-humor this morning, and has already cheered me greatly with reminiscences of happier days."

"Indeed?" I said, looking at the fellow curiously. "He has quickly forgotten the baleful portent of last night. I thought the daylight would yield him new heart."

"And why not? 'T was but a cloud, as all of us know now, — though I confess it terrified me greatly at the time. You yourself seem not even yet to have wholly shaken off its terror."

"'T is not the supernatural that so troubles me," I rejoined. "As you may perceive yonder, Captain Wells rides forth with blackened face to what he deems to be certain death. I acknowledge, Mademoiselle, that I look forward to a serious clash of arms before we are rid of the redskins, in spite of their pledges; and shall therefore keep close beside you, hopeful that my arm may show you better service than my tongue before nightfall."

Her eyes had grown grave as she listened; for I spoke with soberness, and there crept into them a look that thrilled me. Before either could speak again, Ensign Ronan rode up beside me.

"Wayland," he questioned anxiously, "what is this I hear about a strange portent in the eastern sky last night? Saw you anything terrifying there?"

"'T was no more serious than a cloud which

chanced to assume the form of a monster, and its aspect was most terrifying until we understood the nature of its formation. Then it became merely an odd memory to weave a tale about. Mademoiselle here saw it, and remains in most excellent spirits nevertheless."

He lifted his hat to her, and stared hard at De Croix, who barely nodded to his greeting.

"By Heavens!" he exclaimed, as if much relieved, "it seemed to me as if Nature had conspired with those red demons yonder to sap our courage, when first I heard the rumor. I am so convinced that there is trouble afoot, that my nerves are all a-tingle at such mystery."

"Are the savages gathering without?"

"Ay! they are in mass of hundreds, awaiting us at the foot of the mound, and have been since day-break. See! the sentries are being called down, and the men are at the gate levers. I must be back at my post."

He held out his hand, and I clasped it warmly, feeling my heart go out instantly to the brave, impetuous lad.

"You ride this day with the rear-guard," he said, lingering as if loath to go, "and my duty lies with the van. We may not chance to meet again, but the God we spoke about together last night will strengthen our hearts to meet their duty. It matters not where men

die, but how. Good-bye, Mademoiselle! Captain de
Croix, I wish you a most pleasant journey."

With doffed hat, he struck spurs into his nettle-
some horse, and was gone; while the ringing notes of
the bugle called the waiting column to attention.

I watched with deepening interest all that was
taking place before me. The heavy log-gates were
unbarred, swung slowly inward, and left unguarded.
Captain Heald uttered a single stern word of command, and Captain Wells, with a squad of his Miamis
pressing hard at his horse's heels, rode slowly through
the opening out into the flood of sunshine. Captain
Heald and Mr. Kinzie, side by side, with Mrs. Heald
mounted upon a spirited bay horse a yard in their rear,
followed close; and then to Lieutenant Helm's grave
order the sturdy column of infantrymen, heavily
equipped and marching in column of fours, swept in
solemn curve about the post of the gate, and filed out
through the narrow entrance. The regular tramp-
tramp, the evident discipline, and the confident look
of the men, impressed me. While I was watching
them, the small garrison band began suddenly to play,
and the smiling soldier faces clouded as they glanced
around in questioning surprise.

"Saint Guise!" ejaculated De Croix, uneasily;
"it is the Dead March!"

I marked the sudden look of terrified astonishment
in Mademoiselle's eyes, and dropped my hand upon

hers where it rested against the saddle-pommel. Ensign Ronan spurred swiftly back down the column, with an angry face, and hushed the ill sound by a sharp order.

"Another tune, you fool, or none at all!" he said, peremptorily. "The foul fiend himself must have assumed charge of our march to-day."

As the column marched away, the groaning wagons one by one fell into line behind it, until at last our own turn came, and De Croix and I, each with a hand upon the bridle-rein of Mademoiselle's spirited horse, rode between the gate-posts out to where we had full view of that stirring scene below.

It was a fair, bright morning, with hardly so much as a fleecy white cloud in all the expanse of sky; glorious sunlight was flashing its prismatic colors over a lake surface barely ruffled by the faintest breeze. Never did Nature smile more brightly back into my eyes than then, as I gazed out over the broad plain where the glow of the summer reflected back in shimmering waves from the tawny prairie and glittering sand. With all its desolation, it was a picture to be treasured long; nor has a single detail of it ever left my memory.

How vast the distances appeared through that clear, sun-illumined atmosphere, and how pronounced and distinctive were the varied colors spread to the full vista of the eye, contrasts of shine and shadow no human brush, however daring, would venture to depict on canvas. A primitive land this, idealized by distance, vast in its wide, sweeping plains, its boundless sea, its leagues of glistening sand, and, bending over all, the deepest, darkest arch of blue that ever mirrored so fair a picture of the wilderness.

Scattered groups of cottonwood trees, the irregular mounds and ridges of sand, the silvery ribbon of river, merely emphasized the whole, and gave new meaning to what might else have been but sheer desert waste. I knew little then of what other years had seen within these solitudes and within the circle of my view; yet scraps of border legend came floating back into memory, until I recalled the name of many an old-time adventurer, — La Salle, Joliet, Marquette the Jesuit, — who must have camped beside that very stream out yonder.

The column had halted as our last laggards cleared the gate; and for a moment we rested in silence upon the side of the slope, while the long line was being re-arranged for travel. The Indians, in seemingly disorganized masses, were already enveloping the head of the column with noisy clamor, and Wells was having difficulty in holding his Miami scouts to their proper position. A few scattered and skulking savages, — chiefly squaws, I thought at the time, — were stealthily edging their way up the slope of the slight rise, eager to begin the spoliation of the Fort as soon as we had deserted it.

Wild and turbulent as was the scene, I perceived no alarming symptoms of hostility, and turned toward Mademoiselle with lighter heart. Her dark eyes were full of suppressed merriment as they encountered mine.

"I thought you would sit there and dream all day," she said pleasantly; "and I hardly have the heart to blame you. 'T is indeed a fair scene, and one I almost regret leaving, now that the time to do so has come. Never before has its rare beauty so strongly appealed to me."

"'T is the great distance outspread yonder which renders all so soft to the eye," I answered, glad to reflect her mood; "yet Captain de Croix and I know well 't is far less pleasant travelling over than to look at here. We think of the swamps, the forests, the leagues of sand and the swift rivers which will hinder our progress."

"I hardly imagine," she murmured softly, "that Captain de Croix is guilty of wasting precious time in reflection upon aught so trivial this morning. He has been conversing with me upon the proper cut of his waistcoat, and I am sure he is too deeply engrossed in that subject to give heed to other things."

I glanced at him and smiled as my heart glowed to her gentle sarcasm, for surely never did a more incongruous figure take saddle on a western trail. By

what code of fashion he may have dressed, I know
not; but from his slender-pointed bronze shoes to his
beribboned hat he was still the dandy of the boulevards, his dark mustaches curled upward till their tips
nearly touched his ears, and a delicately carved riding-
whip swinging idly at his wrist. He seemed to have
already exhausted his powers of conversation, for he
remained oblivious of our presence, fumbling with one
yellow-gloved hand in the recesses of a saddle-bag.

"By Saint Denis, Sam!" he exclaimed, angrily,
to his black satellite, "I can find nothing of the
powder-puff, or the bag of essence! *Parbleu!* if they
have been left behind you will go back after them,
though every Indian in this Illinois country stand
between. Come, you imp of darkness, know you aught
of these?"

"Dey am wid de pack-hoss, Massa de Croix," was
the oily answer. "I done s'posed you would n't need
'em till we got thar."

"Need them! Little you know the requirements
of a gentleman! Saint Guise! Why, I shall want
them both this very day! Ride you forward there, and
see if they cannot be picked out from among the other
things."

"See, Monsieur!" cried Mademoiselle suddenly,
one hand pressing my arm, while she pointed eagerly
with the other, "there goes the boat with Mistress
Kinzie and her children! That must be Josette in the

bow, with the gay streamer about her hat. She did wish so to ride with us, but Mr. Kinzie would not permit it."

The boat had but just cleared the river mouth, and was working off-shore, with half a dozen Indians laboring at the oars.

"Yet Josette has by far the easiest passage, as we shall learn before night," said I, watching their progress curiously. "I imagine you will soon be wishing you were with them."

"Never, Master Wayland!" she cried, with a little shudder, and quick uplifting of hands to her face as if to shut out the sight. "Memory of the hours when I was last on the lake is still too vivid. I have grown to dread the water as if it were an evil spirit. See! the column resumes its march, and the savages are moving beside us as might a guard of honor."

It was as she had said. The long, hard journey had begun; and slowly, like some great snake torpid with a winter's sleep, the crawling column drew forward. We at the rear rode down the incline and out upon the level plain, every step an unconscious advance toward battle and death.

CHAPTER XXV

IN THE JAWS OF THE TIGER

E chatted carelessly about many things, as we rode slowly onward, our un-guided horses following those in advance along the well-marked trail close be-side the water along the sandy beach. Mademoiselle was full of life and bubbling over with good-humor; while De Croix, having found the essentials of his toilet safe, grew witty and light of speech, even interesting me now and then in the idle words that floated to my ears, — for he managed to monopolize the attention of the young girl so thor-oughly that after a little time I sat silent in my saddle, scarce adding a word to their gay tilt, my eyes and thought upon the changing scene ahead.

I know not why, as I reflect calmly upon the incidents of that morning, I should have grown so confident that the savages meant us fair; yet this feeling steadily took possession of me, and I even began to regret that I had not stayed behind in quest of her for whom I had come so far. Surely it was hopeless for me to dangle longer beside Mademoiselle, for De Croix knew so well the little ins and outs of social intercourse that I was like a child for his play. Moreover, it was clear enough that the girl liked him, or he would never presume so to monopolize her attention. That she saw through much of his vain pretence, was indeed probable; her words had conveyed this to me. Nevertheless, it was plain she found him entertaining; he was like a glittering jewel in that rough wilderness, and I was too dull of brain and narrow of experience to hope for success against him in a struggle for the favor of a girl so fair and gay as this Toinette.

I thought the matter all out as I rode on through the sunlight, my eyes upon the painted savages who trooped along upon our right in such stolid silence and seeming indifference, my ears open to the light badinage and idle compliments of my two companions. Yes, it would be better so. When the Indians left the column at the head of the lake, I would invent some excuse that might allow me to accompany them on their return, and I would remain in the neighborhood of the Fort until Elsa Matherson had been found.

Just in front of us, a large army wain struggled along through the yielding sand, drawn by a yoke of lumbering oxen. The heavy canvas cover had been pushed high up in front, and I could see a number of women and children seated upon the bedding piled within, and looking with curious interest at the stream of Indians plodding moodily beside the wheels. Some of the little tots' faces captivated me with their expression of wide-eyed wonder, and I rode forward to speak with them; for love of children is always in my heart.

As I turned my horse to draw back beside Mademoiselle, my eyes rested upon the stockade of the old Fort, now some little distance in our rear; and to my surprise it already swarmed with savages. Not less than five hundred Indians, — warriors, all of them, and well armed, — tramped as guards beside our long and scattered column, yet hundreds of others were even now overrunning the mound and pouring in at the Fort gates, eager for plunder. I could hear their shouting, their fierce yells of exultation, while the grim and silent fellows who accompanied us never so much as glanced around, although I caught here and there the glint of a cruel, crafty eye. The sight made me wonder; and I swung my long rifle out from the straps at my back down across the pommel of my saddle, more ready to my hand.

The trail we had been following now swerved nearer the lake, deflected somewhat by a long high ridge of beaten sand, separating the shore from the prairie. Here the two advancing lines of white and red diverged, the Indians moving around to the western side of the sand-ridge, while Captain Wells and his Miami scouts continued their march along the beach. There was nothing about this movement to awaken suspicion of treachery, for the beach at this point had narrowed too much for so great a number moving abreast, and it was therefore only natural that our allies should seek a wider space for their marching, knowing they could easily reunite with us a mile or so below, where the beach broadened again. Their passing thus from our sight was a positive relief; and so quiet did everything become, except for groaning wheels and the heavy tread of horses, that Mademoiselle glanced up in surprise.

"Why, what has become of the Indians?" she questioned. "Have they already left us?"

I pointed to the intervening sand-ridge.

"They move parallel with us, but prefer to walk upon the prairie grass rather than these beach pebbles. For my part, I would willingly dispense with their guard altogether; for in my judgment we are of sufficient strength to defend ourselves."

"Ay, strong enough against savages," interposed De Croix, his eyes upon the straggling line ahead; "yet if by any chance treachery was intended, surely I never saw military formation less adapted for repelling sudden attack. Mark how those fellows march out yonder!—all in a bunch, and with not so much as a corporal's guard to protect the wagons!"

I was no soldier then, and knew little of military formation; but his criticism seemed just, and I ventured not upon answering it. Indeed, at that very moment some confusion far in front, where Captain Wells led his scouts, attracted my attention. We must have been a mile and a half from the Fort by this time, and I recalled to memory the little group of trees standing beside the trail where we had halted on our journey westward to enjoy our earliest glimpse of Dearborn. At first I could make out little of what was taking place ahead; then suddenly I saw the squad of Miamis break hastily, like a cloud swept by a whirling wind, and the next instant could clearly distinguish Captain Wells riding swiftly back toward the column of infantry, his head bare, and one arm gesticulating wildly. In a moment the whole line came to a startled and wondering pause.

"What is it?" questioned Mademoiselle anxiously, shading her eyes. "Have the Indians attacked us?"

"God knows!" I exclaimed, clinching my rifle firmly. "But it must be,—look there!"

Wheeling rapidly into line, as if at command, although we could hear no sound of the order, the soldiers poured one quick volley into the sand-ridge on their right, and then, with a cheer which floated

265

faintly back to us, made a wild rush for the summit.
This was all I saw of the struggle in front, — for,
with a cry of dismay, the Miamis composing the rear-
guard broke from their posts beside the wagons and
came running back past us in a panic of wild terror.
I saw Sergeant Jordan throw himself across their line
of flight, striking fiercely with his gun, and cursing
them for a pack of cowardly hounds; but he was
thrown helplessly aside in their blind rush for safety.

"Wayland! De Croix!" he shouted, staggering
to his knees, "help me stop these curs, if you would
save our lives!"

It was a fool thing, yet in the excitement I did
it, and De Croix was beside me. Two or three of the
settlers on foot rallied with us, and together we struck
so hard against those cowering renegades that for the
moment we held them, though their fear gave them
desperation difficult to withstand. I recall noticing
De Croix, as he pressed his rearing horse into the
huddled mass, lashing at the faces of the fellows merci-
lessly with his riding-whip, as if thinking Mademoiselle would admire his reckless gallantry.

A wild yell, with the mad thrill of the war-whoop
in it, suddenly assailed our ears; the Miamis broke
to the left like a flock of frightened birds, and my
startled glance revealed a horde of naked Indians,
howling like maniacs, and with madly brandished
weapons, pouring over the sand-ridge not thirty feet

away from us. With a shout of warning, which was half a curse at my own mad folly, I drove the spurs deep into my horse's side in a vain endeavor to fling myself between them and the girl. Hardly had the startled animal made one quick plunge, when we were locked in that human avalanche as if gripped by a vise of steel. A dozen dark hands grasped my bridle or clutched at me, their swarthy faces fierce with blood-lust, the eyes that fronted me cruel with passion and inflamed by hate. I heard shots not far away; but we were all too closely jammed to do more than fight in a desperate hand-to-hand struggle with club and knife.

The saddle is a poor place from which to swing a rifle, yet I stood high in my wooden stirrups and struck madly at every Indian head I saw, battering their faces till from the very horror of it they gave slowly back. I won a yard — two yards — three, — my horse biting viciously at their naked flesh, and lashing out with both fore-feet like a fiend, while I swept my gun-stock in a widening circle of death. For the moment, I dreamed we might drive them back; but then those devils blocked me, clinging to my horse's legs in their death agony, and laughing back into my face as I struck them down.

Once I heard De Croix swearing in French beside me, and glanced around through the mad turmoil to see him cutting and hacking with broken blade, pushing into the midst of the *mêlée* as if he had real joy in the encounter. While I thus had him in view, a knife whistled through the air, there was a quick dazzle in the sunlight, and he reeled backward off his horse and disappeared in the ruck below.

Never in a life of fighting have I battled as I did then, feeling that I alone might hope to reach her side and beat back these foul fiends till help should come to us. The stock of my rifle shattered like glass; but I swung the iron barrel with what seemed to me the strength of twenty men, striking, thrusting, stabbing, my teeth set, my eyes blurring with a mist of blood, caring for nothing except to hit and kill. I know not now whether I advanced at all in that last effort, though my horse trod on dead bodies. Only once in those awful seconds did I gain a glimpse of Mademoiselle through the mist of struggle, the maze of uplifted arms and striking steel. She had reined her horse back against a wheel of the halted wagon, and with white face and burning eyes was lashing desperately with the loaded butt of her riding-whip at the red hands which sought to drag her from the saddle.

The sight maddened me, and again my spurs were driven into my horse's flanks. As he plunged forward, some one from behind struck me a crushing blow across the back of the head, and I reeled from my saddle, a red mist over my eyes, and went hurling face downward upon the mass of reeling, tangled bodies.

CHAPTER XXVI

THE FIELD OF THE DEAD

HE fierce plunging of my horse in his death agony, and his final pitching forward across my prostrate body, were doubtless all that saved my life. Yielding to their mad desire for plunder, the savages scattered when I fell, and left me lying there for dead. I do not think I quite lost consciousness in those first moments, although everything became blurred to my sight, and I was imprisoned by the weight above me so that the slightest effort to move proved painful; indeed, I breathed only with the greatest difficulty.

But I both heard and saw, and my mind was intensely occupied with the rush of thought, the horror of all that was going on about me. How I wish I might blot it out, — forget forever the hellish deeds of those dancing devils who made mock of human agony and laughed at tears and prayers! It was plain,

269

as the wild cries of rejoicing rose on every side, that the Indians had swept the field. The distant sound of firing ceased, and I could hear the pitiful cries of women, the frightened shrieks of children, the shrill note of intense agony wrung from tortured lips. Close beside me lay a dead warrior, his hideously painted face, with its wide, glaring, dead eyes, so fronting me that I had left only a narrow space through which to peer. Within that small opening I saw murder done until I closed my eyes in shuddering horror, crazed by my own sense of helplessness, and feeling the awful fate that must already have befallen her I loved.

God knows I had then no faintest wish to live; nor did I dream that I should see the sun go down that day. Death was upon every side of me, in its most dreadful forms; and every cry that reached my ears, every sight that met my eyes, only added to the frightful reality of my own helplessness. The inert weight of the horse stifled me so that I drew my short breath almost in sobs; nor did I dare venture upon the slightest attempt at release, hemmed about as I was by merciless fiends now hideously drunk with slaughter. Once I heard a man plead for mercy, shrieking the words forth as if his intensity of agony had robbed him of all manliness; I saw a young woman fall headlong, the haft of a tomahawk cleaving open her head, as a brawny red arm gripped her by the throat; a child, with long yellow hair, and face distorted by terror, ran past my narrow outlook, a naked savage grasping after her scarcely a foot behind. I heard her wild scream of despair and his shout of triumph as he struck her down. Then I lost consciousness, overwhelmed by the multiplying horrors of that field of blood.

It is hard to tell how long I lay there, or by what miracle of God's great mercy I had escaped death and mutilation. It was still day, the sun was high in the heaven, and the heat almost intolerable, beating down upon the dry and glittering sand. I could distinguish no sound near at hand, not even a moan of any kind. The human forms about me were stiffening in death; nor did any skulking Indian figures appear in sight.

From away to the northward I could hear the echo of distant yelling; and as I lay there, every faculty alert, I became more and more convinced that the savages who had attacked us had withdrawn, and that I alone of all that fated company was preserved, through some strange dispensation of Providence, for what might prove a more terrible fate than any on that stricken field. With this thought there was suddenly born within me a fresh desire for life, a mad thirsting after revenge on those red demons whose merciless work I had been compelled to see. Yet if I hoped to preserve my life, I must have water and air; a single hour longer in my present situation could only result in death. Fortunately, such relief, now that

I felt free to exert myself and seek it, was not so difficult as it had seemed. The heavy horse rested upon other bodies as well as my own, so that, little by little, I succeeded in dragging myself out from beneath his weight, until I was finally able to lift my head and glance cautiously about me.

I pause now as I sit writing, my face buried in my hands, at the memory of that dreadful field of death. I cannot picture it, nor have I wish to try. I took one swift glimpse at the riven skulls, the mangled limbs, the mutilated bodies, the upturned pleading faces white and ghastly in the sunlight, the women and children huddled in heaps of slain, the seemingly endless line of disfigured, half-stripped bodies stretching far down the white beach; then I fell upon my face in the sand, sobbing like a baby. O God, how could such deeds be done? How could creatures shaped like men prove themselves such fiends, such hideous devils of malignity? It sickened me with horror, and I shrank from those dead bodies as if each had been a grim and threatening ghost.

Necessity presently overcame the dread possessing me; and slowly, seeking to see no more than I must of the awful scenes about me, I struggled to my knees, and peered around cautiously for signs of skulking Indians. Not a living creature was near enough to observe me. To the northward the savages were swarming about the Fort, and it was evident that they had left everything to search for plunder. My uncovered head throbbed under the hot sun, and my hair was thick with clotted blood; scarce a hundred feet away was the blue lake, and on my hands and knees I crawled across the beach to it, forgetful of everything else in my desire to roll in the cool sweet water.

I realized that it would be far safer for me to remain there until darkness shrouded my movements; but I felt so revived by the touch of the water that the old desire for action overcame considerations of personal safety. Before night came I must somehow gain possession of a rifle, with powder and ball; and I must discover, if possible, the fate of Mademoiselle. I cannot describe how, like a frightened child, I shrank from going again amid those mutilated corpses. I started twice, only to crawl back into the water, nerveless and shaking like the leaf of a cottonwood. I knew it must be done, and that the sooner I attempted it the safer would be the trial; so at last, with set teeth and almost superhuman effort, I crept up the beach among the silent, disfigured dead once more.

With little trouble I found the wagon against which I had seen Mademoiselle draw back her horse in that last desperate defence. It was overturned, scorched with flame, its contents widely scattered; while about it lay the bodies of men, women, and children. A single hasty glance at most of these was sufficient; but a few were so huddled and hidden that

I was compelled to move them before I thoroughly convinced myself that Mademoiselle was not there. I finally found her horse, several rods away, lying against the sand-ridge; but she whose body I sought with such fond persistency was not among those mangled forms.

Faint and sick from the awful scene, with head throbbing painfully, I sank down upon a slope of sand where I was able to command a clear view in either direction, and thought rapidly. I was alone with the dead. Of all those lying silent before me, none would stir again. Not a savage roamed the stricken field, — though doubtless they would again swarm down upon it as soon as the sacking of the Fort had been completed. I must plan, and plan quickly, if I would preserve my own life and be of service to others. And life was worth preserving now, for there was a possibility, — faint, to be sure, yet a possibility, — that Toinette still lived. How the mere hope thrilled and animated me! how like a trumpet-sound it called to action! She had told me once of friendships between her and these blood-stained warriors; of weeks passed in Indian camps on the great plains, both with her father and alone; of being called the White Queen in the lodges of Sacs, Wyandots, and Pottawattomies. Perchance some such friendship may have intervened to save her, even in that fierce *mêlée*, that carnival of lust and murder. Some chief, with sufficient power to dare the deed, may have snatched her from out the jaws of death, actuated by motives of mercy, — or, more likely still, have saved her from the stroke of the tomahawk for a far more terrible fate.

This was the thought that brought me again to my feet with burning face and tightly clinched teeth. If she lived, a helpless prisoner in those black lodges yonder, there was work to be done, — stern, desperate work, that would require all my courage and resource-fulness. Firm in manly resolve, and rendered reckless now of contact with the dead, I crept back among the bodies in eager search for gun and ammunition. For a long time I sought vainly; the field had been stripped by many a vandal hand. At last, however, I turned over a painted giant of a savage whose head had been crushed with a blow, and beneath him discovered a long rifle with powder-horn half filled. As I drew it forth, uttering a cry of delight at my precious find, my eyes fell upon a pair of bronze boots, with long narrow toes, protruding from beneath a tangled mass of the slain. It was no doubt the tomb of De Croix; and without so much as a thought that he could be alive, I drew the bodies off him and dragged his form forth into the sunlight.

Merciful Heaven! his heart still beat, — so faintly, indeed, that I could barely note it with my ear at his chest. But life was surely there, and with a hasty glance about to assure me that I was unob-served, I ran to the lake shore. I returned with hat full of water, with which I thoroughly drenched him, rubbing his numbed hands fiercely, and thumping his chest until at last the closed eyes partially opened, and he looked up into my anxious face, gasping painfully for breath. His lips moved as I lifted his head in my arms; and I bent lower, not certain but he was dying and had some last message he would whisper in my ear.

"Wayland," he faltered feebly, "is this you? Lord, how my head aches! Send Sam to me with the hand-mirror and the perfumed soap."

"Hush!" I answered, almost angry at his flippant utterance. "Sam is no doubt dead, and you and I alone are spared of all the company. Do you suffer greatly? Think you it would be possible to walk?"

"I have much pain here in the side," he said slowly, "and am yet weak from loss of blood. All dead, you say? Is Toinette dead?"

"I know not, but I have not found her body among the others, and believe her to be a prisoner to the savages. But, come, De Croix," I urged, anxiously, "we run great risk loitering here; there is but one safe spot for us until after dark, — yonder, crouched in the waters of the lake. The Indians may return at any moment to complete their foul work; and for us to be found alive means torture, — most likely the stake, — and will remove the last hope for Mademoiselle. Think you it can be made if you lean hard on me?"

"*Sacre!* 't will not be because I do not try, Master Wayland," he answered, his voice stronger now that he could breathe more freely, and with much of his old audacity returned. "Help me to make the start, friend, for every joint in my body seems rusty."

His face was white and drawn from agony, and he pressed one hand upon his side, while perspiration stood in beads upon his forehead. But no moan came from his set lips; and when he rested a moment on his knees, looking about him upon the dead, a look of grim approval swept into his eyes.

"Saint Guise, Wayland," he said soberly, "'t was a master fight, and the savages had it not all their own way!"

It made me sick to hear such boasting amidst the horror that yet overwhelmed me, and I drew the fellow up to his feet with but little tenderness.

"God knows 't is sad enough!" I answered, shortly. "Come, there are parties of Indians already straying this way from the Fort yonder, and it behooves us to get in hiding."

He made the distance between us and the water with far less difficulty than I had expected, and with a better use of his limbs at each step. In spite of vigorous protest on his part, I forced him out from the shore until the water entirely covered us, save only our faces; and there we waited for the merciful coming of the night.

CHAPTER XXVII

A GHOSTLY VISION

HE touch of the water brought renewed life to De Croix. This was shown by the brighter color stealing into his cheeks, as well as by the more careless tone that crept into his voice. The lake proved shallow for some considerable distance off shore, and I compelled the Frenchman to wade with me southward, and as far out as we dared venture, until we must have reached the extreme limit of the field of massacre. Indeed, I fully believed we had passed beyond the point where the attack had first burst upon Captain Wells's Miamis; for I could perceive no sign of any bodies lying opposite us against the white background of sand. As the night drew on, squads of savages wandered over the scene of slaughter, despoiling the stiffening corpses, and taking from the wagons whatever might suit their fancy. Yet

we were now so far removed that we could distinguish little of their deeds, although the sound of their voices echoed plainly enough across the water to our ears.

As time passed, the numbness that had paralyzed my brain, either from the cruel blow that felled me or the terrible shock my nerves had experienced, gradually passed away, and our situation became more vivid to my mind. I thought again of all who had gone forth that morning filled with hope and life. I had, it is true, known none of them long, but there were many in that ill-fated company who had already grown dear to me, and one was among them who I now knew beyond all question was to remain in my heart forever.

I recalled the faces one by one, with some tender memory for each in turn. I thought of the brave Captain Wells, with his swarthy face, and Indian training, who had proved himself so truly my friend for my father's sake; of Captain Heald, the typical bluff soldier of the border, ready to sacrifice everything to what he deemed his duty; of Lieutenant Helm, grave of face and calm of speech, always so thoughtful of his sweet girl bride; and of young Ronan, loyal of heart and impetuous of deed, whose frank manliness had so drawn me to him. And now all these brave, true comrades were dead! Only five or six hours ago I had spoken with them, had ridden by their side; now they lay motionless yonder, stricken down by the

basest treachery, their poor bodies hacked and mutilated almost beyond recognition. I could scarcely realize the awful truth; it rested upon me like some horrible
dream, from which I knew I must soon awaken.

But it was Mademoiselle, — Toinette, with the
laughing eyes and roguish face, which yet could be so
tender, — whose memory held me vibrating between
constant dread and hope. Living or dead, I must
know the truth concerning her, before I felt the slightest consideration for my own preservation. If I lived,
it should be for her sake, not mine. Plan after plan
came to me as I stood there, my face barely raised
above the water level, praying for the westering sun to
sink beneath the horizon. Yet all my plans were so
vague, so visionary, so filled with difficulties and un-
certainties, that at last I had nothing practical outlined
beyond a firm determination in some way to reach
the Indian camp and there learn what I could of its
black secrets. I wondered whether this rash hare-
brained Frenchman would aid or hinder such a purpose; and I glanced aside at him, curious to test the
working of his mind in such a time of trial.

"Saint Guise!" he exclaimed, marking my look,
but misinterpreting it; "the sun has gone down at
last, and there seems a chill in the air where it strikes
my wet skin. It is in my thought to wade ashore,
Master Wayland, and seek food for our journey, as
I can perceive no savages near at hand."

"It will be safer if we wait here another half-hour," I answered, almost inclined to smile at the queer figure he cut, with his long, wet hair hanging down his shoulders. Then I added, "What journey do you contemplate?"

He gazed at me, his face full of undisguised amazement.

"What journey? Why, Mon Dieu! to the eastward, of course! Surely you have no wish to linger in this pleasant spot?"

"And is that the way of a French soldier?" I asked, almost angrily. "I thought you made the journey westward, Monsieur, for the sake of one you professed greatly to admire; and now you confess yourself willing to leave her here to the mercy of these red wolves. Is this the way of it?"

I spoke the words coolly, and they cut him to the quick. His face flushed and his eyes flashed with anger; yet I faced him quietly, though I doubt not I should have felt his hand upon me had we been better circumstanced for struggle.

"How know you she lives?" he asked sullenly, eying the rifle I still held across my shoulder.

"I do not know, Monsieur, except that her body is not upon the field yonder; but I will know before I leave, or give my life in the search. And if you really loved her as you professed to do, you would dream of nothing less."

"Love her?" he echoed, his gaze upon the sand, now partially obscured in the descending twilight. *"Sacre!* I truly thought I did, for the girl certainly has beauty and wit, and wove a spell about me in Montreal. But she has become as a wild bird out here, and is a most perplexing vixen, laughing at my protestations, so that indeed I hardly know whether it would be worth the risk to stay."

Hateful and selfish as these words sounded, and much as I longed to strike the lips that uttered them so coolly, yet their utterance brought a comfort to my heart, and I stared at the fellow, biting my tongue to keep back the words of disgust I felt.

"So this is the measure of your French gallantry, Monsieur! I am sincerely glad my race holds a different conception of the term. Then you will leave me here?"

"Leave you? *Sacre!* how could I ever hope to find my way alone through the wilderness? 'T would be impossible. Yet why should we stay here? What can you and I hope to accomplish in so mad a search amid all these savages? You speak harsh words, — words that under other conditions I should make you answer for with the sword; but what is the good of it all? You know I am no coward; I can fight if there be need; yet to my mind no help can reach Toinette through us, while to remain here longer is no less than suicide."

I saw he was in earnest, and I felt there was much truth in his words, however little they affected my own determination.

"As you please, Monsieur," I answered coldly, turning from him and slowly wading ashore. "With me 't is not matter for argument. I seek Mademoiselle. You are at perfect liberty either to accompany me or to hunt for safety elsewhere, as you wish."

I never so much as glanced behind, as I went up the beach, now shrouded in the swift-descending night; but I was aware that he kept but a step behind me. Once I heard him swear; but there was no more speaking between us, until, in the darkness, I stumbled and partially fell over a dead body outstretched upon the sand.

"A Miami, judging from the fringe of his leggings," I said briefly, from my knees. "One of the advance guard, no doubt, brought down in flight. 'T is good luck, though, De Croix, for the fellow has retained his rifle. Perchance if you be well armed also, it may yield you fresh courage."

"*Parbleu!* 't is not courage I lack," he returned, with something of his old-time spirit, "but I hate greatly to yield up a chance for life on so mad an errand. More, Master Wayland, had this firearm been in my hands when you flouted me in the water yonder, your words should not have been so easily passed over."

The stars gave me a dim view of him, and there was a look in his face that caused me to feel it would be best to have our trouble settled fully, and without delay.

"Monsieur," I said sternly, laying my hand upon his shoulder, and compelling him to front me fairly, "I for one am going into danger where I shall require every resource in order to preserve my life and be of service to others. I have already told you that I care not whether you accompany me or no. But this I say: we part here, or else you journey with me willingly, and with no more veiled threats or side looks of treachery."

"I meant no harm."

"Then act the part of a man, Monsieur, and cease your grumbling. The very life of Mademoiselle may hang upon our venture; and if you ever interfere or obstruct my purpose, I will kill you as I would a dog. You understand that, Monsieur de Croix; now, will you go or stay?"

He looked about him into the lonely, desolate shadows, and I could see him shrug his shoulders.

"I go with you, of course. *Sacre!* but I have small choice in the matter; 't would be certain death otherwise, for I know not east from west in this blind waste of sand."

I turned abruptly from him, and strode forward

across the sand-ridge out into the short prairie grass beyond, shaping my course westward by the stars. However revengeful the Frenchman might feel at my plain speaking, I felt no hesitancy in trusting him to follow, as his life depended upon my guidance through the wilderness.

My mind by this time was fairly settled upon our first movement. The only spot that gave promise of a safe survey of the Indian camp, where doubtless such prisoners as there were would be held, I felt sure would be found amid the shadows of the west bank of that southerly stream along which the lodges were set up. From that vantage point, if from any, I should be able to judge how best to proceed on the perilous mission of rescue.

While we were feeling our way forward through the darkness, a great burst of flame soared high into the northern sky, the red light radiating far abroad over the prairie, until even our creeping figures cast faint shadows on the level plain.

"Saint Guise! They have set fire to the Fort!" exclaimed De Croix, halting and gazing anxiously northward.

"Ay, either to that or to the agency building," I answered. "It was not there I expected to find the prisoners, but rather hidden among those black lodges yonder whence all the shouting comes. 'T is torture, De Croix, which has so aroused those devils; and it will soon enough prove our turn to entertain them, if we linger long within this glare."

"You have a plan, then?"

"Only a partial one at present, — 't is to put the safeguard of the river between us and those yelling fiends. Beyond that it will all be the guidance of God."

The stream proved to be a narrow one, and the current was not swift. We crossed it easily enough, without wetting our stock of powder, and found the western bank somewhat darkened by the numerous groups of small stunted trees that lined it. I moved with extreme caution now, for each step brought us in closer proximity to those infuriated tribesmen who were holding mad carnival in the midst of their lodges. I felt sure that our pathway along the western shore was clear, for the most astute chief among them would hardly look for the approach of enemies from that quarter; but I was enough of a frontiersman not to neglect any ordinary precautions, and so we crept like snakes along at the water's edge, under the shadow of the bank, until much of the wild scene in the village opposite was revealed to our searching eyes.

It was a mad saturnalia, half light, half shadow, amid which the fierce figures of the painted warriors passed and repassed in drunken frenzy, making night hideous with savage clamor and frenzied gesticulations. I would have crept on farther, seeking a place for crossing unobserved, had not De Croix suddenly grasped me by the leg. As I turned, the play of the flames from across the water struck upon his white face, and I could read thereon a terror that held him motionless.

"For Christ's sake, let us go!" he urged, in an agonized whisper. "See what those demons are about to do! I fear not battle, Wayland, as you know; but the scene yonder unmans me."

It is hard for me to describe now what then I saw. The entire centre of the great encampment was brightly lit by a huge blazing fire, around which hundreds of Indians were gathered, leaping and shouting in their frenzy, while above the noise of their discordant voices we could distinguish the flat notes of the wooden drum, the dull pounding of which reminded me of the solemn tolling of a funeral bell. What atrocities had been going on, I know not; but as we gazed across at them in shuddering horror, forth from the entrance of a lodge a dozen painted warriors drove a white man, stripped to the waist, his hands bound behind him. As he stumbled forward, a bevy of squaws lashed him with corded whips. I caught one glimpse of his face in the light of the flames; it was that of a young soldier I recalled having seen the evening before within the Fort, playing a violin. He was a brave lad, and although his face was pale and drawn by suffering, he fronted the crazed mob that buffeted him with no sign of fear, his eyes roving about as if still seeking some possible avenue of escape. Once he sprang suddenly aside, tripping a giant brave who grasped him, and disappeared amid the lodges, only to be dragged forth a moment later and pushed forward, horribly beaten with clubs at every step.

On a sudden, that shrieking, undulating crowd fell away, and we could see the young man standing alone, bound to a stake, his body leaning forward as if held to its erect posture merely by the bonds. The limp drooping of his head made me think him already unconscious, possibly dead from some chance fatal blow; but as the flames burst out in a roar at his feet, and shot up, red and glaring, to his waist, he gave utterance to one terrible cry of agony, and it seemed to me I gazed fairly into his tortured eyes and could read their pitiful appeal. Twice I raised my rifle, the sight upon his heart, — but durst not fire. No consideration of my own peril held back the pressure of the trigger, — 't was the remembrance of Mademoiselle. It was beyond my strength of will to withstand such strain long.

" Come," I groaned to De Croix, my hands pressed tightly over my eyes to shut out the sight, " it will craze us both to stay here longer, nor dare we aid the poor fellow even by a shot."

He lay face downward on the soft mud of the bank, and I had to shake him before he so much as moved. We crept on together, until we came out through the thick bushes into the open prairie, and faced each other, our lips white and our bodies shaking with the horror of what we had just seen.

"Mon Dieu!" he faltered, "'t will forever haunt me."

"It has greatly undone me," I answered, striving to control my voice, for I felt the necessity of coolness if I hoped to command him; "but if we would save her from meeting a like fate, we must remain men."

"Then, for God's sake, find some spot where I may rest for an hour," he urged. "My brain seems reeling, and I fear it will give way if I remain in sight or sound of such horrors."

In spite of all I had seen, it was still my desire to creep in among the deserted lodges while darkness shrouded the outermost of them; but I felt that some safe hiding-place must first be found for my companion. To attempt to take him with me while in such a nervous state would be only to invite disaster.

"De Croix," I asked, "know you if the Indians have destroyed the house that stood by the fork of the north river, where the settler Ouilmette lived?"

"I marked it through Lieutenant Helm's field-glass yesterday. 'T is partially burned, yet the walls still stand."

"Then 't will serve us most excellently to hide in, for there will be naught left within likely to attract marauders. Think you that you could find it through the night?"

He looked at me, and it was easy to see his nerves were on edge.

"Alone?" he gasped brokenly. "My God, no!"

There was seemingly no way out of it, for it would have been little short of murder to leave him alone on that black prairie, nor would harsh words have greatly mended matters. We were fully an hour at it, creeping cautiously along behind the scattered bushes until we passed the forks and swam the river's northerly branch. The action did him good, and greatly helped to steady my own nerves, as the uproar of the savages died steadily away behind us.

At last we came out upon a slight knoll, and found ourselves close beside the low charred walls of what remained of Ouilmette's log-cabin. 'T was a most gloomy and desolate spot, but quiet enough, with never the rustle of a leaf to awake the night, or startle us.

"Have you got back your nerve, Monsieur?" I asked, as we paused before the dark outline, "or must I also help you to explore within?"

"'T is not shadows that terrify me," he answered, no doubt thoroughly ashamed of his weakness, and eager to make amends; "nor is it likely that anything to affright me greatly is behind these walls."

I lay prone in the grass at the corner of the cabin,

my eyes fixed upon the distant Indian village, where
I could yet plainly distinguish numberless black figures dodging about between me and the flames; while
further to the east, the greater blaze of the Fort buildings lighted up, in a wide arc, the deserted prairie. I
gave little consideration to De Croix's exploit, — indeed, I had almost forgotten it, when suddenly the
fellow sprang backward out of the open door, a cry of
wild terror upon his lips, and his hands outstretched
as if to ward off some unearthly vision.

" Mon Dieu! " he sobbed hoarsely, falling upon
his knees. " 'T was the face of Marie! "

CHAPTER XXVIII

AN ANGEL IN THE WILDERNESS

E acted so like a crazed man, grovelling face downward in the grass, that I had to hold him, fearful lest his noise might attract attention from our enemies.

"Be quiet, De Croix!" I commanded sternly, my hand hard upon him, my eyes peering through the darkness to determine if possible the cause for his mysterious fright. "What is it that has so driven you out of your senses?"

He half rose, staring back at the black shadow of the dim doorway, his face white as chalk in the starlight and faint glare of the distant fires.

"'T was the face of a dead woman," he gasped, pointing forward, "there, just within the door! I saw her buried three years ago, I swear; yet, God be merciful! she awaited me yonder in the gloom."

"Pish!" I exclaimed, thoroughly disgusted at his

weakness, and rising to my feet. "Your nerves are unstrung by what we have been through, and you dream of the dead."

"It is not so!" he protested, his voice faltering pitifully; "I saw her, Monsieur, — nor was she once this day in my thought until that moment."

"Well, I shall soon know if there is a ghost within," I answered shortly, determined to make quick end of it. "Remain here, while I go into the house and see what I can find."

For a moment he clung to me like a frightened child; but I shook off his hands a bit roughly, and stepped boldly across the threshold. That was an age when faith in ghostly visitations yet lingered to harass the souls of men. I confess my heart beat more rapidly than usual, as I paused an instant to peer through the shadowy gloom within. It was a small, low room, with a litter of broken furniture strewing the earthen floor; but the log walls were quite bare. The flicker of the still blazing Fort illuminated the interior sufficiently to enable me to make out these simple details, and to see that the place was without living occupant.

There was only one other apartment in the building, and I walked back until I came upon the door which separated the two, and flung it open. As I did so I thought I saw a shadow, the dim flitting of a woman's form between me and the farther wall; but as I sprang hastily forward, grasping after the spectral vision, I touched nothing save the rough logs. Twice I made the circuit of that restricted space, so confident was I of my own eye-witness; but I found nothing, and could only pause perplexed, staring about in wonder.

It occurred to me that my own overtaxed nerves were at fault, and that if I was to accomplish anything before daylight I must say nothing likely to alarm De Croix further.

" Come, Monsieur!" I said, as I came out and shook him into attention, " there is naught within more dangerous than shadows, or perchance a rat. Nor have I any time longer to dally over such boyishness. I had supposed you a soldier and a brave man, not a nerveless girl to be frightened in the dark. Come, there is ample hiding-space behind the walls, and I purpose leaving you here to regain some measure of your lost courage while I try a new venture of my own."

" Where go you?"

" To learn if I may gain entrance to the Indian camp unobserved. There can be no better time than while they are occupied yonder."

He looked uneasily about him into the dark corners, shuddering.

" I would rather go with you," he protested, weakly. " I have not the heart to remain here alone."

"Nevertheless, here you stay," I retorted shortly, thoroughly exasperated by his continued childishness; "you are in no spirit to meet the perils yonder. Conquer your foolishness, Monsieur, for I know well 't is not part of your nature so to exhibit fear."

"'T is naught alive that I so shrink from; never have I been affrighted of living man."

"True; nor have I ever found the dead able greatly to harm. But now I go forth to a plain duty, and you must wait me here."

I did not glance back at him, although I knew he had sunk dejected on a bench beside the door; but with careful look at the priming of my rifle, I stepped forth into the open, and started down the slight slope leading to the river. A fringe of low, straggling trees hid my movements from observation by possible watchers along the southern bank; nor could I perceive with any definiteness what was going on there. The fires had died down somewhat, and I thought the savage yelling and clamor were considerably lessened.

I confess I went forward hesitatingly, and was doubtful enough about the outcome; but I saw no other means by which I might hope to locate Mademoiselle definitely, and I valued my own life now only as it concerned hers. The selfish cowardice of De Croix — if cowardice it truly was — served merely to stir me to greater recklessness and daring, and I felt ready to venture all if I might thereby only pluck her from the grasp of those red fiends. As I crept through the fringe of bushes which lined the bank, my eyes were on the darkened upper extremity of the Indian camp, and all my thoughts were concentrated upon a plan of entrance to it. I may have been somewhat careless, for I had no conception of any serious peril until after I had crossed the stream, and it certainly startled me to hear a voice at my very elbow, — a strange voice, beautifully soft and low.

"You have the movement of an Indian; yet I think you are white. What seek you here?"

I turned quickly and faced the speaker, my rifle flung forward ready for action. The light was poor enough there amid the shadows, yet the single glimpse I had told me instantly I faced the mysterious woman of the Indian camp. For a moment I made no response, held speechless by surprise; and she questioned again, almost imperatively.

"I asked, why are you here?"

"I am one, by the grace of God, spared from the massacre," I answered blindly. "But you? — I saw you within the Indian camp only last night. Surely you are not a savage?"

"That I know not. I sometimes fear the savage is part of all our natures, and that I am far removed from the divine image of my Master. But I am not an Indian, if that is what you mean. If to be white is a grace in your sight, I am of that race, though there

296

are times when I would have been prouder to wear the darker skin. The red men kill, but they do not lie, nor deceive women. I remember you now, — you were with the White Chief from Dearborn, and tried to approach me when Little Sauk interfered. Why did you do that?"

Her manner and words were puzzling, but I knew no better way than to answer frankly.

"I sought Elsa Matherson, — are you she?"

The girl — for she could certainly have been little more — started perceptibly at the name, and bent eagerly forward, peering with new interest into my face.

"Elsa Matherson?" she questioned, dwelling upon the words as though they awoke memories. "It is indeed long since I have heard the name. Where knew you her?"

"I have never known her; but her father was my father's friend, and I sought her because of that friendship."

"Here?"

"At Fort Dearborn, where she was left an orphan."

"How strange! how very strange indeed! 'T is a small world. Elsa Matherson! — and at Dearborn?"

Was it acting, for some purpose unknown to me, — or what might be the secret of these strange expressions?

"Then you are not the one I seek?"

She hesitated, looking keenly toward me through the dim light.

"I have not said who I may be," she answered evasively. "Whatever name I may once have borne was long ago forgotten, and to the simple children about me I am only Sister Celeste. 'T is enough to live by in this wilderness, and the recording angel of God knows whether even that is worthy. But I have been waiting to learn why you are here, creeping through the bushes like a savage! Nor do I believe you to be altogether alone. Was there not one with you yonder at the house? Why did he cry out so loudly, and fall?"

"He imagined he saw a ghost within. He claimed to have recognized the face of a dead woman he once knew."

"A dead woman? What is the man's name? Who is he?"

"Captain de Croix, an officer of the French army."

She sighed quickly, as if relieved, one hand pressed against her forehead, and sat thinking.

"I know not the name, but it seems strange that the chance sight of my face should work such havoc with his nerves. Spoke he not even the name of the woman?"

"I think he cried some name as he fell, but I recall it not."

AN ANGEL IN THE WILDERNESS

"And you? You are only seeking a way of escape from the savages?"

For a moment I hesitated; but surely, I thought, this strange young woman was of white blood, and seemingly an enthusiast in the religion I also professed, and I might safely trust her with my purpose.

"I am seeking entrance within the encampment, hoping thus to rescue a maiden whom I believe to be prisoner in the hands of the Indians."

"A maiden, — Elsa Matherson?"

"Nay, another; one I have learned to love so well that I now willingly risk even torture for her sake. You are a woman, and have a woman's heart; you exercise some strange power among these savages. I beg you to aid me."

She sat with clasped hands, her eyes lowered upon the grass.

"Whatsoever power I have comes from God," she said solemnly; "and there be times, such as now, when it seems as if He held me unworthy of His trust."

"But you will aid me in whatever way you can?"

"You are sure you love this maiden?"

"Would I be here, think you, otherwise?"

She did not answer immediately, but crept across the little space separating us until she could look more closely into my face, scanning it earnestly with her dark eyes.

"You have the appearance of a true man," she said finally. "Does the maid love you?"

"I know not," I stammered honestly, confused by so direct a question. "I fear not; yet I would save her even then."

I felt her hand touch mine as if in sudden sympathy.

"Monsieur," she spoke gravely, "love has never been kind to me, and I have learned to put small trust in the word as it finds easy utterance upon men's lips. A man swore once, even at the altar, that he loved me; and when he had won my heart he left me for another. If I believed you were such a man I would rather leave this girl to her fate among the savages yonder."

"I am not of that school," I protested earnestly. "I am of a race that love once and forever. But you, who are you? Why are you here in the midst of these savages? You bear a strange likeness to her I would save, but for the lighter shade of your hair."

She drew back slightly, removing her hand from mine, but with gentleness.

"It would do you little good to know my story," she said firmly. "I am no longer of the world, and my life is dedicated to a service you might deem sacrifice. Moreover, we waste time in such idle converse; and if it be my privilege to aid you at all, I must learn more, so as to plan safely."

"You have the freedom of the camp yonder?"

"I hardly know," she responded sadly. "God has placed in my poor hands, Monsieur, a portion of His work amid those benighted, sin-stained creatures there. Times come, as now, when the wild wolf breaks loose, and my life hardly is safe among them. I fled the camp to-night, — not from fear, Christ knows, but because I am a woman, and too weak physically to bear the sight of suffering that I am helpless to relieve. It is indeed Christ's mercy that so few of your company were spared to be thus tortured; but there was naught left for me but prayer."

She stooped forward, her hands pressed over her eyes as though she would shut out the horror.

"Yet know you who among the whites have thus far preserved their lives?" I urged, in an agony of suspense. "Were any of the women brought alive to the camp?"

"It was my fortune to see but one; nor was I permitted to approach her, — a sweet-faced girl, yet she could not be the one you seek, for she wore a wedding-ring. She was saved through the friendship of Black Partridge, and I heard that she is a daughter of the Silver-man."

"Ay! Mrs. Helm! Thank God! But was she the only one?"

"Truly, I know not; for I was forced away from sight of much that went on. Little Sauk has a white maiden hidden in his lodge, who was brought from the battle. I have not seen the girl, but know this through others who were angry at his good-fortune."

" Could we reach there, think you, unobserved? "

She rose, and gazed anxiously across the stream, her face showing clear and fair in the faint light of those distant fires, while I caught the glimmer of a pearl rosary about her white throat and marked a silver crucifix resting against her breast.

" It will be life itself you venture in such an attempt," she said softly, " even its loss through torture; yet 't is a deed that might be done, for the Indians are fairly crazed with blood and liquor, and will pay small heed to aught save their heathen orgies."

" Then let us venture it."

She turned slightly and looked at me intently, her dark eyes filled with serious thought.

" Yes, we will go," she responded at last, slowly. " If through God's grace we may thus preserve a life, it will be well worthy the sacrifice, and must be His desire."

For another moment we waited there silently, standing side by side, gazing anxiously across the dark water, and listening intently to the varied discordant sounds borne to us on the night air. I know not what may have been in her thought; but upon my lips there was a silent prayer that we might be safely guided in our desperate mission. I wondered still who this strange young woman could be, so surrounded by mystery, a companion of savages, and still gentle and refined in word and manner. I dare not ask again, nor urge her confidence; for there was that of reserve about her which held me speechless. I glanced aside, marking again the clear pure contour of her face, and my look seemed instantly to arouse her from her reverie.

"I expect little trouble until we near the centre of the camp," she said, thoughtfully. "'T is dark amid the northern lodges, and we shall meet with no warriors there unless they be so far gone in intoxication as to be no longer a source of danger. But come, friend, the longer we tarry the less bright grows the hope of success."

A slender bark canoe rested close beneath the bank, and she motioned me into it, grasping the paddle without a word, and sending the narrow craft with swift, silent strokes across the stream. The other shore was unprotected; so, hesitating only long enough to listen for a moment, much as some wild animal might, she crept forward cautiously into the black lodge-shadows, while I instantly followed, imitating as best I could her slightest movement. We met no obstacle to our advance, — not even the snarls and barkings of the innumerable curs, usually the sleepless guardians of such encampments of savages. I soon saw that as we crept around lodge after lodge in our progress, the light of the blazing fires in our front grew constantly brighter and the savage turbulence more pronounced.

At last the girl came to a sudden pause, peering

cautiously forward from beneath the shadow of the lodge that hid us; and as I glanced over her shoulder, the wild scene was revealed in each detail of savagery.

" 'T is as far as you will dare venture," she whispered, her lips at my ear. " I know not the exact limit of our progress, but the lodge of Little Sauk lies beyond the fire, and I must make the rest of the distance alone."

" But dare you? " I questioned uneasily. " Will they permit even you to pass unharmed? "

She smiled almost sadly.

" I have many friends among them, blood-stained as they are, and little as I have accomplished for the salvation of their souls. I have been with them much, and my father long held their confidence ere he died. I have even been adopted into the tribe of the Pottawattomies. None are my enemies among that nation save the medicine-men, and they will scarce venture to molest me even in this hour of their power and crime. Too well they know me to be under protection of their chiefs; nor are they insensible to the sanctity of my faith. Ay, and even their superstition has proved my safeguard."

The expression of curiosity in my eyes appealed to her, and as if in answer she rested one hand upon her uncovered head, the hair of which shone like dull red gold in the firelight.

" You mean that? " I asked, dimly recalling something I had once heard.

She shook the heavy coiled mass loose from its bondage, until it rippled in gleaming waves of color over her shoulders, and smiled back at me, yet not without traces of deep sadness in her eyes.

" 'T is an Indian thought," she explained softly, "that such hair as mine is a special gift of the Great Spirit, and renders its wearer sacred. What was often spoken most lightly about in other days has in this dread wilderness proved my strongest defence. God uses strange means, Monsieur, to accomplish His purpose with the heathen."

She paused, listening intently to a sudden noise behind us.

" Creep in here, Monsieur," she whispered, quickly lifting an edge of the skin-covering of the lodge. " A party is returning from the Fort, perchance with more prisoners. Lie quiet there until I return; it will not be long."

I crawled through the slight opening into that black interior, turning to hold open the flap sufficiently to peer forth once more. I knew not where she vanished, as she faded away like a shadow; but I had hardly secured refuge, when a dozen painted warriors trooped by, shouting their fierce greeting. In the midst of them, half-stripped, and bleeding as if from freshly inflicted wounds, staggered a white man; and as the firelight fell full upon his haggard face, I recognized De Croix.

CHAPTER XXIX

A SOLDIER OF FRANCE

HAT followed was so extraordinary and incredible that I hesitate to record it, lest there be those who, judging in their own conceit, and knowing little of savage Indian nature, may question the truth of my narration. Yet I am now too old a man to permit unjust criticism to swerve me from the task I have assumed.

The extreme of misery that overwhelmed me at the moment when I beheld my comrade driven forward like a trapped beast to a death by torture, found expression in a sudden moan, which, fortunately for me, was unnoted amid the shouts of greeting that arose around the fire when those gathered there caught sight of the new-comers. Instantly all was confusion and uproar; a scene of savage debauchery, unrelieved by a redeeming feature or a sign of mercy. It was as if poor

306

De Croix had been hurled, bound and gagged, into a den of infuriated wolves, whose jaws already dripped with the blood of slaughter. Gleaming weapons, glaring and lustful eyes, writhing naked bodies, pressed upon him on every side, hurling him back and forth in brute play, every tongue mocking him, in every up-lifted hand a weapon for a blow.

The fierce animal nature within these red fiends was now uppermost, fanned into hot flame by hours of diabolical torture of previous victims, in which they had exhausted every expedient of cruelty to add to the dying agony of their prey. To this, fiery liquor had yielded its portion; while the weird incantations of their priests had transformed the most sober among them into demons of malignity. If ever, earlier in the night, their chiefs had exercised any control over them, that time was long since past; and now the inflamed warriors, bursting all restraint, answered only to the war-drum or made murderous response to the superstition of their medicine-men.

The entire centre of the encampment was a scene of drunken orgy, a phantasmagoria of savage figures, satanic in their relentless cruelty and black barbarity. Painted hundreds, bedecked with tinkling beads and waving feathers, howled and leaped in paroxysms of fury about the central fire, hacking at the helpless bodies of the dead victims of earlier atrocities, tearing their own flesh, beating each other with whips like wire, their madly brandished weapons flashing angrily in the flame-lit air.

Squaws, dirty of person and foul of mouth, often more ferocious in appearance and cruel in action than their masters, were everywhere, dodging amid the writhing bodies, screaming shrilly from excitement, their long coarse hair whipping in the wind. Nor were they all Pottawattomies: others had flocked into this carnival of blood, — Wyandots and Sacs, even Miamis, until now it had become a contest for supremacy in savagery. 'T was as if hell itself had opened, to vomit forth upon the prairie that blood-stained crew of dancing demons and shock the night with crime.

A dead white man, — the poor lad whose early torture we had witnessed, — his half-burnt body still hanging suspended at the stake, was in the midst of them, a red glare of embers beneath him, the curling smoke creeping upward into the black sky from about his head like devil's incense. In front of this hideous spectacle, regardless of the mutilated body, sat the ferocious old demon I had seen the evening previous, his head crowned with a bison's horns, his naked breast daubed with red and yellow figures to resemble crawling snakes, his face the hideous representation of a grinning skull. Above all other sounds rang out his yells, inciting his fellows to further atrocities, and accompanied by the dull booming of his wooden drum.

It was into this pack of ravening beasts that poor

De Croix staggered from the surrounding shadows; and they surged about him, clamoring for place, greeting their new-found victim with jeers and blows and hoots of bitter hatred, viciously slashing at him with their knives, so that the very sight of it turned me sick, and made me sink my head upon my arms in helplessness and horror. A sudden cessation in the infernal uproar led me to peer forth once more. They had dragged the charred and blackened trunk of the dead soldier down from the post where it had hung suspended, and were fastening De Croix in its place, binding his hands behind the support, and kicking aside the still glowing embers of the former fire to give him space to stand. It was brutally, fiendishly done, with thongs wound about his body so tightly as to lift the flesh in great welts, and those who labored at it striking cruel blows at his naked, quivering form, spitting viciously into his face, with taunting words, seeking through every form of ferocious ingenuity to wring from their helpless victim some sign of suffering, some shrieking plea for mercy. Once I marked a red devil stick a sharpened sliver of wood into the Frenchman's bare shoulder, touched it with fire, and then stand back laughing as the bound victim sought vainly to dislodge the torturing brand.

Whatever of shrinking fear De Croix may have exhibited an hour before, however he may have trembled from ghostly haunting and been made coward by contact with the dead, he was a man now, a soldier worthy of his uniform and of his manhood. Merciful God! but it made my heart swell to see the lad, as he faced those dancing devils and looked coolly into the eyes of death. His face was indeed ghastly white in the fire-glow, save where the red stains of blood disfigured it; but there was no wavering in the bold black eyes, no cowardly shrinking from his fate, no moan of weakness from between his tightly pressed lips. Scarce could I think of him then as being the same gentle exquisite that rode on the westward trail in powdered hair and gaudy waistcoat, worrying lest a pinch of dust might soil his faultless linen, — this begrimed, blood-stained, torn figure, naked to the waist, his small-clothes clinging in rags from his thighs, his head bare and with long black locks streaming to his shoulders. Yet it was now, not then, he won my respect and honor.

Once I saw him strain desperately at the cords in a mad endeavor to break free, his flashing eyes on the demons who were torturing him beyond endurance. Well I knew how he longed to lay hand on any weapon, and thus die, battling to the end; had he succeeded, I doubt not I should have been at his side, forgetful of all else in the struggle. The deer-skin thongs, as unyielding as iron, held him fast. I ground my teeth and dug my nails into the earth to hold me from leaping forward in hopeless attempt at rescue, as a huge brute struck him savagely with clinched hand across the lips.

Suddenly, as if in response to some low spoken order, the jostling horde fell aside from before him, leaving a narrow space unoccupied. I had no time to wonder at this movement before a tomahawk, whirling rapidly and flashing like a ruby in the red glare, went hurling forward, and buried its shining blade deep in the post an inch from the prisoner's head, the handle quivering with the force of impact. Again and again, amid yells of derision and encouragement, they threw, twice bringing token of blood from the grazed cheek and once cleaving the ear nearest me as if by a knife-blow. In spite of all, De Croix sneered at them, mocked their efforts, taunted them with their lack of skill, no doubt seeking to infuriate them and cause the striking of a merciful death-blow.

I trembled as I gazed, held there by a fascination I could not overcome, shading my eyes when I saw an arm uplifted to make a cast, and opening them in dread unspeakable as I heard the dull impact of the blow. Never in my life have I seen such marvellous nerve as this French gallant displayed in those awful moments; standing there motionless, with never a tremor, no twitching of a muscle, his scornful eyes following the deadly steel, his lips jeering at the throwers, as he coolly played the game whose stake was death. At last some savage cast from farther

back amid the mass of howling contestants; I failed
to see the upraised hand that grasped the weapon, but
caught its sudden gleam as it sped onward, and De
Croix was pinned helpless, the steel blade wedging his
long hair deep into the wood.

A dozen screaming squaws now hustled forward
the materials for a fire; I saw branches, roots, and
leaves, piled high about his knees, and marked with a
shudder the film of blue smoke as it soared upward
ere the flame caught the green wood. Then suddenly
some one kicked the pile over, hurling it into the faces
of those who stooped beside it; and the fierce clamor
ceased as if by magic.

I staggered to my knees, wondering what it could
mean, — this strange silence after all the uproar.
Then I saw. Out from the shadows, as if she herself
were one, the strange girl who had been my companion
glided forward into the red radius of the flame, and
faced them, her back to De Croix.

Never shall I fail to recall her as she then appeared, — a veritable goddess of light fronting the
fiends of darkness. With cheeks so white as to seem
touched with death, her dark eyes glowed in consciousness of power, while her long, sweeping tresses rippled
below her waist, gleaming in a wild red beauty almost
supernatural. How womanly she was, how fair to
look upon, and how unconscious of aught save her
mission! One hand she held before her in imperious

gesture of command; with the other she uplifted the crucifix, until the silver Christ sparkled in the light.

"Back!" she said clearly. "Back! You shall not torture this man! I know him. He is a soldier of France!"

CHAPTER XXX

THE RESCUE AT THE STAKE

HE word uttered by the strange woman was one to conjure with even then in the Illinois country. Many a year had passed since the French flag ruled those prairies, yet not a warrior there but knew how the men of that race avenged an injury, — how swift their stroke, how keen their steel.

I watched the startled throng press closely backward, as if awed by her mysterious presence, influenced insensibly by her terse sentence of command, each dusky face a reflex of its owner's perplexity. Drunken as most of them were, crazed with savage blood-lust and hours of remorseless torture of their victims, for the moment that sweet vision of womanly purity held them motionless, as if indeed the figure of the Christ she uplifted before their faces had taught them abhorrence of their crimes.

But it was not for long. To hundreds of those
present she was merely an unknown white woman;
while even to those who knew her best, the Pottawattomies, she appeared only as one who came to
balk them of their revenge. They may have held her
person inviolate amid their lodges, and even have
countenanced her strange teaching; but now she had
ventured too far in attempting thus to stand between
them and their victim. They held back a single moment, halted by her fearlessness, rendered cowardly
by vague superstitions regarding her religious power;
but after the first breathless pause of dumb astonishment and irresolution, voice after voice arose in hoarse
cries of rage and shouts of disapproval. There was
a surging forward of the straining red line, while in
their front howled and gesticulated the hideous old
medicine-man, his painted face distorted by passion,
eager to grasp this auspicious moment to cast down
forever one who had sought to end his superstitious
rule among the tribe. I marked how she drew back
as they advanced, retreating step by step, — not, indeed, as if she feared them, but rather as if some defi-
nite purpose led her movement. Her eyes never
wavered, her hand still uplifted the gleaming cross,
as she retreated slowly, until she stood directly before
De Croix, where he hung helplessly staring at her with
an expression of fear in his face strangely at variance
with his late show of desperate courage.

"Back!" she cried again, but now in a deeper and fuller voice that sounded like a clear-toned bell above the uproar. "I tell you I will kill this man with my own hand before I permit you to put further torture upon him!"

An instant only did this threat halt the gathering rush. Some one voiced an Indian insult, and there came a fierce surging forward, although no warrior among them seemed eager to lead in the attack. I saw the woman lift her hand, and caught the glimmer of a steel blade; and even as I sprang erect, partially flinging aside the obstructing flap of the lodge, an Indian, stalking silently forth from the shadows, faced the mob, standing motionless within a foot of the desperate girl, and with his back toward her. One glance at that tall thin figure, the stern face, the long white hair, told me it was the great war-chief of the Pottawattomies, Gomo; and I sank back trembling from the reaction of that moment's strain.

His words were calm, deliberate, commanding; but the angry roar with which they were greeted made me fear the horde he faced so resolutely was now beyond control. He smiled, his thin lips curling in derision as he gazed with contempt into the threatening faces pressing closer upon every side.

"Fear not," he murmured aside to the watchful woman, and resting one hand upon her arm. "Cut loose the prisoner!"

She turned instantly to her task, while he spoke briefly the names of his chiefs; and as each was called in turn, a warrior came from among the mass and silently stood beside him. A dozen came forth thus, stalwart, grim-faced braves, many with fresh scalps dangling at their belts.

Gomo now spoke again, using the French tongue, that all present might better grasp his meaning.

"Brothers," he said gravely, "this squaw is Pottawattomie. She was adopted by our people and lives in our lodges. Pottawattomies are friends to Frenchmen; there is no war between us. Why should Wyandots and Sacs wish to burn a Frenchman?"

For a moment no one ventured to reply; the mob stood halted now, robbed of its leaders and its courage, even the noisy medicine-man silenced before this stern array of protecting chiefs. Loose as was Indian discipline and tribal authority, even in drunkenness those desperate warriors dared not openly disregard such a display of power.

"Have the Pottawattomies spoken well?" questioned the old chief, sternly, "or have our words wronged our brothers?"

A giant of a fellow, whose broad face and huge head seemed disproportionate even to his big body, his long coarse hair profusely ornamented with shells and beads flashing gaudily in the firelight, pushed his way out from among the silent mass.

"Gomo, the great war-chief of the Pottawattomies, has spoken well," he said in a deep voice that
rolled like distant thunder. "The Wyandots did not
know; they war not with Frenchmen, nor harm the
women of the Pottawattomies. The Great Spirit hath
made us brothers, and we have smoked together the
pipe of peace."

Gomo moved forward with Indian dignity, and
exchanged solemn greeting with the new-comer.

"It makes the hearts of the Pottawattomies light
to hear the words of Sau-ga-nash," he said gravely.
Then he turned and waved his hand to his clustered
warriors. "Release the Frenchman, and place him
for safety in the council lodge. Pass the woman free.
It is the will of our chiefs."

The council lodge! I glanced about me apprehensively; surely this must be the same tepee in which
Captain Heald and I had met the chiefs! There were
no signs of ordinary Indian occupancy, and now as
I looked about me the firelight from without revealed
clearly the shading of those grotesque figures I recalled as having been sketched upon the outer covering. So it was here that De Croix was to be confined!
I crept back hastily, dropping into place the loosened
flap through which I had been peering. A skin or
two were lying on the grassy floor; and I grasped the
larger of these, drawing it over me while I rolled
as closely as possible against the farther wall, hoping

desperately that no Indian guards would be posted within.

The uproar outside continued, as if there were still opposition to the commands of the chiefs; but presently, as I peeped through a hole in the skin held over me, I perceived a sudden flash of light as the flap covering the entrance was drawn aside. I saw a number of dark hands thrust within, a savage face or two peering for a moment about the darkened interior; but to my inexpressible relief only one body was thrust inside, with such violence, however, as to cause the man to fall face downward at full length. The next instant the lodge was again wrapped in utter darkness. By God's mercy I remained undiscovered, and was alone with De Croix.

For a short time, assured as I was of this fact, I did not venture to creep from my place of concealment, or make my presence known to my companion. What ears might be listening, I knew not; nor dared I trust too much to the Frenchman's already over-taxed nerves. He did not move from the position where he fell; but I could hear him groan and sob, with now and then a broken ejaculation. Without, the yelling and uproar grew perceptibly less, although an occasional outburst gave evidence that the carousal was not wholly ended. Finally I pushed back the robe that covered me, now grown uncomfortably warm, and crept cautiously toward the place where I knew him to be lying. It was intensely dark, and I was still fearful lest he might cry out if I startled him.

"De Croix," I whispered, "make no alarm; I am Wayland."

"Wayland!" I could mark the amazement in his tone, as he instantly sat upright, peering through the gloom in the direction whence my voice came. *"Mon Dieu!* You are here? You saw all of it?"

"Ay," I answered, reaching out and groping in the darkness until I grasped his hand. "You have had a hard time, my lad; but the worst is over, and hope remains for us both."

He shuddered so violently I could feel the spasm shake his body.

"'T was not the dying," he protested; "but did you see her, Wayland? Merciful God! was it really a living woman who stood there, or a ghost returned from the other world to haunt me and make living worse than death?"

"You mean the sister who interposed to save you?" I asked. "She was as truly alive as either of us. Think you she is not a stranger?"

He groaned, as if the confession was wrung from him by the terror of eternal torment.

"Mon Dieu! She is my wife!"

"Your wife?"

"Ay, my wife, — Marie Faneuf, of Montreal."

"But how comes she here, Monsieur, living in

the Pottawattomie camp? And how comes it that you sought another in this wilderness, if you were already long wedded?"

"Saint Guise! but I cannot tell you," and his voice shook with the emotion that swept him. "'T is like a black dream, from which I must yet awaken. She died, I swear she died; the sisters told me so at the convent of the Ursulines, whither she fled to escape my unkindness, — for I did her wrong; and I stood by the grave as the body they called hers was lowered into the ground. For all these years have I thought it true; yet the girl yonder was Marie. But you, Wayland, — know you aught of her?"

"Only that she guided me hither in search of Mademoiselle. On the way we conversed, and she let me know that she had dedicated her life to the service of these Indians, seeking to save their souls."

"'T is like enough; she was ever half a nun, and most religious. Yet made she no mention of me, and of my crying out at the house? — for I must indeed have seen her there!"

"She asked me your name, Monsieur, and when I told her she said she recalled it not. Knew she you by some other?"

He did not answer, though I could mark his heavy breathing, as if he strove with himself for mastery. Nor did I speak again, eager as I now was to arrange some plan for the future; for this man was certainly in no condition to counsel with.

I know not how long I may have rested there in silence, seeking vainly in my own mind for some opening of escape, or means whereby I might communicate with Mademoiselle. Would the strange woman forget me now, or would she venture upon a return with her message? If not, I must grope forward without her, hampered as I should be by this unnerved and helpless Frenchman. Outside, the noise had almost wholly ceased, — at least, close to where we were, — and I could perceive that a slight tinge of returning day was already in the air, faintly revealing the interior of the lodge.

As I sat thus, drifting through inaction into a more despairing mood, the rear covering of the tepee moved almost imperceptibly, and I turned hastily to seek the cause, my heart in my throat lest it prove an enemy, perhaps some stealthy savage still seeking the life of De Croix. It was far from being light as yet, but there was sufficient to show me the faint outline of a woman's figure. The Frenchman had seemingly heard nothing; and I rose quickly and faced her eagerly.

"You have found her?" I questioned anxiously. "I beg you tell me that she yet lives!"

"Hush! you speak too loud," was the low reply. "The one you seek is, I think, confined within the

lodge of Little Sauk, and thus far remains unharmed.
I have not been able to reach her, but she has been
described to me as young, with dark hair and eyes,
and as having been dragged from a horse near the
rear of the column. Think you she is the one you
seek?"

"I do indeed!" I cried, in a rapture of relief.
"Where is this lodge in which they hold her?"

She hesitated to answer, as if she somewhat
doubted my discretion.

"It is the third from the fire, in the row west
of this," she said at last. "But it is already daylight,
and you must lie hidden amid these skins until another
night, when I will strive to aid you. You will be safe
here, if you only keep hidden; and I have brought
with me food for you both."

I had quite forgotten De Croix, in my eagerness to
learn news of Mademoiselle; but now I realized he
had risen to his knees, and was gazing at our visitor
through the dim shadows as if half fearful even yet
that she was but a spectre. In that gray dawn his face
was ghastly in its whiteness, — the dark lines under
his eyes, his matted hair, and the traces of blood upon
his cheek, yielding a haggardness almost appalling.

"Marie!" he sobbed, catching his breath between
the words as if they choked him, "Marie, in God's
name, speak one word to me!"

I saw the girl start, looking around at him with

eyes widely opened, yet with an expression in them I could not fathom; it was neither hatred nor love, though it might easily have been sorrow.

"Marie," he urged, rendered despairing by her silence, "I have done you wrong, great wrong; but I thought you dead. They told me so, — they told me it was your body they buried. Will you not speak a word of mercy now?"

Dim as the light was, I saw her eyes were moist as she gazed down upon him; but there was no faltering in her voice.

"You were right, Monsieur le Marquis," she said slowly, "Marie Faneuf is dead. It is only Sister Celeste who has aided in the preservation of your life in the name of the Master. Make your acknowledgment to the Mother of Christ, not to me, for such mercy."

I knew not when she passed out, or how; but we were alone once more, and De Croix was lying with his face buried in the short grass.

CHAPTER XXXI

A SEARCH, AND ITS REWARD

SLEPT at last, soundly, for several hours, lying well hidden behind the skins at the back of the lodge. There seemed nothing else to do; for poor De Croix had no thought other than that of the woman who had just left us, and I was exhausted by hours of excitement and toil. He was asleep when I awoke, lying just as I had left him, his face still buried in the short trodden grass that carpeted the floor.

It was so quiet without that I listened in vain for a sound to indicate the presence of Indians. Silence so profound was in strange contrast with the hideous uproar of the preceding night, and curiosity led me finally to project my head from beneath the lodge covering and gain a cautious glimpse of the camp without. The yellow sunshine of the calm summer afternoon rested hot and glaring on the draped skins of the tepees, and on the brown prairie-grass, trampled by hundreds of passing feet. I could perceive a few squaws working lazily in the shade of the trees near the bank of the river; but no other moving figures were visible. Several recumbent forms were within my sight, their faces toward the sun, evidently sleeping off the heavy potations of the night. Otherwise the great encampment appeared completely deserted; there were no spirals of smoke rising above the lodge-poles, no gossiping groups anywhere about.

It was plain enough to me. Those of the warriors capable of further action were elsewhere engaged upon some fresh foray, while the majority, overcome by drinking, were asleep within their darkened lodges. Surely, daylight though it was, no safer moment could be expected in which to establish communication with Toinette. With night the camp would be again astir; and even if I succeeded in reaching her at some later hour it would leave small margin of darkness for our escape. Every moment of delay now added to our grave peril, and there was much planning to be done after we met. Possibly I should have waited, as I had been told to do; but it was ever in my blood to act rather than reason, and I am sure that in this case no cause remains for regret.

I must confess that my heart beat somewhat faster, as I crept slowly forth and peered cautiously around the bulging side of the big lodge I had just left, to assure myself no savages were stirring. It was not that I greatly feared the venture, nor that a sense of danger excited my nerves; but rather the one thought in my mind was that now my way lay toward Mademoiselle. How would she greet me? Should I learn my fate from her tell-tale eyes, or by a sudden gleam of surprise in her lovely face? These were the reflections that inspired me, for a new hope had been born within me through the forced confession of De Croix.

There was little danger of exposure while I advanced through the shelter of the lodges, for I was always under partial cover. But I waited and watched long before daring to pass across the wide open space in the centre of which the fire had been kindled. The torture-post yet stood there, black and charred, while the ground beneath was littered with dead ashes. The bodies of three white men, two of them naked and marked by fire, lay close at hand, just as they had been carelessly flung aside to make room for new victims; yet I dared not stop to learn who they might have been in life. The sight of their foul disfigurement only rendered me the more eager to reach the living with a message of hope.

I moved like a snake, dragging my body an inch at a time by firmly grasping with extended hands the tough grass-roots, and writhing forward as noiselessly as if I were stalking some prey. There were times when I advanced so slowly it would have puzzled a watcher to determine whether mine was not also the body of the dead. At length, even at that snail's rate of progress, I gained the protection of the tepees upon the other side of the camp, and skulked in among them. The lodge just before me, blackened by paint and weather, must be the one I sought. I rested close within its shadow, striving to assure myself there was no possibility of mistake. As my eyes lifted, I could trace in dim outline the totem of the chief faintly sketched on the taut skin: it was the same I had noted on the brawny breast of Little Sauk.

Never did I move with greater woodland skill, for I felt that all depended upon my remaining undiscovered; a single false move now would defeat all hope. Who might be within, concealed by that black covering, was a mystery to be solved only by extremest caution.

Inch by inch I worked the skin covering of the tepee entrance up from the ground, screwing my eye to the aperture in an effort to penetrate the shrouded interior. But the glare of the sun was so reflected into my eyeballs, that it left me almost blind in the semi-gloom beneath that dark roof, and I could distinguish no object with certainty. Surely, nothing moved within; and I drew myself slowly forward, until half my body lay extended upon the beaten dirt-floor. It was then that I caught a glimpse of a face peering at me from out the shadows,—the face of Toinette; and, alas for my eager hopes of surprising her heart and solving its secrets! the witch was actually laughing in silence at my predicament. The sight made my face flush in sudden indignation; but before I could find speech, she had hastily accosted me.

"Good faith, Master Wayland! but I greet you gladly!" she said, and her soft hand was warm upon mine; "yet it truly caused me to smile to observe the marvellous caution with which you came hither."

"It must have been indeed amusing," I answered, losing all my vain aspirations in a moment under her raillery; "though it is not every prisoner in an Indian camp who could find like cause for merriment."

Her eyes grew sober enough as they rested inquiringly on my face, for all that they still held an irritatingly roguish twinkle in their depths.

"It was the expression upon your face which so amused me," she explained. "I am not indifferent to all that your coming means, nor to the horrors this camp has witnessed. More than that, you appear to me like one risen from the dead. I have truly mourned for you, John Wayland. I lost all power, all desire for resistance, when I saw you stricken from your horse, and often since my eyes have been moist in thoughts of you. No doubt 't was but the sudden reaction from seeing you again alive that made me so forgetful of these dread surroundings as to smile. I beg you to forgive me; it was not heartlessness, but merely the way of a thoughtless girl, Monsieur."

It had been impossible for me to resist her cajolery from the beginning; and now I read in her eyes the truth of all she spoke.

"There is naught for you to forgive, Mademoiselle," I answered, drawing myself wholly within the tepee and resting on my knees. "But are you quite alone here, and without guards?"

"For the present, yes. Little Sauk has been gone from the camp for some hours. They watch me with some care at night, — yet of what use can their guarding be? If I should get without the lodge, escape would be hopeless for a girl like me. But now tell me about yourself. Are you also prisoner to the Indians? Surely I saw you struck down in that mad mêlée. 'T was then I lost heart, and gave up every hope of rescue."

"No, I am not a prisoner, Mademoiselle. I fell, stunned by a blow dealt me from behind, but was saved from capture by the falling of my horse across my body. I am here now of my own will, and for no other purpose than to save you."

"To save me! Oh, Monsieur! it would make me blush really to think I ranked so high in your esteem. Was it not rather that other girl you came to seek, — the one you sought so far through the wilderness,

only to find hidden in this encampment of savages?
Tell me, Monsieur, was she by any chance of fate the
heroine who last night plucked Captain de Croix from
the flames of torture?"

"You know, then, of his danger and deliverance?"
I said, not feeling eager to answer her query. "'T was
a most brave and womanly act."

"A strange exercise of power, indeed, Monsieur,"
and she looked directly into my eyes; "and the savages tell me she claimed to have knowledge of him."

Surely I had a right to relate the whole story of
De Croix's confession; yet somehow I did not deem
it the manly thing to do. Rather, I would let her learn
the truth in God's own time, and from other lips than
mine. Perchance she would respect me more in the
end for keeping silence now. But in this decision I
failed to consider that hasty words of explanation
might naturally lead her to believe the existing friendship mine instead of his.

"We met her across the river in the darkness last
night," I answered. "At my request, she acted as my
guide into the Indian camp."

The expression in her eyes puzzled me; nor could
I interpret the sudden flush that lent color to her
cheeks.

"You are frank, Monsieur," she said quietly, "and
doubtless 't is better so. But the strange situation of
this young woman has much of romance about it, and

interests me greatly. How chances she to be here?
Surely she cannot be of Indian blood?"

"She holds connection with some sisterhood of
the Church, as I understand, and has lived for some
time amid the Pottawattomies, seeking to win the
heathen to Christ."

"A Catholic?" she asked, her eyes brightening
with deeper interest.

"Such is my understanding, though in truth she
never said as much to me. Indeed, we spoke little,
Mademoiselle, for our path was in the midst of peril,
even before the capture of poor De Croix upset all our
plans."

"Doubtless," she answered with a slight trace of
sarcasm in the soft voice. "But Captain de Croix, —
he was not seriously injured, I trust? Where have the
savages confined him? And know you what they in-
tend as to his future?"

"He will forever bear some scars, I fear," I answered, wondering dully at the calmness of her inquiry. "I have just left him sleeping quietly in the
council tent. Know you anything of what fate has
befallen other of our friends of the garrison?"

Her eyes grew sad. "Only what little I have
learned through the taunting of my own captor," she
answered, her voice trembling. "Captain Wells is
dead, together with Ensign Ronan and Surgeon Van
Voorhees. Both Captain Heald and his wife were

sorely wounded, and they, with Lieutenant Helm, are prisoners somewhere in the camp; but the Lieutenant's wife is safe with the Silver-man's family across the river. The Indians hold these in hope of ransom, and wreak their vengeance upon the common soldiers who were so unfortunate as to fall into their hands alive. Yet few, I think, survived the massacre."

"You have doubtless guessed aright. I noted with what fearful spirit of revenge the savages dealt with some of their captives, while sparing others. Surely you, for instance, have met with but little hardship thus far at the hands of Little Sauk?"

She glanced up at me, with a touch of the old coquettishness in her dark eyes and a quick toss of her head, while one white hand smoothed her soft hair.

"Think you then, Monsieur, I do not look so ill?"

In spite of every effort at control, my heart swept into my eyes; she must have read the swift message, for her own drooped instantly, with a quick flutter of long lashes against her cheeks.

"I have already told you how greatly I admire you," I faltered, "and you make no less fair a picture now."

"Then I shall not tempt you to add to your compliment," she hastily responded, rising to her feet, "for I like loyalty in a man better than mere gallantry of speech. You ask me about Little Sauk. He holds me for ransom, — although Heaven knows 't will prove but waste of time, for I am aware of no one in all the East who would invest so much as a dollar to redeem me from Indian hands. Yet such is his purpose, as told to me this morning."

"Perchance, then," I urged, doubtfully, "you may prefer remaining quietly here rather than risk the peril of trying to escape?"

She looked at me keenly, as if in wonder at my words; and I could see that her eyes were moistening with the sudden rush of feeling.

"You are either dull of comprehension, John Wayland," she said, a bit pertly, "or else you understand me less than any man I ever knew. If I seem brave and light of heart amidst all this horror, 't is merely that I may not utterly break down, and become an object of contempt. I feel, Monsieur, I am not devoid of heart nor of the finer qualities of womanhood. Prefer to remain here? Holy Mother of Christ! It would be my choice to die out yonder on the prairie, rather than stay here in these Indian lodges. There is no peril I would not face joyfully, in an effort to escape from this place of torture and barbarity. I confess that an hour ago I cared not greatly what my end might be; I had lost heart and hope. But now your coming, as of one risen from the dead, has brought back my courage."

"You will go, then, whenever and wherever I say?"

She stepped forward with her old frank confidence, resting both hands in mine, her eyes upon my face.

"Out yonder in the night, and amid the sand, John Wayland," she said earnestly, "I remember saying I would travel with you whithersoever you wished. I know you far better now than I did then, and I hesitate not at taking upon myself the same vow."

What power then sealed my lips, I know not. Doubtless there is a fate in such matters, yet 't is strange the light of invitation in her eyes did not draw me to lay bare my heart. In naught else had I a drop of coward blood within my veins; while here I hesitated, fearful lest her pleading face might change to sudden roguishness, and she laugh lightly at the love that held my heart in thrall. Truly, the witch had puzzled me so sorely with her caprices, her quick change of mood, her odd mixture of girlish frankness and womanly reserve, that I knew not which might prove the real Toinette, — the one to trust, or the one to doubt. So I stood there, clasping her soft hands in mine, my heart throbbing, yet my tongue hesitating to perform its office. But at last the halting words came in a sudden, irrepressible rush.

"Toinette!" I cried, "Toinette! I could forget all else, — our danger here, the horrors of the night just passed, the many dead out yonder, — all else but you."

She gave a sudden startled cry, her affrighted eyes gazing across my shoulder. I wheeled, with quick intuition of danger; and there, just within the entrance of the tepee, the flap of which he had let fall behind him, in grave silence stood an Indian.

CHAPTER XXXII

THE PLEDGE OF A WYANDOT

A SINGLE glance told me who our unwelcome visitor must be. That giant body, surmounted by the huge broad face, could belong to none other than the Wyandot, Sau-ga-nash, — him who had spoken for the warriors of his tribe before the torture-stake. He stood erect and rigid, his stern, questioning eyes upon us, his lips a thin line of repression. With a quick movement, I thrust the girl behind me, and faced him, motionless, but with every muscle strained for action. The Indian spoke slowly, and used perfect English.

"Ugh!" he said. "Who are you? A prisoner? Surely you cannot be that same Frenchman we helped entertain last night?"

"I am not the Frenchman," I answered deliberately, vainly hoping his watchful eyes might wander about the lodge long enough to yield me chance for a spring at his throat, " though I was one of his party. I only came here to bring comfort to this poor girl."

" No doubt she needs it," he replied drily, " and your way is surely a good one. Yet I doubt if Little Sauk would approve it, and as his friend, I must speak for him in the matter. Do you say you are also a prisoner? To what chief? "

" To none," I answered shortly, resolved now to venture all in a trial of strength. He read this decision in my eyes, and stepped back warily. At the same instant Toinette flung her arms restrainingly about my neck.

" Don't, John! " she urged, using my name thus for the first time; " the savage has a gun hidden beneath his robe! "

I saw the weapon as she spoke, and saw too the angry glint in the fellow's eye as he thrust the muzzle menacingly forward. As we stood thus, glaring at each other, a sudden remembrance made me pause. " Sau-ga-nash "? — surely it was neither more nor less than a Wyandot expression signifying " Englishman." That broad face was not wholly Indian; could this be the half-breed chief of whom I had so often heard? 'T was worth the chance to learn.

" You are Sau-ga-nash? " I asked, slowly, Toinette still clinging to me, her face over her shoulder to front the silent savage. " A chief of the Wyandots? "

He moved his head slightly, with a mutter of acquiescence, his eyes expressing wonder at the question.

"The same whom the Americans name Billy Caldwell?"

"'T is the word used by the whites."

I drew a quick breath of relief, which caused Mademoiselle to release her grasp a little, as her anxious eyes sought my face for explanation.

"Recall you a day twelve years ago on the River Raisin?" I asked clearly, feeling confident now that my words were no longer idle. "An Indian was captured in his canoe by a party of frontiersmen who were out to revenge a bloody raid along the valley of the Maumee. That Indian was a Wyandot and a chief. He was bound to a tree beside the river bank and condemned to torture; when the leader of the rangers, a man with a gray beard, stood before him rifle in hand, and swore to kill the first white man who put flint and steel to the wood. Recall you this, Sau-ga-nash?"

The stolid face of the listening savage changed, the expression of revengeful hostility merging into one of undisguised amazement.

"That which you picture has not left my memory," he answered gravely.

"Nor the pledge you gave to that white captain when he brought you safely to Detroit?" I queried, eagerly.

" Nor the pledge. But what has all this to do here? "

" Only, Sau-ga-nash, that I am Major David Wayland's son."

The Indian sprang forward, his eyes burning fiercely; and thinking his movement to be hostile, I thrust the girl aside that I might be free to repel his attack. But he did not touch me, merely peering eagerly into my face with a keen questioning look that read my every feature.

" You have the nose and forehead," he reflected aloud; " yes, and the eyes. Before the Great Spirit, I will redeem my pledge; a chief of the Wyandots cannot lie."

He paused, and I could mark the varied emotions that swayed him, so deeply was he moved by this strange discovery. Unconsciously my hand clasped Mademoiselle's, for now I felt that our fate hung on his decision.

" 'T is a hard task, Master Wayland," he admitted at length, almost wearily, " but for your father's sake it shall be done. I see only one way for it, and that by water. Know you anything about the management of boats? "

" Only as I have paddled upon the Maumee," I answered, doubtfully, " although I handled a small sail when a mere boy in the far East."

" 'T will suffice if the fair weather hold, as is likely

at this season. At least it may be risked. The land trails are crowded by Indians from far-off tribes, hastening hither in hope of fight and spoils. More than a hundred came in to-day, painted for war, and angry because too late. You could not escape encountering such parties, were you to flee by trail eastward; nor would they show mercy to any white. The Silver-man has returned to his home north of the river; but 't is all that we who are friendly to him can do to keep these warriors from attacking even there. 'T is the Indians from far away that make the trouble; and these grow more numerous and powerful each day. We keep a guard at the house to save the Silver-man and his family; and were more whites to seek refuge there, we should lose all control. There is still safety at the mouth of the Saint Joseph River, and 't is there you must go. The venture must be made to-night, and by water. Is it known to any Indian that you are alive and within this camp?"

"To none."

"That is well; we can work best alone. Now listen. At midnight, Master Wayland, a boat, prepared for the trip, will await you, hidden under the ruins of the Agency building. The river flows under the flooring deep enough for the purpose, and I will place the boat there with my own hand. Beyond that, all must rest upon your own skill and good fortune. You will wait here," and he glanced about anxiously for some means of concealment, " lying behind those robes yonder, until the hour."

" Here? " I questioned, thinking instantly of my duty to De Croix. " But I would first have speech with the Frenchman. He is my friend, Sau-ga-nash. Besides, I have left my rifle in the council lodge."

The face of the savage darkened, and his eyes gleamed ominously as they roamed questioningly from my face to Toinette's.

" I said you were to stay hidden here," he answered shortly, his tone showing anger, and his hand pointing at the robes. " Many of the sleeping Pottawattomies are again astir without, and you could not hope to gain the council lodge undiscovered. What care I for this Frenchman, that I should risk my life to save him? I pledge myself only to Major Wayland's son; and even if I aid you, it is on condition that you go alone."

" Alone, say you? " and I rested my hand on Mademoiselle's shoulder. " I would die here, Sau-ga-nash, and by torture, before I would consent to go one step without this girl."

The half-breed scowled at me, drawing his robe about him in haughty indifference.

" Then be it so," he said mockingly. " 'T is your own choice. I have offered redemption of my pledge."

I started to utter some harsh words in answer; but before I could speak, Toinette pressed her soft palm upon my lips in protest.

"Refuse him not," she murmured hastily. "'T is the only chance; for my sake, do not anger him."

What plan her quick wit may have engendered, I did not know; but I yielded to the entreaty in her pleading eyes, and sullenly muttered the first conscious lie of my life.

"I accept your terms, Sau-ga-nash, harsh as they are."

He looked from one to the other of us, his face dark with distrust and doubt.

"You are not mine to dispose of," he said sternly to the trembling girl, who visibly shrank from his approach, and clung once more to me. "You are prisoner to Little Sauk; nor will I release one thus held by the Pottawattomies. They and the Wyandots are brothers. But I trust you, and not the word of this white man. Pledge me not to go with him, and I will believe you."

She glanced first at me, then back into the swarthy, merciless face. Her cheeks were white and her lips trembled, yet her eyes remained clear and calm.

"I give you my word, Sau-ga-nash," she said quietly. "While I am held as prisoner by Little Sauk, I will not go away with John Wayland."

Little as I believed these words to be true at the time, the sound of them so dulled me with apprehension that I could only stare at her in speechless amazement. It seemed to me then as if the power of reason had deserted me, as if my brain had been so burdened as to refuse its office. I recall that Toinette almost compelled me to lie down against the farther side of the lodge, placing a pile of skins in front of me and assuming a position herself where she could occasionally reach across the barrier and touch me with her soft hand. No doubt she realized the struggle in my mind, for she spoke little after the departure of the half-breed, as if anxious to permit me to figure out the future for myself. Little by little I faced it, and came to an irrevocable decision. It was to be Toinette or nothing. While it might be true that she was in no immediate danger, and possibly could be safely ransomed if I once escaped to civilization, yet the risk of such venture and delay was too great; nor would my love abide so vast a sacrifice on her part. I thought to say this to her; but there was a look of firm decision in her sweet face, as her dark eyes met mine, that somehow held me silent. I felt that in her own heart she must already know what action I would choose, and the final moment would prove sufficient test for her evident determination. Reassured here, my thoughts turned to De Croix; but that was useless. I could send no message to him; he was no longer in especial peril, and perhaps would not willingly desert his newly found wife even to escape the savages. Nay, — it was to be Toinette and I, now and forever.

THE PLEDGE OF A WYANDOT

I do not clearly remember at this day what it was we spoke about in the brief whispering that passed between us while we waited there. Neither of us felt like voicing our real thoughts, and so we but dissembled, making commonplaces fill the gaps between our silences. The night found us undisturbed, and it shut down so darkly within the narrow confines of the lodge that I lost all trace of her presence, but for an occasional movement or the sound of her low voice. Without, the rapidly increasing noise indicated a return of many savages to the camp, until at last a fire was kindled in the open space, its red flame sending some slight illumination where we were, but not enough to reveal the interior of the lodge. An Indian brought the girl some food, entering and leaving without uttering a sound; and we two ate together, striving to speak lightly in order to make the coarse meal more palatable.

Suddenly I became aware of a faint scratching upon the skin of the lodge, at my back. At first I supposed it to be some wild animal, or possibly a stray dog; but the regularity of it showed a purpose of some kind. Could it be De Croix? Or was it the half-breed with some secret message he dared not deliver openly? I lifted the lodge covering slightly, and placed my lips to the aperture.

"Is some one there?" I whispered cautiously "Who is it?"

"I am Sister Celeste," came the immediate low reply. "Are you the white man I guided?"

"Ay," I answered, rejoicing at this rare good fortune, "and I beg you to listen to what I say. There will be a boat awaiting us beneath the old Agency building at midnight. You must be there with De Croix."

"De Croix?"

"Yes; I know not if that be his name to you, but I mean the Frenchman whose life you saved. Will you take him thither at midnight, together with the rifle I left in the council lodge?"

For a moment she did not answer. Doubtless it was a bitter struggle for her thus to agree even to meet the man again. At last she made reply, although I could plainly mark the faltering of her voice.

"The man of whom you speak shall be there," she said, "unless some accident make it impossible."

As I drew back my head, and sat upright, Mademoiselle spoke questioningly.

"With whom were you conversing just now, Monsieur?"

"The young woman of whom we have spoken so often," I answered thoughtlessly. "She has pledged herself to bring De Croix to the meeting-place."

"Indeed!" she exclaimed, with accent so peculiar I knew not how to interpret it. "It almost makes me desire to form one of your party."

346

CHAPTER XXXIII

AN INTERVENTION OF FATE

ORM one of our party?" I echoed, believing I must have misunderstood her words. "Surely, Mademoiselle, you cannot mean that you take your promise to the half-breed so seriously as voluntarily to remain in captivity?"

"Yes, but I do, Monsieur!" and the tone in which she said it was firm with decision. "The Indian asked my pledge in all solemnity, and has gone away trusting to it. My conscience could never again be clear did I prove false in such a matter. You also made a pledge, even before mine was given; was it not your purpose to abide by it?"

"No," I answered, a bit shortly. "I merely agreed to his proposition at your expressed desire that I should, and because I believed you had framed some plan of escape. Have you such small respect for me, Mademoiselle, as to think I could consent to leave you here alone and at the mercy of these red fiends? Have I risked my life in coming here for no other end than this?"

I felt her reach her arm across the pile of skins lying between us, and grasp my hand within her own.

"But, dear friend, you must!" she said, pleadingly, her softly modulated voice dwelling upon the words as if they came hard. "Truly you must, John Wayland, and for my sake as well as your own. I am comparatively safe here, — safe at least from actual physical harm, so long as the savages dream that the sparing of my life will yield them profit. You have no right to remain in such peril as surrounds you here, when by so doing you benefit no one. You have father and mother awaiting in prayer your safe return to them yonder on the Maumee; while I, — I have no one even to ask how sad my fate may be. Think you that because I am a girl I must therefore be all selfishness? or that I would ever permit you thus to sacrifice yourself unnecessarily for me? No, no, Monsieur! I will remain prisoner to Little Sauk, for my sacred word has been pledged; and you must go, because there are others to whom your life is of value. Nor need you go empty-handed, for the one you have sought so far and long seems now ready enough to travel eastward with you."

Scarcely had her voice ceased, leaving me struggling to find fit words to change her mad decision, when a rough hand flung back the entrance flap, and the naked body of an Indian, framed for a single instant against the light, lurched heavily through the opening. Even that brief glimpse told me the man had been drinking to excess; while for the moment, as I huddled down closer behind my robes, I was unable to make out his identity.

"Where white woman?" he ejaculated gruffly, as he paused, blinded by the darkness. "Why she not come help me?"

His quick ear evidently caught the slight rustle of the girl's skirt as she rose hastily to her feet, for with a muttered Indian oath the savage lurched forward. I could scarcely make out the dimmest shadow of them in the dense gloom, yet I seemed to know that he had grasped her roughly, though not the slightest sound of fear or pain came from her lips.

"Ugh! better come!" he muttered, a veiled savage threat growling in his tone. "You my squaw; cook in my lodge; get meal now."

"But where? and how?" she asked, her voice trembling perceptibly, yet striving to placate him by a seeming willingness to obey. "I have nothing here to cook, nor have I fire."

"Indian squaw no talk back!" he retorted angrily. "This way I show white squaw to mind chief!"

I heard plainly the brutal blow he struck her, though even as she reeled back she managed to stifle

349

the scream upon her lips, so that it was barely audible. With one bound I was over the barrier of robes and clutching with tingling fingers for the brute. I touched his feathered head-dress at last, and he must have supposed me his helpless victim, for with a grunt of satisfaction he struck once again, the blow meeting my shoulder, where he judged in the dark her face would be.

"White squaw mind now — "

I had him gripped by the throat before he ended, and we went down together for a death-struggle in the darkness, from which each realized in an instant both could never rise again. My furious grip sobered him, and he made desperate efforts to break free, struggling vainly to utter some cry for rescue. Once I felt him groping at his waist for a knife; but I got first clasp upon its hilt, though I twisted helplessly for some minutes before I could loosen his hold at my wrist so as to strike him with the blade. His teeth closed upon my hand, biting deep into the flesh like a wild-cat, and the sharp sting of it yielded me the desperate strength I needed to wrench my hand free, and with one quick blow the knife I clutched cut deep into his side, so that I could feel the hot blood spurt forth over my hand. I held him in a death grip, for I knew a single cry meant ruin to all our plans, until the last breath sped, and I knew I lay prostrate above a corpse. It had been so swift and fierce a contest that

I staggered half-dazed to my feet, peering about me as if expecting another attack. I was steadied somewhat by the sound of a low sob from the darkness.

"'T is well over with, Toinette," I murmured hastily, my voice trembling from the strain that still shook me.

"Oh, John! John Wayland! And you are truly unhurt of the struggle?" It was scarcely her voice speaking, so agitated was it. "Have you killed him?"

"Yes," I answered, finding my way cautiously toward her, and speaking in whispers. "I had no other choice. It was either his life or yours and mine. Knew you the savage?"

"It was Little Sauk," she replied, clinging to me, and growing somewhat calmer from my presence. "Oh, what can we do now?"

"There remains but one thing, and that is to accept the chance that Providence has given us. There remains no longer a shadow of excuse for your staying here, even by your own reasoning. You are no longer prisoner to Little Sauk. Your pledge has been dissolved by Fate, and it must be God's will that you go forth with me. What say you, Mademoiselle?" And I crushed her hands in mine.

I could feel her slight form tremble as I waited her reply, and believed she peered across my shoulder through the darkness, imagining she saw the dead Indian's form lying there.

351

"Do you truly wish it?" she questioned at last, as though warring with herself. "Think you she would greatly care?"

'T is a strangely perverse thing, the human mind. As there dimly dawned upon me a conception of her meaning, — a knowledge that this seemingly heart-free girl cared enough for me to exhibit such jealousy of another, — I would not undeceive her by a word of explanation.

"I certainly do wish it," was my grave answer, "nor does it greatly matter what the desire of any other may be. This is not an invitation to a ball, Mademoiselle. I beg you answer me; will you go?"

She looked toward me, wondering at my words.

"Yes," she said simply. "Has the time come?"

"I have no certain means of knowing; but it cannot be far from the hour, and we shall be much safer without."

I took the Indian's knife with me, wiping the long blade upon the pile of skins, and placing it convenient to my hand within the bosom of my hunting-shirt. It was dark enough back of the lodge away from the glare of the fires, and we rested there well within the shadow, for some time, while I scanned the surroundings and planned as best I might our future movements.

"Was it from dread of venturing once more upon the water that you held back so long?" I asked

her, seeking rudely to delve into the secret of her
reserve.

"Have you ever found me of cowardly heart,
Monsieur?" she questioned in return, parrying with
quick skill, "that you should think any bodily terror
could hold me back? If I had reasons other than those
already given, they were worthy ones."

"You are not afraid of the perils before us?"

"No," she answered; "my heart beats fast, but
't is not from fear."

Only a few scattered lodges had been raised to the
eastward of where we were, nor did these show any
signs of life. We crept forward with painful slowness,
partially hiding our movements by following a shallow,
curving gully, until we had gained the extreme limits
of the encampment, where we crawled out into the
gloom of the surrounding prairie. Not until then did
either of us venture to stand erect, or advance with
any degree of freedom.

Directly ahead of us there was nothing by which
I could safely guide our course. The flat sameness of
the plain offered no landmarks, while the night sky
was so thickly overcast as to leave no stars visible.
Nor was there light of any kind, save that of the fires
in the camp we had just left. I hesitated to risk the
open prairie thus unaided, lest we should wander
astray and lose much valuable time; so, although it
measurably increased our peril of encountering parties

of savages, I turned sharply northward, keeping the bright Indian fires upon our left, and groping forward through the gloom toward where I knew the main branch of the river must lie. It was neither the time nor place for speech. I held her hand closely while we moved onward silently, carefully guarding each step lest by mischance it should bring betrayal. Once, after we had reached the river and were moving eastward again, a party of Indians passed us, coming so silently out of the black void, in their soft moccasins, that I had barely time to hold her motionless before they were fairly upon us. I counted nine of them, moving rapidly in single file, like so many black ghosts. We waited with wildly throbbing hearts, listening for fear others might follow in their trail.

We were almost beside the walls of the factory building before either of us was aware of its proximity. Even then, as I lay prone on the earth and studied its dim outlines, they possessed nothing of familiarity, for the high-pitched roof had fallen in and carried with it the greater portion of the upper walls, leaving a mere shell, shapeless and empty. I rested there, gazing at it, and wondering how best we might proceed to find our way beneath where the boat was to be moored, when I felt Mademoiselle's fingers press my arm warningly. Scarcely a yard away, on a ridge of higher ground, two dim figures came to a sudden pause.

" I perceive naught of the presence of your friends

as yet, Monsieur," spoke a soft voice, " but I will remain until certain of the outcome."

"Then your decision is unchanged?" asked the
other, in deeper accent, full of earnest pleading. "All
is to be over between us from this hour? And you
deliberately choose to devote your life to the redemption of these savages?"

"We have discussed all this at length, Monsieur
le Marquis, as we came along, and, as you fully know,
my choice is made beyond recall. I am here to serve
you to-night, because it seems to be a duty given unto
me by some strange Providence; and I have relied
upon your courtesy to make it as little unpleasant as
possible. I pray you, beseech me no more. The girl
I once was lives no longer; the woman I now am has
been given a special mission by God, too sacred to be
cast aside for aught that earth has to offer her of happiness. We part in kindness, Monsieur, — in friendship even; but that which was once between us may
never be again."

There was no answer; even the reckless audacity
of a courtier was silenced by that calm final dismissal.
It was Mademoiselle who spoke in swift whisper, her
lips at my ear.

"Speak! who is she?"

"The woman of whom you have heard so often,
—the missionary in the Indian camp."

"Yes, I know," impatiently; "but I mean her
name?"

"She calls herself Sister Celeste; I have indeed heard mention of another, but it abides not in my memory."

"You deceive me, Monsieur; yet I know, and will speak with her," was the quick decision. "Mother of God! 't is a voice too dear ever to be forgotten."

She was beside them with a step, seeming no doubt a most fair vision to be born so instantly of the night-shadows.

"Marie Faneuf!" she exclaimed, eagerly. "I know not by what strange fortune I meet you here, but surely you will not refuse greeting to an old friend?"

The girl drew hastily back a step, as if her first thought was flight; but ere such end could be accomplished, Mademoiselle had clasped her arm impetuously.

"Marie!" she pleaded, "can it be possible you would flee from me?"

"Nay," returned the other, her voice trembling painfully, as she struggled to restrain herself. "It is not that. Dear, dear friend! I knew you were among the few saved from Dearborn. The American hunter told me, and ever since have I tried to avoid you in the camp. 'T was not for lack of the old love, yet I feared to meet you. Much has occurred of late to make the keeping of my vow most difficult. I have been weak, and grievously tempted; and I felt scarce strong enough, even though protected by prayers, to withstand also my deep love for you."

Their voices insensibly merged into French, each speaking so rapidly and low that I could get little meaning of it. Then I noted De Croix, half lying upon the ground, his head hidden within his hands. With sudden remembrance of the work before us, I touched his shoulder.

"Come below, Monsieur, and help me search for the boat," I said, kindly, for I was truly touched by his grief. "It will help clear your mind to have some labor to accomplish."

"I dare not, Wayland!" he answered hoarsely, and the face he uplifted toward me was strangely white and drawn. "I must stay with her; I dare not leave her again alone, lest she escape me once more. She is mine, truly mine by every law of the Church, — my wife, I tell you, and I would die here in the wilderness rather than permit her longer to doom herself to such a fate as this."

His words and manner were so wild they startled me. Surely, in his present frame of mind he would prove useless on such a mission as that before us.

"Then remain here, Monsieur!" I said, "and do your best to win her consent to accompany us. No doubt Mademoiselle will aid you all that is in her power."

357

CHAPTER XXXIV

A STUMBLE IN THE DARK

LOOMY as the hole was, there was no help for it. I could perceive nothing below, not even my hand when held within a foot of my eyes; nor had I the slightest previous knowledge of the place to guide me, even had not the fire ruins above effectually blocked every passage-way with fallen débris. Listening however intently, my ears could distinguish only the faint lapping of the river as it crept about the log piling on which the house had been built; but beyond this dim guidance, I had to feel my way forward with extended hands and groping feet. Swinging to my back the rifle that De Croix had brought, and casting an inquiring glance backward at the little group huddled upon the bank, almost invisible even at that short distance, I grasped the piling nearest me and slid down into the unknown darkness.

My feet found solid earth, although as I reached

out toward the left my moccasin came in contact with
water, which told me at once that only a narrow path
divided the steep bank of the excavation from the en-
croaching river. The floor above was originally low,
so that I could easily touch the heavy supporting
beams; and I had felt my way scarcely a yard before
coming in contact with a serious obstruction, where
the weakened floor had sagged so as almost to close
the narrow passage. This caused me to wade farther
out into the water, testing each step carefully as I
followed the sharp curving of the shore-line. I had no
fear of meeting any living enemy within that silent
cave, my sole doubt being as to whether the half-breed
chief had fulfilled his promise and brought the boat, my
gravest anxiety to discover it early and get my party
safely away before the Indian encampment learned
the truth.

I must have reached the apex of the little cove,
moving so cautiously that not a ripple of the water
revealed my progress, and feeling for each inch of way
like a blind man along city streets, when my knee suddenly struck some obstacle, and seeking to learn what
it might be, I muttered a silent prayer of thanksgiving
as I touched the unmistakable sides of a boat. It was
a lumping, awkward craft, rudely fashioned, yet of a
seeming length of keel and breadth of beam that set
my heart beating with new joy, as I wondered if it
was not the same craft in which the Kinzie family

put forth upon the lake the morning of the massacre.
This seemed very likely, for there could hardly be two
such boats at hand, where the Indian water-craft were
slender, fragile canoes, poorly fitted for serious battle
with lake waves. Doubtless this was the only vessel
Sau-ga-nash could find suitable for the venture, or he
would never have chosen it for the use of a single man,
as it was of a size to require the services of several
paddles. Yet the thought meant much; for this very
lack of water-craft was likely to render pursuit by the
baffled savages impossible, if only once we got fairly
away from the shore.

With these reflections driving swiftly through my
brain, I ran one hand hastily along the thwarts of the
boat, seeking to discover if paddles had been provided,
or even a sail of any kind. I touched a coil of rope, a
rude oar-blade so broad as to seem unwieldy, a tightly
rolled cloth, — and then my groping fingers rested on
the oddest-feeling thing that ever a startled man
touched in the dark. It was God's mercy I did not
cry out from the sudden nervous fit that seized me.
The thing I touched had a round, smooth, creepy feeling of flesh about it, so that I believed I fingered a
corpse; until it began to turn slowly under my hand
like a huge ball, the loose skin of it twitching yet
revealing no human features to my touch. Saint An-
drew! but it frightened me! I knew not what species
of strange animal it might prove to be, nor whence its

grip or sting might come. Yet the odd feeling of it was strangely fascinating, — I could not let it go; the damp flesh-like skin seemed to cling to my fingers in a horrible sort of magnetism that bound me prisoner, the cold perspiration of terror bursting from every pore, even as my other hand, trembling and unnerved, sought in my shirt for the knife of Little Sauk.

As I gripped the weapon, the thing began to straighten out, coming up in the quick odd jerks with which some snakes uncoil their joints after the torpidity of winter. My hand, finding naught to grasp, slipped from the smooth round ball, and as it fell touched what seemed an ear, and then a human nose.

"Merciful God! 't is a man!" I gasped, in astonishment and yet relief, as I closed upon his throat, madly determined to shut off his wind before he could give alarm.

"Cuss the luck!" he gasped hoarsely, and I let go of him, scarcely able to ejaculate in my intense surprise at that familiar voice.

"Burns? For Heaven's sake, Burns! can this indeed be you?"

For an instant he did not speak, doubtless as greatly perplexed as I at the strange situation.

"If ye 're Injun," he ventured at last gravely, "then I 'm a bloody ghost; but if by any chance ye 're the lad, Wayland, which yer voice sounds like, then it's Ol' Tom Burns as ye 're a-maulin' 'round, which seems ter be yer specialty,—a-jumpin' on unoffensive settlers in the dark, an' a-chokin' the life outer them."

The growling tone of his voice was growing querulous, and it was evident that his temper, never quite childlike, had not been greatly improved by his late experiences as an Indian captive.

"But Burns, old friend!" I persisted heartily, my courage returned once more, "it was surely enough to stir any man to violence to encounter such a thing in the dark! What in Heaven's name has happened to leave you with such a poll? What has become of your hair and beard? Is their loss a part of Indian torture?"

There was a low chuckle in the darkness, as if the old rascal were laughing to himself.

"Injun nuthin!" he returned with vehemence. "Thet's jist my way of sarcumventin' the bloody varmints. I shaved the hull blame thing soon as ever they let me loose, an' then played loony, till thar ain't no Injun 'long the shore as 'd tech me fer all the wampum in the Illini country. 'T ain't the fust time I saved my scalp by some sech dern trick. I tell ye, it's easy 'nough ter beat Injuns if ye only know how. By snakes! I'm sacred, I am, — specially teched by the Great Spirit. I tell ye, ter be real loony is dern nigh as good in an Injun camp as ter hev red hair like thet thar little Sister Celeste with the Pottawattomies. She knows her business, you bet; an' so does Ol' Burns know hisn!"

A STUMBLE IN THE DARK

His mention of her name instantly recalled me to the little group waiting above us, and doubtless already worried at my prolonged absence.

"Burns," I interrupted, "this is no time for reminiscences. I am here seeking some means of escape out of this place of horror. What were you doing down here?"

"Sorter contemplatin' a sea v'yage," he said, dryly. "'T was rec'mended by my doctor fer the growth o' my har. So, snoopin' 'round yere in the dark, an' not over fond o' Injun com'any, I found this yere boat. Jest got in ter see how 't was fixed, when ye jumped down yonder. Reckon I 'd kinder like ter wet 'er up an' see wot she 's like."

"Good! so would I. This boat was placed here for that very purpose. Now listen. The young woman you just mentioned, that Indian missionary with the auburn hair, is above yonder, together with another young white girl rescued from the massacre, and the Frenchman, De Croix. We have come here, on pledge of a half-breed chief that this boat would be ready for our escape. And we have no time to waste, for we may be followed at any moment."

"They ain't seen ye stealin' outer the camp?"

"No, but in doing it I was compelled to kill Little Sauk, and the others may find his body at any time."

For a moment the sly old borderer made no response, and I knew he was quietly turning over the complicated situation in his own mind preparatory to intelligent action. I heard him step from the boat into the shallow water.

"All right, lad! I understand," he said heartily, his former indifference vanished. "Derned if I would n't jist as soon leave that Parley-Voo behind; but I 'm with ye, an' I reckon Ol' Burns 'll give them thar redskins another dern good jolt. Take hold here, boy, an' we 'll run this yere man-o-war outside, where we kin ship the rest o' her crew."

The back-water rippling among the old piling was shallow, but the boat had little aboard and floated free, so that we worked it forward with little difficulty until we succeeded in rounding the slight promontory and held its bulging sides close against the mud wall. Leaving Burns to keep it in place, I crept silently up the bank.

"Come!" I whispered, making my way to the side of Mademoiselle more by instinct than sight. "The boat we sought is here and ready! I have even found a boatman to aid us, in the form of Ol' Burns, who, you remember, aided De Croix and me at the time of our famous race. Let us waste no more of the night here, but do the rest of your talking in greater safety on the water."

They came with me down to the edge of the stream without a word of protest. I had taken Mademoiselle in my arms and lifted her slight form into the boat, when she turned suddenly, as if by an unrestrainable impulse, and held out her hands toward the dim figure of the silent girl who yet remained motionless several feet away.

"Marie!" she said, anxiously, "it may be wrong of me to urge it, but I beg you to think again in this grave matter. Surely such horrible massacre as you have witnessed must absolve you from your vow, and yield you freedom to return eastward with those you love."

The other did not respond to this passionate appeal, but stood facing us silent as a statue.

"What mean you, Mademoiselle?" I asked. "Will not this Sister Celeste consent to leave the Indians?"

"Nay, she has made a sacred vow of religion which binds her to this sacrifice. I implore you, John Wayland, urge her to go with us! 'T is but waste of her life here. She is an old schoolmate of mine, and 't will be hard to leave her alone in this wilderness. Captain de Croix, she was far from being a stranger to you in those other days at Montreal, — will you not add your entreaties to ours?"

I saw him step forward toward that quiet bowed figure, and she straightened perceptibly, even in the darkness, as he drew near. His words were in French, and spoken so low I missed their meaning; yet we all heard plainly her calm answer, while marking the faltering accents of her lips.

" Dear, dear friend! " and I felt her eyes, blinded by tears, were seeking out Mademoiselle through the gloom, " it breaks my heart to answer you nay in this hour of sore trial to us both. Yet my vow to God is more sacred than any earthly friendship; nor could peace ever again abide in my heart were I to break the vow so lightly. My duty is here, be it for life or death; and here I must abide until the Master sets me free."

Then, addressing De Croix, she continued sadly, " No, Monsieur, the sense of duty that presses upon me and yields me such strength is beyond your comprehension. I bid you go back to that world of light and gaiety you have always loved so fondly, and think no more of me. To you I am, even as you have supposed, a dead woman, yet happier far in this sad exile than I ever was in that gilded social cage where men laugh while they break the hearts that trust them. My Indians are indeed cruel, but there is a deeper cruelty than that of bloodshed, and I prefer the open savagery of the woods and plains to things I have known in city life. So it must be good-bye, Monsieur!"

I was looking directly at her when she uttered these last words of dismissal, yet as she ended she vanished into the black night beyond, I knew not how. A moment before, two figures had been standing

there, De Croix's and hers; and although my eyes
never once wavered, suddenly there remained but one,
that of De Croix, peering forward with bent body as if
he also knew not how or when the girl had vanished
from his side. I was staring yet, half believing it was
but a trick of my eyes, when suddenly, like phantoms
from the mist, a half-dozen naked figures topped the
high bank before me. It was the work almost of a
second. I caught Burns's low cry of warning from
where he sat watching within the boat.

"Run!" I shouted to De Croix. "To the boat,
quick! The savages are upon us!"

He made no motion, and I grasped him. Rarely
have I laid so heavy a hand on one in friendship; but
I lifted him from off his feet and flung him bodily into
the boat's bottom, scarce waiting till he struck before
I had my shoulder against the stern to send the craft
free from shore. I know not what mischance caused
it, whether I slipped upon a stone or tripped over a
hidden root; but as I shoved the boat far out into the
dark current of the river, instead of springing after it,
as I had meant to do, I toppled and plunged headlong
down at the edge of the stream.

CHAPTER XXXV

THE BATTLE ON THE SHORE

HAT followed was long a famous story on the border, and I have even read it written out most carefully in books purporting to tell the history of those troublous times. None of them have it as I recall the details of the incident, although it all occurred so rapidly that I myself can hardly tell just how 't was done.

I know that I scrambled again to my knees, resting half in the water, my purpose being to fling myself into the river in an effort to regain the boat. But it was already out of sight in the dense gloom, while not the slightest sound reached me for guidance. Beyond this, I had no time for much save action. Above me, upon the high bank not three yards away, I saw several Indian forms peering over; and then others, three or four, I am uncertain which, sprang lightly down within a yard of where I crouched in waiting.

THE BATTLE ON THE SHORE

My father gave me a frontier maxim once, which ran, " If you must fight, strike first, and strike hard." The words flashed in my memory, and I put them to the test straightway. These prowling savages were apparently unaware of my predicament; their sole thought was with the boat floating away lakeward down the stream. At all cost, they must be blocked in any purpose of pursuit. These were the thoughts that darted through my brain like fire through stubble. How many opposed me, how desperate would be the struggle, were matters of which I did not stop to think. I could at least busy them until the fugitives were safe; after that, it was God's affair, and theirs. My rifle was wet and useless from my recent tumble; but before the group at the water's edge even saw me I was fairly upon them, striking fiercely with my gun-stock, and two savages went down, shrieking from pain and surprise, before so much as a return blow reached me.

It was not a noisy battle; from the outset it was too fierce and rapid for any waste of breath. Never did I need my strength of body more, nor did the long training of my father come in better play. I made that long rifle-barrel both club and sword, knife and axe in one, striking, thrusting, clubbing, in the mad fury with which desperation bids a man battle for his life. I had no thought to live, but was determined that if I went down to earth many a painted savage should

lie there with me. The enshrouding darkness proved
a friendly help; for as I backed in closer against the
bank, I gained a fair view of my opponents, while
keeping myself more hidden. Again and again they
charged upon me, joined now by the others from
above; but the circling iron I swung with tireless arms
formed a dead-line no leaping Indian burst through
alive.

Once a hurtling tomahawk half buried itself in my
shoulder; a long knife, thrown by a practised hand,
pierced the muscles of my thigh, and stuck there quivering, till I struck it loose; and twice they fired at me,
the second shot tearing the flesh of my side, searing it
like fire. Yet I scarcely realized I was touched, so
fiercely was the battle-blood now coursing through
my veins, so intense the joy with which I crushed
them back. I grew delirious, feeling the rage to slay
sweep over me as never before, giving me the crazed
strength of a dozen men, until I lost all sense of defensive action, and sprang forth into their midst as
might an avenging thunderbolt from the black sky.
Never had I swung flail in peaceful border contest as
I did that murderous iron bar in the dark of the river-
shore, driving them back foot by foot against the high
bank which held them helpless victims of my wrath.
I struck again and again, my teeth set together in
bulldog tenacity, my breath coming in gasps, the
streaming blood from a deep cut over my eyes half

blinding me, yet guided by fierce instinct to find and smite my foes. I trod on limp bodies, on writhing forms, and felt my weapon clash against iron rifle barrels and clang upon uplifted steel; but nothing stopped me, — no cry of terror, no plea for mercy, no clutching hand, no deadly numbing blow.

God knows the story of that fight, — how long it lasted, by what miracle 't was won. To me it is — and was — little more than a dim haze of strange leaping figures, of fierce dark faces, of maddened cries of hate, of uplifted hands, of dull-clashing weapons. I seemed to see it all through a red fog whence the blood dripped, and I lost consciousness of everything save my unswerving duty to strike hard until I fell. At last out from the maelstrom of that wild *mêlée* but a single warrior seemed to face me; and some instinct of the fight caused me to draw back a pace and wipe the obscuring blood away, that I might see him better. It came to me that this was to be the end, — the final duel which was to decide that midnight battle. He and I were there alone; and the stars bursting through the clouds gave me faint view of him, and of those dark, silent forms that lined the shore where they had fallen.

A chief, a Pottawattomie, — this much I knew even in that hasty shrouded glance. Writers of history affirm my opponent was Peesotum, the same fierce warrior whose cruel hand slew the brave Captain

Wells and wrenched his still beating heart from out the mutilated body. All I realized then were his broad sinewy shoulders, his naked brawny body, his eyes ablaze with malignant hate. He was the first to close, his wild cry for vengeance piercing the still night; and before I knew it, the maddened savage was within the guard of my rifle-barrel, and we were locked in the stern grapple of death.

It was knife to knife, our blades gleaming dull in the dim light of the stars, each man gripping the uplifted wrist of the other, putting forth each last reserve of strength, each cunning trick of fence, to break free and strike the ending blow. Back and forth we strove, straining like two wild animals, our moccasined feet slipping on the wet earth, our muscles strained, and sinews cracking with intensity of effort, our breath coming in labored gasps, our bodies tense as bowstrings. Such merciless strain could not endure forever, and, strong as I was in those young days, the savage was far stronger and less exhausted by the struggle, so that inch by inch he pressed me backward, battling like a demon, until I could see the cruel gleam of his eyes as I gave slowly down. It was God who saved me, for as I fell I struck the sharp shelving of the bank, and the quick stoppage swung the savage to one side and below me, so that, even as he gave vent to an exulting yell of triumph, wrenching his hand loose from my weakening clasp to strike the death-blow, I whirled and forced him downward, his face buried in the stream.

Those who write history say the rescuing warriors discovered him alive. I know not; but this I swear, — I held him there until every struggle ceased, until answering yells from the westward told me others were already close at hand, and then, breathless and trembling from the struggle, blinded by blood and faint from wounds, I sprang forward into the night-shadows, dimly conscious that my sole hope for escape lay lakeward. I ran but feebly at first, skirting the partially destroyed stockade of the old Fort, with its litter of debris, and stumbling constantly in the darkness over the obstructions that lined the river bank. As my breath returned, and I somewhat cleared my eyes of blood, I saw better; and at last ran from the darker soil on to the white sand of the beach.

There were now many stars in the sky, with the moon struggling feebly to break through the haze; but to my anxious glance nothing was visible upon the water. Surely the boat must have floated to the river-mouth by this time, — surely the force of the current would have accomplished that; nor was it likely that Ol' Burns would draw far away from shore until assured of my fate. The wild shouting told me that savages from the camp had already found their dead. A moment more would place them on my trail, hot for revenge; and there was no course left me but to

take the water, before their keen eyes found me out.
I waded out, seeking thus to get far enough from shore
to baffle their search, when suddenly a quick spark of
light winked from the blackness in front of me. Surely
it could be nothing less than a signal, the swift stroke
of flint on steel, — no doubt in the faint hope it would
prove a beacon to me in my need.

Desperate as the chance was, it was still a chance,
and to my mind the only one. I glanced behind; a
dim figure or two dotted the white sand, and my heart
lifted a silent prayer to God for guidance. A second
later I was beyond my depth, breasting the unknown
waters, swimming steadily toward the place where
that mysterious spark had glimmered. Once again it
flashed, the barest glimpse of light through the intense
gloom; and I pressed on with new vigor, certain now it
was a real beacon. But I was so weakened by wounds
and spent from exertion, and such desperate work is
swimming fully clad, that my progress proved slow;
and twice I was compelled to pause, paddling slowly
on my back, in the buffeting of the waves, in order
to gain strength to renew the struggle. I almost lost
heart in the black loneliness, as the swirling water
swept me back and confused me with its ever-tossing
motion. Once I went down from sheer weakness,
choking in a cloud of spray that swept my face; and
doubtless I should have let the struggle end in despair
even then, had not the spark leaped up once more

through the deep haze; and this time so close was it that my ears caught the clashing of the flint and steel.

With the new hope of life thus given me, I pushed grimly forward, using the silent Indian stroke that never tires, my eyes at the surface level where the light of the moon glimmered feebly. At last I saw it, — the black lumpy shadow of the boat. I must have splashed a little in my weakness and excitement, for I plainly perceived the figure of a man hastily leap to his feet, with an oar-blade uplifted threateningly above his head.

"Don't strike, Burns!" I managed to cry aloud. "It's Wayland."

The next moment, with scarce so much as a breath remaining in my battered body, I laid hand upon the boat's side, and clung there panting and well-nigh spent. I felt his hands pressed under my arms, and then, with the exercise of his great strength, he drew me steadily up, inch by inch, until I topped the rail, and fell forward into the bottom of the boat. An instant I rested thus, with tightly closed eyes, my head reeling, my breath coming in sobs of pain, every muscle of my strained body throbbing in misery. Scarcely conscious of what was being done about me, I could still realize that arms touched my neck, that my head was gently lifted to a softer resting-place, and that a hand, strangely tender, brushed back from my forehead the wet tangled hair. The touch was thrilling;

and I unclosed my wearied eyes, looking up into the sympathetic face of Mademoiselle. The faint moonlight rested upon it gently, touching her crown of hair with silver; and within the dark depths of her eyes I read clearly the message I had waited for so long.

"Toinette!" I murmured, half conscious.

She bowed her head above me, and I felt a sudden plash of tears that could not be restrained.

"Do not try to speak now, John!" she whispered softly, her finger at my lips. "I can only thank the good God who has brought you back to me."

I made no effort to say more; I could only lie in silence and gaze up at her, pressing the hands resting so frankly within my own. Indeed, we needed no words in that hour; our hearts had spoken, and thenceforward we were one.

Suddenly the heavy boat lurched beneath us, to some quick impetus that sent a shudder through every inch of it; and I heard a heavy splash alongside, which instantly brought me upright, anxiously grasping the rail.

"May Heaven help him!" cried Burns excitedly, and pointing out at the black waters. "The Frenchman has gone overboard!"

"Overboard?" I echoed, striving to regain my feet. "Did he fall?"

"Fall? No; it was a dive off the back seat here. Save me! but he went into it like a gull."

We sought for him long and vainly, peering over those dark swirling waters, calling his name aloud, and striking flint on steel in hope to guide him by the spark. Nothing appeared along the rolling surface, no answering cry came from the black void; De Croix had disappeared into the depths, as desperate men go down to death. Suddenly, as I leaned over, sick at heart, peering into the dimness, Toinette drew near and touched me softly.

"Let us not mourn," she said, in strange quietness. "No doubt 't is better so."

"How?" I questioned, shocked at her seemingly heartless words. "Surely you cannot rejoice at such a loss?"

"'T is not a loss," she answered firmly, and the soft moon-rays were white upon her face. "He has only gone back to her we left behind; it was the beckoning hand of love that called him through the waters. Now it is only ours to pray that he may find her."

CHAPTER XXXVI

IN THE NEW GRAY DAWN

Y anxious glance wandered from the face I so dearly loved, out where those dark restless waters merged into the brooding mystery of the black night. How unspeakably dreary, lonely, hopeless it all was! Into what tragic unknown fate had this earliest comrade of my manhood been remorselessly swept? Was all indeed well with him? or had the Nemesis of a wrong once done dealt its fatal stroke at last? The voices of the night were silent; the chambers of the great tossing sea hid their secret well. Had this gallant and reckless young soldier of France, this petted courtier of the gayest court in Europe, whose very name and rank I knew not, succeeded in his desperate deed? Had he reached yonder blood-stained shore, lined with infuriated savages, and found safe passage through them to the side of the woman he had once called wife, and then forgotten? Or had he found,

378

instead, the solemn peace of death amid the swirling waters of this vast inland sea, so many leagues to the westward of that sunny land he loved? These were the thoughts that shook me, as I leaned out above the rail, her dear hand always on my shoulder. Never have the circling years found voice, nor the redeemed wilderness made answer.

"Possibly it might be done," I admitted slowly. "'T is scarce farther than I swam just now, and he is neither weary nor wounded."

We all realized it was a useless peril to remain there longer, and I sat at the helm and watched, while Burns, who developed considerable knowledge in such matters, fitted the heavy sail in place. With the North Star over the water for our guidance, I headed the blunt nose of the boat due eastward into the untracked waters.

I confess that my memory was still lingering upon De Croix, and my eyes turned often enough along our foam-flecked wake in vague wonderment at his fate. It was Mademoiselle who laid hand softly on my knee at last, and aroused my attention to her.

"Why did you tell Sister Celeste that you came to Dearborn seeking Elsa Matherson?" she questioned, her clear eyes intently reading my face.

"I had even forgotten that I mentioned it," I answered, surprised at this query at such a time. "But it is strictly true. While upon his death-bed Elsa

379

Matherson's father wrote to mine, — they were old comrades in the great war, — and I was sent hither to bring the orphan girl eastward. I sought her as a brother might seek a sister he had never seen, Mademoiselle; yet have failed most miserably in my mission."

"How failed?"

"In that I have found no trace of the girl, and beyond doubt she perished in the massacre. I know not how, but I have been strangely baffled and misled from the first in my search for her, and it was all to no purpose."

For the first time since I had fallen dripping into the boat, a slight smile was visible in the dark eyes fronting me.

"Why hid you from me with such care the object of your search?"

"I hid nothing, Mademoiselle. We spoke together about it often."

"Ay, indeed you told me you sought a young girl, and your words led me to think at first it must be Josette, and later still the Indian missionary. But not once did you breathe the name of the girl in my ears. The dwellers at Dearborn were neither so many nor so strange to me that I could not have aided you in your search."

"You knew this Elsa Matherson?"

"I am not so sure of that, Master Wayland," she

returned gravely, her eyes wandering into the night.
" Once I thought I did, but she has changed so greatly
in the last few days that I am hardly sure. A young
girl's life is often filled with mystery, and there are
happenings that turn girlhood to womanhood in a
single hour. Love has power to change the nature as
by magic, and sorrow also has a like rare gift. Do you
still greatly wish to find this Elsa Matherson? "

" To find her? " and I gazed about me incredulously into those flitting shadows where the waves
raced by. " Ay, for I have dreamed of her as of a
lost sister, and it will sadly grieve those at home to
have me return thus empty-handed. Yet the thought
is foolishness, Mademoiselle, and I understand not why
you should mock me so."

She drew closer, in the gentle caressing way she
had, and found my disengaged hand, her sweet face
held upward so that I could mark every changing
expression.

" Never in my useless life was I farther removed
from any spirit of mockery," she insisted, soberly;
" for never before have I seen the presence of God so
clearly manifest in His mysterious guidance of men.
You, who sought after poor Elsa Matherson in this
wilderness, looking perchance for a helpless orphan
child, have been led to pluck me in safety out from
savage hands, and yet never once dreamed that in
doing so you only fulfilled your earlier mission."

I stared at her, grasping with difficulty the full significance of her speech.

"Your words puzzle me."

"Nay, they need not," and I caught the sudden glitter of tears on her lashes; "for I am Elsa Matherson."

"You? you?" and I crushed her soft hand within my fingers, as I peered forward at the quickly lowered face. "Why, you are French, Mademoiselle, and of a different name!"

She glanced up now into my puzzled face, a bit shyly, yet with some of the old roguishness visible in her eyes.

"My mother was indeed French, but my father was an American soldier," she said rapidly, as if eager to have the explanation ended. "You never asked my name, save that one night when we first met amid the sand, and then I gave you only that by which I have been most widely known. None except my father ever called me Elsa; to all others I was always Toinette. But I am Roger Matherson's only child."

It was clear enough now, and the deception had been entirely my own, rendered possible by strange chances of omission, by rare negligence of speech — aided by my earlier impression that she whom I sought was a mere child.

"And 't was Sister Celeste who told you whom I sought?" I asked, for lack of courage to say more.

"Yes, to-night, while we waited for you beside the ruins of the old factory. Oh, how far away it all seems now!" and she pointed backward across the waters. "Poor, poor girl! Poor Captain de Croix! Oh, it is all so sad, so unutterably sad to me! I knew them both so well, Monsieur," and she rested her bowed head upon one hand, staring out into the night, and speaking almost as if to herself alone; "yet I never dreamed that he was a nobleman of France, or that he had married Marie Faneuf. She was so sweet a girl then, — and now to be buried alive in that wilderness! Think you that he truly loved her?"

"I almost have faith that he did, Mademoiselle," I answered gravely. "He was greatly changed from his first sight of her face, though he was a difficult man to gauge in such matters. There was a time when I believed him in love with you."

She tossed her head.

"Nay," she answered, "he merely thought he was, because he found me hard to understand and difficult of conquest; but 't was little more than his own vanity that drew him hither. I trust it may be the deeper feeling that has taken him back now in face of death to Marie."

"You have indeed proved hard to understand by more than one," I ventured, for in spite of her graciousness the old wound rankled. "It has puzzled me much to understand how you so gaily sent me forth to a mission that might mean death, to save this Captain de Croix."

It was a foolish speech, and she met it bravely, with heightened color and a flash of dark eyes.

" 'T was no more than the sudden whim of a girl," she answered quickly, " and regretted before you were out of sight. Nor did I dream you would meet my conditions by such a sacrifice."

" You showed small interest as you stood on the stockade when we went forth! "

" You mean when Captain de Croix and I leaned above the eastern palisades? "

" Ay, not once did your eyes wander to mark our progress."

Her eyes were smiling now, and her face archly uplifted.

" Indeed, Master Wayland, little you know of the struggles of my heart during that hour. Nor will I tell you; for the secrets of a girl must be her own. But I marked each step you took onward toward the Indian camp, until the night hid you, — the night, or else the gathering tears in my eyes."

The sudden yawing of the boat before a gust of wind drew my thought elsewhere, and kept back the words ready upon my tongue. When once more I had my bearings and had turned back the plunging bow, she sat silent, deep in thought that I hesitated to disturb. Soon I noted her head droop slightly to the increased movement of the boat.

"You are worn out!" I said tenderly. "Lean here against me, and sleep."

"Indeed, I feel most weary," was her drowsy reply. "Yes, I will rest for a few moments."

How clear remains the memory of those hours, while I sat watchful of the helm, her head resting peacefully on my lap, and all about us those lonely tossing waters! What a mere chip was our boat in the midst of that desolate sea; how dark and dreary the changeless night shadows! Over and over again I pictured the details of each scene I have here set forth so poorly, to dream at the end of a final home-coming which should not be alone. It was with heart thankful to God, that I watched the slow stealing upward of the gray dawn as the early rays of light crept toward us across the heaving of the waters. It was typical of all I had hoped, — this, and the black shadows fleeing away into the west. Brighter and brighter grew the crimsoning sky over the boat's bow, where Burns lay sleeping, until my eyes could distinguish a far-off shore-line heavily crowned with trees. I thought to rouse her to the glorious sight; but even as I glanced downward into the fair young face, her dark eyes opened in instant smile of greeting.

"'T is the morning," she said gladly, "and that dark, dark night has passed away."

"For ever, Mademoiselle; and there is even a land of promise to be seen out yonder!"

She sat up quickly, shading her eyes with her hand as she gazed with eagerness toward where I pointed.

"Think you we shall find shelter and friends there?"

"The half-breed chief said there were yet white settlers upon the Saint Joseph, Mademoiselle; and the mouth of that river should be easily found."

She turned toward me, a slight frown darkening her face.

"I wish you would not call me Mademoiselle," she said slowly. "It is as if we were still mere strangers; and you said Elsa Matherson was to be as your sister."

I bent over her suddenly, all my repressed love glowing in my face.

"Toinette!" I whispered passionately, "I would call you by a dearer name than that, — by the dearest of all dear names if I might, for you have won my heart in the wilderness."

For a single instant she glanced shyly up into my face, her own crimson at my sudden ardor. Her eyes drooped and hid themselves behind their long lashes.

"Those who sent you forth seeking a sister might not thus wish to welcome Elsa Matherson," she said softly.

"'T is a venture I most gladly make," I insisted, "and would seal it with a kiss."

Her eyes flashed up at me, full of sudden merriment.

"The unpaid wager leaves me helpless to resist, Monsieur."

.   .   .   .

The soft haze of Indian summer rested over the valley of the Maumee. We rode slowly along the narrow winding trail that hugged the river bank; for our journey had been a long one, and the horses were wearied. Burns was riding just in advance of Toinette and me, his cap pulled low over his eyes, his new growth of hair standing out stiff and black beneath its covering. Once he twisted his seamed face about in time to catch us smiling at his odd figure, and growled to himself as he kicked at his horse's flanks.

It was thus we rounded the bend and saw before us the little clearing with the cabin in the centre of its green heart. At sight of it my eyes grew moist and I rested my fingers gently upon the white hand that lay against her saddle-pommel.

"Fear not, dear heart!" I whispered tenderly. "It is home for both alike, and the welcome of love awaits you as well as me."

She glanced up at me, half shyly as in the old way, and there was a mist of tears clinging to the long lashes.

"Those who love you, John, I will love," she said solemnly.

WHEN WILDERNESS WAS KING

It was Rover who saw us first, and came charging forth with savage growl and ruffled fur, until he scented me, and changed his fierceness into barks of frantic welcome. Then it was I saw them, even as when I last rode forth, my father seated in his great splint chair, my mother with her arm along the carved back, one hand shading her eyes as she watched our coming.

This is not a memory to be written about for stranger eyes to read, but as I turned from them after that first greeting, their glances were upon her who stood waiting beside me, so sweet and pure in her young womanhood.

" And this, my son? " questioned my father kindly. "We would bid her welcome also; yet surely she cannot be that little child for whose sake we sent you forth? "

I took her by the hand as we faced them.

" You sent me in search of one whom you would receive even as your own child," I answered simply. "This is Roger Matherson's daughter, and the dear wife of your son."

What need have I to dwell upon the love that bade her welcome? And so it was that out of all the suffering and danger, — forth from the valley of the shadow of death, — Toinette and I came home.

THE END

Good Fiction Worth Reading.

A series of romances containing several of the old favorites in the field of historical fiction, replete with powerful romances of love and diplomacy that excel in thrilling and absorbing interest.

A CCLONIAL FREE-LANCE. A story of American Colonial Times. By Chauncey C. Hotchkiss. Cloth, 12mo. with four illustrations by J. Watson Davis. Price, $1.00.

A book that appeals to Americans as a vivid picture of Revolutionary scenes. The story is a strong one, a thrilling one. It causes the true American to flush with excitement, to devour chapter after chapter, until the eyes smart, and it fairly smokes with patriotism. The love story is a singularly charming idyl.

THE TOWER OF LONDON. A Historical Romance of the Times of Lady Jane Grey and Mary Tudor. By Wm. Harrison Ainsworth. Cloth, 12mo. with four illustrations by George Cruikshank. Price, $1.00.

This romance of the "Tower of London" depicts the Tower as palace, prison and fortress, with many historical associations. The era is the middle of the sixteenth century.

The story is divided into two parts, one dealing with Lady Jane Grey, and the other with Mary Tudor as Queen, introducing other notable characters of the era. Throughout the story holds the interest of the reader in the midst of intrigue and conspiracy, extending considerably over a half a century.

IN DEFIANCE OF THE KING. A Romance of the American Revolution. By Chauncey C. Hotchkiss. Cloth, 12mo. with four illustrations by J. Watson Davis. Price, $1.00.

Mr. Hotchkiss has etched in burning words a story of Yankee bravery, and true love that thrills from beginning to end, with the spirit of the Revolution. The heart beats quickly, and we feel ourselves taking a part in the exciting scenes described. His whole story is so absorbing that you will sit up far into the night to finish it. As a love romance it is charming.

GARTHOWEN. A story of a Welsh Homestead. By Allen Raine. Cloth, 12mo. with four illustrations by J. Watson Davis. Price, $1.00.

"This is a little idyl of humble life and enduring love, laid bare before us, very real and pure, which in its telling shows us some strong points of Welsh character—the pride, the hasty temper, the quick dying out of wrath. . . . We call this a well-written story, interesting alike through its romance and its glimpses into another life than ours. A delightful and clever picture of Welsh village life. The result is excellent."—Detroit Free Press.

MIFANWY. The story of a Welsh Singer. By Allan Raine. Cloth, 12mo. with four illustrations by J. Watson Davis. Price, $1.00.

"This is a love story, simple, tender and pretty as one would care to read. The action throughout is brisk and pleasing; the characters, it is apparent at once, are as true to life as though the author had known them all personally. Simple in all its situations, the story is worked up in that touching and quaint strain which never grows wearisome, no matter how often the lights and shadows of love are introduced. It rings true, and does not tax the imagination."—Boston Herald.

For sale by all booksellers, or sent postpaid on receipt of price by the publishers, **A. L. BURT COMPANY,** 52-58 Duane St., New York.

Good Fiction Worth Reading.

A series of romances containing several of the old favorites in the field of historical fiction, replete with powerful romances of love and diplomacy that excel in thrilling and absorbing interest.

WINDSOR CASTLE. A Historical Romance of the Reign of Henry VIII. Catharine of Aragon and Anne Boleyn. By Wm. Harrison Ainsworth. Cloth, 12mo. with four illustrations by George Cruikshank. Price, $1.00.

"Windsor Castle" is the story of Henry VIII., Catharine, and Anne Boleyn. "Bluff King Hal," although a well-loved monarch, was none too good a one in many ways. Of all his selfishness and unwarrantable acts, none was more discreditable than his divorce from Catharine, and his marriage to the beautiful Anne Boleyn. The King's love was as brief as it was vehement. Jane Seymour, waiting maid on the Queen, attracted him, and Anne Boleyn was forced to the block to make room for her successor. This romance is one of extreme interest to all readers.

HORSESHOE ROBINSON. A tale of the Tory Ascendency in South Carolina in 1780. By John P. Kennedy. Cloth, 12mo. with four illustrations by J. Watson Davis. Price, $1.00.

Among the old favorites in the field of what is known as historical fiction, there are none which appeal to a larger number of Americans than Horseshoe Robinson, and this because it is the only story which depicts with fidelity to the facts the heroic efforts of the colonists in South Carolina to defend their homes against the brutal oppression of the British under such leaders as Cornwallis and Tarleton.

The reader is charmed with the story of love which forms the thread of the tale, and then impressed with the wealth of detail concerning those times. The picture of the manifold sufferings of the people, is never overdrawn, but painted faithfully and honestly by one who spared neither time nor labor in his efforts to present in this charming love story all that price in blood and tears which the Carolinians paid as their share in the winning of the republic.

Take it all in all, "Horseshoe Robinson" is a work which should be found on every book-shelf, not only because it is a most entertaining story, but because of the wealth of valuable information concerning the colonists which it contains. That it has been brought out once more, well illustrated, is something which will give pleasure to thousands who have long desired an opportunity to read the story again, and to the many who have tried vainly in these latter days to procure a copy that they might read it for the first time.

THE PEARL OF ORR'S ISLAND. A story of the Coast of Maine. By Harriet Beecher Stowe. Cloth, 12mo. Illustrated. Price, $1.00.

Written prior to 1862, the "Pearl of Orr's Island" is ever new; a book filled with delicate fancies, such as seemingly array themselves anew each time one reads them. One sees the "sea like an unbroken mirror all around the pine-girt, lonely shores of Orr's Island," and straightway comes "the heavy, hollow moan of the surf on the beach, like the wild angry howl of some savage animal."

Who can read of the beginning of that sweet life, named Mara, which came into this world under the very shadow of the Death angel's wings, without having an intense desire to know how the premature bud blossomed? Again and again one lingers over the descriptions of the character of that baby boy Moses, who came through the tempest, amid the angry billows, pillowed on his dead mother's breast.

There is no more faithful portrayal of New England life than that which Mrs. Stowe gives in "The Pearl of Orr's Island."

Good Fiction Worth Reading.

A series of romances containing several of the old favorites in the field of historical fiction, replete with powerful romances of love and diplomacy that excel in thrilling and absorbing interest.

GUY FAWKES. A Romance of the Gunpowder Treason. By Wm. Harrison Ainsworth. Cloth, 12mo. with four illustrations by George Cruikshank. Price, $1.00.

The "Gunpowder Plot" was a modest attempt to blow up Parliament, the King and his Counsellors. James of Scotland, then King of England, was weak-minded and extravagant. He hit upon the efficient scheme of extorting money from the people by imposing taxes on the Catholics. In their natural resentment to this extortion, a handful of bold spirits concluded to overthrow the government. Finally the plotters were arrested, and the King put to torture Guy Fawkes and the other prisoners with royal vigor. A very intense love story runs through the entire romance.

THE SPIRIT OF THE BORDER. A Romance of the Early Settlers in the Ohio Valley. By Zane Grey. Cloth. 12mo. with four illustrations by J. Watson Davis. Price, $1.00.

A book rather out of the ordinary is this "Spirit of the Border." The main thread of the story has to do with the work of the Moravian missionaries in the Ohio Valley. Incidentally the reader is given details of the frontier life of those hardy pioneers who broke the wilderness for the planting of this great nation. Chief among these, as a matter of course, is Lewis Wetzel, one of the most peculiar, and at the same time the most admirable of all the brave men who spent their lives battling with the savage foe, that others might dwell in comparative security.

Details of the establishment and destruction of the Moravian "Village of Peace" are given at some length, and with minute description. The efforts to Christianize the Indians are described as they never have been before, and the author has depicted the characters of the leaders of the several Indian tribes with great care, which of itself will be of interest to the student.

By no means least among the charms of the story are the vivid word-pictures of the thrilling adventures, and the intense paintings of the beauties of nature, as seen in the almost unbroken forests.

It is the spirit of the frontier which is described, and one can by it, perhaps, the better understand why men, and women, too, willingly braved every privation and danger that the westward progress of the star of empire might be the more certain and rapid. A love story, simple and tender, runs through the book.

RICHELIEU. A tale of France in the reign of King Louis XIII. By G. P. R. James. Cloth, 12mo. with four illustrations by J. Watson Davis. Price, $1.00.

In 1829 Mr. James published his first romance, "Richelieu," and was recognized at once as one of the masters of the craft.

In this book he laid the story during those later days of the great cardinal's life, when his power was beginning to wane, but while it was yet sufficiently strong to permit now and then of volcanic outbursts which overwhelmed foes and carried friends to the topmost wave of prosperity. One of the most striking portions of the story is that of Cinq Mar's conspiracy; the method of conducting criminal cases, and the political trickery resorted to by royal favorites, affording a better insight into the statecraft of that day than can be had even by an exhaustive study of history. It is a powerful romance of love and diplomacy, and in point of thrilling and absorbing interest has never been excelled.

For sale by all booksellers, or sent postpaid on receipt of price by the publishers, A. L. BURT COMPANY, 52-58 Duane St., New York.

Good Fiction Worth Reading.

A series of romances containing several of the old favorites in the field of historical fiction, replete with powerful romances of love and diplomacy that excel in thrilling and absorbing interest.

DARNLEY. A Romance of the times of Henry VIII. and Cardinal Wolsey By G. P. R. James. Cloth, 12mo. with four illustrations by J. Watson Davis. Price, $1.00.

In point of publication, "Darnley" is that work by Mr. James which follows "Richelieu," and, if rumor can be credited, it was owing to the advice and insistence of our own Washington Irving that we are indebted primarily for the story, the young author questioning whether he could properly paint the difference in the characters of the two great cardinals. And it is not surprising that James should have hesitated; he had been eminently successful in giving to the world the portrait of Richelieu as a man, and by attempting a similar task with Wolsey as the theme, was much like tempting fortune. Irving insisted that "Darnley" came naturally in sequence, and this opinion being supported by Sir Walter Scott, the author set about the work.

As a historical romance "Darnley" is a book that can be taken up pleasurably again and again, for there is about it that subtle charm which those who are strangers to the works of G. P. R. James have claimed was only to be imparted by Dumas.

If there was nothing more about the work to attract especial attention, the account of the meeting of the kings on the historic "field of the cloth of gold" would entitle the story to the most favorable consideration of every reader.

There is really but little pure romance in this story, for the author has taken care to imagine love passages only between those whom history has credited with having entertained the tender passion one for another, and he succeeds in making such lovers as all the world must love.

CAPTAIN BRAND, OF THE SCHOONER CENTIPEDE. By Lieut. Henry A. Wise, U. S. N. (Harry Gringo). Cloth, 12mo. with four illustrations by J. Watson Davis. Price, $1.00.

The re-publication of this story will please those lovers of sea yarns who delight in so much of the salty flavor of the ocean as can come through the medium of a printed page, for never has a story of the sea and those "who go down in ships" been written by one more familiar with the scenes depicted.

The one book of this gifted author which is best remembered, and which will be read with pleasure for many years to come, is "Captain Brand," who, as the author states on his title page, was a "pirate of eminence in the West Indies." As a sea story pure and simple, "Captain Brand" has never been excelled, and as a story of piratical life, told without the usual embellishments of blood and thunder, it has no equal.

NICK OF THE WOODS. A story of the Early Settlers of Kentucky. By Robert Montgomery Bird. Cloth, 12mo. with four illustrations by J. Watson Davis. Price, $1.00.

This most popular novel and thrilling story of early frontier life in Kentucky was originally published in the year 1837. The novel, long out of print, had in its day a phenomenal sale, for its realistic presentation of Indian and frontier life in the early days of settlement in the South, narrated in the tale with all the art of a practiced writer. A very charming love romance runs through the story. This new and tasteful edition of "Nick of the Woods" will be certain to make many new admirers for this enchanting story from Dr. Bird's clever and versatile pen.

For sale by all booksellers, or sent postpaid on receipt of price by the publishers, **A. L. BURT COMPANY, 52-58 Duane St., New York.**